The HEART *of* STONE

—— *A NOVEL BY* ——
BEN GALLEY

COPYRIGHT

HOSPB1
ISBN: 978-0-9935170-2-0
1st Edition 2017 - Published by BenGalley.com
Cover Design by Shawn T. King

ABOUT THE AUTHOR

Ben Galley is a purveyor of dark fantasy from rainy old Brighton, England. Harbouring a near-fanatical love of writing and fantasy, Ben has been scribbling tall tales ever since he was knee-high. When he's not busy day-dreaming on park benches or arguing the finer points of dragons, he works as a self-publishing consultant, helping fellow authors from all over the world to publish their books.

For more about Ben, visit his site **www.bengalley.com**, say hello at **hello@bengalley.com**, or follow Ben on Twitter **@BenGalley** and Facebook **@BenGalleyAuthor**.

OTHER BOOKS BY BEN GALLEY

The Scarlet Star Trilogy
Bloodrush
Bloodmoon
Bloodfeud

The Emaneska Series
The Written
Pale Kings
Dead Stars - Part One
Dead Stars - Part Two

The Written Graphic Novel
Shelf Help

SUGGESTED LISTENING

Below is a playlist of songs that fuelled and inspired me whilst writing, plotting, and generally steepling my fingers over *The Heart of Stone*. Enjoy.

Mountain At My Gates
FOALS

Damn Nation
LOWER THAN ATLANTIS

We Could Forever
BONOBO

Empty Gold
HALSEY

Unstoppable
SIA

Megalomaniac
INCUBUS

The Enemy
MEMPHIS MAY FIRE

Heretics & Killers
PROTEST THE HERO

My Obsession
KILLSWITCH ENGAGE

Maggie's Farm
RAGE AGAINST THE MACHINE

Slow Dance
ARCANE ROOTS

Welcome Home, Son
RADICAL FACE

To My Mother
THOMAS NEWMAN

The Funeral
BAND OF HORSES

Yet Onward We Marched
JOY WANTS ETERNITY

Casey's Song
CITY AND COLOUR

Follow the playlist at **www.bengalley.com/heart-of-stone**

This book is dedicated to the warriors.
You know who you are.

THE
ICE-RAFTS

DESTRIX

DISPUTED

BEGRAD

THE
YAWN

HARTLUND
(THE SIX ISLANDS)

BRAAD

NORMONT

THE
BLUE
MOUNTAIN
SEA

THE
DUELLING
DOZEN

BAY OF SOULS

THE Realm

LEZEMBOR

CHANARK

THE
THUNDER
-SHORES

HINGE OF THE
WORLD

THE GOD'S RENT

SECOND
SEA

THE DIAMOND
MOUNTAINS

HASPLA

IFL

KHANDRI

NARWE

KHANDRI
AFFELA

THE
DUNEPLAINS

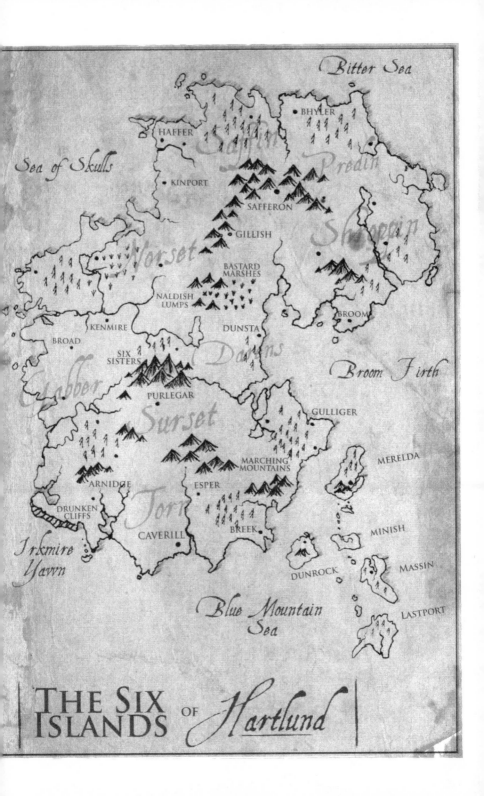

Bitter Sea

Sea of Skulls

BHYLER

HAFFER

KINPORT

Predth

SAFFERON

Shippen

GILLISH

Norset

BASTARD
MARSHES

NALDISH
LUMPS

BROOM

KENMIRE

DUNSTA

BROAD

Clabber

Downs

Broom Firth

SIX
SISTERS

PURLEGAR

GULLIGER

MERELDA

Surset

MARCHING
MOUNTAINS

ARNIDGE

ESPER

Torn

MINISH

DRUNKEN
CLIFFS

CAVERILL

BREEK

MASSIN

Irkmire
Yawn

DUNROCK

LASTPORT

Blue Mountain
Sea

THE SIX
ISLANDS OF *Hartlund*

The HEART of STONE

PRELUDES

FIRST

'Keep still!' a voice demanded. 'Keep still or it will take root in the wrong place, mercy me!'

He remained motionless as the soft hands dug inside his mouth; checking, shuffling, fixing. His face felt so wide, so open. He could feel his body tingling, as though he wore the dying embers of a fire.

'There!'

He felt the fingers crawl back to his chin and cheeks. *Always touching.*

'Bite down, and slowly mind!'

His jaw did the work for him, clicking back into place under the guiding hands; teeth crunching, finding their nests. The tongue began to burn in the pit of his mouth.

There came a clanking as the room swivelled about him. Something tugged at him without touching, pulling at every corner of his body. He felt heavier than a mountain.

'It is time to open your eyes, my new friend!'

His eyelids were impossible at first, but with some searching and testing, he cracked them open, and let the light flood in.

When the colours had finished dancing, and the stabbing pain had receded, a small shape coalesced in front of him. A wizened thing it was, with glass circles in its eyes and a black robe smirched with rock-dust on its back.

The room was long, full of complicated contraptions made of wood and hooks and rope. Tools littered every available surface. The floor was carpeted in stone chips. Along one wall, window-holes had been cut into the rock, and light spilled over intricate arrays of articulated metal arms which hung from the ceiling, and cogs in the walls, made for turning.

Something was howling in the room. Constant yet undulating in pitch. It made his skin shiver.

'Move. Try your limbs,' said the wrinkled figure, a man.

He turned his head, making strange noises, feeling his bones grate. He turned the other way, and the same sound chased his movement. He looked down, and began to writhe.

Stone. He was made of stone.

The old man dashed forwards and threw a hand to a lever.

Ropes went to work on him, dragging his arms apart until he was spreadeagled and held fast. Yet still he wriggled. Every move filled his head with a crunching and rattling. His eyes darted back and forth. He glared wildly at each of his rope-bound extremities.

He was nothing more than an intricate series of stone plates, bound in the shape of a man. Each plate was dense and tightly packed, like the fibres of a muscle.

'Calm yourself, curse it!' the man cried, waving his arms. 'CALM!'

His fingers were jagged shards of rock, curling against his will as the binds tightened around his wrist.

'I said, calm yourself!'

His feet were practically hooves.

It took time to bite back the fear that drove the urge to break his bonds and rip the stone from his limbs. As the spasms grew weak, he found stillness, and resorted to dangling in the ropes' hold. It was then that he tried his throat.

His first words were nothing but a mashed-up muddle that ricocheted from his rock lips.

The old man came closer, peeling the glass from his eyes. 'You spoke! Mercy me, you're a fast one.'

'Haeerm!'

'Concentrate on shaping the lips. Use your cheeks. Try it again!' The man was climbing onto him now.

'Whaarg!'

'The lips, damn it!'

'Why?'

That startled the wrinkles out of the man. He retreated, wringing his hands, eyes searching the floor.

'There must have been a mistake,' he said. 'Fourteen golems, and you're the first to ask "why".'

SECOND

Arguing was a familiar song to her. She'd heard it every day since she'd learnt her first words; and a few years before that, too, when it had all been formless noise and anger. Just something to make her wail in her cot. Words had flown across the room like daggers; from the wild tantrums by the fire to the seething soliloquies when she had been tucked up in sheets.

Da used to tell her such simple bedtime stories; the kind that drew sparkling things behind the eyelids. Stories where witches wore black and all heroes carried swords. They were made of such clear and comforting lines. Something to believe in.

But the arguments had made everything blurry. They showed her that in real life, heroes sometimes wore black, and even witches carried swords.

Tonight, her da wore his long robes; the dark ones with silver fur. He weaved no fantasies; just venom and spittle, his red face burning bright like a coal.

Usually, she would plant a grubby finger in each ear, guarding against the poisonous details. Now, those fingers were entwined on her lap, as still as a gravestone. Only her eyes moved; her darting, slicing eyes. They carved up every sentence and branded it into memory.

Somehow she knew that tonight she needed to listen.

'You want me to say I don't love you? Well listen up, then. I don't! I never did. Who could, in their right mind? Who could bear to live with it? It's your mother's blood. Her peasant curse living on through you, ruining everything for us. Spit on it, Mil! Spit on this whole thing!'

The slam of the door that followed would echo in her ears for many years to come. At night, when the thatch creaked and the lanterns had burnt to ash, she would hear it. She had no clue of the significance then, but she would in time.

She broke her gaze to fetch a cloth for her mother. It was usually now that the whimpering came; the tears and the snot. Then the incessant cleaning, or cooking; something good for a distraction. Then silence, angled up against the wall by the door, her head to the stone. Mam would always laugh after a moment or two, and come to hug her long and tight. They were the only bruises her parents ever gave her, and there was something good in that.

3

But no tears came. Not a drip nor a glint. Mam stayed put, her hand outstretched to the door-handle, as if snagged on something. It took an age for it to drop. Then she moved closer to press her palms against the old wood, stained by soot and use.

'Da's gone again,' said the girl.

The hands moved to throttle a dishcloth. 'That he has, Lesk. That he has.'

The girl hopped to her feet and stood in the middle of the room. Her hands crawled behind her back. There was a new taste to the cottage air; different from the usual stink of the cooking spit and the corner bucket. Something sour. Something dead.

'He'll be back by sun setting,' she said.

Mam nodded for a long while, and it was as though every dip of her head wound her up tighter, like the clockwork toys that hung in Old Kinny's window. At long last, she turned, straightening up to somewhere between calm and proud. She said nothing; just smiled in a way that made her lips flutter.

Now came the hug. Mam must have been too tired for the tears and the wailing and the cleaning.

When her mother's arms wrapped around her, the girl felt a stiffness in them. They were too gentle, too light. She felt lips brush her ear; so close she flinched when the words came spilling. They were hushed and tightly bunched.

'Tomorrow. Next Sowing. Maybe when you're as old and as wrinkly as I am, a man will come to find you, Lesky. He will tell you the Architect has called upon you. He will sell you stories of righteous rewards, of a place in the highest towers of the Forge, just for you. He will promise wonder, travel, and the chance to make the world a better place. He will flatter you, tell you how special you are.' A finger prodded her in the back. 'And all of it except the last will be a lie, my little miss.'

Mam withdrew to look the girl in the eyes. It was a hard, mean stare; the sort that was rare for such a smile-crinkled face. The girl felt the weight of the gaze, but she held onto it; too rapt to turn away.

'And when that day comes, I want you to run like your back is on fire.'

'I—'

'Just promise. One nod, and we'll never speak of it again.'

She gave her a nod, and the matter was buried. Mam took the girl's face in both hands and touched their foreheads together.

'You're different, Lesky. Don't ever stop believing that you can change the world, dear. Not ever.'

THIRD

Even the sun refused to look upon the scene. Its last rays had slid from the high stained windows, leaving the cavernous hall full of clawing shadows. And here she was, thinking the room could grow no fouler.

'I say again,' she said. 'The rule applies to Zealots only, clear and simple.'

'Once again you dare to lecture us on our own edicts!' Vullen screeched.

She gave him the same look she had been pouring onto his counterpart, the miserable-faced Lockyen.

'I am just repeating it as it's written down in ink and parchment. The Manual makes no mention of gl—'

'Silence!'

It was good to see Treyarch Daspar had finally broken his pondering. His chin had been affixed to his fist for some time now. He reclined in his great seat and hummed.

'Consecrator Lockyen, remind me. I believe Glimpse Techan was once a zealot, was he not?'

Lockyen thumbed his chin for show. She wanted to leap up the steps of his chair and dig a fingernail into his eye for the cheek of it.

Eleven years she had trod the halls of the Blade of the Architect, carving missionaries out of acolytes and lectors. Seven since she'd earned her scars and furs. And barely one since she'd found Techan, sitting alone in Caverill's docks and staring at the sea so hard he'd turned his eyes the colour of blood. He said he'd tried to turn himself into a ship, or a glider; anything that could help him escape.

She almost smirked, at the thought of their first fight. He had done himself proud despite nearly pitching himself into the sea. But Lockyen's words kept her face stormy, kept her blood boiling. This was no place nor time for jollity. A laugh hadn't been heard inside the Treyarch's Hall for half a millennium. She didn't think it likely it would hear one soon.

'For two years, before he disappeared north over the Sisters. A zealot, through and through.'

It was cold, without the paint-scatter sunlight. 'You can't be suggesting that still applies?' she asked.

'I don't remember excusing him from the ranks. Do you, Lockyen? Vullen?'

The Consecrators both shook their heads, still feigning puzzlement.

Too cold. A shiver crawled up her back. 'Treyarch, please! If I had known this would be your judgement, I would never have—'

Daspar sighed. 'And yet you never consulted me.' He ran a hand through his thick waterfall of yellow hair. 'I cannot, in the eyes of the Architect, allow it to continue now it has come this far.'

She cocked her head. 'This far? Trust me, it's a minor thing, Treyarch. Nothing more!'

'Hanigan!' yelled Daspar, shocking her with the suddenness of it. 'It is not a minor thing at all.'

A man who looked to be part wardrobe shuffled into the room. There was another man dangling from his ham of a fist. A man who, this time, had not done himself proud.

She hadn't heard the guards move up behind her. Vullen's subtle work, no doubt. They seized her before she could take more than one step.

Techan was dumped on the marble. Blood already filled his ears, and was smeared across his face in ghastly stripes, where his shaggy hair had soaked in it. His glimpse-robes were cut at the collar, revealing bruises that almost matched the dark of his cloth. A smell—similar to burnt flesh— had wafted in with them. She knew it well, and that only made her struggle more.

'You...' The words died on her tongue.

Daspar wagged a finger. 'Careful now, Zealot Frayne. You know what has to happen.'

She flashed her teeth at the man. To tell the truth, she hadn't the faintest idea; just a growing sense of bewilderment, turning colder with every moment.

'I don't understand.'

'"No fruits shall Zealots bear between them."' Daspar let the words dangle for a moment before they came crashing down. They might as well have been rocks, for the way she slumped in the guards' grip.

'Lies!'

Daspar heaved himself forward to make sure she saw the cut of his expression; to see just how stony it was. 'I am only repeating it as it is written down in ink and parchment, Ellia. The Architect's wisdom is the only fruit you need bear.' He waved a hand. 'Especially when it concerns a bastard conceived of secrets and skulking. You knew precisely what you were doing, and now you'll watch what your disobedience means for those who you, dare I imagine, *love*.'

The poison was carried in on a silver tray. She saw no servant; not even the two other zealots trailing behind it, not even the shattered expression on Techan's face. Just the bottle; a smoked-glass vial the size of her littlest finger, stoppered by a bright-red cork.

She wasn't sure whether they had forced her jaw open, or she had let them. As they tilted her head back, she clung to one mercy. The bitter spew being poured down her throat was not a cheap tincture from some alleyway vialman. The powdered herbs were expensive. Nobody spends coin on a corpse, especially before the corpse is made a corpse. Death is the cheapest thing going.

When the last drip had dropped, they left her to double up and howl.

The order was a distant holler to her, but she caught it all the same.

'And now the bastard's father!'

Hanigan was a professional at least. When it comes to executioners, it's the little touches that can make the difference between clean and kind, gurgling and messy; like making a long cut tucked high into the jaw instead of a ragged little nick low over the windpipe. She'd seen people take almost an hour to die that way; a long time with a lungful of blood instead of air.

She watched the man pitch onto his side, mirroring her as she writhed. He went silently. Perhaps one stuttering cough, and that was it.

To Daspar, his Consecrators, the zealots, and the troll of a man standing over Techan's corpse, it would have seemed a cold parting. And yet even through the pain, she could feel his thoughts slamming against hers in his final moments. Emotions drowned her as though she'd been left under a waterfall. Before she tumbled into a black oblivion, she promised these men one thing. The word chased her into the darkness.

Vengeance.

1

'What is man, if not a shell for the Architect's imagination?'

FROM THE BLESSED MANUAL OF THE ARCHITECT
VORE, VERSE 1

37TH FADING, 3782 - HARTLUND

The day that gripped the Irkmire Yawn was a foul one.

The strip of sea was strangled with eager winds, the air choked with icy drizzle, and the sea boiled to a spray.

The only mercy the Yawn could offer the valiant men of the glorified barge was its size. The gap between Irkmire and the soaring cliffs of Hartlund was barely eight leagues at its skinniest point. The journey may have been a detestable wash of rain and saltwater, but it was a brief and relatively steady one. The *Bilgesnapper* was a stout craft. Its squat shape and mean, flat prow bludgeoned the waters aside, bothered not a penny by the swell.

With the sails stripped almost bare, and the belowdecks crammed with two-score of sweating rowers, the rest of the barge's crew had taken to sulking below the gunwales. They blew into their hands and grimaced through the murk. Each of them rocked back and forth in odd and silent unison, slave to the monotonous canter of the sea.

'There ain't nought miserabler than a Lundish fading's day,' wheezed an old sailor, trussed up in two thick coats and still shivering. His olive skin spoke of a southern heritage and time spent in the sun. Even the seawater and drizzle hadn't managed to bring a chill to it.

Ole Jub was right. The others around him murmured in agreement, each of them pulling at their collars, as if the mere sight of Jub made them all feel the cold a little keener.

Another sailor took up the chatter, eyes wide and urgent under the brim of his floppy brown hat, which had wilted in the wet. He had a worry in him, and was eager to see it voiced. He was not alone; a few of the sailors around him shared the same awkward expression.

'Ain't even some good pouches at the end of this, did you 'ear? We should be gettin' double for the danger,' he hissed. 'Spit on it all!'

A woman's voice shushed him from the stairwell, just a few bodies behind. She was barely audible over the wind and slapping waves. 'Oh, give it a rest, will you, Norbin? You're twitching over a spot of rain. You've seen worse.'

Norbin wasn't thankful for her words. He shot her a baleful look over his shoulder. 'An' I told you to shut it, Kein. Ain't the weather I'm worried about, and you knows it.' His eyes fell back to the deck as another soldier came edging past, spear low. Norbin needn't have worried; the man was too preoccupied with the... *thing*.

That was the only word for it.

When the soldier had passed, he snuck another look at the great lump sitting square in the centre of the deck, beside the mast. There was an empty circle around it, made out of fear. Nobody—not one soldier, not one sailor—dared to come within an oar's length of the thing. If that wasn't reason enough to worry, Norbin didn't know what was.

Kein had never been one for letting up. She shuffled along the deck, clearly keen to be heard. 'What's wrong? You afraid of old-magic?'

There came a bark from the aft-castle. 'Quiet down there!'

As if to punctuate the order, a stray wave stole over the gunnels and splashed their huddle. The sailors moaned as cold water seeped under collars and into the throats of boots, finding new crevices to chill.

'Deffing Yawn,' swore Norbin. He was about to give Kein another piece of his mind when a noise stole away his words. It sounded like the popping of knuckles, or the low grumble of a distant landslide. The chains rattled once and then fell still again.

Norbin jabbed a finger at it. 'See? It's laughing at us!' He cast a look back at Kein, now crouched behind him. Her face was puckered into a smirk. 'I'm tellin' you, it ain't right. I didn't sign my name on no line for this. Evil is what it is. Architect spit on it!'

Kein laughed at that. 'Bet you're glad for the wet, hmm? Can't see you pissin' your breeches then, can we?'

The others chuckled. Norbin spat on the deck.

'Tell me why's it chained up, then,' he said. 'And why they're all giving it a wide berth.'

'Could tip over the side, bein' so heavy n'all,' ventured another shipmate. He was a tall lad, tall enough to poke above the gunnels and receive more drizzle than he deserved. His cheeks were scrunched up so tightly his eyes were two thin slivers.

Norbin whirled on him. 'You can pipe down, Spew! Before I take back that blanket I gave you.'

Spew threw up his hands. 'That ain't fair!'

'Cap'n doesn't want it moving around, is all,' said Kein.

Norbin scoffed. 'Fawl-piss! It's bloody dangerous, that's why. The *snapper* is solid as a harbour. Alright, 'ow many soldiers we got on this ship, eh? Why are all they needed then? It's a demon, I'm tellin' you.'

Laughter.

'It's a machine for the war, you deffer.'

'Yeah, something special for the Truehards.'

'I don't care. Their war ain't my war.'

'Oh no, that's right. You're the man whose only home is the sea, ain't you?'

'You can shut it as well, Fargle!'

'Well it's about time somebody mentioned it.'

'You've told us four times this week already.'

'Be *quiet* down there!' First mate Botch, eager to stretch his chords as usual. 'We're coming out of the deep waters. See to!'

The crew begrudgingly saw to it. Apparently a little more begrudgingly than management would have liked.

'I said SEE TO, you ingrates!' roared Botch.

'Yessir!' The crew scurried across the deck, giving the cargo a wide berth, although they still allowed themselves a quick glimpse through the ring of soldiers.

The *Bilgesnapper* nosed into a shallow crescent of grey beach that lay in the shadow of the Drunken Cliffs. A gaggle of people waited on the sand, maybe half a dozen at most.

Norbin stretched his neck upwards to gaze at the rocks, as was his habit whenever they came to Hartlund by this route. They had sailed the Yawn less and less in recent months. Something to do with the Lundish being penniless.

The Drunken Cliffs were aptly named; only alcohol could elicit such an angle from its victims. The slabs of grey granite were pressed tightly together, halfway fallen like slumping books on a shelf. Their lofty heights were covered by dark green grass, and the barely visible threads of a small crowd. Between them and the beach, a jagged yet impressive footpath ran in a zig-zag through the rock.

Now that the barge had been swallowed by the shadow of the rock, the day seemed even gloomier and wetter than before. Fortunately for Norbin, he was on anchor duty, and that meant a scrap of shelter behind the fat capstan, to the side of the bow and under a walkway.

From there, he could get another decent eyeful of the thing; as big an eyeful as the murk could afford, at least.

If he peered hard enough, he could make out contours beneath the green tarpaulin, and gauge the girths encircled by the chains. The soldiers had taken a liberal approach with the irons. The thing was practically clothed in them.

Norbin silently begged it to move, as if to prove it was not some sort of rain-crafted mirage; a trick of the sea-spray.

'Master Ghurn!' yelled Botch.

Norbin raised a hand. 'Yessir?'

'To the bow, you, and Miss Simpkins!'

'Yessir!' Norbin inwardly groaned, but did as he was told.

Kein scurried past him, always eager to lick an arse whenever one was presented. Norbin glowered at her as he put one hand on the cog and one hand on the brake.

'Hold oars!' yelled the captain. Hecka was her name; a Graden who'd inherited the *Bilgesnapper* from her dead father. She sailed it as though it were his tombstone.

The big barge shuddered as the oars were held fast, bucking the momentum.

'Boat oars!'

There was a squeaking of painted wood on wet metal as the oars were brought in. They stuck on the shale beneath the waters.

'Hold!'

Norbin always like to count. His challenge was to see if he could make the crunch land on three. To his private infuriation, he was always slightly out.

With a loud scraping, the flat bottom of the barge met the beach, pressing the scattered pebbles into the sand.

'Door!' came the order.

Norbin released the brake and held the pressure of the cog for a moment before gently loosing it. The snub-nosed bow slowly peeled away from the ship, forming a ramp between the deck and the damp sand.

'All yours, Captain Jenever!' called Hecka.

'Thank you, Madam,' said a hoarse voice amongst the soldiers.

Norbin toyed with his thumbs behind his back, squeezing them between fingers. He could tell Kein was looking at him, but he didn't give her the satisfaction of meeting her gaze. He could feel what little colour he had left in his face draining away.

From there, at the bow, he could finally understand the architecture of the chains. His eyes tumbled down the outlines of the thing. *Head. Shoulders. Arms.*

'Right, then,' said the soldier captain, stepping forward to tap the hulking cargo with the butt of her sword. It felt far too solid for flesh. The sailors hugged the gunwales as the men in armour stepped forward. They brought their spears up, one by one. 'Time for you to wake up!'

The sound came again; that rumble, like fawl bones cracking. It sent a shiver down Norbin's spine. The thing didn't deign to move. It felt as though it was taunting them.

'I said, wake up!' The captain poked again.

The thing moved. Its form shifted under the tarpaulin, head twitching to the side.

'Now behave!' Jenever warned it, bringing her sword-tip to bear.

The only answer she got was a noise that sounded like two rocks grinding together.

'It's time for you to meet your new owner,' said Jenever, as she signalled to her men. 'You four, see to those chains. Don't let them out of your grasp.'

The thing seemed to have other ideas. Slowly, inexorably, before fingers could get to bolts, it rose to standing. The tarpaulin was ripped aside. Chain-links unfurled as if they were made of rusted wire. Chunks of planking sprang forth, skittering across the deck. The soldiers stood frozen in awe.

The monster was immense, standing at least nine foot-lengths tall without being generous. Its flesh was made of slabs of stone knitted together, ashen-grey with veins of misty blue, shifting with every crunch and shiver of its swollen limbs. Its shoulders were as broad as a battering ram, and its fingers were jagged shards, stained black like a fireplace and shining like marble at the tips.

Norbin felt his gaze being drawn towards the thing's jagged face; heavy-jawed and angular. He could not avoid those eyes; bewitching points of light that seemed to escape scrutiny, floating in two deep-set black hollows. They fixed him with a cold look as he passed, and the sailor felt his chin quiver as the stone beast marched down the ramp with purpose.

Norbin knew then that he would die a different man than the one who had started the day picking weevils from crackers. He would go to his grave knowing that it was not man which the Architect had built in his image, but this great monster who had pierced his soul in the time it took to share a glance.

2

'War drives men to great things. Great evils, great sacrifices, great bravery. But also great innovation.'

FROM WAYS OF THE HASP, BY ALBIN CROSSIT

37TH FADING, 3782 - HARTLUND

With a mighty thud, his foot dug deep into the sand. It blended almost perfectly with the grey hues of the grit. It looked as if he was rooted to the earth, like some growth that had sprouted to scare the sea-goers.

The shouting of the soldiers was just noise to him. In his many years, he had learnt that most of the sounds that skinbags make are useless clamour. *Or lies.*

He spied a brown pebble sitting in a puddle and bent to pick it up. Spears waggled in his face as he did so, but he paid them no heed. Transitions were often tense for both parties. He wasn't exactly the brand of mercenary people were used to.

'Hold it there!' It was the one with all the metal on her. She wore at least double the armour of any of her men, and waved her sword about like a riding whip.

The pebble was an interesting one, speckled with flecks of crystal. His stone fingers wrapped around it, feeling its smooth grain, living its ages. This was a cold land, a bitter land, an old land that had seen too many years for its own good.

'Put it down!' ordered the suit of armour. A spear was tucked under her arm, its point wavering. 'I said, put it down.'

The pebble was tossed to the sand. Task had already learnt enough from it. The woman could have the pebble, though he doubted she could glean its secrets. *Only stone can truly know stone.*

The others on the beach had grown impatient. They were striding across the sand towards the ring of spears. They wanted a better look at their new monster.

The suit of armour saluted them as they approached, clicked her boots together and covered her eyes with her palm.

A skinny man with a circle of glass wedged in one eye elbowed his way between the soldiers. He wore a formal suit with a long coat that brushed the sand. Not a single hair sprouted from his head.

'My, my! If my lungs hadn't already been emptied by this wind and blasted cold, this would be leaving me breathless, gentlemen.'

'It's a bloody giant!' said another; a pudgy man with a suit of plate-mail and a pointed helmet. There was a long musket at his side, held with white knuckles.

The beast shrugged his shoulders. The crunching of rocks almost sounded like a growl.

A woman came forwards. She was slender, wrapped in a long green coat lined with fur. Her fiery red hair thrashed in the pestering winds. 'It is not a giant, Sergeant. It is a blue golem of Wind-Cut. In the flesh, so to speak.'

'Do you mind?' asked the glass-eyed man, stepping closer. *A brave one, him.*

The golem held out a hand, nodded, and watched as the man gently touched the pitted stone, then felt the edges of his thick fingers. 'Each like a knife in its own right. Marvellous! You've done us proud, Baroness. Dartridge will be pleased.'

The woman bowed her head. 'All I care about is how the younger Dartridge is going to handle this. It's a monster.'

'Dartridge.' The golem tested the word. His voice was rasping, lacking in depth. He spoke again to bring a rumble to the name, like distant thunder. 'Dartridge is the new master.'

'It speaks!' Glass-eye exclaimed, raising both hands. The armpits of his suit ripped in the process and he cursed. 'Spit on it! Where have all the good tailors of this country gone to?'

'Normont, most likely,' said the woman. 'There is a war on, you know.'

'Cowards!'

The golem flexed his hands.

Glass-eye had finished tutting at his suit and was now readjusting the circle of silk tied about his neck. 'Yes, Mr Golem. General Huff Dartridge the Third is your new owner. He awaits you at his camp. It's a bit of journey, I'm afraid.'

The woman rolled her eyes. 'You can't call him "Mr Golem". Do you have a name… golem?'

'Task, of Wind-Cut,' he said, spitting out the consonants. He only had trouble with the soft ones. Stone lips weren't built for words.

14

Glass-eye motioned to the cliffs. 'A fine name. Now, I say we get toddling. Can we trust you, golem? No more breaking of chains? Nor necks for that matter?'

Task nodded.

'Fantastic! Onwards, then. Out of this infernal rain.'

They followed Glass-eye, as he headed for the chiselled gap in the cliffs. They walked in single file with Task at their centre, spears clamouring at his back. Task wondered if they believed their spears could hurt him, or if the wood and weight just gave them the courage they needed. They'd soon realise how useless they were. *They always did.*

The stairs were too small for him, so he took three at a time; sometimes four, if he felt adventurous. Their climb passed slowly to the drone of clanking armour and the pound of Task's feet on the stone. Three times they doubled back on themselves, and three times Task ran his fingers against the cliff-rock, tasting every eon of its crushed layers.

Glass-eye hovered by his arm. 'I realise I have yet to introduce myself. I am Councillor Dast, envoy to the King and his Council.'

Task nodded. Dast went on. 'You know, I do hope the wagon we procured will be up to the task, pardon the pun. Ha!' He seemed pleased with himself, as if he was the first man in four hundred years to think of that joke.

The man with the gun spoke over his shoulder. 'The general assured me it could hold the weight of several cannons, so I trust it will be fine.'

'I feel sorry for the firns that have to pull it,' cackled Dast.

A larger group of soldiers and watchers greeted them at the summit of the slanted cliffs. Their jaws dropped and slowly rose again. Their eyes stayed wide. It was as if Task was too big to take in all at once.

The soldiers poked him towards a nearby cart. Four large beasts with fur and scales sat in hames and traces, shackled to a stout wooden wagon. Several other cloth-covered wagons waited nearby. Lanterns glowed within them.

The firns were strange beasts, full of meat and long in the spine. They had stubby tails and ridged backs, and pointy heads, held low. Their scales were an ochre-brown; diamond-shaped and overlapping like fine armour. Their bellies and long legs were wrapped in a dark, mottled fur. They chuntered in the cold, their steaming breath snatched away by the wind. Sharp teeth poked from leathery mouths. Stubby claws stamped in the mud.

A few sacks of sand had been piled onto the wet grass, arranged like a set of steps. Task tested one with a foot before stepping down. He felt them creak and wheeze before he knelt on the wagon's bed. The wheels groaned, but held steady, and Task arranged himself into a sitting position. Another tarpaulin was draped over him, but they left him enough room to stare out.

'Hope you don't mind the rain!' said Dast, before nipping into his wagon, into the dry.

The whips cracked and Task tilted his head to face the direction of the wind, letting the drizzle whip his face. He allowed himself one of his private smiles.

He loved the rain.

The silent countryside rolled by at a stately pace. Every now and again, when the wind wasn't rushing over his craggy features, he would get a glimpse of his new land.

Hartlund, he had heard it called. From what he knew of maps it was a fractured world in the northwest of Normont, at the far reaches of the Accord.

Task had never been this far north. Though the weather seemed pleasant enough, the cold was a constant prickle, seeping into his stone. Not even in the darkest hours of a frigid desert night had he felt this type of coldness. It emanated from the ground like a mist.

The countryside was a permanent wash of green. Though the trees were skeletal and naked, and the daylight murky, the rolling hills and stretching fields of grass were a deep emerald. Stone walls divided up the land, made of flat blocks piled atop one another, much like his own construction. Task scrutinised every one of them.

Most of the land seemed abandoned. Fields that had been sowed now rotted in the chilly air. Livestock seemed a rare sight, but here and there, beasts would low and snuffle at them through broken fences. There were more of the firn creatures, and smaller horned versions, but with fluff instead of scale. They were fat enough, despite their wild looks. It looked like the grass had been doing its job, even if the fences had failed theirs.

The verdant expanses were punctuated by churches with squat spires and cottages with thatched roofs. A few people came out to peek at the tramping soldiers and the wobbling wagons. Task saw the worry in their faces, the whiteness of their knuckles as they clutched babes and grimy children. A few even came to their doors with muskets or clubs. The soldiers let them be, not even sparing them a glance. Task clenched his fists all the same. It seemed the cold was not the only thing that had seeped into this land. He could taste the fear in the air.

Here and there, as they wove a merry pattern down dirt paths walled with hedgerows, and cracked flagstone road, he caught the signs of battle. Of death. The last tendrils of fire hovering over a village; the stench of firepowder in a valley; craters in the earth where cannonballs had met the ground; hills churned to mud where countless boots had come marching.

At one point they trundled through an abandoned town, and Task rattled with every bump its cobbled streets had to offer. All the doors were barred with planks, and embers still smouldered in the streets where fires had blazed. Every one of the crooked buildings was dark and empty. They leant over the street as if in mourning, walls and thatch punctured with holes from cannon and musket. A few bodies still lay in doorways, their hands crooked, faces more bone than skin.

Task caught glimpses of ragged children hiding in alleys, mud and fear on their faces. They were as white as parchment in their torn clothes. Alone and hungry.

As they ambled back into the country, escaping the gloom of the town, Task wondered what had eaten the soul of Hartlund. What had brought this country to rot and rust and worry?

There was only one reason to be fond of soldiers in Task's mind: they could never hold their tongues. A tongue to a golem was a very precious thing, not to be wagged about or left unchecked. But soldiers liked to gossip. Task had gleaned a fair few whispers on the long journey from Lezembor, but none of them helpful.

All he knew was that this land was in the grip of a civil war. The people had taken a dislike to its crown, formed their own armies and called for battle. He would be fighting for a king's general. A Truehard, he'd heard them branded. *A royalist.*

Another general. Task had fought for many in his lifetime, and he had yet to find one he liked. Flesh and stone did not mix; like water and fire. *You either get steam or one dies.*

There was one thing he enjoyed holding onto during every transition, and that was the glimmer of hope. The dogged hope that this master would be different; that their war would be different.

The golem snorted at the countryside. Four hundred years, and he was still waiting.

General Huff Dartridge the Third was pacing. He liked to pace. He thought it showed determination. Standing still spoke of indecision.

'We'll show it around first. Let it get the lay of the camp. Just in case it needs anything.'

A burly man to his left cleared his throat. He stood easy, with his arms folded behind his back, staring at an insect that was busy headbutting the lantern. 'What exactly would a golem need, sir? Water, perhaps?'

'Just in case, Manx, just in case. It may want me, at times.' Dartridge wagged a finger for extra emphasis.

'Of course, sir.'

'And, Glum. Have you found a berth for it?'

'I 'ave, sir,' said a sour-looking attendant slumped at the back of the room. 'Over by the stables, there's a patch of spare paddock. Seems only fair. Beasts with the beasts.'

The general nodded. 'It will have to do for now.'

'Will it be wanting a mattress, sir? Straw?' said Manx, still enraptured by the moth.

'I doubt it, Captain,' said Dartridge, before huffing and snatching the moth from the air mid-stride. He crumpled it up in his hands, grimaced at the mess, and flicked it to the wood. 'I want nobody bothering it.'

'Not a soul, sir.'

'It's mine, understand?'

'Absolutely, sir!'

Dartridge came to a halt, hands on hips, foot tapping. 'How long?'

Glum took out a pocket watch. 'Within the hour.'

'Right, off with you then. To the gate to keep watch. Let me know the moment it arrives.'

'Yessir!' the pair duetted, before making themselves scarce.

After making a mental note to order Glum to bathe the next time he saw him, he went to the mirror and checked his uniform. A clean uniform, even in a time of war, is a sign of composure and meticulousness. Huff liked that word. *Meticulousness.*

He nudged a fibre from his shoulder and patted his blonde hair back into place. It was always sneaking out of shape on wet days.

With his appearance in check, Huff fetched his favourite pistol from his cabinet and affixed it to his belt. He took a seat at his desk; if it could really be called a desk. It was more of a glorified folding table. Then he templed his fingers.

For almost an hour he waited, letting his thoughts wander through the future, painting pictures of his forthcoming victories. He was grinning by the time the captains came to call on him.

'General, sir. It's arrived,' said Manx.

Glum nodded. 'Your new toy, sir.'

Dartridge shot Glum a mean look. 'It is not a toy, Captain. It is a *weapon.*'

Glum saluted, covering his eyes. 'Right you are, sir.'

'Well, where is it?'

Manx jerked a thumb over his shoulder. 'Comin' up the southern road, all slow and tired by the looks of it.'

'It looks big, sir. *Very* big.'

The general pointed the way, letting his two captains fall in behind him. Together, they cut through the saluting crowds of Truehard soldiers, making straight for the southern gates. Huff let the smile grow on his cheeks again and injected a little strut in his stride. It was a momentous day, after all. The turn of the war, to be precise. Even the drizzle couldn't bother him today.

'Open the gates!'

The stout doors revealed a drab road snaking out into the countryside, and on it, a trail of wagons and soldiers, crawling at walking pace. Fortunately, they were close, but Huff still fidgeted with every pace they took.

'Welcome back!' he said, once the dignitaries had extricated themselves from their individual wagons and come to stand in the shadow of the wooden gates. 'Not too awful a journey, I trust?'

'Miserable,' Councillor Dast grumbled, flicking raindrops from his coat collar.

Dartridge turned to Baroness Frayne. Her face was courteous yet impassive.

'Baroness?'

'Far too long. He is at the back of the line.'

Dartridge raised an eyebrow. He hadn't considered genders. 'He?'

'Sounds like a he to me,' said Sergeant Collaver, shouldering his musket.

'Well, then,' said the general, clapping his hands together. 'Let's see what my father has procured for me. For us. Bring it forward!'

A whip cracked, unseen, and the bobbing noses of four firns came into view. Something monstrous sat on their wagon. Huff's heart performed a brief dance.

'Jenever! Take that tarpaulin off it. Off *him*, that is. Does he have a name?'

'He calls himself Task,' Frayne told him.

'How apt.'

'Indeed,' said the Baroness, still devoid of emotion as always. Her cheeks had been pinched red by the cold.

'Come forward, sir!' Huff ordered, waving a hand for the sheet to be dragged away.

His eyes widened as the light found the dark stone. The golem's muscles bulged, revealing every pit and rift of the stone skin. His flesh was knitted from thin blades of stone, stacked tightly together. They moved like clotted liquid as he pushed himself from the wagon and came to tower over the huddle. He must have been nine foot-lengths tall, maybe brushing ten. He was the very definition of towering.

'Incredible!' Huff mouthed, voice stolen. 'How does one build such a thing?'

Frayne had the answer. 'Piece by piece, from stones carved with the force of rushing air, each blessed with old charms, so they say.'

'With patience,' the golem corrected her, with a voice like pickaxes meeting granite. His eyes turned on Huff. 'You are the new master?'

The general felt his mouth flap, so he puffed out his chest and said, 'I am.'

Task bent to one knee, coming face to face with him. 'Show me.'

Huff was momentarily mesmerised by the pinpricks of light burning in the golem's hollow eye sockets. He had not expected that. Perhaps he had imagined eyes also made of stone, or dark voids; not these shivering flares that pressed him into the ground whenever he managed to meet them.

Frayne coughed. 'General?'

'Of course,' said Huff, remembering himself. He reached into the pocket of his military jacket and brought forth folded parchment. 'Task! Here we have the signed contract between my father, the king, and I, assigning me as an owner. Here is another contract signed by your late master Ghoffi. When he died, you became mine. My name is General Huff Dartridge the Third. You may call me General, or Master. Whichever you prefer.'

'A master is always a master,' the golem replied, peeling open the document with his colossal fingers.

'Indeed he is,' Huff gulped.

'I am satisfied,' Task rumbled, and stuck out his tongue. It was a strange thing, fashioned from glossy bright-blue stone, like the warmest of summer skies.

Huff stared at it for a moment before shrugging.

Dast sighed. 'You have to touch it, General. Your father sent you instructions for a reason.'

'Ah.' Huff reached out a nervous hand. His eyes were busy sizing up the beast's jagged teeth.

The tongue was cold and hard, exactly as stone should be. He managed only a brush of it before it snapped back into the black void of the golem's mouth.

The monster rose to its feet and bowed.

'Master,' it said. There came a brief splutter of applause from the soldiers. Huff decided he rather liked the sound of "Master." Especially when it was being said by a stone war machine.

Huff bowed back. As he rose, he met the mismatched gazes of his men; some narrowed, others plainly bored. His army was fraying at the edges. It had spent a Fading seesawing between defeat and digging trenches in the frozen ground. That sort of existence will gnaw at even the most determined of men.

Since taking command, just as the first Fading snows were falling, Huff had scrabbled for ways to summon some motivation. Looking back at the jagged stone fingers, he smiled. *Now he had it.* What could be more motivational than the promise of a swift end to a bitter task? And war was the bitterest task of all.

Huff felt the need for a speech. He faced the soldiers.

'Today is a momentous day, my comrades!' he began, recalling the words he had spent half the morning speaking into his mirror. 'I know many of you will be concerned about this new addition to our ranks, but let me reassure you. With my... with this new weapon, this creature, Task, we will finally be able to push the Last Fading back beyond the Six Sisters and reclaim our stolen land. And we will not stop there! We will cut a path straight to Lord Lash's front doorstep before Rising Day, and bring our own warmth to the land! The Truehards will have victory, friends! Victory at last!' Huff punched the air as he cried out.

The silence was awkward.

A few of the soldiers broke into a sheepish cheer. Others clapped as they shuffled about on their cold feet. The rest just chewed tobacco and stared, glassy-eyed like old fawls.

'Shall we let the men get back to their duties, General?' said Collaver, tapping his musket on the ground.

Huff gritted his teeth. 'Yes, Sergeant. I think that would be best.'

Collaver's bellow was loud enough to make even the golem flinch. 'DISMISSED!'

'Come,' said Huff to Task. 'Let us have a few words, you and I.'

'Yes, Master.'

That really did have a good ring to it. Huff found his swagger in three quick strides.

Task caught every stare and grimace the soldiers had to throw at him. Mistrust. Hate, Envy. He had seen them all before. One man spat at his feet as the crowd dispersed. The sergeant, Collaver, clipped the soldier around his head with a gauntlet and sent him packing. Human emotions were naught but a fizzing grenade; dangerous and unpredictable.

Task kept his eyes on his master's back and his feet moving, leaving great prints in the mud.

The mood in the camp seemed sombre. Cold. No music floated between the canvas tents, no clashing of battle practice rang in the wet air. The only noise-maker was a blacksmith, busy beating the life out of a pike blade. Even he paused his clanging to curl a lip at Task's passing. Blacksmiths were all the same. If it couldn't be melted and hammered into shape, they weren't interested.

The road meandered through the mass of conical tents and wagons. Everything was either a soil-brown, or a deep maroon. All around, lanterns hung on poles, swinging in the wind and at least giving the gloom something to contend with. Shields rested against tent-poles, denoting regiments and their place in the camp hierarchy. Queues formed before rickety latrines constructed over deep ditches. Priests in white smocks toured the crowds, offering prayers. Everywhere Task looked, the soldiers seemed entrenched, as if they had been there for years. That might have explained their foul expressions.

Here and there, Task saw a long-bodied creature snaking through the mud: a four-legged thing, a mess of scale and fur with big floppy ears and a whiskered snout. Its sinuous body looked stretched out, like hot glass. He wondered whether it was for eating or for fighting.

There was a slight rise in the centre of the camp where a caravan had been built, like a castle dominating a town. Slowly, they wound their way up to its entrance, where a dozen flags crackled on their poles and twice as many guards stood on alert. The suit of armour from the ship waited with them, a strong pout on her lips.

Task had to duck to squeeze through the doorway. He took up a hunched stance beneath a dangling lantern as the general and the others made themselves at home. The Baroness found a chair by the door, as did Glass-eye, Dast. The others just found spots to stand on, claiming them with a crossing of the arms.

The general sat down to spread his hands over the dark-wood tabletop and smile. 'So, Task. You must be excited?'

Task lowered his brows. Out of the corner of his eye, he could see the woman shaking her head. He was inclined to agree with her. Privately, of course.

'Excited?'

His master waved his hands as if tossing some understanding at him. 'Yes. Excited to begin winning this war for us! To dive in and start making a difference.'

"Excited" wasn't the word that Task would have used for this situation. He made his shoulders crack.

'I am to do whatever a master commands of me.'

'You could command him to be excited,' suggested Dast.

'A good point, Councillor,' said Huff, wagging a finger. 'Golem, are there any limits to our new arrangement?'

Task nodded, then recited in monotone. 'There are three rules I am bound to. I cannot disobey my master, I cannot harm my master, and I cannot harm myself. Those are the three pillars we each must abide by.'

Huff looked pleased with that. He slapped a hand on the desk. 'Well, how about that? Seems a fair deal! Tell me then, what can you do? On the battlefield, I mean.'

'I fight.'

'Of course! But I mean do you have powers? Abilities? Magic?'

Frayne sighed. 'It's a Wind-Cut Golem, Dartridge, I think that's magic enough, don't you?'

Huff deflated. 'You're right, I suppose. Well then, we shall just have to see on the morrow won't we?'

'Tomorrow, Dartridge?' said Dast.

Huff rose to adjust his medallions. 'Yes, *tomorrow*, Councillor. We push forward at dawn. It'll give my men something to do. Golem, how long do you need to prepare?'

'I am always ready.'

Huff clapped his hands. 'Did you hear that? I wish I had ten of these. I must write a letter to my fath—'

'General!' shouted the councillor. 'Are you sure a push tomorrow is wise? What with the men being so out of shape and all.'

'You heard him with your own ears, Dast. He's always ready. That is a model my men will learn to live by. Here…' Huff snatched the helmet from Collaver's head. The man glowered but kept his mouth shut.

'Crush this,' ordered Huff, waving it under Task's nose.

Every time. It was as if a stone beast wasn't truly impressive unless he was breaking things. It was why he had broken his chains at the beach, to get it over and done with. Alas, Huff had not been there to see it.

Task took the helmet in his fingers and effortlessly flattened it into a plate. He handed it back to Huff, who laughed.

'Very good. Very good!'

Baroness Frayne was not so impressed. 'This is a serious matter, Dartridge. It is not just some toy your father's bought you.'

Huff fixed the baroness with a haughty gaze. 'I am in complete agreement, my good Councillor. In fact, I was reprimanding Captain Glum there not moments ago for the same comment.' Over by the door, Glum lowered his head. 'But you should know that my father has instructed me to do what I wish with this weapon, and I intend to do just that.

'For almost half a year now, this army has loitered here, with nothing but skirmish after skirmish. "Barely holding the line", we were. My father's very words. The Last Fading have pushed beyond their limits and now is the time to strike them, before they find support from the Accord and fancy their chances at taking Caverill. I made a promise to my father and the king, and I intend to keep it. I will see this war won, I will see justice served to traitors, and he is my key to achieving this.' He thrust a finger in Task's direction.

Frayne stroked her furs as she got to her feet. 'You have a lot of eyes upon you, General. It would be wise to remember that. I bid you all a good day. Mr Task.'

Task nodded to her, watching how her eyes lingered on him.

'We should get you to your berth,' said Huff, pointing towards the door. 'Manx, Glum. Escort our new friend out.'

The sky had turned to rain during their thankfully brief meeting. Task raised his head as he was led from the caravan and down a long, winding path to the edge of the camp. Half a dozen rough stables had been constructed out of spare tents and fence-posts. Some were large, others skinny and wilting. Their paddocks seemed the focus; hundreds of beasts snuffled in pens that must have stretched for a quarter-league, maybe more. It was hard to tell in the haze.

Task was shown to the skinniest of the strange buildings. There were two paddocks; one empty and the other playing host to a trio of the scaly beasts that had dragged him here. They didn't look too pleased with the new arrangements, and snuffled as the golem approached, bleating and entangling themselves.

'I've had a paddock cleared for you, so you have your own space,' Huff was explaining. 'Privacy, if needed.'

Task looked up and down the path, eyeing the handful of skinbags who were braving the wet. Puffs of vapour emanated from their huddles; breath and smoke, both snatched by the breeze. Task rumbled his gratitude, deep in his belly. It did seem quieter than the rest of the camp, though that was probably for the soldiers' sake, not his. Besides, he had seen worse berths.

Huff showed him the gate. 'You are to stay here until we fetch you.' He took one step before swivelling back. 'Do you sleep?'

'I do.'

Huff hummed, as if considering why in the Realm a golem needed sleep. 'Then we will wake you at first light. What about water? Shelter?'

'Neither.'

'Then I bid you a fine evening, Mr Golem. Welcome to the Truehard army, and to the king's fight!' He strutted away, back to the comfort and dry of his caravan.

Task flicked the gate of his paddock open and settled down into a crouch. For a while, he let the rain dribble down his features as he watched the camp revolve around him. He listened hard to the clanking of carts, the murmur of voices, the drumming of feet.

It was only when the beasts grew comfortable with his presence that he moved, shifting to his backside and letting his cold legs stretch out in the mud and rotten hay. He tested the fence with his weight, found that it held, and allowed himself to rest. The creatures soon graduated from fear to curiosity. They came to snuffle at his stone and wonder at the magic that made him. One even began to lick the rainwater from his shoulder.

'Always thirsty, that'n,' said a small, hollow voice. ''Specially when the sky is leaking.'

Task flicked his head with a grind of stone, finding a small thread of a skinbag leaning on his fence. Her arms lay flat on the wood and her chin balanced on her knuckles. The moonless-black hair that clung about her skinny face was dripping wet. She didn't seem to care.

Task rumbled, a fraction surprised. 'You're a quiet one.' It took a special pair of feet to sneak up on a golem. Or the knack of being a ghost. 'I didn't hear you. Well done. Now leave me alone.'

Skinny Skinbag tilted her head, working her gums. 'Where's your ears, then?'

Task tapped a stone finger to the side of his head, where a small fissure split the skin.

The girl clearly wasn't pleased with the answer. She bounded the fence in one hop and trudged across the mud to stare at the spot in question.

'That ain't no ear I've ever seen before.'

Task leaned away from her probing fingers. She had no fear in her. That was unusual, and in Task's book, unusual meant dangerous.

'Well, have you ever seen a golem before?' he asked, trying to flash teeth.

'No. But I've seen a jork and cafflesnout. Two of those!' Her chest swelled and a smile flashed across her muddy face.

'I don't know what those are. Now, go away—'

The girl cut across him. 'Well, I don't know what a golin is, so now we're even.'

'Golem.'

The girl plonked herself right down next to him, staring at his knobbled knees. 'Where you from?'

Task looked around at his surroundings as if to check. 'Far, far away from here. Lezembor. Haspia. Khandri. Pick one.'

'I'm also from far away. Now we got something in common. Mam says you got to have five things in common to be best friends.'

The girl stood up and stuck out a hand. Task had seen skinbags do this countless times, but he had rarely been offered the gesture himself. Stone fingers didn't make for the kindest shake. Still, being treated like some sort of plague victim suited him fine. The less he touched them, the less he knew. Their ugly lives already seeped into his skin like ink through wet paper.

'You got to shake it.'

Task scrunched up his face, taking an age to reach out a single stone finger. She wrapped it tightly with hers and he shook it as quick as he could.

Her skin felt like cloth, and her life bit into him. Bright colours snapped in his mind, but he pulled away before he could make sense of them.

'Lesky,' she said, face curious. 'That's my name. Lesky, not Pesky, like my master calls me.'

'Task.'

'That's that, then. Now, don't you go botherin' my fawls.'

And with that, she hopped back over the fence and disappeared into the stables, leaving Task alone to wonder at the strangeness of small humans. Harmless, they were. The darkness of humanity would settle in once their bones were grown and their faces chiselled into adulthood, but for now they were a purer creature. He sighed, refusing to dwell.

Before he closed his eyes, he found another pebble in the mud and held it tight between thumb and finger. He hummed a low note as it gave up its secrets.

A cold land, indeed.

3

'The Last Fading's masters hide upon their ghost ship, so far undiscovered by my carracks. The Bastion is a mighty vessel, and I do not understand how it can hide so. I say we let them grow confident, while we continue to patrol the Bitter Sea. We will sink Ebenez and his upstarts eventually.'

WRITINGS OF CAPTAIN KOFF, OF THE KING'S FIRST FLEET

38TH FADING, 3782 - TRUEHARD CAMP

The smell of a war-camp latrine is bested only by the smell of one being torn apart.

Task was wrestled from his slumbers by the wafting stench. He had smelled it even in his scattered dreams, full of water as always. The crash and yells had dragged him fully into wakefulness.

His hollow eyes sprang open to find one of the fawls staring down at him, a sliver of drool dangling from its mottled lip. It bleated as Task reached out a hand and pushed his face from the paddock mud.

An icy mist had snuck into the camp at night, and now it wrapped the pointed tents and lantern-poles with its cloth, dulling the edges of the dim morning. The sun had barely climbed over the horizon, and the lanterns still cast fuzzy auras in the murk.

Task peered around for the source of the noise. Further down the path it looked as if a latrine had collapsed mid-removal, throwing several soldiers into a ditch. Indignant shouts came floating on the wooly air. Shapes sank to the soil, crumpled by laughter. Officers waved sticks for order.

Though the rest of the camp was hidden by the mist, if Task strained he could hear the muffled din of hammers and axes, the snuffling of beasts and the running of feet. It seemed General Huff was eager to get moving.

Task climbed to his feet, scattering the fawls. He crunched his neck back and forth, and stood at gate, arms dangled by his sides, shoulders hunched as usual. In the privacy of his morning, he allowed himself a deep yawn. Sleep had been shallow. The dreams always pounced when he slept on strange soils.

He stayed that way for some time, scratching at his stones that had yet to wake up, while the stables were broken down into wagon and wheels around him. He was mostly ignored. A wide berth formed around him and stayed there. Mistrusting glares formed its edges.

Lesky weaved in between the taller bodies, carrying steaming cups and wearing a vexed frown. She had mentioned a master, and there he was: a balding man with a beard on his cheeks and plague-scars beneath his eyes. He threw orders at her and the other workers like an bowman dispatched arrows.

'Don't forget anyone!... You mind that lantern, lad! They won't give me another... Don't stand there, girl!... Mind my bloody head!... No, your *other* left, you bloody deffer!'

And so on. Task immediately disliked the man, with more than the usual disgust he held for the skinbags. Bullies were a breed that would have made his hackles rise, if he'd had any. He fixed the stable-master with a thin stare.

'And what are you looking at, you great lump of rock?'

Task did not answer. He simply kept staring. It had taken a few decades to discover the effect of still eyes and a quiet tongue. Now, watching men crumble under the weight of his gaze was one of his few indulgences.

The stable-master wrinkled a lip as he took the bait. He began to walk closer. A few workers slapped at his sleeve, urging him on. They were keen to see the golem in action, so long as it didn't involve them. Ganner had volunteered, as far as they were concerned. They flung out a few vacant warnings, in case it all turned sour.

'Ain't worth it, Ganner!'

'Huff'll have you on bog duty for the next week.'

But Ganner wasn't to be deterred. 'I'm going to teach this dumb beast some manners.'

Task's eyes followed the man in his march to the paddock gate. The golem stretched to his full height and watched Ganner wilt in his shadow.

'Now look here, beast. You keep those unholy eyes of yours off me, off all of us! I don't want no old-magic sneaking into my mind, corruptin' me. We were doing just fine before you came along. Don't need you gettin' in the way, do we, lads?'

'You tell him, Ganner!' said a soldier, a little bolder now he had seen a man challenge the golem without being turned to a bloody smear.

'This ain't your war, beast!' shouted another.

Task raised a hand, making Ganner skip away from the fence. A few of the others flinched as well; an added bonus.

Seeing the broad curve in the golem's lips, the stable-master spat in the mud and stalked back to the soldiers, muttering. 'Freak o' bloody nature... Pesky! More glugg!'

Task caught Lesky's hazel gaze as she scampered out from behind a crate. There was an emotion in her eyes he had not seen in a while. It looked almost apologetic.

It took almost an hour for Huff to arrive, and by then, the camp was almost packed away. The mist rose with the sun, though it still clung to the hollows and ditches as best it could. Task caught glimpses of powder-blue through the unravelling clouds.

His master appeared in a clatter of feet and metal, leading a phalanx of guards. Huff was short of breath and red in the face from the weight of his glittering armour. The general had put oil in his hair and moustache to make them shine, and it caught the light as deftly as the plate armour that encased him.

Sergeant Collaver strutted at his side, musket glued to his shoulder as usual, and glass-eyed Dast hovered behind. The woman with the furs, Frayne, was nowhere to be seen.

'There he is!' said Huff, as if the golem might have wandered off in the night.

Task bowed his head in greeting.

'Ready for your first day?'

'I am always—'

Huff waved his hand, cheated of his excitement. 'Yes, I know. You're always ready. I mean are you... Oh, never mind.' He paused to acknowledge the salutes of the nearby soldiers. 'I'm told we are almost ready to move out. It has been far too long since we trod a road that pointed north.'

When Task offered an even blanker expression than usual, Huff elaborated. 'I forget you're a foreigner, so to speak. Since the enemy, the Last Fading, overran the middle counties, the lines of battle have hardly moved in a year. They have scouting forts, you see, watching us.' Huff pointed in two random directions. 'The moment we mobilise, they come marching. It's time we turned the tables on them, don't you think?'

Task nodded, wondering what furniture had to do with war.

The general seemed excited. 'You will travel with the first riders. I want you hidden behind their line, understand? I intend to keep you a surprise as long as I can.' Collaver nodded in appreciation, his new helmet sliding about his bald pate. Dast yawned.

It was a tactic that Task was more than familiar with. His last master, Ghoffi, had been fond of shield walls and of hiding Task behind them. When the arrows stopped falling, that was the sign to start killing.

He felt an old weight settle over his chest. He cleared his throat to shift it, startling Huff.

'Do you understand your orders, golem?'

'I do.'

'Then you leave immediately, before this damn fog lifts and the Fading guess what we're up to. Do me proud, Task. Do me proud.'

Huff even went as far as to clap Task on the arm as he lumbered through the gate. He winced despite his gauntlet, and his guards sniggered.

'Silence!' Huff yelled before storming back the way he'd come. It was a clever trick of those in charge, to always appear busy.

'This way, golem,' said Collaver, nodding his head down the path. Task followed, thankful for the chance to stretch his legs. His stones tended to settle when they weren't being used.

They walked in silence at first, broken only by Collaver's bellowing whenever he saw something not to his liking. Apparently, there was a lot of that going around.

'These soldiers need some sport,' said the sergeant. 'Gettin' too lazy for their own good. You ever fought in Hartlund before?'

'Never.'

'That's right. You've been fightin' for the Borians. Down in the Hinge? The general mentioned that. How does Hartlund compare?'

Humans were obsessed with comparing things. Their fleshy brains seemed wired for measuring. It was a trait that had permeated his stone over the centuries, and become an irritating habit of his own.

'It's wetter.'

'Mm, I expect so. You can blame the God's Rent for that. You know what that is, yes, out in the Blue Mountain Sea? We get the brunt of its sway here. All the storms and all the rain. Good for the crops, though. Which is why the Khandri and the rest of the 'Armony are spittin' poison currently.' He sighed, as if bemused by Realm politics. 'So, I imagine you must have seen a fair few battles in your time, eh? Especially sharing a few borders with the Dozen.'

Task could remember every sparking blow. Every spatter of gore. Every white face staring down at parts now missing. Stone holds onto its memories.

'A fair few.'

'Ten? No, let me guess. Thirty?'

Task shook his head.

'Sixty?'

'More.'

'A hundred?'

'More.'

Collaver tipped back his new helmet and scratched his sweaty forehead.

Task offered an explanation, to put the man at ease. 'I was built for the Diamond Wars.'

'Well, that makes sense. You got some years on you, haven't you? Lucky you're stone, golem, otherwise you'd look like shite.'

Task didn't know what to say to that. He grunted and let Collaver fall into a thoughtful silence.

'Who are the Last Fading, anyway? What does a Last Fading look like? I have not been told much about this war.' They could have been centaurs for all he knew.

The sergeant snorted. 'Huff likes to leave the details to his men. He's a gentleman with a big and noble brain, that one. He's busy focusin' on the important stuff, not on the mini... the mintage. No, the minush...?'

'Minutiae.'

'That's the one. Well, in answer to your question, the Fading are the scum who turned their back on the Boy King Barrein when he first took the throne to the Six Islands. His father had been in the ground barely a year when they made their grab for power. Greedy rich folk and business owners, all upset over taxes and whatnot. All his Highness wanted to do was rebuild the country. But, no! They banded together and bribed thousands of workers to march on Caverill, pitchforks and muskets in hand, sellin' them lies about the king's birthright. They retreated, of course, but them folk have been tryin' to kill us off ever since. Their masters sit all pretty like on a ship in the Bitter Sea.'

'And to answer your other question, Fading look just like you or I... us. Except they dress in grey where we dress in russet and gold. Similar armour, I suppose, but theirs is Braaden-made, bought with stolen gold no doubt. Ours is Lundish through and through.' Collaver thwacked his metal chest for good measure.

'I see.'

Coin. It nipped at the heels of power and religion in the ranking of why wars are fought. *How many had those three spawned across the millennia?*

'Rule of thumb. If we shoot at it or slash it to bits, it ain't ours.'

'I'll remember that.'

They passed through a mighty arch in the wooden palisade, big enough even for Task. Outside the bustle of the camp, the air was colder but quieter. A score of men stood with their beasts. These were not firns for wagons; Task knew a war-beast when he saw one. They were heavily-muscled, their scales taut over broad backs. Their fur shaved tight to vein-rippled skin. Drool hung from their panting jaws, steam leaking from lips lined with ivory teeth. No harness or wagon for these; instead they had been adorned with mail and plate, just like their riders. Horned saddles had been lashed to their ridged backs. Task could feel the trembling in their bodies. Not fear, but the desire to move, to start the hunt.

While the big creatures merely whinnied at him, the riders looked insulted by the golem's presence. They muttered between themselves, mouths hidden behind their visors and gauntlets.

Before Task could walk any further, one of the riders swaggered up to Collaver. He had a sharp cut to his jaw and cheeks, similar to the general. Noble-born, no doubt. He gave the sergeant no salute.

'I don't like this, Collaver,' he said.

'You don't have to like it, Lancer, you just have to do what you're told.'

The officer looked over at Task's thick legs. 'You know we ride fast, right? Anything else is suspicious at best. That thing won't be able to keep up with the firns.'

Task couldn't help but chuckle.

'You stick together. Those are your orders.' Collaver looked tired of backchat and complaints.

'Fine, but at the first sign of trouble, I'm not looking after it.'

'The general wants us to call it by its name.'

That brought the other riders to a splutter. 'It has a *name*?'

'We'll talk about this later, Architect spit on it! Just do your job.'

The officer worked his jaw for a moment before consenting. He covered his eyes.

'Sergeant.'

Collaver adjusted his musket before leaving. 'Lancemaster. Task.'

'Follow on then, beast,' said the rider, without meeting the golem's eyes.

Task cut a slow path to the centre of the group while the riders sought their saddles. With sharp whistles, the firns came to life, scratching at the dirt and shaking their mail. The Lancemaster raised and lowered his weapon, and the beasts sprang into action, galloping across the rumpled countryside.

Task felt like the crockery on a table, standing still as the cloth was whipped from under it.

But he was happy to let them go. He wanted to give them some distance. Making a point often requires patience. He waited until the first cry of laughter floated back to his ears.

Then he moved.

Flattening his hands into blades, he took a few ponderous lunges before settling into a pounding rhythm. His feet struck the earth like meteorites. Wet soil sprayed up behind him.

With each loping stride, his massive bulk lent him momentum, pushing him faster and faster. Within a musket shot, he was gaining on them. Within two, he was at their back.

The look on the first rider's face was a perfect picture, but the Lancemaster's expression was Task's favourite. It was a kind of grim and grudging acceptance that skinbags liked to wear when they were wrong and in far too much company for a scowl.

The man waved his hand in a circle and the riders closed in around Task, forming a wall of thrumming muscle and steel. He kept their pace, following every twist and turn of their route, driving through streams and bounding fallen walls.

By the time he was guided through a thicket of thorns, Task had the impression that the Lancemaster was testing the golem against the might of his powerful mounts. But he didn't return a single look. Instead, he busied himself learning the landscape, testing every rock that touched his fingers, digging the mud with his heels to gauge its give. The heat of grinding stones coursed through him like dripping sweat.

It took little time for the countryside to grow flat and marshy. Some of the morning's mist had clung to life here, in the shadow of the plain. The Lancemaster presented a fist, and gradually the company slowed to a trot, then halted.

'Smell something, Lancer?' asked one of the riders, a woman with a wine stain running along her jaw.

'Something's off, that's for sure.'

Task dropped to his knee and placed a hand to the mossy earth. It was faint, but it was there.

'Vibrations in the ground. Feet and boots.'

The Lancemaster sneered. 'Onwards, but slowly like.'

The company broke into a gentle canter, closing in even tighter around the golem. Task could feel his awareness sharpening. He felt every grain of air rushing over his craggy skin, every squelch of the moss between his stubby toes.

He felt the tingle of anticipation rise, and with it, the usual temptation. He held himself tightly, keeping himself level.

The rumble built slowly, tinged with the muted clank of armour. 'Arms!' the Lancemaster cried, throwing a look over his shoulder at Task as he spurred his firn into a gallop. Lances jutted forward as the riders fanned out into a line, Task hidden at the centre.

He spied their shapes in a gap between the galloping firns. A hundred maybe, sent to harry the front guard before the full Truehard army arrived. They were a rabble of riders and foot soldiers, their copse of spears aimed low and bristling.

As the distance between the lines shrunk, the roar of two waves about to clash rose higher. Battle cries ripped from throats, Truehard and Fading alike. Only Task remained silent, letting the heat of his body fuel his concentration. He clamped his jaw shut, clenched his stones and angled his head.

A pebble's toss before the jagged edges of Fading spears, the galloping firns split in half. Moss flew as their tough claws skidded. Left and right they broke, tearing off at right angles to the enemy lines. In the swirling mist, the golem loomed in their wake, arms swinging like pendulums.

The battle cries withered in an instant.

Task met them like a cannonball, eyes narrow. Their spears were swept aside like bundles of twigs. Their blades simply splintered against his skin. Their bodies were cast aside like broken dolls.

Two firn-riders braved his reach, swinging axes as their mounts leapt in mighty arcs. They were folded paper to him. He seized the beasts by their necks and brought their heads together with a sickening crunch. They collapsed into twitching heaps at his feet, tongues lolling and blood leaking. The riders were trampled under his steps as he powered on, singular and unstoppable. One simple goal powered him.

Destruction.

His moves were wild but mechanical. Each slash and punch was savage, yet calculated; as precise as a blade. It was not a finesse that came from enjoyment, but duty and grim practice.

Task cut a swathe into the centre of the Fading ranks, and paused to let his stones cool. They pressed in, driving spears and bayonets into his arms and chest. Task claimed them as his own, dragging their owners forward to meet his fists. He broke their distant game, forcing them into the short. The masses surged inwards in a frantic push, and Task welcomed them all.

Sparks flew from every sword-cut. Stone-chips sprayed with every bite of the axes, and yet Task dealt with each soldier in turn. He was merciless. His first master had taught him two lessons: shock and awe. Now, he passed on that wisdom. The men were wheat to him, ready to be cut and counted. Cheap. Meaningless.

With every blow, he sank deeper and deeper into the recesses of his mind, holding on to his concentration tightly, like a shield, in case the rage came calling. In case he slipped and gave in. The merest inkling of it was enough to make him twitch, and shift his focus back to battle.

Only one soldier fought with a skill he could respect. An older, grizzled man with a double-bladed axe. He ducked the golem's swings with an agility that belied his years, breaking chunks from Task's legs with every pass. A cold stabbing lanced up his thighs, over and over; the golem's only measure of pain.

He knew this game. Many a knight had played it with him over the years. He feigned another jab at the soldier. This time, as he ducked, Task brought his other fist swinging from the ground up. He almost took the man's head clean off. There was a crack, a spurt of blood, and the soldier joined his kind in the mud.

Just like every other hero and sword-master who had come to test him.

It was tough, being near-indestructible.

The lines broke like a loaf in hungry hands, scattering in all directions. They ran, feet slip-sliding on the gore that soaked the long grass, fear carved so deep into their faces Task wondered if it would ever leave. The firn-riders harried them as they ran, skewering a few for good measure. The ones that stayed put up a half-hearted fight, as though they had resigned themselves to being pulverised into the next life. Before long, Task was left standing in a spiral of carnage, steaming like the squeamish mist that now recoiled from the scene.

'Architect's piss, beast!' said the Lancemaster. He could not take his eyes off the mess of bodies and armour. He spat on the ground and rode away, signalling for his riders to form up.

With a sigh, Task sagged back into his usual hunch and let his eyes half-close as he checked his arms and thighs, noting the fresh notches in his stone where the blades had bitten deep. He was almost impressed.

He stretched his arms to the ground and curled his fingers into claws. He tensed them, making them crack softly. He could feel them in an instant. Every tiny shard and splinter of stone—wherever it lay in the blood, mud and moss—began to quiver.

Task bent his fingers to fists with a sharp snap, and his pieces flew and tumbled back to him. They sniffed out every groove and gap left in his skin, and scuttled to fill it. Within the space of a breath, the golem was whole again.

A sharp whistle made him turn. The Lancemaster beckoned once more. They had aimed their beasts back across the plain, towards the safety of numbers.

Not a word of appreciation nor a single congratulatory comment was given as he rejoined the lines. They didn't surround him this time. Instead they stayed a good spear's length away, and stared at the bloody paint with which Task had decorated himself.

Cigars flared in the smoky gloom of the caravan. Two fat tallow candles sat in their holders, each vying for attention.

All sat but one: Lancemaster Taspin. He stood in front of the desk, hands clasped behind his back, thumbs working his knuckles. Huff was busy lighting his next cigar. He had already burnt through one, and even though it had put a spin in his head, he had the taste for it. Huff had noticed that men of power always seemed to have a cigar at hand, and he was eager to enforce the stereotype.

'Savagely, would be your answer, General, sir.' It wasn't often a lowly officer was asked to report personally, and it had set a hoarseness to the man's voice. 'The beast tore through their lines like a beggar through a steak.'

'Savage, you say?' Huff raised an eyebrow. Dast and Frayne appeared to be intrigued as he was. 'Unchecked? Bloodthirsty? Feral?'

'It ripped apart men as easy as I would unbuckle a belt. Broke spears like blades of grass. And that was only from what little I saw. We were fighting them at the flanks, you see.'

'How many?' asked Frayne.

'There were about a hundred of them, Milady.'

'No. How many did he kill?'

'Sixty. Seventy, maybe.'

'Didn't you count, man?' said Dast.

The Lancemaster turned to answer the councillor directly. 'There wasn't much left to count, Milord, if I'm to be honest.' Perhaps it was the smoke, but the soldier had taken on a pale turn.

'Effective then, would you say?' said Huff.

'But so's a catapult, sir. Or a ram. I don't see why—'

Huff tapped his ash in an empty glass, bringing silence. 'Are you comparing my golem to a siege engine, Lancemaster?'

'No, sir. I merely—'

'Would you say he was effective in battle, as a weapon? I asked you here for a report, not a commentary on battlefield equipment.'

Taspin ground out the words. 'Yes, sir. As a weapon, he is brutal. The most effective I've ever seen. The Fadings didn't stand a bloody chance.'

Huff waved his hand. 'Then you are dismissed.'

Once the Lancemaster had left the room, Huff looked around, from his captains to his esteemed guests; the thorns that had pestered him day after day. 'Well, I must say I'm rather pleased.'

'Looks like you pulled it off, Dartridge,' proclaimed Dast. 'A successful first test.'

Huff beamed. 'The first day of a new war, gentlemen. And lady.'

'I still wouldn't proceed too fast, General,' said Dast.

Huff's face fell into a scowl. Oddly, Frayne was wearing the same expression. 'And why would you say that, Councillor? Did you not hear the Lancemaster's report? Finest weapon he's ever seen. We press forwards!'

The councillor swirled his drink. 'Did you not read the instructions your father had written for you?'

He shrugged. 'I skimmed.'

Dast tutted. 'You must bear in mind that golems can be beaten. What do you think happened to the rest of them?'

The answer was elusive. Frayne elaborated.

'They died in battle, or through trickery, just like any man or woman. Cut a golem's tongue out and it's no more than the scraps it was made from. There are few enough left to prove they are not invincible.'

A worrisome inkling arose in the general's head. 'I thought you said he was the last golem.'

'The last of his kind,' said Frayne. 'The last surviving Wind-Cut Golem. Not the last of them all.'

Dast grumbled at that. 'Why in the Realm do you think he was so damned expensive?'

Huff followed his thread of thought. 'Then presumably could the Fading manage to procure one. Or us another?'

'Impossible,' said Dast, over the rim of his cup. 'It took us almost a year to find one, never mind several. Am I correct, Baroness?'

Frayne nodded. 'It took more than a year, and a man to die. The Council and the Mission exhausted every one of my extensive connections. You can rest assured, all the others are spoken for, or far too expensive for the likes of the Fading rabble.'

'Rarer things come with higher price tags,' offered Manx.

Dast rose to his feet, as if height could improve his argument. 'You should let the men get back into shape before throwing them and that golem into battle again. They're either too fat or too skinny, from what I've seen. And altogether too lazy. Take it slowly, I say. We want to win, not waste our men. Patience, Dartridge. It's a lesson your father learned well.'

For once, Huff wished he could shimmy out from under his father's shadow. Dast was forever draping it over him.

The baroness seemed to be on his side tonight. Perhaps she was not so intolerable after all.

'I have to disagree, my good Councillor,' she said. 'I believe haste is of the essence. We should strike before the rumours of Task begin to spread.'

Dast slurped at his glass, spilling some down his front. 'Frayne, you do not know war as the General and I do. You know trade and politics. You would not be here without the Grand-Captain's strongly-worded letters. What he sees in you will always escape me.'

The look on her face was acidic. Huff decided to intervene.

'I believe the hour is late, Councillor. Baroness. Perhaps you had better get some rest. We have a big day tomorrow.'

'Training, I trust.' Dast took his time in leaving, making a point of his old bones.

Frayne paused at the doorway, eyes still pinched into that dangerous look. Huff was about to extend his gratitude to her, when she cut him off.

'Remember, dear General, we Lundish have a proud and fearsome reputation to uphold, especially with all the uproar in the capital. Nobody wants to see another year of war. So, if I were you, I would ignore that drunken old fool, and press forwards as fast as possible, making your mark. Or, one word from myself, and your father will be on the next wagon out of Caverill, ready to see this war done. That glorious victory you pine for? It will be all his. So, take my advice. We don't want another repeat of the ravine incident, do we?'

Frayne turned, furs swirling as the curtain closed after her, leaving Huff to scowl, and irritably suck at what was left of his cigar.

When every item in the room had been scrutinised and glowered into submission, Huff turned to his desk. His hands wandered over the leather finish, spidering down to a drawer. A twist of the key, and his fingers were rummaging through the sheafs of paper. A brown folder landed on the leather, almost matching its hue. He stared at it in the candlelight for some time before dashing it to the floor with the back of his hand.

'Spit on all of them!'

Say one thing for the scrap of a stable girl, the little skinbag was persistent, despite his usual gruff orders of, 'go away!' and, 'go away or I'll eat you!'

Tonight she brought him a fire. Kindling and branches, to be precise. Task's effort and a saw-toothed scrap of metal had provided the sparks.

It wasn't often that Task got to bask in the glow of a fire that wasn't eating its way through a building, or clinging to the backs of the unfortunate. Skinbags were precious about who they allowed to gather around their flames.

A couple of Diamond Knights had let him join their circle once upon a time. Then a yarl-trader, looking for some company on a frigid desert night, and a chance to wag his tongue a while. And Ghoffi, of course, his blue eyes always bewitched by the flames, never moving as he waxed long and lyrical about his upbringing. But then he would grow bored, and make Task hold his hand in the fire and melt cheap copper in his palm. When the golem held his fingers up to the light he could see the dull sparkle of metal still stuck between his stones.

Then there was this girl. This little waif made of angles and knobbly joints. Her jet-black hair looked like resin in the orange firelight. Like Ghoffi, she too stared long and hard at the flames.

His stable tonight was stretched between a half-moon made of three wagons, acting like a pen for the beasts, both flesh and stone. With the camp spread over the curve of the hill, the stables, gunsmiths and washer-huts had been stuffed down on the flat, where a gnarled forest encroached on the mass of tents. The muddy paths were quiet and mostly empty. Jaunty music had sprung up on the hill, and the soldiers had gone to drink and revel in their new surroundings. Only the strays and drunkards staggered past them now.

'Do they not clean you?' enquired Lesky.

'Do they...?'

'Clean you. After you fight. I assume you did fight today, otherwise you wouldn't be covered in all of... that.' She wiggled a finger and made a face. Lit by the flames, Task was a russet brown, splashed head to toe in gore. 'Unless it's actually mud. But I'm pretty sure I saw you before sunset and you was definitely a dark red, and that looks like a finger.' She pointed at a spot under his arm.

Task looked down. She was right. The gruesome article was lodged in a gap between his stones. He twisted sharply, and there was a quiet squish amid the rattle of rock.

Lesky stuck out her tongue. Task half expected her to leave. Most skinbags would have usually retreated at that point. But she stayed. He guessed she had seen more than her fair share of violence in her short time.

'They should clean you. With a bucket and a bit of cloth, like we wash the fawls and firns. It'd take a while though. With all them cracks.'

Task grunted. 'Never been cleaned.'

'Why not?'

'Rain washes it away. Or I wade into rivers. My last master, Ghoffi, he didn't like that. He wanted me to look fearsome.'

'You're already pretty scary as you are.'

Task shuffled, uncomfortable. He had made few friends in his time. In fact, he could count the number of humans he'd ever liked on one hand, even without the thumb. Ever since his first master had shown him the true face of humanity, barely a year awoken, he had known the cost and danger of making friends. And this girl—this skinny, grubby girl—was far too familiar for his liking.

'Are you scared of me?'

The girl snorted. 'I don't get scared. Mam thinks the Architect forgot that part when he built me. Fear, that is.'

Task knew the same could be said of him. The difference was that his Architect had been a man, and not some almighty thing in the sky. 'Perhaps mistakes aren't only reserved for the mortal, then. My first master said I was built wrong.'

''Ow many masters have you had, then? I've had two.'

'Eighteen.' Task let all their faces flash through his mind.

Lesky tried to whistle, but ended up just blowing instead. 'And now you're Huff's.'

'He is my Master.'

She poked the flames. 'He's a funny one. Ganner says he's a prissy deffer. Ganner doesn't like people with money. He says the poor are the ladder the rich climb. Says that Huff is going to get us all killed trying to impress his daddy.'

'He seems fine to me.' He had endured worse masters than Huff. *Much worse.* 'He has been... polite.'

'I don't trust him. But I don't trust nobody.'

'Something else we have in common.'

Lesky flashed some little white teeth. 'See, we're getting along just fine. That's two now. Halfway.' She counted on her fingers, confused.

Task narrowed his eyes. 'You aren't going to leave me alone, are you?

'No.'

'And you aren't scared in the slightest, are you?'

'Nope.'

'Fine.'

'Are all people normally scared of you?' She said it with a hint of pride, knowing the answer might prove her special.

'Scared. Angry. Cruel. People don't like me very much. This is the longest conversation I have had for a long time.'

'Why don't they like you? Aren't you here to help? People should be kind and thoughtful to those that come to help.'

Boots trudged past the paddock, and Task looked up. The soldier kept his head down and cap low, maybe a few glances snuck here and there. Task's eyes followed him as he spoke.

'People don't like the reflection of what I am to them. I may be different, all stone and dust instead of skin and blood. But they still see themselves. Copied. Faked in stone. They see their Architect's work in something that isn't flesh, and they can't help but be offended by it, scared by it. Fear breeds hate.'

Like Task himself, these words had been chiselled, shaped and polished over the decades. He had spent years watching the skinbags—their men, their women, their wriggling, whining offspring—and built every glance and fleck of spit into this reason.

Lesky pondered for a moment, chin on fist. 'Nah, that ain't it.'

Task fixed her with a stare.

'It ain't true, I say.'

'Why?'

''Cos *I* like you.'

Task wriggled out of her logic, not knowing what to do with the compliment. 'You wouldn't if you were a soldier.'

'That's it, then.'

'What?'

'Maybe they don't like you because you're better than them. They know they can't beat you. Mam says jealousy is the recipe for hate. As well as fear, of course.'

Task couldn't help but smile. 'Your mam is a wise woman.'

'More 'n wise. She always seems to know a thing 'afore it happens.' She poked at the fire, pleased with herself. 'People may hate

41

you, but they ignore me. Unless they want something, like Ganner always does.'

'I'd rather be ignored than hated.'

The girl flashed another smile. 'I like it 'cos it makes me invisible. You? You're big. You stand out in a crowd. Even if you bent down you'd still be a great big lump. Me? I can disappear. And you know what that means?'

'What?'

Lesky tapped her nose. 'I hear all the secrets.'

A voice made them both flinch. 'Best to be careful with secrets, little girl,' said the woman in furs. 'They can get you killed.'

She strode to the gate, leaning her elbows against it. She wore a thin smile on her powdered face. Task had never understood the need to wear a mask like this. His fractured features were his and his alone. He had no need to hide them.

'Making friends, Mr Task? Along with you now, girl. No secrets for you tonight.'

'Yes, Baroness.'

Lesky scuttled away without question.

'Look at that!' said Frayne. 'She even knows who I am. I'd better watch out for that one, hadn't I?' The thin smile lingered. She seemed curious. 'Tell me, do you feel the warmth, golem?'

'I do.'

Her hand moved to the latch of the gate. 'May I?' she asked, while already moving to stand near the fire. Her furs and bright hair burned in the shifting light.

'We have not been formally introduced. My name is Baroness Ellia Frayne. Call me Ellia.'

Task declined to touch her offered hand. 'You know mine.'

'Indeed I do. In fact, I have just come from the general's tent, where you were discussed at length. He is rather impressed with you. Has he mentioned it?'

The golem tilted his head. 'Vaguely.'

He remembered Huff's first sight of him. The man's smile had been so wide Task had half-expected his jaw to snap.

'We've been waiting a long time for your arrival. Ghoffi kept you close, didn't he? Even when we asked for an audience, he ignored us.'

'He had many enemies.'

Ellia nodded. 'Yes, and the one that finally got him was his heart, I hear. Popped in the middle of the night. Unfortunate for him, but fortunate for us. And you, for that matter. You're going to be part of history, Mr Task.'

Task had seen enough history to know how it was made. History was a bloody mess, scraped up and strained into the books of the people who made the mess in the first place.

Ellia stepped closer. Her moss-coloured eyes searched his face. 'You really are remarkable. Huff doesn't know what he has. But I can see you're a blade, not a hammer. A fine blade for cutting and paring, not something to be thrown against a shield-wall. He'll make a battering ram out of you, not a saviour or a miracle.'

Task nodded.

'Tell me, how old are you? Ghoffi's details were sketchy, and all your other masters are long dead.'

It was a hard question to evade. 'I awoke in twenty-three sixty-one.'

Ellia was quick with her numbers. 'Four hundred and twenty-one years. By the Architect's spit, you've seen your fair share of history already, haven't you? And "awoke"? How clever of the Windtrickers. You were built for the Diamond Wars, so I read?'

'By Belerod of Wind-Cut, for the Khandri mines.'

'Built for the Khandri, and now you fight for one of the Accord. How curious.' She settled into a crouch. 'Has Huff even told you why you're here?'

Task shook his head. Ellia tutted sharply.

'That man. He has grit for brains. You fight for Hartlund, Mr Task. For the king, for the Truehards and for the continuation of this great kingdom's way of life. On the way here from the cliffs, you surely saw the strays standing at the doors of their cottages. Did you see their wide eyes? Nine long years, this civil war has raged, and it's torn the Lundish in two. Don't fight for Huff. Fight instead for our survival. All we want is for it to end, and to have our homes back.'

'I see.'

There was always a spiel. Always one blazing brand of truth. He had heard them all, from stolen yarls to insulted gods, Task had learnt to nod along, and let them talk; let them believe he cared about the endless plight of humanity. Mortality was a curse in a foreign tongue to him. It meant nothing. He had his own curses to worry over.

Ellia studied him, then rubbed her hands. 'I thank you for your fire, Task. Sleep well, if you do so.'

Task bowed his head, wondering what she had come to glean, and whether he had given it to her. People like this always wanted something.

'And you, Baroness.'

She lingered behind the gate. 'That girl is right, you know. Huff is not to be trusted.' And with that, she squelched into the night, leaving him to sit and ponder her words and warnings.

Task thought of those wide eyes, peering from door-cracks. He remembered their white knuckles, fingers tight around their clubs and rope-knives. He wondered whether this Lundish war was any different from the three dozen or so he'd seen before, whether these Truehard veins ran hotter and truer; whether he might finally find a cause he could rally behind, to blunt his chore of wreaking carnage.

To do some good.

4

'The power to glimpse and gaze runs in older bloodlines. Once the magic of kings and princes, it bled into the common folk through unwise dalliances. The ability to read a mind, or understand a future are powers unfit for peasants and farmers. So it was that His Holiness the Treyarch Shunt decreed that all known glimpses be acquired or otherwise disposed of.'

FROM LETTERS FOUND IN THE MISSION'S ARCHIVES

41st FADING, 3782 - SAFFERON FORTRESS

The tunnel had a stink to it. A wretched stench, seeping out of the dank walls.

Carafor Westin trudged the muddy path as quick as he could manage. By the time he reached the office door he had almost brought a handkerchief to bear.

A smart rap on the door and the snarl of a rabid wark bade him to enter. Westin saw to the door sharpish, making sure to close it behind him. Lord Lash was a barrel of rage that morning. His cheeks were bruising purple, his fists clenched with bloodless ferocity. The dark hair, normally so coiffed and waxed, fell about his forehead and ears in stubborn strands which swished angrily about his furious face.

'Lord Lash, sir!' Westin greeted him, bowing as low as possible.

'Just the man I wanted to see!' Lash tested his knuckles against his desk. 'And about bloody time, too!'

'My apologies, Lord. With the rains, there was flooding—'

'Flooding, my arse!'

'Yes, Milord.' Westin bowed again for good measure.

It was then that he realised they were not alone in the room. He had been transfixed by Lash's burning gaze, as a hunter stares at a rearing firn.

A woman in broken armour raised a buckled gauntlet to cough. Westin flinched at the sight of her. The soldier's metal was smeared in mud and dried blood. She stood at a slant, as if one leg was gradually giving up on life.

'Carafor Westin.'

She saluted, covering her eyes. 'Shield-chief Junes.'

'Pleasure.'

'*Executor* Westin should not be so cavalier with his titles.' Lash peeled a finger from the vice of his knuckles and jabbed it at Junes. 'You need to listen to her report. Nothing else, until you hear this.'

'Fair indeed,' Westin agreed, watching the chief grimace out of the corner of his eye. The story was clearly a difficult one to tell.

The finger wagged some more. 'Go on, Chief. Tell him what you told me.'

The chief's voice was hoarse from the first word. Westin sought a seat as she began.

'I fought with Forty and Two company, the Wayward Morals. A spear and shield battalion under General Crast. We were to stop the Truehards in their tracks using a valley as an advantage. It was a perfect set-up, all designed for slaughter. Shields across its mouth, high on the slope, with bowmen on the rocks above.' Junes bit her lip. 'It was a slaughter, indeed.'

'I take it—'

'Shh, Westin!' Lash hissed at him. Westin bit his tongue to keep it from moving.

'The Truehards have some kind of new weapon. It crushed our lines once night had fallen, breaking through our shield-wall with a swipe of its fist. Soldiers flying left and right. My line was scattered, broken and left in the mud. I drove a spear into its side but all that shattered was my blade.'

Westin was rarely confused. He was a learned man with a quick brain between his ears. But here he felt he was missing a trick.

'I'm sorry. You mentioned a weapon. But you said "fist". What kind of weapon are we talking about?' Westin's gaze switched between the chief and Lash. Junes shivered.

'They have a golem, Carafor!' barked Lash. 'A deffing golem!' He gripped the dirty wheels of his chair and pushed himself away from the desk. His chair had developed a rusty squeak over the past few weeks; something fallen loose in that contraption of wood and iron. The noise had grown to grate on any and all who knew his presence.

'A *what*?' said Carafor. *Surely not.*

'A golem.' Lash growled as he thwacked away at his wheels, trying to batter the chair into silence. 'Did your father never tell you any stories?' Junes had found her voice again. 'It stood eight foot-lengths high, maybe nine. It was made of stone, by my reckoning. Glowing eyes that freeze you to the mud.'

'Stone, you say?'

'It tossed me aside and left me in the dirt with the rest of them. We lay there, dazed and powerless, as the dead fell all around us, on top of us.'

It was there that Junes broke. Not cries and tears; just a paling of the face, a hollowing of the eyes. Though she stood in their presence, she was still there, face in the mud, listening to the roar of bloody chaos all around.

'That'll be all, Shield-chief,' said Lash. 'You get yourself a room in the west quarter. A beer, a bath and some tongue-wagging will see you right. Hear me?'

'Yes, Lord Lash. Thank you, sir.' Junes marched from the room, holding her head high.

'Brave woman,' Westin mumbled. He hadn't been prepared for this calibre of conversation so early in the day.

'Far too much bravery ends with a blade in the back, these days,' said Lash. 'She was one of the lucky ones.'

'But surely you have to question her story. A *golem*, Milord? I've been led to believe they are just figments of...' Westin's voice trailed upon seeing the creases in Lash's face.

'Then you've been led wrong. Figments of folklore, they are not, Westin. You're an Executor, you should know better than to dismiss the written word. From what I've gathered, it's a Wind-Cut Golem.'

'Wind-what, sir?'

'Only the finest of bloody golem-kind, Westin! Built by the Windtrickers during the Diamond Wars, for the Khandri and Hasp kings, when the Accord went on its fool's errand. The Windtrickers carved their stone with nought but wind and old-magic, and they built them to fight like devils risen. Wild things they were in battle, mad with bloodlust. Men have bankrupted kingdoms, traded their princes and princesses, even sold their own mothers to own a golem.'

'But that would make them several hundred years old. If they did exist then surely they're all d—'

'I don't have time for surelys, Westin! The Truehards have a golem. I don't care how they got one, or where. I care simply that they have one, and that it is ripping apart my troops with its bare hands. Its bare hands! That is the fact of the matter. A fact that I... *we*, now have to contend

47

THE HEART OF STONE

with!' He raised a fist to the ceiling and brought it down to punish the desk once more. He let the echoes die as he stared at the dirt floor, eyes still wide, his mouth a thin white line.

'We were so close to the end.'

Westin picked at his chapped lips in thought. 'How many times have we come up against this golem?'

'Judging by the severity of the reports, four losses in three days. Junes survived our last encounter.'

'I can picture the faces around the Last Table now.'

'Damn the Table! They don't give me enough to fight men, never mind golems!'

An idea bloomed in Westin. Even as he spoke, it grew shape. 'It's been a long and bitter war, my Lord. I came here this morning to tell you that the private funds are all but exhausted. The Table is as penniless as our soldiers. I know you despise it, but every move, every body, every damn musketball must now be accounted for if we are to win.'

Lash fixed him with the withering gaze he used when bureaucracy was in the air. 'And I've said it to the masters a thousand times, to Ebenez himself! You can't run a war like one of their damn companies! My dead mother, Architect save her, moves with more alacrity than they do. All this talk of golems will send them into a spiral of uselessness. By the time the Last Table makes its decision, the beast will be knocking at my very door.'

Westin took a stand. 'Perhaps if we were to take them a solution, and present it alongside the problem, it may serve to grease the wheels. I know you've been itching for a last push, Lord Lash. This could be your chance.'

Lash wheeled himself in a small circle around his office. The rage still burned behind the eyes, but a silence had come to his tongue. He motioned for Westin to continue.

'If the Truehards have a new weapon, then we fight it with one of our own.'

'If you're suggesting another golem, you can shut your trap right now. If they aren't all dead, then we hardly have the coin for one.'

'No, my Lord,' said Westin. 'I'm suggesting a man. A warrior. A man who is no stranger to smiting creatures of old. A man for whom a golem would be no challenge. A man who killed the Last Dragon.'

Lash knew the stories well enough. 'You're suggesting the Knight of Dawn? Alabast.'

'Precisely. We need a champion of our own. I'd suggest Everlong, but he has long since fallen off the map, so to speak.'

Lord Lash mulled over Westin's words. 'And you think the tongue-waggers and purse-pinchers will sanction it?'

'Lady Auger has already spoken his name to the Table, several months ago now. She suggested him as a way to rally the army's efforts. Master Ebenez deemed it too expensive.'

'I'm surprised she even graced you with a visit. What's more, I look forward to hearing why she had no knowledge of this golem.'

'She will no doubt have her reasons, my Lord. In any case, the name of Dawn will still be fresh in their minds, and besides, what have they to lose now?' Westin paused to wink. 'That's the good thing about mercenaries.'

'What?'

'If they die, you don't have to pay them.'

42ND FADING, 3782 - CAVERILL

'Many a day has passed since you graced these steps, Baroness,' Lord Baragad said in his hollow drone, sounding like a ghost with a spot of mortplague. The curve of the mighty roof caught its echo, dragging it out.

Ellia bent a knee and swept her arms wide. 'Far too many.'

'We trust the frontier has not proved too dangerous?'

'I am pleased to report that the danger has been considerably reduced over the last few days.' She smiled.

'I take it this is due to our new friend?' barked another voice, this one bludgeoning and bold. She looked up to the wide balcony to meet the squint of its owner.

'Indeed.'

Grand-Captain Gorder Dartridge had a face like a dinner plate; almost perfectly round, still smudged with vestiges of dinner. His cheeks and bald head were adorned with red blotches; the kind that would always flourish the moment he was angry, which was often. He was more *wide* than fat. Ellia felt it a shame that his son the general hadn't inherited any of his stature. *Perhaps then he wouldn't have grown up to be a pompous sack of air with legs.*

Clinging to the grand-captain's nose was a small moustache; a mere strip of salt and pepper, once blonde. His eyes were clouded with cataracts, but Ellia knew how little they bothered him. She had seen the quickness in his gaze the moment she had first met him, more than a decade ago. But that didn't stop him conning others. Playing the blind old fool was one of the elder Dartridge's favourite games, especially here at King's Council.

'No interruptions, Dartridge,' said the chubby figure on the throne, which was set high in the wall, besieged on all sides by bronze-coloured curtains and dark mahogany. It looked as though the Boy King had begun to test his voice, and in more ways than just volume. Ellia inwardly rolled her eyes. Power and a youth in constant search of limits are never a good combination.

'Of course, my Liege.' Gorder held up a hand in apology.

Once Lord Baragad, the head of the Council, had finished with his preposterous bowing, he motioned for Frayne to continue.

She made sure her report was long yet empty, like a riverbed in the hottest days of reaping. It was a game she played often. Meander enough to distract them, but keep the detail as featureless as stranded dust and shale. *Just enough to keep the questions at bay, and hold the smiles of the king and his council.*

Ellia started with the golem, praising him and his prowess. No details of his manner, just the blood and body count; that was all they needed. While they were grinning, she praised Huff for his swift action and decisiveness. Victory was the theme here, and once it was introduced, she dragged them deeper with details of supply hiccups and latrine issues, of armour manufacture and ideas for more efficient mangles.

They always seemed to grow sleepy at the subject of paying for things.

Baragad interjected. 'I believe we shall have to stop you there, Baroness. But we thank you for your... *meticulous* report. I'm afraid His Majesty has many more items on his agenda.'

Ellia offered him, and His Majesty of course, another bend of her knee, and stood still as the balcony was cleared, to the tune of shuffling feet and grumblings about lunch.

She caught the eye of the grand-captain as he left, and met him at the foot of the great wooden stairs that hugged the wall.

Gorder pointed her down an adjoining corridor. 'Shall we?'

As they strolled down a shorter flight of steps and into a corridor, Gorder's meaty hand draped over the crook of Ellia's arm.

'A fine report indeed, Ellia. Very detailed, and yet as enlightening as the mewling of a dullard farmboy.'

She smiled. 'Precious details are for ears that deserve them.'

Gorder tutted, as was his habit, and tugged her through a door. Sunlight drenched them, forcing them to blink.

The grand-captain sighed. 'Go on, then. Tell me of my idiot offspring. Being too rash with our new weapon, I imagine? Lacking in honour? Give me something that won't make me blush when I mention his name.'

Ellia shook her head. 'Absolutely not, my Lord. He presses forward eagerly, yes, but at a steady and careful pace, taking my advice. He has truly come on leaps and bounds since…' She paused, dangling awkward memories in front of the grand-captain.

Gorder was never in the mood for subtlety. 'Since he drove a hundred of my soldiers into a ravine chasing what he thought was a scouting party.'

'I suppose that in the rain, a pack of wild cralligs could, in theory, look like a Fading scouting party.'

'Fawl-piss! Where is my army? You were as vague as a morning mist in there.'

'Thirty leagues into the Fading's claimed land by now. Maybe twenty south of Purlegar and the Six Sisters. Huff aims to claim the town as a new outpost by the end of the week.'

'The mountains will give him trouble.'

'He has a plan, I'm sure.'

'If it's not "use the golem", then consider me impressed. It's that damnable Dartridge fire. Gets it from his mother.' Gorder hawked and spat, sending something with a black carapace tumbling into a nearby water trough. He snickered.

Ellia walked away from his grip and crossed her arms. 'I'm surprised to hear that.'

Gorder inclined his head. The windows might have been foggy but the lights within still burned brightly. 'You don't think it's a poor trait?'

'I see the same trait in you. Your son is keen to end it swiftly. Given that all the Council and the Mission can blabber on about is the Khandri's ambassador touring the Accord, I think that's prudent. You and I know there is more to win here than just the war. Reputation, as Dast is so fond of saying. Though I call it profit. That is why we all trust, or rather hope, that Huff will do his job and end this one.'

'Not deff it up, you mean.'

The baroness tugged at her furs. There was a northern breeze today, and it had an edge on it. 'Precisely. However, might I point out that you were the one who suggested Huff for the position of general. We should trust in your son.'

The old man traced an arc with his arm. 'Do you know how long I've watched the servants tend this garden?'

Ellia's gaze roved over the topiary and drooping stems. Here and there, greenhouses dotted a merry path through the flowerbeds, pots and troughs. Brown and moss-green it may have been now, but come rising and sowing, Ellia knew how it could explode into colour. 'Many years.'

'Forty and five years, I've watched this garden. Forty and five years, I've watched its ebb and flow, its dance between the seasons. It's already outlived two kings and will probably see two more before it withers. And do you know why I have devoted so much of my time to it, even though I will be but a brief interlude in this garden's memory?'

She tapped her chin. 'I would hazard a guess it is something to do with the peace and quiet, and your dislike of your fellow man. Your misanthropic ways.'

Gorder chewed on that for a moment. His glazed eyes searched her face, then he chuckled. 'Well. Perhaps. This garden is a far more worthy expense of my time than battling the incompetence of that Council. Of men with long swords and small hearts. Of the world. People let you down, Ellia. They always will. But this garden? This garden is immortal. All you have to do is tend it, and watch it. It's simpler.'

He emphasised his point by nipping off a bite-riddled leaf. 'Huff is too proud and eager to prove himself. He has no time for-level headed sense. Were we not desperate and dangling at the end of a nine-year-long rope, you know I would not have given him the golem. I should be up there, keeping an eye on our investment alongside you, instead of that old codger, Dast.'

Ellia watched him root about in the flowers for a moment, chuntering to himself. 'Might as well throw myself in the God's Rent, and be done with it all. Before the Khandri come knocking.'

It wouldn't be the first time the Rent had swallowed a willing victim. Its swirling gullet had become a place of pilgrimage for thousands over the centuries.

Ellia knew the corrosive nature of doubt; how it ate away at a man like a fungus does a tree. How it ate and ate until he began to wobble. And as any wood-cutter will warn, a wobbling tree is a dangerous thing. She needed the good grand-captain to be steady.

'Huff will not disappoint you if you give him enough time. Cut him short, and you will never know if he could have proven you wrong. Besides, Gorder, your health.'

The captain rubbed his swollen stomach for a time, then blew a sigh. He got back to the business of idle wandering.

'You spin a good yarn, Ellia Frayne, and even though I know you're spouting fawl-shite, I'll trust you. Now, tell me more about our new weapon. How is the thing doing? Has our hard work bore fruit?'

Ellia sighed, making Gorder look up, an eyebrow raised.

'It is a strange creature, as dutiful as it is imposing. Vicious in battle. A Lancemaster, Councillor Taspin's boy, called it the most effective weapon he has ever seen. As Ghoffi promised, it is slaved to rules and obeys its master no matter what. It returned drenched in Fading blood the evening I left for the city.'

'Big?'

'Nine foot-lengths, maybe more.'

'And it can talk?'

'Like you or I.'

'How many has it killed?'

'Almost seventy on the first encounter alone. Hundreds since.'

'Architect's hammer!'

'He does have a strange way about him. He is dutiful, but quietly so. Almost sullen.'

'Sullen? It's stone. Stone shouldn't be sullen.'

'Ghoffi's letters did mention a... personality, as it were.' Ellia flashed him a sideways look. 'But fear not, the king has spent his money well.'

Gorder hawked again. 'The Mission's money, you mean. This war has made us no richer than the mud-dwellers and the deffing peasants. The Mission has the king by his hairless balls.'

The captain paused his idle wandering to fix a frayed knot of twine that was failing to do its job of holding up flowers. He took a reel of brown string from his coat pocket, making his medals jangle. The grand-captain was never caught in wrappings other than full uniform.

'Just the other week, those two scrotum consecrators of his, Lockyen and Vullen, were demanding more churches in Caverill once the war is won. I've long desired to burn them all to the ground.'

'I believe the Mission would call that heresy,' said Ellia. 'And it comes with a vial of poison. Or a crucible of hot lead, if you are not so fortunate.'

Gorder snorted. 'If they're so concerned about us winning the war before the ambassador's arrival, then they wouldn't dare take back the golem. Besides, their days are short. Soon, I can burn whatever I want to the ground.'

It was then that Ellia saw a shade of him she had never seen; one she expected more from Huff than his father. For a moment, he was nothing but a petulant child, enveloped in a coat of skin and fat. She cleared her throat, glancing around.

'As you say, we won't have to suffer them for long.'

Gorder finished his knot and stood straight. 'Long enough, in my books. There'll be no country left at this rate! We'll have no spoils to share.'

'Then we shall have a blank slate to build upon. You, I, your son, and any other that we deem worthy of our new council.'

Gorder clapped his hands. 'There could be another opportunity there, Baroness. If my son doesn't get his head lopped off before this war is over, he'll be in want of a wife...' He let the suggestion trail away, probably because he could see the stiffness in her.

'I'm flattered, of course,' she said, aching to bray with laughter. She turned the talk to the wider world. 'Speaking of relationships, is there word on what the king intends to do with the ambassador, when she arrives?'

'Probably let Baragad do the talking. Here seems the likely venue.'

'How perfect for us. No news on what the ambassador wants?'

'Word from the west is that their minds have not changed. More trade routes or more trouble. Strife never truly dies, Ellia. Now, Flummish at the house could rustle up lunch if you haven't eaten? I know the wives will be pleased to see you.'

Ellia was otherwise engaged. 'More business with the Council, I'm afraid. Then back to the army.'

'Keep an eye on that boy of mine.'

She bowed as he saluted, covering his eyes. 'Fear not. I'll keep his head safely on his shoulders.'

Gorder tutted as she turned away.

Through the great hallways and bulging corridors, she weaved her way back out into the chill. Her stately carriage—bronze, trimmed with black—waited at a kerb. The drivers hopped back into their seats.

'Baroness!' they chorused, tipping their hats.

'The Blade of the Architect, sharpish.'

Whips cracked as the door slammed. The carriage lurched into life, wooden wheels crunching the gravel. Its innards were dark behind the grey curtains. Ellia busied herself with her gloves before opening her mouth.

'The Council has no complaints. Nobody suspects.'

The pale, bald man sitting opposite her hummed, deep and long. She could hear his smile in his voice. 'Compartmentalisation, see? It works. The Hasp have a term for it. *Etara swarne*. Literally means "to build walls".'

'Well, I've built mine. It's time to start goading Huff into action. We have a war to win, after all.'

She spied a nod, and said no more, turning her head to watch the city pass.

Caverill squatted on the edge of a slanted cliff, clinging to the slope before the sheer edge. The Grave sat beyond it; a hollow crater half-swallowed by the sea, dug by some god of forgotten ages, before the Architect changed the face of the Realm with his hands and brought the Rent to power the ocean.

Two soaring needles pierced the ashen sky above the capital, each vying for height and attention. They were skinny pyramids, built of the pockmarked stone which had made Hartlund famous. Buildings and battlements huddled like barnacles to their roots.

If one looked closely, the southern tower was ever so slightly shorter, and wider at the base. Its stone had a brownish hue, and its windows glowed with torchlight, even in the afternoon. It was said that the lights of the Blade of the Architect never went out; there was always one lantern burning.

The other tower was Castle Sliver, home of the Boy King and his entourage. The centuries had painted its features a solemn grey, and worn swirls in the brick. Its blunted head was bulbous, and sported a steel crown. Save for the mountains, it was the highest point in all of Hartlund. The perfect place for a king to lay his young head at night.

The firns strained against the harsh slope of the city. The going was slow, giving Ellia a chance to examine the streets and the filth that smeared them. Some of the filth even moved around, wearing dresses and work-clothes, bonnets and boots.

The people of the city looked as glum as the weather hanging above them. Where markets had once brayed their bargains to the masses, now repurposed crates and sackcloth sleeping-bags had taken up residence. Where noble, shining knight-guards had once stood in doorways and under arches, now men in long coats lurked, whispering amongst themselves, slyly doling packages to any skinny wreck with the bravery or the craving to approach them.

Caverill had once been a vibrant city. Her ports had been full to bursting every day of the week. But nine years of war strangles a city in invisible ways, until the day it chokes its last, until the neck-bones snap. Ellia did not give Caverill much time.

'All the more reason to continue as planned,' said the man in the shadows, lending voice to her thoughts.

Ellia threw him her most acidic look. She had been letting her guard down. 'I've asked you repeatedly not to bridge without my consent, Spiddle. Do I have to ask again?'

'It's my job.'

'You're a glimpse. Your job is to sniff out heretics and steal secrets, not to meddle with the minds of zealots.'

'Watch all, catch all. That's our motto. We're the ones who keep you zealots in check.'

'It's a violation,' said Ellia, before turning back to the dismal view. 'I'll have you written up.'

Spiddle leaned forward, his sharp features tasting light. He was a knife of a man, all angles and crooked lines. 'Have me written up? Throwing another body under the cart, are we? Overconfidence, Zealot. It'll be the death of you.'

'You're a glimpse, not a gazer. Better you remember that.'

That kept the impertinent sod quiet, at least until they shuddered to a stop in a courtyard at the base of the Blade.

'After you,' he said, as the drivers saw to the doors. Ellia stepped out into the shadow of the tower, feeling the pinch of the breeze again. She licked her lips and tasted salt. A raindrop struck the back of her hand.

A huge man in a long fur jacket came out to greet them. He had a steel-hard face and a square stature that had no time for fat.

'Frayne. Spiddle.' The gravelly tone told of a life spent in raised voice. Master Hanigan Cane was an authority on shouting, having spent several decades training blithering Church-Knight recruits into fearsome weapons.

'Cane,' they said in unison.

'Spiddle, the Treyarch wants you now. Frayne, you report in an hour.'

'Very good, Cane. I'll refresh in my chamber. It's been a long journ —'

'Prayers. Fifty verses of the Manual I believe will suffice. It's been far too many days since you've passed my threshold. Far too many since you've communed with our good lord, I'd wager.'

Ellia forced a smile onto her face. 'It is tough to find peace in some places.' She bowed. 'As you wish.'

Cane clicked his tongue, and the two went their separate ways; one left, one right. Ellia kept her back straight and her pace confident. If Cane had looked closely, he might have seen the tightness of her jaw, and the way her teeth ground together.

Ellia loathed communing with anything. Especially the good lord himself. Twenty and one years she had given the Mission, and she had her own way of worshipping the Architect: through blood and toil, and not necessarily her own.

5

'The golems were originally status symbols. Simple magic tricks to entertain and boast to travellers. When a golem one day defended a Chanark king against an assassin, they began to be used for war. A race started, one to build bigger and better machines of war. From stone, to bone, to wood, to mud, to flesh, golems have fought alongside men for decades. They are made to wreak havoc. In Haspia, where the finest golem-builders in the Harmony reside, the word golem means "chaos".'

FROM TREATISES OF THE NARWE HARMONY 3012, AUTHOR UNKNOWN

18TH REAPING, 3361 - WIND-CUT, HASPIA

The room was the kind of hot that hands could wade through. It was like dragging a palm through pond water.

The wind screamed like a tortured child. He covered his ears, but its undulations cut right through him. He could feel his stones shivering with its caterwauling.

He shouted. 'Must it be so loud?'

But his master could not hear him; he had metal cups clamped to his ears, stuffed with haswe fur. Belerod commanded the contraption with ease, flicking levers and wrenching handles as though he were conducting some intricate dance of puppets. Like those he had seen in the market.

The screaming came from outside the small window. Task took a curious step, his movements slow and liquid. The room felt slanted.

Through the glassless frame he watched the pincers sway with the wind. They had between their claws a shard of rock the span of his hand. In their grip, it weaved a monotonous path through the rushing air, dipping over and over into the thin stream of dust hurtling past the *window. Every time the rock met it, there would be a screech, and the rock would be cut across another surface. A dozen more turns, and the rock was a thin shard of polished grey, flecked with mica.*

Belerod began to furiously stamp on a pedal. With every strike of his heel, the screaming lessened. The thin blade of dust faded, and was gone. The wind calmed to a disgruntled moan.

'Out of the way, you great lump! Go stand over there.'

His legs crumbled with every step, but he made it to the edge of the room.

Beside him on the wall, hanging from ornate hooks, were skeletons of all shapes and sizes. There were huge ones, hunched and fearsome, with long snouts and curving teeth; and spindlier things with bones as fine as straw. He looked down at his plates of pitted stone, and felt alone amid the macabre display.

Belerod carried the shard to a half-finished monster at the end of the room: a golem almost twice his height, with long, twisted arms, and claws of white marble.

With great care, his master placed the shard on a table. Taking up a chisel, he carved two lines in its surface, like a slanted cross, and then took it to the tall golem. The shard slid into an empty slot in its forearm and with a curved tool, Belerod levered it into position. There came a sharp crack once it had stuck fast.

'That'll do just fine,' he said, barely audible over the wind. He dusted off his hands and walked along the skeletons, fingers occasionally brushing a toe, or testing a skull.

'Do you see now, what it means to be a golem?'

'No, Master.'

Belerod sighed. 'You are built! Carved by man with wind and sand and the blessings of Haspha. Not grown like these bones.'

Yes, Master.' His tongue felt sluggish. He had to prise it from the floor of his mouth.

Belerod's face grew stormy, his eyes thin. 'You are manufactured at our wish alone, not by the coupling of two bodies, as these were. As I was. As all humans are.'

'I understand, Master.'

'Therefore, golem, you have no soul. You are bent to a will beyond yours. You are owned. You belong to your maker, and that is I. That means one duty for you and one duty only: to obey. That is the purpose of you. Anything other is inexcusable. That is why we shall have no more issues. No more misbehaviour.'

The golem bowed his head. Belerod stood a hands-breadth from him, fingers threaded behind his back, head up, face glowering. His head span, confused, knotted. A rising roar began to join the moan of wind.

'If I hear you have been found wandering the courtyards again, I will have you demolished. I do not care if you want to see the rain! You have much work to do. A great many things to learn. I have not failed a single order and I will not have you ruin that reputation. We will make a Wind-Cut Golem of you yet!' Belerod was shouting now, and yet the roar almost drowned him out.

'Fighting, tactics, weapons...'

The stone roof was buckling. Cracks spread like lightning forks.

'...Manners, etiquette...'

Water began to pour down in great dark curtains, grey-green and full of froth. He felt it lap at his knees. Belerod stood there, up to his waist now, robe stained darker with every wave, his long grey beard tugged by the current.

'...and most importantly, maintenance...'

The golem felt the water lift him, try to bear him away. He tensed his stones and grunted with effort.

Belerod was gone, but his voice still floated over the cacophony of water and wind.

'It will be quite the task. That is what I should call you. Task.'

Before the room was swallowed, he saw it; somewhere in the flash of bubbles and debris. A spinning maw of water, leagues across, black as death at its centre and rumbling like a mountain twisted from its roots.

43RD FADING, 3782 - TRUEHARD CAMP

Task awoke with a grunt, lashing at the nearest thing with his fist. The fencepost shattered at its waist, tearing half the slats down and making the fawls bray with fear.

Lesky was a quick little thing; leaping from her bag to the doorway in the space of two startled blinks. 'What in the Realm...?'

She yawned, fighting to keep her eyes open.

Task shuffled onto his knees and tried to prop up the post by holding its two shattered ends together. It didn't work. He looked back to Lesky to find her shaking her pillow-tousled head. The new dawn painted her face a dusty pink.

'Architect's arse! Ganner's going to eat you alive. And me.'

'I think I would be hard to chew.'

THE HEART OF STONE

Lesky smiled at that at least. Task's peculiar dreams had foxed him, put him in a stupor. He shook his head with a rattle and bit down on his tongue to stir some of the magic.

The energy lurched through his skull in a heartbeat, making him shiver. One of his masters had once compared it to the sensation of eating too much ice too quickly. *Skinbags were fragile creatures.*

'I'll fix it.'

'You will alright. I'll go get the things. Meanwhile, you'd better keep Trix, Mix and Flix all safe n'sound, otherwise Ganner'll have another reason to get you in front of Huffy.'

'Why do ski… humans insist on using nicknames? Are your names not sufficient?'

Lesky put a finger to her chin. 'Maybe sometimes their parents didn't do a good enough job o' namin' them in the first place. Close, but not close enough.' She grinned, impressed with herself.

'Right.' It made no sense, but he nodded all the same.

'Now you stay there, you silly creature. And watch them fawls.'

He took up a stance at the broken fence, watching the creatures with slitted eyes. Nobody ever talked to him like a… Task frowned. *Like a human.* Monster, beast, or thing, he was to most. He wagered the girl wanted something. They were always nicer when they wanted something.

Barely five minutes passed before the stable-master managed to rouse himself from hungover dozing. He came stamping to the doorway, and his ruddy face blossomed red in an instant.

Task stood a little taller as Ganner marched towards him, finger raised like a sword. If there was one human emotion Task did not like, it was rage. He had seen far too much of it in his long years, both in the wild eyes of men, and glowing at the corners of his own.

'It was only a matter of time! That's what I said to 'is Generalship. Only a matter of time before he breaks something or wounds a fellow, sir, I said. And look what you've gone and done. Who's got time to fix that?'

'I will fix it,' said Task, staring down at the man, marvelling at how the morning light bounced off his pate, and the lingering stink of glugg.

'Deffing spit on it, *you*? Fix a fence? You can't just pull off somebody's head and huzzah! A fence is fixed. Yeah, that's right. I heard the stories about you.' Ganner moved to jab Task in the arm. The golem jerked forward, stones snapping. The stable-master skipped backwards, a little white chasing the red out of his cheeks.

'Now look 'ere!'

Task spoke in a deep rumble. 'I'll fix the fence. I'll also keep the fawls from escaping. All I need to do this is Lesky. Not you, Ganner. Nor your foul breath.'

Ganner went to spit some more venom, but the stern cut of the golem's jaw must have put him off. 'Well, somebody ought to watch you, and it ain't going to be me! Pesky, you runt! Come sort this bloody mess out! Heel!'

Task had heard that word used for the long, floppy-eared beasts that scampered around camp. They belonged to the soldiers, it seemed; bred not for war or food but for company. Protection, even. Warks, they were called. They moved long and low to the ground, sleek as pipes, with patches of scales between the fur and whiskers.

Lesky came running, a short spar of wood in her hand. She stood to attention. Ganner clipped her around the head, making Task growl.

''Ow many times have I got to tell you? You ain't no soldier! Watch him, and make sure he fixes that fence.'

'Right you are, Master.'

'That's better.' Ganner gave her a parting shove before he left them to it, grumbling to himself about going above and beyond his duties. The stable's makeshift door slammed behind him. Barely a moment passed before they heard the clink of bottles.

Task looked down at Lesky. She harrumphed at him.

'You're doin' all the work. I get to supervise. That's what it's called. Su-per-vish-on. Anyways, do you know what you're doin'?'

'I built many walls and fences in Yalazar, during the Diamond Wars.'

'You keep talkin' about these wars, but I really don't know what they are.'

'They were—'

Lesky cut him off with a wag of her finger. 'So you can build a fence?'

'Yes.'

'So that means you can mend a fence?'

'Yes.'

'Good,' she said with a grin. 'You can show me. I need to learn.'

Task threw her a look as he began to poke around the back of the stable. First, they needed wood. Then something to affix it with.

'Why do you need to learn?'

'Why do you learn anythin'? To get better, you big lump.'

Task winced at the sound of that name. It was too familiar for him. But he was curious now.

'Why fences?' he said, as he poked around between two barrels where two lengths of wood were hidden.

When he turned back, Lesky had drawn herself up to her full height, barely reaching his waist. She puffed her chest out and set a twinkle in her eye.

'Because one day I'm goin' to have Ganner's job. That's why I need to know more than he does. Because then I can get another stable, and another, and so on. Until I've got a whole bunch of stables, with dozens of fawls and firns and four-legged things. Some will be for the army. Some for rent n'buy. Some to ride for fun. And there'll be healers at every stable, to help other animals. And it'll all be mine. An' I'll be rich. Like a queen!'

Task was impressed. 'You've got it all planned out.' He almost envied her. Humans could plot these paths, hope and dream, test their boundaries if they wished. Task did not like to think of his boundaries. Of the few he bore, one he had spent his lifetime avoiding like a madness, and the other was so distant it was not worth testing.

'Mam says you've got to have a plan. Have a few goals to aim fer. Otherwise you just float around, movin' sideways, she says. Not achievin'. That's the word she used. So that's my plan, and I'm going to achieve it.' She leant forward, holding a hand, blade-like, up to her mouth. 'Don't tell Ganner.'

Task played secretive. 'I see.'

He broke off the two lengths of wood and clasped them in one fist, then loped back to the broken fence. The fawls had become curious, sniffing the wreckage. Lesky chased them back in with a whistle.

'Cheeky deffers!'

Task began to measure up the spar, choosing the longer of the two. With a hard yank, the broken post came loose and was tossed aside. The spar was angled into the hole and lined up with the horizontal planks. With one finger, he began to carve out long slivers of wood, making a nest for the joint. The wood was damp, and it took no time at all.

Lesky watched as he drove the spar deep into the earth. With a few wiggles and some brute strength, the fence was whole again.

Lesky gave it a kick for good measure. To Task's relief, it seemed sturdy. He decided not to test it with his foot.

'That took no time at all,' she said, as she poked at the grooves.

'Imagine doing fifty leagues of fence twice this height,' said Task. If he thought hard enough, he could still feel the heat of the Khandri sun on his neck. It had been too hot even for the golems. The oasis water had bubbled and hissed on their skin. One had cracked an arm.

'Look who it is,' Lesky pointed up the hill of the camp. Huff was winding his way down to them, encircled by his captains and sergeants.

The early sunlight glinted off their armour. It seemed the further north they pressed, the shinier the officers became.

Lesky crossed her arms, squinting up at him. 'Do you have a plan, golem?'

Task jutted out his jaw as he thought. It was just for show, to see if he could waste enough time for Huff to interrupt. Task knew perfectly well what he wanted: two goals that had stirred him since his creation. But he dared not tell Lesky at that moment. Against his instincts, he didn't wish to scare this particular skinbag away. It was a feeling so old and forgotten it felt almost new.

Once the general drew close enough, he shook his head. 'I'll tell you later.'

Huff caught Lesky's scowl and clearly wasn't fond of it.

'Shoo, little lady! This is grown-up business, and not for your tiny peasant ears. Not that your mind could comprehend it.' The general nudged Captain Glum, and the man offered a one-sided grimace. Task's stones rattled in annoyance.

Lesky did as she was told. She scuttled around the other side of the stable, and was gone.

'We have a big day ahead of us, Task. A big day indeed. Our first major battle in almost a year, or so my scouts tell me. The Fading have finally come out of their holes to fight, and we are ready for them! Rather exciting, don't you think?'

'He said he's never—'

'I know!' Huff spat the words at Jenever, who frowned, leaving the spittle to dangle on her cheek. 'In any case, a big day indeed.'

Task nodded. 'You said that.'

Huff pouted. 'Yes, well. It'll be a fine day for it. Ground's firmed up after all that confounded rain, as luck would have it. Clear and sunny and no room for tricks, eh?'

'No, sir,' came the chorus from around him.

Huff patted Task on the arm. 'We'll have you in the centre with the spears. We'll blast them with muskets and cannon as we approach, and then you'll hit them hard by driving a hole right through their ranks. I want you to wreak havoc, Task. I want you to make them wish they had died in their dreams and never woken up this morning. I want word of our new recruit to spread through the Fading ranks and make every one of them tremble in their deffing boots!' Huff ground a fist into his palm. He seemed far too exhilarated by this prospect. 'The captains here will be escorting you to the gates. We move out in one hour.'

Task ignored the clench of his innards and nodded. 'Yes, Master.'

'Good chap. Can I call you chap? Too Lundish for you?'

'My name is T—'

'Yes, alright!' snapped Huff.

It was always best to play dim-witted around any master. Large things are expected to be fools, as if the Architect could not have blessed them with both brain and brawn. Anything contrary to that belief tended to worry his masters.

By the time his wagon came to a halt, half the army had already dug its spears and shields into the dirt. Lines were formed, body after body, until the fields were full of squares and triangles, all clamouring for space.

They didn't spare a moment. Task was ushered out of the wagon and pointed down a trampled path towards the battle-lines. All around him, cannons were being pitched, their spikes driven deep into the ground by huge mallets. Task frowned at the cannonballs, piled in pyramids next to the fuses. Indiscriminate killers, they were; bouncing through battle with no care for what they damaged. One had taken off his arm, several decades ago, and he had not yet forgiven them.

'Down you go, golem,' Jenever was saying, dragging Task out of his memories.

As he walked, he could feel the heartbeats through the earth, roaring together in ragged unison. No matter how many battles he had been a part of, each one had felt the same. His own heart—if whatever was inside him could be called a heart, or even an organ at all—held a different beat; a slow rumble of concentration, of forced calm.

From simply giving it thought, he felt the agitation trying to rise again. It was not a fear of battle, but of what battle demanded of him; the edge it asked him to walk. Ghoffi had become lazy in his old age, but here in this cold and wet land, the business of war was booming. Almost a week now he had spent with the Truehards, and already he'd seen four battles. Fighting had always been a grim job, but although spilling guts was depressing, the true issue lay deeper inside himself. It was becoming harder to avoid losing control, to avoid slipping over the precipice he had constructed in his mind long ago: the line between calm and rage that he always trod in battle.

Task set his jaw and kept moving. The grass scattered before his feet as he strode across the field. Jenever barked occasional orders at the lines still forming around them. They came together with a precision Task had not seen before; sliding back and forth, standing straight and tall, clanking their shields as the captains and their huge charge lumbered past.

As he walked, Task read the muddle of faces that stared at him: the curious ones, the frowning ones, the ones in mid-curse, even the quietly thankful ones that were glad they had a golem on their side, not facing one themselves.

He felt it then: the thrumming in the ground. It was deeper than the vibrations around him. *Further away.* As the murmurs rose, he looked up at the trailing hills a league away, at the metal that had begun to glint on their slopes.

Jenever bellowed. 'There they are! Get ready!'

All too abruptly, Task surged to the front line, where the spears bristled and the soldiers wore serious faces. The first rank into battle was never a comfortable place to be, for neither flesh nor stone. Priests of some order did their best to assuage the fear, touring the lines, waving golden hammers over the troops, their white smocks edged with fur and smeared with dirt.

Trumpets blew from the ridge behind them. A shiver ran through the armoured masses.

'Onwards!' came the order, howling from the mouths of officers. Task turned to find that Jenever and the others had retreated, and the path of shields closed in behind them with the tramping of feet. Task shrugged. *Those in charge are always fond of guarding the rear.*

The army began to move, lurching forwards like a startled beast. One line yanked the next forwards until the formations slowly spread across the field, like creatures obsessed by shape and uniformity.

The pace built gradually; first a quick swagger, then an awkward jog. Then, the trumpets blared for a full charge and they were pelting through the grass.

Task ran at the very centre, his grunting stone beating out a rhythm with the war drums. Their canter filled the air, driving the masses forward, building a frenzy. Several started to yell and roar, wordless noises of violence. Task felt the pressure build inside him, too. He bucked against it between his strides, striving for numbness.

The cannons spoke then, concussing the countryside with thunderous blasts. Purple smoke billowed as black shapes raced across the powdered sky. Where they crashed back to earth, plumes of dirt and body parts rose from the Fading's lines. Screams joined the blare of the charge.

The enemy cannons replied with a crackle. It came as no surprise they aimed for the centre of the lines. Straight for the fabled golem.

Only one of the barrage managed to hit Task, but not before he hit it first. His fist shot out like a piston, into the face of the cannonball. There was an almighty thud, and the stone lump was crushed under marching feet. Task felt the echoes of the impact dance around his body.

They were so close now. Task could see their faces grimacing behind their grey shields. He saw their eyes widen at the sight of him charging forwards like a mountain sliding from its roots. Their musketballs peppered him; just the grains of a sandstorm. The smoke hid the lines for a fleeting moment.

Task drove forwards, putting a gap between him and the Truehards. As the noise rose to fever pitch, he swung his arms wide, fingers crooked, and wrestled his mind to calm.

The numbness fell as he collided with the Fading lines, muting the thunder of clashing armour, the screams of the first-dead, and the cold chime of a hundred blades on rock. Task was cold in his carnage, digging a trench deep into the Fading formation. Truehards poured in after him, widening the gap.

He was like an axe biting into wood. The soldiers were saplings to him, bending and snapping with every thrash of his hands. Armour crumpled like old bark in his grip. Though shards flew from his legs, lucky strikes biting at him, he paid them no heed. He paused to let them pull back for a charge. The spears and pikes came first, as the others held back to cock muskets and send iron to nip at his stone.

The golem felt the grin spread across his face, felt himself lose his grip and slip for a brief moment. He lunged to the side, giving a soldier the full power of his fist. The man folded in two, sailing into the ranks pressing behind him. He swung again, downwards this time, making a grotesque shape out of two swordsmen trying desperately to evade his reach. Back and forth he fought, through the constant press and wriggle of bodies, his limbs dripping wet. He could taste nothing but the stink of fear and the broken, leaking bodies of the already-dead.

'None can escape me!'

Task clenched himself, dragging himself back from the edge. *I will not. I will not*, he chanted to himself between the punches. Once more he became a machine, whirling through the war dances of the Hasp, the ones that had been branded into his memory. *Forward, cut, break, left, crush.* Task ducked and whirled, waded and pressed. When he had broken through to the back of one regiment he tackled the next. And still the Truehards kept pressing behind him.

A shrill whistle broke through the noise, and the Fading's army expanded its ranks, releasing some of the pressure of the panic. It was a fine tactic, forcing Task to move more, and allowing riders into the fray. *Clever, indeed.*

An immortal carries a morbid fascination with any scent of death. A longing, Task would have called it; a longing to feel close to something mysterious. To be a golem was to live life largely unchallenged. Time, disease, war, vicious hunting accidents. Task feared none of these. But should something come close, if something offered up a worthy challenge, even threaten his existence, he found himself greeting it with warmth.

Though his rules forbade him from harming himself, there was still the skill of others to be relied upon.

Task paused again, letting the beat of the cannons match the thrum of his stones, hot from the action. He spied firn-riders galloping towards him, now withdrawn from the flanks. Three rode in a line in front of the rest. Their lances shone in the sunlight.

Task crouched, forcing the riders to lower their aim. As more musketballs ricocheted from his skin, he waited, holding his breath until they were almost on top of him.

With a roar he exploded from the dirt. As the lances shattered on his stone, his fists flew outwards—left! right!—two blows to the front two firns' jaws that sent them skidding to the grass. The final beast leapt for the golem with a snarl, and Task introduced his forehead to its nose. It collapsed with a whine. The riders lay pinned and dizzy.

Again and again, he was charged. Riders and musket-carriers, spears and swords, each falling back as the other pressed him. They believed they could tire him, as if he was a wind-up contraption that would eventually die of slack cogs. He wanted to show them he was not made that way. Slowly but surely, he built a pile of bodies for them to climb.

It was then that the Fading's cannons began to fire. Cannonballs exploded all around him, showering him with black dirt, pulverising men and firns alike.

Confused shouts pierced the thunder. 'Fading! We're Fading!'

Task wrenched himself around to face the nearest hill, where the gun-crews crowded around their cannons like fat children huddled over gleaming cakes. They knew precisely what they were doing, who they were firing upon. Task held no love for these skinbags, foe or friend, but that was deplorable; to turn against one's own in battle. Whatever respect he nurtured for the Fading wilted and died. His anger flared, and he fought it back with a snarl, but not completely. He let himself flirt with the brink.

As another barrage spewed from the black cannon-mouths, Task began to run. A cannonball struck next to his foot, blowing his shin away with pure force of impact. It barely slowed him; he simply switched to a hobble as he clenched his fists. He felt the snap of the stone-shards tumbling back to him and in a flash he was running once more.

They were firing sporadically now. Their movements were frantic, their aim random. Only one shot landed a hit; right in the ribs, blowing part of his side away. Clouds of grass and soil bloomed around the golem.

The first cannon was ripped from its mount and repurposed as a battering ram, slung under Task's arms. The great brass guns screeched like tortured bells as they were broken from their fixings. *One, two, three...* all the way to twenty. Task charged through them all.

A wayward spark managed to find some powder on the last cannon. Fire plumed with a whoosh, then something more substantial was ignited. With a concussion that knocked even Task to his knees, the firepowder blew the cannon from its mount, breaking its back in an instant. The cloud of smoke and soil enveloped him, like a storm with pebbles and stones for rain.

Task felt the thrumming in his chest grow stronger. Though he'd pushed and pressed and buried the temptation, he could still feel the flicker of enjoyment. Part risk, part want for chaos; he allowed himself just a sample of it.

The gun-crews had scattered like autumn leaves. Through the smoke, Task hunted them, seizing them by the arms and throwing them down the hillside. The officers that dared to face him found their jaws broken by his fingers, or their collars and throats ripped clean away. A fitting punishment, Task thought, for those that dared to give such murderous orders.

When the last of them had taken their breaths, Task hauled his cannon to the edge of the rise, where the grass fell away like a waterfall. Below him the fighting still raged, but with a keen eye, and a stomach for the sights between the fighters, it was clear the Truehards had broken the Last Fading.

He glared down at the turning tide of grey and spattered red. He bared his teeth as he lay hands to the cannon's mouth. A roar ripped from him as he hefted it into the sky. It soared across the grass, landing with a wail. Task eyed the hole it cut into their lines.

If this was to be the measure of the Fading, then he would welcome them to his crushing embrace with open arms and zero qualms. Death may have been his business, but murder and cowardice were different disciplines, reserved for those without decency. This was a twisted brand of chivalry, he knew; but it had been his for centuries, and like a rope-walker's pole it kept him balanced. Besides, once stone gets a hold on something, it's impossible to prise it away.

6

'They say a Destrix will sell his mother for a song, and kill his brother over a loaf. Truer words have never been spoken of their kind. If they're not murdering each other, they're murdering their neighbours, squabbling over territory, or generally being nuisances. A flux on all of them!'

FROM A DIARY FOUND IN AN ABANDONED MONTISH WAR CAMP

44TH FADING, 3782 - GURNIGEN, BRAAD

There is only one thing in the Realm that can cure the vicious hangover notoriously affiliated with gutwine, and that is more gutwine.

Alabast Flint swayed as he reached for the decanter. He waggled it next to his ear and was rewarded with a suggestive splosh. He blew a sigh of relief, groping for a glass that wasn't stained with lip-paint or dubious smudges.

He picked out the one that looked least likely to give him whipsores and stumbled around looking for something to wipe it with. He looked down at his bare body, shrugged, and used a shirt from the floor. It didn't look like one of his. Borian silk was never his taste.

The wine slopped eagerly into the glass, almost reaching its brim. With some trouble, Alabast tossed the decanter onto a couch, lifted the glass to his lips, and slurped like a thirsty wark.

He made it halfway before he came up for a breath. He stared up at the stained glass window, and its delightful scene of farming nonsense: fawls hooked up to ploughs, and a no-doubt witty proverb in old Braad wrapping round their legs. He grinned at it, licking his gums. No matter how sophisticated the Braaden thought they were, with their velvet-clad culture and their bulging banks, they were still just a bunch of filthy peasants.

Alabast curled his lip. 'Deff them all.'

The empty glass saw its way to the table, despite his unresponsive feet. He grabbed another decanter, and poured again until all it had to offer were rosy drips. Alabast hummed. *Two glasses it would have to be.* His usual remedy was three.

He laid a hand on the desk to steady himself as he opened his mouth and craned his neck to drink. With dribbles escaping down his chin, he gurgled down the wine and set the glass back down with a thud, snapping the stem. Tutting, he placed both pieces in a drawer.

Alabast staggered over to the discarded clothes with startling accuracy, as if he had been fuelled by the alcohol. He had been considering that possibility more and more recently, and whether it was a sign to shape up. He shook the horrid thought from his head. He couldn't get blind drunk on vegetables, exercise and a good night's sleep.

He found his boots and breeches curled up in a ball beneath a chair. His own shirt turned out to be at the foot of the bed, one arm lingering in an ash-bucket. He grimaced, shook it clean and slid his arms into the sleeves.

Somehow, his jacket had found its way up onto a corner of the four-poster bed. He had to climb on the mattress to reach it.

A groan emanated from one of the two lumps under the covers. Alabast shrugged again, and laced his boots. He didn't remember them being this muddy. *Had he been running?* He grinned as the memory floated back to him.

Braaden thugs don't like to get their nice attire all mucky. Prissy, they were. The mud suited Alabast just fine, if it meant avoiding a beating.

The mail was last, a new addition. It may have been heavy, and a little uncouth for his liking, but he thought it suited him better than a knife in the back. He hefted it over his head and let its weight descend over him, then he dragged on his jacket over the mail, and staggered for a moment before finding his balance. It felt like a cannonball covered in crushed glass was rolling about his empty head. *Damn cheap gutwine.*

A snore came from the covers, and Alabast's eyes flicked to the cabinet beside the bed. Keeping his boots quiet on the wood, he crept over and wiggled open the drawer with a finger. His coin-purse sat there, beside a little dagger. *His* little dagger; the one he kept hidden in his jacket.

Deffing thieving whores.

'I'll be having those, methinks,' he whispered to himself, sweeping both from the drawer. He ran his fingers through his waxy hair, slicking it back over his skull.

Alabast followed the muddy footsteps out of the door, down the corridor, and out into the streets. He blinked in the sun, which was already high in the sky. Its rays added more glass to the cannonball. He winced, bowed his head and joined the throngs of people, falling into their slow march.

It was a simple enough task, and yet somehow he kept veering into others. Once or twice they cursed him, and he glared. A few saw the crest on his mail and backed away. At least his legend still had some credit to it; unlike his bank accounts.

Flashing a quick look over his shoulder, Alabast made his way south over the muddy canals and deeper into the honeycomb city.

If there is a place in Gurnigen that a man can lose himself, it's in the alleys of the Fjorn Three-Leagues, a triangular patch of buildings at the elbow of two wide canals. There they say the difference between nothing and anything is the amount of coin in one's pocket. It's a place where fog lingers and shadows have names and voices, where shops black their windows and employ heavies at their doors. It's a place where the buildings lean and the lanterns glow green with the salt spread by the wanderers.

Alabast had grown wary of the strange little women that hobbled around in big coats; coats with plenty of places for hiding things. They also say of the Three-Leagues that the wanderers can sell you your own soul. It had taken barely a day for that to make sense to Alabast. Having his pocket-watch lifted had been a big hint.

And the salt! Oh, how their little tradition bothered him. The women wandered from lantern to lantern, feeding salt to the flames and painting them an emerald-green. All night and morning they did this, until the sun rose to its zenith and they skulked back to whatever drain they called home.

Alabast hurried on, burrowing into the twists and turns of the narrow alleys. He kept his gaze away from the sunlight and fixed on the signposts; a complex set of glyphs that had taken months to learn.

The Fountain of Sense was a tiny tavern set between two looming buildings. Alabast waded inside, through the stools and their slumped patrons. The barkeep had a sluggish look in his eyes. His shoulders where hunched so high they were level with the ragged tips of his ears.

Alabast held up two fingers, and the barkeep turned to the taps. Two tankards of spiced beer followed, overflowing onto the bar. He flicked over a couple of coins and took his drinks deeper into the tavern.

Once he'd found a secluded booth, Alabast rested his head against the wood and rolled his skull across the warped planks. With every sip of his tankard, his rambling thoughts became quieter. By the time he'd reached the dregs of the first tankard, he would have sworn the spices were medicinal. He reached for the second.

A ship. That's what he needed. A dirty great big ship going somewhere that had heard of his legend, but knew nothing of his bad credit with the Destrix. Or the Braaden. Or the Borians. Alabast swirled his beer and bared his teeth. Maybe south, to the Montish coasts. Or to the Eager Islands, where the Rent brought nothing but tropical sunshine. Retire, maybe.

Or a horse. Wagon, if he was lucky. East to Begrad perhaps. Spend the summer in the Gamav. He still knew a few names there; names that mattered. Names he could leech off for a while. Bally the Grin wasn't likely to chase him over the border. The Destrix and the Graden are not the best of friends.

Where to run to. This was the choice his life had boiled down to. Not which cathouse to rut in, which sunset ball to attend, or which colour horse suited his armour best, but the direction in which to scarper, like a coward.

Alabast was just about to rest his forehead on his arm when he saw a shape moving through the gloom. From the crook of his eye, he watched it choose a nearby table. There was an assuredness to the man's movements that told Alabast he wasn't drunk; not yet at least. Maybe he was simply a late starter. *If you want to drink all day, you have to start in the morning.*

He peered into the fog, trying to catch the cut of the man's clothes, but it was too murky to pick out anything other than a long coat, flat cap, and a taste for wine.

That was enough to tip him off. Destrix would never drink a beer they hadn't brewed themselves. Gutwine, however, they had a passion for. Alabast felt a mixture of surprise and worry; mainly at the fact that the *Fountain* actually served wine, and secondly, that he had been found. Bally was at it again. The cathouse madam had probably tipped her off.

Damn wagging tongues!

Alabast felt the weight of his tankard. It was a shame it wasn't glass, but if he had learned anything in his years, it was that life largely revolved around not getting what you want. He held the tankard by his side, hoping it might offer some sharp edges if the situation got ugly.

A scuff of a boot drew his gaze. A second shape emerged from the haze and took a seat, at a bench across from the first man. Another sharply dressed fellow with a taste for grape juice. Alabast buried his face in his arm.

The three of them sat in silence, listening to the screeching of the flutt. Every now and then, he would catch them peering through the murk at him. He would match their posture and they would turn away.

His second beer practically evaporated. Even though he ached for a third, he had decided it was time to find another hole. Preferably one in the hold of a boat.

Ship, it was.

Gripping a tankard in each tense fist, Alabast rose to his feet. It was no surprise that the first man stood with him, leaving his glass on the table. Alabast squared against him, finding the man taller, and just a little bit wider. He inwardly groaned.

The man wasted no time with small talk. He marched across the grim floorboards and prodded Alabast hard in the chest, making him totter backwards.

'Bally wantsin to see you,' he hissed, in a thick Destrix accent. Now, Alabast could see the swirling tattoos around the man's throat, between his ruffle and his grimace.

At least he wasn't there to kill him. Bally clearly wanted the pleasure for herself. That sparked a bit of confidence.

'If she wants money, I'll meet her with it on my own terms. Later.'

'When, later?'

'Tomorrow morning.'

The Destrix spat. 'None deal. Today!'

Another poke of the chest; even more painful than the last.

Alabast raised his chin. 'Tonight, then. Two bells past sunset.'

Plenty of time to find a ship.

The Destrix seemed to be having trouble comprehending the concept of anything other than today. He worked his lips.

'No! Today. Bally won't like tonight. None tomorrow. *Today.* We knowsin of you and yous slipperin' ways.' Manicured hands groped for him, seizing his arm.

Alabast swiped them away with his tankards, rapping the man's knuckles.

'Back off, I say!'

The next swing caught the Destrix in the nose, spattering blood across his fancy shirt. It halted him for a moment, just long enough for the other man to come stomping over. He was a muscular sort, tall and young, but with no tattoos at his collar.

Alabast brandished his tankards at him. 'You stay there!'

'Sir Alabast!' said the man. Lundish by his clipped enunciation.

A fist slammed into Alabast's jaw and made his eyes roll up. Stars crackled in the darkness. The world span like the Rent itself.

'Stop!'

Strong fingers grabbed his collar.

'Stop, I say!'

With every blink, the room was restored piece by piece. It was on its side, but at least the stars had gone. He saw bared teeth and a bloodied fist close to his face. He winced, bracing for the blow.

The second man stamped his foot, and both the Destrix and Alabast turned. From the floor, Alabast could see the difference in the cut of the man's clothes. Old-fashioned. Something a Destrix would never be caught in. A Lundish cut.

He was now speaking to the thug. The words were sluggish in Alabast's ears, but he caught them all the same.

'Hear me out, before you render him unconscious. I'm not here to cause you any bother. Rather, to make you and your master an offer. Bally, was it?'

'Aye.' The Destrix spat blood.

'Allow me to make you an offer on this man's behalf.'

Alabast raised an eyebrow.

'And whys you wantsin to help this piece a' shite?'

'Let's just say he's as important to us as he is to you. More so, in fact.'

The Destrix tapped his nose. 'Owes you, too, does he? Maybes Bally can works with that. She says either coin or his good'n self.'

He released his grip and Alabast slumped to the floor. As he felt a fresh wave of pain roll across his jaw, he wondered which Lundishman he owed money to, and how in the Realm he had forgotten.

'Good,' said the second man. He reached into his coat and produced a sheaf of Braaden promise-slips and a small quill. 'How much does he owe?'

'One and six thousand ardens.'

The colour drained from the Lundishman's face. To his credit, he kept hold of the pen and parchment.

'One and six...'

'...thousand ardens.'

Alabast had a way with sums, especially when there was coin involved. He knew that Lundish coin had lost its favour. The sum translated to almost two and four thousand Lundish tants. A minor fortune.

The Destrix waited close with crossed arms while the man filled out the slip. As soon as it was written, he snatched it from the pad, then held it up to whatever light the tavern could muster, and nodded.

The Lundishman offered a hand, but it only made the Destrix sneer. He left without another word or glance.

Once the pen and promise-slips had been stowed, the man helped Alabast to a nearby chair. He wiggled his jaw, feeling the crunch of sinew.

He knew it would be agony on the morrow. *Might as well take the chance to speak now.*

'Do I owe you money?'

'No.'

'Then I take it you want my services.'

'Precisely.' The man didn't seem so sure now.

By the bloody Architect, it had been a while.

Alabast slapped a palm on the table. 'Well, first I'll need another drink after that debacle. Then you'll sit. I'll ask who I'd be working for, what they want, and what would be in it for me. You'll then remind me of the fact I'm the only man for the job and I'll sigh and make a big fuss about saying yes. All of which leads to me getting most of what I want. Sound good?'

The man extended a hand. 'Carafor Westin. Executor of the Last Table.'

'Alabast Flint, the Knight of Dawn.' He narrowed his eyes. 'Executor as in...?' He drew a finger across his throat.

The man waved his hands and chuckled. 'Fear not, Alabast. The only things I execute are orders, and the only damage I'd do is a paper-cut.'

'Ah.'

Westin smiled, bobbing up and down on the spot.

Alabast propped his chin on his hand, and wiggled a finger in the direction of the bar. 'The drink?'

'Of course.' Westin saw to it promptly, bringing back another glass of wine and a frothing beer. Once he was settled, and Alabast had taken a long gulp of the warm beer, they got to business.

'Right, yes,' said Westin. 'Who and why. I am honoured to work for the Last Fading. I assume that you're up to date on the current state of Hartlund?'

'I'm surprised you Lundish even remember, given how long you've been fighting. Let me see. Crippled by nine years of futile war between stuck-up boy kings and broken businesses?'

Westin frowned. 'That's the one. I work for the broken businesses. Or, as I would put it, the jilted lords and ignored voices. Standing up for what is right.'

The chuckle came with a shower of froth. 'Of course.'

'As for what I want. The Last Fading have sent me here to hire you, Alabast. To use you in our struggle against the Truehards. They have proven... difficult of late.'

'And so what's in it for me?'

'Board, food and honour. We have just cleared your debt, after all.' He eyed the tankard in the knight's hand. 'And perhaps drink can be arranged.'

The downward slant of Westin's gaze tickled Alabast in a way he didn't like.

'How *difficult?*'

Westin blew a sigh. 'Well, the Truehards have recently bought a fighter of their own.'

'Who is he? Is it that putrid Karananse? Or the Wooden Knight?'

'Neither. He's Hasp. We think.'

'Hasp?' Alabast scratched his temple.

Westin nodded.

The knight slammed the tankard down on the table. 'Spit it out, man! There are other employers waiting to snap me up, other damsels in distress.'

What he really meant was that other taverns needed his coin.

Westin spat it out alright, like a bothersome pip. 'It's a golem.'

'A golem?' As in...' Alabast gestured again, shaping something large and massive over his head. His heart had taken on a nervous tick. He knew the stories of golems well enough. A mad baron with a grudge against some warlord once asked him to slay one for him. That conversation had been shorter than this one, despite the pretty price.

'Yes, one of those.'

'Made of what? Bone? Dirt?'

Westin bobbed his head. 'Stone, so we understand.'

'I do *flesh*, Westin. Something a sword can cut.'

'The Fading have the utmost faith in your fighting ability. After all —'

'If you're about to say I'm the right man for the job...' Alabast began to push himself away from the table.

Westin rose first. 'You slew the Last Dragon, a beast with iron scales and an acid tongue. Surely your average golem would be an easy task for one such as the Knight of Dawn.'

'There is nothing average about a golem, Mr Westin.'

'It is slow and clumsy, and we think that if we trap it, you can cut out its tongue. Our Lord Lash hears that is the way to kill them.'

Alabast was becoming irritated. 'Can't be done. I won't be bullied and bought into a role involving suicide. I have my integrity to think about.'

Westin smirked at that, looking around at the dinge of the tavern. 'Of course you do.'

'What exactly does that mean?'

The executor patted his pocket. 'Tell me, do you know where to find this Bally? I need to arrange a reversal of fees.'

That got Alabast to his feet. 'Good luck with that, Mr Westin. I don't see how Bally the Grin is going to let you dangle your Lundish coin under her nose then whisk it away.'

'Oh, but you see the Destrix have a stake in the outcome of the war. Those who won't join us... They ruin the benefits. Bally will have an extra interest in you now that the cost of my journey has been added. And these fine drinks.'

'You...' Alabast's brain had soaked up too much beer. As had his tongue. It tumbled over the blocks of Westin's threat, teasing out the result. 'They'll kill me.'

'Either a gang of thugs, or a Wind-Cut Golem. Your choice.'

Alabast drew himself up to his full height. 'I want payment, on top. Thirty of your tants a week.'

'Ten,' said Westin, quick as a flash.

'Twenty.'

'Twelve, or I walk out the door and start asking if anybody knows a Mrs Grin.'

Alabast stuck out a stiff hand, his thumb tucked in the Braaden way. 'Fifteen.'

Westin grasped the hand firmly. 'There is a carrack waiting at the dock. Lundish colours. *The Jealous Tide*. Can you remember that?' Westin's eyes flicked to the tankard.

'It just so happens I was thinking of catching a ship. When?'

'One hour.'

Alabast was about to complain that he wouldn't have time to collect his belongings, when he remembered he carried all he owned; all except his sword, which was most likely still at the bottom of the Gurn river, where he'd thrown it in a drunken rage two nights ago.

Alabast bowed low. 'One hour, Mr Westin, and I'll be yours.'

'The Fading's, actually.'

'Whoever. As long as they're paying.'

It was the motto of every mercenary.

7

'Bare your soul to another, and they will know your dreams. Bare your heart, and they will know your love. Bare your mind, and they will know your evils.'

FROM WRITINGS OF THE CHANARK HERETIC NA'YAMI, AN INFAMOUS GLIMPSE

44TH FADING, 3782 - TRUEHARD CAMP

'No, the *Chanark* are part of the Harmony. Not the Chunk, Glum.'

'Oh,' said the man, confused again.

Huff viewed his captains at an angle, his head slanted on his open hand, elbow to the desk. They were arguing in the corner, thinking he was busy with paperwork, or gazing off into the distance, as was his habit. Today his distance was blocked by two fools in chainmail, bickering the finer points of Realm politics.

'They're starving. God's Rent doesn't give them rain like it does with us. They're farming in desert.'

Glum scratched his chin. 'Yes, but it's our sea. Our crops.'

Huff's patience gave out. 'Are you two quite finished? Or should I call you a priest, Glum, and inform him of heresy?'

The captains came to attention, quick as a blink. Manx had a clever look on his face.

'Actually, sir. I was about to tell Glum about the Khandri ambassador some of the officers have mentioned. Word from Caverill, sir.'

Huff pushed his head upright. 'Were you, indeed? I wonder, what is your opinion on such a matter?

Manx had a think. 'Well, they're clearly spying. Gauging our strength, seeing what we're made of. Under the guise of politics, sir. I don't think we should let her land on our shores.'

The general shook his head slowly. 'Aren't there some orders to be given? Some latrines that need washing?'

Manx and Glum looked around as though checking the caravan for any sign of latrines or lax soldiers. Huff whispered for mercy.

A thud and a crackle of stone interrupted any further belittling. Jenever entered first, towing a rope that reached upwards to the golem's neck.

'Captain! Do you care to explain the rope? Is this some wark you're taking for a stroll?'

Jenever looked hurt, as if she had expected to be showered with praise. 'I thought... You were angry about him wandering off, so I thought —'

'You thought a rope would be a good idea?' Huff sprang to his feet, pressing his knuckles to the desktop. 'A *rope*? At least have the wits to fetch a chain. Get that off him!'

Task bowed to let the captain retrieve the leash. Huff could have sworn he heard a chuckle amongst the rattling of stone.

The general flicked a finger. 'Task! Front and centre. I must have words with you.'

'Words?' said the golem.

'Yes, words. And I command you to salute me, from now on.'

The golem rolled his shoulders. 'I do not salute. I am not a soldier.'

The beast was being impertinent now.

'I am your master.'

'I am held at the bidding of a master by law of magic. A salute has never been needed.'

'Well it is now, curse it! I'm making a new rule.'

Task took his sweet time to comply. He raised his arm and covered his eyes for a moment. Huff decided that would have to do.

'First of all,' said Huff, taking his seat with a squeak, 'it was a fine performance on the field yesterday. I couldn't have hoped for better, I really couldn't. We have taken over ten leagues in all. Ten!' Here Huff raised a hand. 'However. One matter has been brought to my attention. You, Task of Wind-Cut, abandoned our forces to go beat up some cannons and their crews. Is that correct? Am I to believe these rumours are true?'

'There were about three thousand witnesses—'

'Manx!' Huff had found his temper fraying more in recent days. Every sunrise brought him new troubles, new complaints, new gripes. Even in the evenings, in his brief moments of peace, he was forced to deal with poltroons. He had begun to nurture a desire to see them impaled.

Once again, the golem hunched. He seemed unsettled, as if the fire of battle ran through him still. Huff leaned back in his chair.

'Task?'

'They were firing into their own men.'

Huff looked around as if a bad smell had wafted in. 'I fail to see the problem with that. Do you, Jenever? Manx? Glum? Or have you fallen asleep standing up? It is becoming difficult to tell the difference, these days.'

'No problem with it, General,' said Glum.

'Thank you. Your point, Task?'

'It's against the rules of war. It's cowardly. Murderous.'

'War is full of cowards, full of murder. Civil wars, most of all. Countrymen fighting countrymen. It brings out the beast in a soldier. Not all, of course. Especially not officers.'

Task grunted at that.

'You broke ranks, Task. You disobeyed orders, and I will not have that.'

'You asked for havoc. I provided it. There were no orders to stay in rank. It was a battle. There is no rank. You have been in battle. You should know what it's like.'

There was an awkward shuffling around the room. Huff could have blamed it on the fabric rustling in the wind, but he was no fool. It was common knowledge that the general had never fought in a battle. He eyed his captains, forcing their eyes to the floor. He puffed himself up.

'Your duty is to do what I tell you, allow me to remind you of that. We could have used those cannons for our own arsenal, deff it!' He felt his temper bloom. 'I'm warning you. Continue to disrespect me, or disobey me, and you will see my unkind side. You do not want that, golem.'

'Yes, Master.' He bowed.

Huff let out a big breath. 'That's better. Much better. Now. On to a lighter subject. What do you think of our adversary, now that you have met the Fading in battle?'

'A clever fighter, Master, but rash.'

Huff was nettled at the clever part, but he held himself back. 'Rash is good! That comes from pride, and we all know that pride leads to a fall.' He thumped the desk. 'We have them by the balls.'

The captains cheered. Every soul in the camp was tired of war. Even Huff wanted out of the mud and marching; as long as he made his name out of it first.

The general wanted more good news. 'And our soldiers? A finer breed, I expect?'

Task hesitated. 'My back was turned for most of the battle. But they are eager.'

'Eager? Just eager, Task? Something more, perhaps?'

'Good with cannons.'

Huff threw up his arms. 'Our soldiers have been fighting for nine long years. They are trim and trained, golem, and nothing less.' He couldn't help his gaze sneaking over to the rotund Captain Glum. 'I doubt there is an army in the Realm that could challenge us.'

'The Riders Farria,' suggested Task. 'They say they are born on horses. Fearsome warriors, who eat the flesh of their own dead. They were formidable.'

Huff snorted.

'Hasp Diamond Knights...'

'Thank you, golem.'

'Khandri Bladewhirlers...'

The fist met the table in anger this time. 'Silence! I will not have heresy in this camp!'

Task had made his point. Manx and Jenever looked insulted.

'The Khandri rejected the Mission and the Architect. They follow their own goddess. As such I will not have myself or my men compared to them. Do you hear me, golem?'

'Yes, Master.'

'Now, away with you! I want you back in your paddock, thinking hard about what I said. We have yet another big day tomorrow. We finally take Purlegar back from the Fading!' He stood with arms folded as the beast was led away by Jenever.

'Impertinent creature.' Huff shook his head at the oafish cohorts in the corner. Even their faces had begun to bother him. 'Go and make yourselves busy! While you're at it, fix up the tents for Dast and the baroness. They will return by sunrise. And yes, I am as thrilled as you are. Begone!'

They shuffled from the door with all the alacrity of a sand dune.

Finally, he had peace. There was only one thing he wanted to do with it. He would write a strongly worded complaint for Frayne. He was promised a war machine, and machines were not meant to talk back.

Purlegar. *A town.* The word put a fresh worry in Task's granite bones. Not the admonishing by Huff, not the hilarious threat of a leash; but a town.

It was remarkable how much the feel of stone at a man's back made his mind falter. With a battlefield, disregarding the sharp blades and deadly company, there was always a place to run; a place to move. In a town there were buildings and streets, walls and corners; all things to get stuck in. A town was like a trap, and however brave the man, stick him in a trap and he will squirm and squeal. Task had seen such madness for himself more times than he cared to recall.

Ignoring Jenever's muttered attempts to ensure he trod the right path, Task marched as if he were alone, striding through the camp with confidence. The thuds of his giant feet brought heads out of tents, turned gazes. Most of them wore the usual sour expression at his passing, but to his surprise, a few grinned and shook fists at him. One soldier even hollered after him, shouting, 'Golem saved my life!'

Task didn't remember saving any lives, but he nodded to the man. Compliments were rare things, and like a child with a sweet, he always held them close, to savour later.

His paddock came around the bend. Jenever hovered around to make sure the latch of the gate was secure, then ambled away. She had barely said a word to Task since they had nosed up the shores of the Yawn. He didn't care. Jenever was just another soldier with a downturned face.

There was a spectrum to the ways humans displayed their dislike. Usually it was disgust, or anger, led by the voice and followed by fists. Or it could be subtler; all vicious games and whispers. Jenever had chosen silence and ignorance. Task returned the same treatment.

The celebrations still hadn't died. Night and day they had cantered on. Music still blared from the centre of the camp, muddled with drunken shouts. A ten-league advance was apparently a big cause for merriment. Task had claimed more on his own in an afternoon.

He crunched his neck from side to side before shuffling up against the fence. The wood creaked as he rested some of his weight against it.

Lesky didn't take long to appear. She must have been waiting for his return, judging by the blanket and the lantern she lugged by her sides.

'Evenin'!'

Her black hair was more tousled and knotted than usual. Little bags hung beneath her eyes.

'Chores all done then?' said Task.

Lesky flashed him a serious look, pointing at the bluer shade around one eye. Task clenched his teeth. 'Ganner's been in a mood since you broke that fence. Not your fault.'

'I broke the fence.'

'You didn't break Ganner, though, did you? Make him all so twisted and mean and drunk all the time?'

'I suppose not.'

'There you are, then. He'll get his comeuppance soon. I can feel it. Mam says I have a sight in me. Like a bit of old-magic. Like you! That's three things we got in common now. We're almost best friends!'

She truly was a strange creature; the like of which Task had encountered only once before. It was the way she carried no fear as she stepped into his paddock; the way she simply talked to him; even the way she looked at him. She actually listened. She even listened without glaring or knitting a frown, or gawping at him like a dolt. Huff could have learnt some lessons from her.

Lesky must have guessed his thoughts. 'What did His Generalness want?'

Task reached out a curious hand to feel the warmth of the lantern. It always took a while, through his stone. He dipped his fingers into the flame. Lesky watched on, fascinated.

'He said he wasn't happy with me breaking the Fading cannons.'

'From what the others have been blabbing about, you won the day.'

Task narrowed his eyes. 'Something tells me the victory is less important than his pride. That morning he was pining for carnage. Now he's upset because I didn't follow orders and caused too much carnage. It's infuriating.'

The girl wriggled forwards. 'So you get feelings like we do?'

'My masters have always said as much.' Task remembered how his first master had put it to him and sighed.

Lesky studied him for a moment. 'You don't look infury... inferlated. Angry.'

Task chuckled. 'It's inside.' He tapped a finger against his chest.

'Yeah, your face don't move about much.'

Task held up his hands, letting her look at his fingers, jet-black like volcanic glass and jagged in the flickering flame. 'But these do.'

Lesky moved as if to touch them, and then thought better of it. He could tell she was fighting her curiosity.

'It's alright,' he said, flattening his hands out to turn the edges away from her. She ran a tentative finger across them.

Task felt her life bleed from her. He could feel her handful of years in the grain of her skin, compressed into flashes of light and colour, snatches of a woman's face and a thatched cottage. He flinched away before he saw too much.

'You can feel that?' Lesky withdrew her hand, holding it as if cold.

'Every crack in your skin. I can feel every breath of wind, every bite of a blade, every drop of blood.'

'But you're stone.'

'I'm also magic.'

'Is that normal for a golem?'

'No.' The reply was gruff. Lesky scrunched up her face.

'Mam says never to pry into others' businesses, so I won't. But she also said that friends talk, and that's why they're friends.'

There was something about this obsidian-haired beast that softened the edges of his mind. All he had to do was let his tongue loose. They sat in silence, until Task cracked.

'Remember you asked what my plan was?'

'Mm.'

'Want to know?'

Lesky shuffled. 'I like knowin' things.'

Task looked up at the stars poking through the furrowed clouds. The moons were low in the sky tonight, their jagged edges balancing on the hilly horizon. He waited until a gaggle of murmuring soldiers had passed. 'I want for only two things: to be free or to die.'

It felt strange giving those thoughts a voice after all the decades he'd spent nurturing them. He waited for Lesky to edge away, or leave. She did neither. Instead, she stared long and hard at the flickering flame and pulled her blanket around her.

'I understand.'

'You do?' Task couldn't imagine any human understanding the workings of his mind.

Lesky sat up straight. 'My da was a slave to something. Summin important in the city. It kept him away for months on end. He had a job to do, just like you got one. Just like I got this job. Don't stop you wanting something different and better. Your job's tough, so what you're wantin' is pretty… tough.' She pondered for a moment, then shrugged.

Task looked at her and she winked.

'I'll 'ave you know I got an old head on these shoulders, Mr Golem, sir. Nothing gets past me. Not even Miss Wanderin' Claws over there. Flix.' She nodded to one of the fawls, now snuffling in its sleep. The beasts had arranged themselves in a pile to keep warm. Task couldn't tell where one started and another began.

'Always makes a run for it, that 'un. Anyways.' She brought herself back to her point, 'You'll understand when you meet my mam. She's the wisest one.'

'Meet her?' Task looked around, as if a woman might have been hiding behind the stable the entire time.

'We're headin' north and east. Once we go past Purlegar, 'round the Sisters, you'll be fighting near my county. The Darens. Wittshire.'

'Purlegar,' Task huffed.

'Know it?'

'Huff is planning to take it tomorrow.'

'You don't sound happy 'bout it.'

'I'm not.'

'Don't like towns?'

Task stared out at the crooked points of the tents. 'I don't like what you skinbags do in them.'

'Like what?'

The memories prickled him. 'Things you wouldn't care to know.'

'Why'd I ask, then?'

Task dug at the dirt with his fingers. 'All the energy and fear of a battlefield squeezed into alleys and thoroughfares. Cruelty and horror, that's all towns know in war.'

'That why you don't like soldiers?'

'It's why I don't like people. They're fickle. Always one slip away from wild.'

'I'm people.'

'You're different.'

Lesky hummed. 'Maybe you just ain't met many of the good ones. Besides, if you only see us "skinbags" in battle, then you're only seein' the bad stuff. You're skewed, like Old Kinny's clockwork toys. If you're always thinkin' we're going to fail you, we always will.'

'Or I've seen people at their worst, and that's the rule every one of them should be measured by.'

Lesky thumbed her nose. 'Then why you talkin' to me?'

Task bent his lip. 'You're not...' She had skewered him good and proper. 'You aren't a skinbag.'

'You know what a promise is?'

Task knew what a promise was. *A thing people liked to break.* 'Of course.'

'You got to make me one.'

The only person Task had ever made a promise to was himself.

'A promise about your goals. And friends got to keep promises, okay?'

'Okay.'

She looked at him with a serious gaze. 'No dyin' on me, okay? Let's go with the free idea.'

Task found himself smiling. He was about to agree when a harsh shriek interrupted their talk. He was on his feet in a blink and a crackle of stone. He moved in front of Lesky as another cry broke the murmur of the camp, closer this time.

He lifted the latch of his gate and stepped onto the muddy path. Heads poked out from tent-flaps. A few soldiers even shrugged on mail and reached for muskets.

Torches clamoured on the path ahead, shouts tumbled before them. As a monster who had seen his fair share of torches and pitchforks, he could recognise a chase in an instant. The wretched squealing was being made by whatever was being chased, and it was getting louder.

Task stood in the centre of the path, fists clenched and ready. He glanced back at Lesky, hovering at the mouth of the paddock, and waved her to get back.

Night-guards swarmed up from behind him. Sergeant Collaver appeared, waving a huge club and missing one boot. His men wisely kept their distance, forming a curve behind the golem.

The thing was close now. Task could see something wriggling in the darkness. It was one of those small scaly beasts; a wark.

This one was terrified. It was so desperate for escape it kept tripping over its own legs. Its breath came in dogged gasps, and its eyes looked fit to pop.

A gang of louts were chasing it, whooping and swinging their torches. A few threw stones as they ran. One caught the wark on its rump and made it shriek even louder.

Task crouched, scooped up the wark and held it by his side. He felt tiny fingers rub against his skin and wrestle the thing away from him. He looked down to see Lesky skipping back to the paddock, the wriggling wark under her arm and a cheeky glint in her eye.

He turned back to the hunters, who had ground to a halt just out of arm's reach. Most looked sorry for themselves at the sight of Collaver and the huge golem, but a handful wore menacing frowns. Task glowered back.

'What in the Realm is this?' said Collaver, marching forwards. 'A day at the races? Who's in charge of you scruffy riders? Speak up!'

The gang split to let a man step up. Task recognised him immediately.

'Lancer Taspin,' said Collaver. 'I should have guessed!'

'And a fine evening to you also, Sergeant,' said Taspin, pausing to sip from a metal flask. 'Out ruining the celebrations as usual, are we?'

'You'd best mind your tongue or I'll have you in front of Huff.'

'The wark stole a sausage, so we thought we'd make it work for it.'

'By terrorising it?' said Task.

'You can talk, big fellow! Stomping around camp all day and keeping my men awake.' Taspin walked closer.

Collaver laughed. 'What are you going to do, Lancer? Sock him in the jaw? Break a stool over his head like you did that Gabber boy?'

'He can try,' said Task, leaning forward to give Taspin a chance.

Collaver roared in the Lancemaster's face. 'The damn thing's howling woke up half the camp, you deffer! I'm surprised the war-drums haven't been sounded yet! Back to your tents, the lot of you! Sleep off that torig. You reek of it.'

Taspin obeyed, but not before spitting at Task's feet.

'You're an abomination, beast. You've done your work now. You can go.'

'That is for Huff to decide, not you!' said Collaver. 'Off! You're lucky I'm not throwing you in gaol for the night!'

When Taspin's men had retreated back into the gloom, the sergeant turned to nudge Task. 'Riders. Think because they're from good families they can piss around and turn war into a pastime.'

Collaver said no more, and dispersed his men. Heads were withdrawn into tents, muskets set back in their racks, lanterns dimmed. Task stood alone in the darkness of the evening, staring up at the Mothers, climbing the sky in the south. The claw-marks across their chalky surfaces had given each them faces over the millennia. Tonight, as always, the moons looked lazy, half-asleep; as if they had lost faith and interest in all they saw below.

'I think I'll name him Shiver,' said a voice. Once again she'd managed to sneak up on him.

'What?'

Lesky chuckled. 'Look! He won't stop.'

The wark was propped up in Lesky's arms, shaking terribly. It's black eyes were still wide and full of fear, but surprisingly that didn't increase as the golem approached. Task reached out a finger and poked its floppy ear.

'Like this,' said Lesky, guiding his finger down the wark's head and along its ridged spine. The little beast seemed to grow calmer with every stroke. 'See?'

Task could feel its fear leaking into his stone. It made him think of what the morrow held, and he withdrew to a corner of his paddock. 'I think I want to rest, Lesky.'

'Suit yourself. Shiver and I are off for a walk.'

'Hasn't he run enough?'

Lesky looked at him as though she'd just asked him the colour of the sky. 'It'll calm his nerves, putting some more exercise into him. I don't just know fawns and firns, Task.'

'Fair enough. Just stay away from those riders.'

Lesky put her hands on her hips. 'You've been here, what, a week? I've been 'ere three years. I know what I'm doin'.'

She smirked, and then, oddly, threw him a salute; a wonderful, childish little thing, and so freely given. Task couldn't help but indulge her. He covered his eyes, and smiled.

Lesky departed in search of twine. The little wark trotted at her feet, now tame again. Task shook his head and closed his eyes. It wasn't long before stillness took hold of him, and dreams spun him old stories once more.

♛

Lesky tutted at the snoring golem; although it was more like grinding than snoring. The sound of a stone-mill turning grain to powder. Mam had taken her to one of those once. She had drawn shapes in the flour.

Lesky turned back to the twine and finished her double knot. She didn't want the wark running off again. The wriggly bugger was quick on its claws.

Shiver was true to his name as she slid the leash over his head. It was a happy shudder, though; like a crallig's purr. She could tell by the way his scales bristled.

She stroked his spine. 'You're a trustin' one. That'll do you both bad and good, says Mam. On we go.'

After a short period of straining at the leash, and flinching here and there at noises, Shiver calmed and stuck to scampering close to Lesky's ankles. He was tall for a wark, and long. Not some junk-breed stray.

She strolled the walls of the camp, keeping to the torch-poles, making sure not to go too fast for the wark's short legs. The creatures didn't need much walking, but she doubted he'd seen much exercise before tonight's chase.

The soldiers she passed paid her no notice. Most were too drunk to bother. Others saw just a dirty stable-waif, not worth looking at. Her mam had been wise to see her put into the king's army, rather than some ragtag division, or at a fort where the men grow "restless", as she put it. Huff and those before him had been strict on such behaviour. The punishment was common knowledge, and it made Lesky pull a face any time it crossed her mind.

'Ick,' she said, sticking out her tongue.

Her wandering took her in a graceful curve to the eastern camp: the riders' enclave. Lesky looked over her shoulder, and contemplated retracing her steps. Shiver still looked keen enough; he was only shaking a fraction at the reek of the riders' bonfires.

Her mam had told her that walking was good for the tongue, and on her travels that night, she had worked up a few words for Lancer Taspin; words that now begged to be set free. *Onwards it was.*

She walked where the light from the fires spewed across the path, daring Taspin to see her, strolling as if she were enjoying the feel of beach-sand between her toes.

Lancer Taspin dared alright. He threw himself out of his chair and marched to cut her off. A half-dozen or so of his riders came behind him, spread as though they were heading into battle.

Lesky turned to meet them, arms crossed. She pasted an expectant look on her face.

'Well if it isn't the golem's pet girl. Now with a pet of her own, I see! It looks rather familiar, don't you think? Perhaps she's come to return what's rightfully ours?'

Taspin raised his hands and his cronies muttered in agreement.

'And here I was thinking decency had all but died out in Hartlund.'

Lesky tutted. 'I've rescued him! Seein' as his last owner thought chasing him to death was a good idea.'

Taspin took a step forward. There was now barely a lunge between them.

'I think you forget your station, peasant.'

Lesky shook her head. 'I think you forget yours.'

Taspin stuck out his chin, stepping closer still. Lesky grabbed Shiver and held him tightly. He had begun to tremble again. Maybe it was the smell of the bonfire, or the torig on the rider's breath. Both of them bothered her.

'You think we're joking, you dirty Darens whelp?' His voice had turned gravelly. 'You'd better give us that wark, or I'll show you what we do to thieves in this enclave.' He massaged his knuckles in front of her face.

'You won't lay a finger on me,' countered Lesky, puffing herself up.

Taspin laughed. 'Oh, won't I? You think your golem can protect you? I don't see him nearby. Do you, gentlemen?'

More murmurs from the henchmen.

The Lancemaster pressed his fists together. 'Just as I thought.'

Lesky took a step back, bringing her feet together. She held up a finger. 'Firstly, you put your firn-stink hands near me, and I'll tell Huff you tried to touch me. You and all your men. I've heard what the washers say 'bout you riders. No woman in the camp will want you once the tongues start wagging in a different direction. Maybe they'll think you've gone bonkers. Plagued in the brain.' She tapped her head, then propped up a second finger. *'Then,* I'll tell Task, and knowin' that great lump, I wager he won't wait till mornin'. He'll come marchin' up that hill before you can get out your sacks. I don't think he'll wait for Huff's order. Probably just do it himself right there n'then.' She let the thought sink in as she mimed the merciless removal of certain precious items usually found in men's breeches.

Lesky paused there, fixing him a stare, as if she could ram her threat into his tiny brain through his eyes; make him see every visceral detail she could dream up. She grit her teeth, and his face twitched. For a moment, she glimpsed the fear in him, hiding beneath the bluster.

She shrugged. 'As for after, that's up to him. Don't think you'd be ridin' again, anyways. So that's why you won't lay a finger on me, Lancer. And that's why you're not havin' this wark. He's in better hands now, and he'll stay in them. That's all this dirty Darens whelp has to say. Goodnight!'

Lesky flashed a smile, swivelled on her heel, and strode away, leaving the riders to their silence. She waited until she had rounded a corner, before coming to a halt. She took a deep breath and held it until the pounding of her heart had found a calmer beat.

'Don't know about you, little snout, but I'm glad that worked.'

And how it had worked! Lesky spent a moment savouring the memory of Taspin's fleeting look of fear. She promised herself she would learn how to paint or draw, so she could hang a picture of it up in her stable one day.

Lesky was about to cackle to herself when she felt an itch upon her lip. She raised a hand and it came away smeared with crimson. She took a moment to stare at it, somewhat confused.

'Just the cold,' she told herself. 'Ain't no blood-flux in this camp. Not in Fading.

She snorted, tasting blood, and hurriedly wiped the rest away. With a tug of the lead, she and the wark were back on the path, hunting for a warm fire.

8

'Find me a man who knows the true cost of spilt blood, and I'll hand him my crown without a quiver in my heart.'

FROM LETTERS OF LUNDISH KING RASPIER, FATHER TO THE BOY KING

45TH FADING, 3782 - PURLEGAR

Ellia Frayne picked over the debris. Her heeled boots wandered over broken beam and tortured stone, cracking the occasional shard of glass. With one hand clasped behind her back and the other forming a visor above her narrowed eyes, she went about her examination with a regal air.

Somewhere, a lonely bell pealed dolefully. Brick-dust floated on the still air like morning fog. The buildings, once proud works of masonry, were now empty shells punctured with jagged holes. The fault of cannon, for the most part; but here and there she spied a wall missing, or the front of a building yawning wide. Marks of a rampaging golem.

The deeper she ventured into the town, the more bodies she found. They lay awkwardly in the rubble, half-buried or curled up on top. The battle had touched all: soldiers, townspeople, beggars, traders, men, women, and some so young it made even Ellia twitch. Their lifeless faces gawped at the dust or the blue sky, never anywhere in between; as if, in their final moments, they had caught sight of their ultimate destination. She trusted enough in her religion to know there were two ways to get to eternity. *Up or down.*

Scarlet jabbers had already begun to arrive. They gathered in mangy flocks upon the rooftops, cawing as they argued over which would get the first peck of flesh.

The jabbers weren't the only guardians of the dead. Truehard soldiers hovered in doorways and under smashed arches, caked in dust and blood. Some stood alone, hunched over cold flasks, while others clustered in groups, swapping fresh memories of the battle. Some were going from door to door with sacks, and Ellia could hear fresh crashing as buildings were searched.

'And he just keeps on running. Bam! Bam! Bam! Walls falling down as if they were rotten wood.'

'Could have been weeks of siege.'

'No mercy, that 'un. He's the Destroyer's work, I bet you.'

'He knocked the gates down in two kicks. Two deffing kicks and we was in!'

'Captains couldn't do a thing about him. He wouldn't stop. Huff had to be called.'

'I heard he ripped one of ours up.'

'Heard he killed six men with a shoe. A shoe!'

Ellia put a jolt into her step. She followed the paths of carnage to the main square of Purlegar, where a long tent had been erected for the officers. The day was unexpectedly warm and clear for the time of year; a sign of an early Rising.

Ellia affixed a warm smile to her face as she approached the huddle. The general and his captains were poring over a map. The golem was pacing along the other side of the square, with that oaf Collaver guarding him.

As if that pile of blubber could stand in the way of stone.

'Gentlemen!'

Huff had a streak of mud down his shirt as if he'd taken a fall, and there was a venomous tint in his eye. Even his slick of hair was frayed and out of place. Ellia was shocked, and pleased, to see how much his patience had eroded in her short absence.

'Ah, Baroness Frayne,' he greeted her, crossing his arms. 'We were beginning to think you had gotten lost, been kidnapped, or perhaps worse. No such luck, I see.'

Ellia's smile only broadened. 'Mercifully, no. The Council demanded more of my time than usual, and besides, the journey grows ever longer the more land you gallantly reclaim for us.'

Huff twitched his moustache. 'While you may not appreciate the great progress we are making here, there are plenty in Caverill who shout my praises, I am sure.'

'Funny, I recall no shouting. Plenty of grumbling.'

'I believe this is a conversation for another time, Frayne. What can I assist you with?'

Ellia sought a stool. 'A report, as it happens.'

Huff wasn't having that. 'Councillor Dast was informed over an hour ago. Perhaps you can talk to him, seeing as you both work for the Council, and ensure your reports are in agreement.'

She smirked. 'There is a reason why two of us are watching you, General. Two points of view. As such, I'd rather hear it from the fawl's mouth, so to speak.'

The general was clearly put out at being compared to a beast. He huffed and left the map with the captains, taking her aside.

'The Fading put up quite the fight as we drew close to the walls. Bombardment started at around nine horns. Captain Manx here had the idea to have the golem hold some of the wagon-bed up as shields for the muskets. It worked well until they brought their own cannons to bear. They must have smuggled them in from the north. They began to tear through our lines, so Task was sent forward. He saw to the gates, tearing them down just before our riders caught the worst of it. I sent two regiments forward with Glum and Jenever.'

Huff took a breath. Ellia caught the pull of his upper lip. 'It became a brawl. Street to street we fought them, tooth and nail. Task was almost useless in the narrow streets. Chasing after one soldier, then the next, letting people slip though his fingers.'

'Townsfolk?'

'People who could pick up arms against my men at any moment. People who didn't even brandish a fist under the Fading's rule.'

'Rich people,' said Glum, overhearing. 'Feeding the Fading with gold.'

Ellia inclined her head. 'I see.'

'I ordered them rounded them up, to be ransomed if possible. Claim the rest in the name of the king.'

She curled her lip. 'Is that why you gave the order to loot the town?'

'As I have reminded you before, Baroness, I have been given license to end this war how I see fit. Would you have me do that without supplies and funding from the capital? I would rather cut the financial legs from under the Fading and restock our own coffers.'

Ellia let the matter go. Irritatingly, he had a point. 'As you wish, General. Continue.'

'We don't know what caused it, or whether it's simply what golems do, but we lost Task to some sort of madness.'

Ellia had to suppress her smile. She had been waiting to hear those words ever since the monster arrived.

The dullard captain butted in. 'Wouldn't stop fightin'. Charging at everything that dared to wave a weapon.'

'Yes. Thank you, Captain Glum. He rampaged through the town, doing wonderful damage, but with complete disregard for the plan. The thing couldn't be stopped. When we tried, he tore a man's arm from his shoulder. Only then did he calm himself. I haven't decided what to do with him yet. For now, he can stay over there until I can trust him. And I will be sending my father a letter about this.'

'If you think that is wise, General. Telling your father of failure.'

Huff's jaw dropped a fraction. 'What failure would that be? Purlegar is ours! The Six Sisters are on our doorstep! We are making greater headway than we have in years, Baroness.'

She sighed, for effect. 'The golem clearly isn't responding to your authority. It hasn't taken to you at all. I would hazard a guess that in your father's eyes, that could be dubbed as failure.'

The ground shuddered as an explosion concussed the far side of the town. It stole the moment Ellia was enjoying so much; watching Huff's cheeks blossom.

'Firepowder, most likely,' said Jenever.

Huff jabbed a finger at the map, eager for a distraction. 'They must have broken into the town hall. Fine news!'

Ellia left them to their pillaging, but Huff caught her.

'And just where are you going, Frayne?'

Ellia didn't even bother to turn. 'To speak with the golem, of course.' She ached to find out what had cracked him open.

'Please refrain from filling his head with any of your Council babble. He is quite mad already, thank you!'

Task saw her coming, saw the purpose in her stride. *Another reprimand on legs.* And yet, when his gaze was bold enough to meet her face, he saw nothing but a friendly smile. It put a pause in his pacing, though he still heaved with ragged breath, still tremored with outrage.

Purlegar had been nothing new. Just a fresh battle for the pile of bloody memories. The soldiers had seen to their duties with viciousness and venom. It had been murder, not battle. Every Purlegar soul without a Truehard mark had been cut down like a flag at a parade long finished. Swords and bayonets had done the main job. Cannon had turned the streets into clouds of rubble.

How could he have not lost control, even for a moment? *What self-respecting—*

'Mr Task!' Her voice shook him from his whirlpool of thoughts.

Although he was painted with entrails and stone-chips, she had stopped just within arm's reach of him. Bold as usual, but respectful.

'Baroness Ellia Frayne,' he said, hoarse even for his stone throat.

'Please,' she said, waving a hand. 'Ellia will do fine.'

Task tried it on for size. 'Ellia.'

'Will you walk with me, Mr Task? I find it easier to have something to tread on while handling difficult topics.' She spoke as if everything was rehearsed, taking a short pause before each sentence as if recalling the next line.

'Fine.'

Together, with Collaver bringing up the rear, they ambled around the edges of the square. It might have been calming, if not for the broken market stalls and crumpled bodies strewn across the flagstones. More than once he had to adjust course to avoid the dead.

Only when they were far away from Huff's awning did she speak. 'A difficult day, I hear? Apparently you went rather... mad, and began stampeding through the streets. Or so says Huff.'

Task bared his jagged teeth, fixing her with a dangerous look.

'For a split second, Madam.'

Ellia smiled at him, fearlessly. 'I take it that makes you angry? Strange. I never knew golems were supposed to feel emotion. As impassive as stone, I heard.'

Task kept his mouth clamped, but Ellia was persistent.

'Huff is wrong, of course. The man is an idiot. I told you not to trust him. This is his fault, not yours.'

Task broke his silence for that. 'How so?' If there was a chance of an excuse for his behaviour, no matter how weak, he would take it.

'He should know your history, as I do, and know that you're different from the others of your kind. Huff's father, the Grand-Captain, demanded to have you in the midst of respectable battle. "Honourable engagement." He sent instructions to his son, although I doubt he read them. Otherwise, he wouldn't have crammed you into this city and forced havoc upon you. Am I correct?'

Task worked through her logic, testing its strength. 'How do you know my history?'

'Your late master, Ghoffi. He sent letters before he died, telling us of a "condition". That there was something more about you than just being good in a fight. Dartridge and the Mission had already bought you by then.'

He knew immediately what she was scratching at. The small boy who picked up his father's sword and stood against Ghoffi. The warlord had laughed, never one for mercy. Age had not mattered to him; he saw people in two states: alive or dead. The boy was in the wrong category for his liking. Not one hour later, Task had snapped, storming the gates of a fortress, giving in to his temptations for the first time in decades. The warlord never looked at the golem the same way again. He'd fallen ill a week later.

The baroness stopped in her tracks, waving Collaver away. She stepped closer, narrowing her eyes at him, staring deep into his pinprick eyes.

'I wonder how a stone learns to feel. Does it just copy human emotions, or can they truly flow through it?' Another step was taken, and her hand snaked out to touch his arm. 'What could make stone care?'

Task shrugged away from the brush of her fingertips, standing tall and covering her in shadow.

Ellia withdrew her hand, held it for a moment, and then shrugged. 'You know why I am here.'

'To report to your king,' said Task, as they began to walk again.

'It's more than that. I'm here to make sure the war is *won* for the king, and to do that, I have to make sure that man...' Ellia paused to jab a finger at Huff. '...does a fine job of it. Using you, of course. I have his father's ear. Do you know what that means?'

Task shook his head.

'One word from me to Gorder Dartridge, and his oaf of a son will be scrubbing barrack latrines in the capital. If he wasn't winning battles, and if it wasn't for you being shackled to him, I would recommend him flayed for his incompetence.'

Task was cheered by this, but he held himself back. 'I see.'

'He's pompous and the army despises him for it. You must have seen it.'

'And yet you let him continue. You leave him in charge.'

The baroness sighed. 'This struggle needs to end as quickly as possible for this island to survive it. Huff has the ambition we need to charge forwards. As a Truehard, I have no love for the Fading, but I'm also Lundish, and I don't want to see my countrymen like this.' Ellia pointed to a corpse with a missing arm, sprawled in a water trough.

'The longer it goes on, the more will die, and by the end there will be no country left. You alone have the might to change that, Task. Not Huff. Not I. *You*. You could end this war in a week if you wanted to. I imagine you've had enough of war? Then help us put an end to ours.'

The golem jutted out his angular chin. 'One more in a long line, Baroness. And what of the next war? And the one after that? You humans are fascinated by the death of your own kind. You bicker as an excuse to battle, caring not what damage it wreaks in the process. There will always be wars. And I will always fight them.'

'The cause we all fight for is not a foolish or needless one, Task. Perhaps in time, you'll see why we're called the Truehards. You're right.

We fight to preserve ourselves against the next war, not to just win this one. The Khandri grow restless, and we wish to survive them.'

'And what makes you any different? Why should the Truehards win over the Fading?'

'Because if we win, we can govern this country as we did before. Rebuild it.' Ellia lowered her voice. 'You speak of the next war, Task. Well, a great war is coming, bubbling up in the south. The Khandri and the rest of the Harmony have grown resentful of the Accord. Dire times are ahead. A country needs a king to stand behind, not a gaggle of rich lords and businessmen. That's how we save lives.'

Task gestured at the square. 'You call this saving lives?'

Ellia held up her hands. 'I will talk to Huff. Tell the buffoon to put a stop to the butchery. You continue doing what you do best. Ignore his orders, Task. Do what you know is right. Concentrate on putting this affliction, this emotion of yours, to good use. Let it burn for something right and truthful. Let it out, I say! It could win us this war, earn you some respite.'

'If you want to save lives, that is not a good idea. The cost is too great. And I cannot disobey my master.'

The baroness tapped her nose. 'But you can bend the rules.'

Task clenched his fists once more. 'I cannot. When will you talk to the general?'

'As soon as he is finished looting the town.'

The golem's knuckles crunched so loudly that she jumped. Task quickly turned his mind to other things to keep it from straying.

'What is this Mission?' he asked, choosing the first thing that came to his head.

Ellia cocked her head. 'Why do you ask?'

'I've seen some priests in the camp. And you mentioned Dartridge and the Mission. What is it?'

Ellia looked the sky in thought. 'They are the Church of the Architect, responsible for making sure the Accord follows its righteous path. Their centre is here, in Hartlund. They have been funding the Truehards for several years now.'

Task knew all about skinbags and their money. There was pointless lunacy in the metal of coins, capable of driving a man to evil. He had often wondered why they simply didn't manufacture more of it, and make everybody happier in the process.

He was calmer now, and so he simply shrugged. 'I've never understood religion.'

Before Ellia could reply, a shout rang out across the square.

'Golem! Here!'

It was Huff, standing with his arms on his hips, captains at his back. If his chin had been raised any more he would have been staring at the sky.

'My master is calling,' said Task, almost as an apology. Ellia bowed and waved him on.

'Think about what I said, and what you could do here. And fear not, I'll have the fool put straight. I'm a keeper of my word, Mr Task.'

Task looked back over his shoulder. 'Then you're a rare breed amongst your kind.'

Huff felt the shudder in the ground as Task stomped towards him, as sullen as any child who'd had his sugar-pie taken away. Though the golem's eyes were fixed on the ground, the general could sense their burning.

If he'd had skin instead of stone, Huff would be staring Task down and piling three weeks of latrine duty onto him. A good officer needs to be able to affirm his authority over every member of his army. He'd read that in one his father's books.

'Stand up straight, Task!'

The wrinkle in that stone lip was enough to kick the wind out of his bravado, and yet Huff persevered. He could feel his captains' eyes upon the situation.

'Now. What's to be done with you? What's the proper punishment for a golem that won't obey its master? I should pin attempted murder of a fellow soldier on you, after what I saw!'

'Cruel men deserve cruel things. One of my masters told me that.'

'I am your master now!' said Huff, pushing himself up to his tiptoes. 'As such, I demand... No, I *deserve* to be obeyed.' Huff held up three fingers. 'Three times I ordered you to cease, and twice you refused me, tearing off a rider's arm in the process. That is abominable behaviour and I will not stand for it in my army. The battle was hard enough without you turning half the town to dust.'

'He was torturing an old man—'

'I don't want to hear it!'

The baroness chose that moment to stick her nose in. 'General! Might I have a word before you continue?'

Huff looked to the sky for a saviour. 'No, you may not, Frayne. I'm busy.'

'I think you'll find it pertinent to the matter.'

His hand flapped like a strangled jabber. 'In a minute! Task, to show that you're truly sorry for your spate of madness, you will help with the clearing of the bodies. The men will surely appreciate that. Sergeant, if you please?'

Task turned on his heel and let Collaver lead him away, a low rumble in his chest.

The general huffed as he turned. 'Yes, Baroness Frayne?'

'Might I have a word with you about the golem, in private?' Frayne glared at the three captains behind Huff.

'It better be important, I'm telling you now…' Huff waved and the captains sauntered away, their curiosity quashed. It was probably for the best; whatever Council nonsense Frayne had for him, it would sail over their heads.

Once they were alone, the baroness crossed her arms and all vestiges of formality fell away, like a shroud wrenched aside.

'You *are* failing, Huff, and you know it.'

The general could only flap his jaw. Frayne didn't give him a chance to form words.

'You're not being firm enough with him. Can't you see he thinks and feels like we do?'

'That's heresy—'

'Do not lecture me on heresy! The stone has emotions. Are you saying you didn't see how angry he was?'

'Angry at *what*? The reason escapes me.'

Frayne sighed and fixed him with a sympathetic look. 'From what he has led me to believe, he thinks you're inept. You and your soldiers. It irritates him. He wants to be left alone.'

In the corners of his eyes, Huff could see his cheeks blooming a deep red rash. 'Excuse me?'

'He told me you're not using him as best you could. He's a war machine, General, created for one thing only. To destroy. All golems are. What do you think the word "golem" means in Hasp? It means *chaos*. This is him trying to do his job. You are holding him back. He may not have said it, but I have the strong impression he thinks you're weak. Possibly cowardly. He is used to warlords and desert kings, not Hartlund generals still sporting their first moustache. Show him that you're not afraid of war, Huff. Unleash him, and show him that you're as good as any master that came before you.'

Huff was a muddle of gleaming possibilities and outrage. The concoction produced no words. For him, that was rather rare.

'Do you see now why I advised against writing to your father?' said Frayne.

'Yes, alright!' said Huff. He smoothed his moustache, wracking his brains as to what in the Realm would curb a golem's scorn. It turned out that Frayne had already given him the answer.

'If he is a machine, then I will treat him as one.'

Frayne nodded, looking satisfied. 'Very well. Meanwhile, Huff, the Council will be pleased to hear of your victory here today, I'm sure. They have been grumbling about the slow speed of the campaign. Let us not forget the imminent arrival of the Khandri Ambassador.'

Huff narrowed his gaze. He had enough to worry about without adding a foreign dignitary to the pile. 'Quite.'

'Quite, indeed. If you carry on like this,' she gestured to the square with a smile, 'I am positive the Council will quiet down. Celebrate you, even. That chest could do with a few more medals, if you ask me.'

Frayne was being unnaturally friendly, but Huff preferred the sound of celebration over grumbling.

And he did rather like medals.

He cleared his throat. 'Well then, Baroness. If that is what I must do to earn respect, then onwards with all speed it shall be. You can tell the Council that.'

The baroness' crallig-like smile widened. 'I will, General.'

9

'The Mission has crept like mortplague across this land. Theirs is a simple ruse. If a man holds the secret to heaven, others will line up to learn it. Add a dash of horrific iconography and the threat of eternal damnation, and there you have it. No wonder their coffers are overflowing, their churches have sprung up in every province, and their missionaries and zealots wander every road.'

CASIX MANIR, GRADEN PHILOSOPHER

45TH FADING, 3782 - PURLEGAR

'The worst part of battle is the mess at the end of it,' said the old soldier, hairless as a white pebble. 'It's all very well crushing a man's skull, but shovelling up what's left is another matter. It hangs heavier on the soul.'

Task didn't know if he had a soul, but he felt the weight all the same. This chore was vile. He wanted to murmur in agreement, but he held back. The others talked, but not to him, as though a grim party had gathered around a boulder. The soldiers' fierce expressions at his arrival still hung in his mind.

The old soldier said no more on the subject, but a younger man had his own wisdom to offer.

'Least we're not one of these poor deffers, and get to go fill our bellies after it.' He nudged a bloodied head with the toe of his boot.

Task ground his teeth, making a few of the men twitch.

''Ow can you eat after this?' said a peaky-looking man at the back of the pack, further down the street. His throat bobbed up and down.

'S'hard work, that's all,' said the younger soldier. 'I just imagine I'm buildin' a stockade or diggin' a latrine.'

'Wading through a latrine, more like,' said a woman with the smudge of a birthmark across her right cheek. Her gaze was locked on her boots. Task's eyes followed it and spied a lonely hand sitting in the dust, fingers like coat-hooks. 'The Destroyer's latrine at that.'

Task kept to his work, lifting the bodies from the soldiers' piles onto an open wagon that somebody had stolen from a grain-house. When it was full, it would be carted off, and he would wait for another. He never had to wait long, but he savoured every break.

For Task, touching the bodies was torture.

No matter how lightly he touched them, nor how swiftly he carted them, they told him their secrets, opened up their last moments. Flashes of axe-heads and the soles of bloody boots. Crunching sounds, the like of which his stone could never make, filled his ears like sharp cracks of desert thunder. He kept to their clothes as best he could.

A soldier called out to him, brandishing a severed arm. 'Hey, golem! One of yours?'

Task kept his eyes down, thanking them silently for choosing humour instead of hatred. He'd had enough of that today.

After two more wagon-loads, he began to flinch at the feel of the bodies. On the next, the soldiers began to notice.

The older man crept forward. 'You alright there, golem?'

'Keep back, Sald. He might snap again.'

'I won't snap,' said Task through his teeth, grabbing a corpse in each hand. He barely got them onto the wagon.

The old soldier leant on his shovel. His face was spattered in blood; some old, some new. Task could tell from the streaks that he'd given up trying to wipe it away.

'Is this difficult for you?' He spoke as if he couldn't believe his own words.

Task looked at each of the soldiers in turn. They had all frozen, with their eyes fixed on him; expressions curious, concerned, or just plain confused.

'How can it be difficult?' asked the younger soldier. 'He's made of stone. He can't be tired.'

'This is difficult labour for the mind as well as the body, Cater,' said Sald. 'For you, golem. I think it's more the former, right? Not all stone, are you?' He stared at the golem for a moment, watching the tremble of Task's huge fingers. He nodded to himself, and held out his shovel.

'You should use this. And, Cater, give him yours.' Sald hinged his hands at the wrist and clapped to show Task his idea. 'Like pincers.'

'What am I going to use?' said Cater.

Sald demonstrated by dragging a corpse to the nearest pile. 'The hands the Architect gave you, silly deffer.'

Once Cater had given in, Task took a shovel in each hand and stood there, eyes switching between them, trying to think of the last time he had been shown such simple kindness by a soldier. Once or twice, perhaps, but always whispered or back-handed, and never in a group. Soldiers are pack animals, and packs have a habit of turning on those who stick out.

Task bowed his head to them, and turned back to his labour.

Sald bowed back before chuckling. 'See? He ain't no demon. Just another soldier.'

'Lancer Taspin seems to think otherwise,' muttered Cater. He grimaced now, trying to use his feet instead of hands.

Sald shook his head. 'Taspin's bent so far backwards tryin' to look down his nose at everyone he can lick his own arsehole. I've seen plenty like him come and go. Educated, so they think they're above the rest of us. Rich, so they don't have to fight as hard. And cruel, because the battlefield ain't enough fun for them.'

'Sounds about right,' said Task. He too had seen his fair share of Taspin's type; enough to make the simple gift of a pair of shovels something to be branded in memory.

Cater kept at it, talking as he chased away a bold scarlet creature with two sets of wings. It cackled at him before flapping back to its brethren on the rooftops. 'He's just an officer. You expect any different from them? Shite rolls downhill, Sald. You should know that with all the years you got under your belt, old man.'

'And wisdom is a long and difficult climb, you ignorant whelp! Remind me, did your wet nurse sign you up, or did you manage it all on your own?'

Cater pulled a face which only deepened as the laughter spread. Even Task took to chuckling. Humour was one human export he actually liked, when it was good-natured. There was escape to be found in the ease of atmosphere that laughter brought. He felt some of that weight lift off his soul.

The woman took up where Sald had left off. 'Taspin can talk all he likes. So can all the others. We'd be shovelling bodies several leagues back if it weren't for this golem. Best decision Huff has ever made.'

'The *only* good decision…' said another, receiving a few affirmative mumbles. Task remembered the baroness' words. *The army despises him.* He thought back to the scrunched-up faces that had first welcomed him to the Truehard camp. Perhaps not all of them had been for him.

'I agree,' Sald said, wincing as a body squelched under his fingers. He carried it close to the ground to keep all its bits from spilling. 'You got a name? Or is it just golem?'

'Task.'

Sald smiled. 'Right name for the right job. Well, Task, meet the Dregs. Simple peasants the lot of us.'

'Dregs?' Task echoed.

'We ain't officers,' said the woman. We ain't trained.'

'And we get all the shite jobs,' said Cater.

'We're the lowest of the low as far as the army is concerned, Task,' said Sald. 'You may fit right in.' He beamed a gap-toothed smile.

Task gave him one of his own; less gap-toothed but more fearsome.

Here were men and women who didn't feel the need to prove their worth. He liked this breed of mankind. Soldiers such as these felt no pressure of position; no need to bully. They just wanted to do their jobs and still be living at the end of it. Task could empathise with that.

'And despite that, you still fight for the Truehard cause?' he asked.

Sald looked as though he knew the depth of the question. 'I don't know much about the politics that has us here mopping up the dead, but the cause of staying alive is worth fighting for, don't you think?'

'I wouldn't know,' said Task, between the thud of two more bodies.

'I suppose not.' Sald crouched down in the muck and scratched his bald head in thought, leaving a smear of grime on his scalp. 'Then put it like this. Imagine you have a home, a family, maybe even a small plot to your name. It's a tough life but it's yours. You pay your taxes, high as they may be, but if you don't, the lord who owns the land will kick you off it. One night you're in the tavern swapping songs and you hear a murmur of war approaching. Civil war, no less. Talk turns sour. As the weeks go on, the talk gets nervous. War finally breaks out. The country divides itself in two. You live in Gabber county. Truehard country, by all accounts. So now you know where you fall, no matter which direction tongues might have wagged in before. There ain't no argument, despite how you feel. It's an allegiance based on the scratches on a map.

'Weeks pass with no sniff of war, until one day you see banners breaching the hilltops. Screams start, you begin to run, and the further you go the higher the smoke behind you rises. You know that's your home, your crops, all you had beside what you're carrying and the hands you're holding. Twice more, that happens, until you're in country you ain't ever seen, living as beggars between camps. One day a man comes around with the king's banner, looking for bravery and a strong sword arm, or a good eye for musket-fire. You've seen a few fights in your time, maybe fought against the Destrix when they ventured west. Then you remember the pillars of smoke, the smell of burnt wheat on the breeze, and the ache in your legs from running. You decide that's not right and something must be done. Three years later and here you are, shovelling the bodies of the people you hope lit the fires. There's nothing noble in our struggle besides wanting back what we once had. We've got no gold or glittering halls to protect. No higher calling of duty or honour. No politics rushing through our veins. Just a warm hearth and the chance to be. Survive or die. That's a peasant's war, my stone friend. That's the cause we're fighting for. Architect spit on it, I'd even fight to pay taxes again!'

Task pondered the man's words as the laughter came and went. The Dregs all seemed to agree.

'I've never had a life to protect. Just masters and their orders,' he said.

The woman chimed in. 'That doesn't mean you don't fight for what's right. Every league you win, another soldier gets his home back.'

Task disagreed. Every blow he'd ever landed in the name of "right" hadn't felt right at all. And every right had its wrongs, many times over.

He gestured to the dead. 'And what about these soldiers? These peasants? What about their homes?'

The Dregs sucked gums and clucked tongues as they thought. In the end, it was Cater who answered him.

'They were on the wrong side of the scratches,' he said.

'He's got a point,' said Sald. 'These are either traitors or Fading who have moved into our lands. Look here! Shroppin jork furs on this one.' He prodded a man's bloodied clothes.

'And I know Norset copper when I see it, too,' said the woman, holding up the arm of another corpse. Its burnished bracelet caught the sun.

'All Fading territories from the outset,' said Sald.

Task remembered Ellia's words, and the broken woman sprawled in a trough. 'They are still your countryfolk.'

Sald worked his way closer to the golem. 'I don't know what you feel, or dare to try and imagine, Task. But I know the look of a man when he's punishing himself. Not too different when you see it in stone, as it turns out.'

Task sighed. 'Baroness Frayne believes I can win this war for the Truehards. Put an end to it quicker.'

The woman spat. 'Well, if the Baroness thinks so, then she must be right!'

'Ah, the Baroness Frayne,' said Cater, mostly to himself.

Sald waved a hand at his comrades. 'Nerenna there don't trust anyone with more than one coin in their pocket, and the young fool can't stop staring at the woman, so ignore the both of them. I'd say Frayne was right. Before you came along we'd barely moved a foot-length in six months. The Fading had us pinned good and proper. Now, a week later, and we're reclaiming Purlegar. I'd say that's progress. Before long we'll be dining at the Last Table!'

A cheer went up from around the corpse-piles, and Task smiled with them. He had to admire their spirit. It felt true to him. Innocent. Even though their blades had cut flesh like the rest. That kindled fresh hope in him. He could not fight for the Truehards; not for Huff. But he could fight for men and women like these. Men and women who were shackled by the sway of their betters, just like him. In that moment, for the first time for centuries, he felt camaraderie.

The bodies seemed a little lighter after that.

Huff appeared later, right on cue, as the clouds began to darken. They hung over the city like a sullen mood, threatening to pour at any moment. Like the Dregs, Task always kept one eye on the weather, waiting for the first drop of moisture. He doubted they watched it for the same reason.

'Nearly finished, I see?' called the general. Manx, Glum and Jenever hovered at his back.

The soldiers snapped to attention. Shovels clattered to the ground as they covered their eyes. Task lowered his corpse and stood there, waiting for instruction.

Huff raised an eyebrow. 'At ease. Task, I believe we talked about this? Or will you defy me yet again?'

The golem tried to hide his sigh as he obliged him, giving Huff a rough salute.

'That's better,' said Huff, leaning on the wagon's handles. He applied a fraction too much pressure and the wagon shifted, just enough to make him jump. He cleared his throat. 'Back to work!'

The soldiers returned to their grim toil.

'Task, I shall personally escort you back to the camp. Make sure you don't find any trouble along the way.'

'Will we not be using the town, Master? It is more fortified.'

Something flashed over Huff's face. Task could see his tongue dragging over his teeth. 'We shall, but some of the camp will be stationed outside due to the lack of room.'

'The stables.'

Huff smiled. 'Like the stables. Well done.'

'And if the Fading counter-attacks?'

The general smoothed his moustache. 'Then you will be there, won't you? Now that's enough questioning of my orders! That is not your job!' Huff's voice rose in volume with every word until he was shouting once again. Task wondered why he originally thought him a quieter man.

Task straightened his back, eliciting a crunch. 'Yes, Master.'

'Good. You are trying my patience, golem. I will not have you doubt me!'

'I do not doubt you, Master.'

Huff scowled. Task had never been good at lies.

Cater caught Huff's eye. The lad was still grimacing, despite giving up his shovel four hours ago. He was trying to drag a body with one hand in a vain effort to keep the other from being soiled.

'My, my,' said Huff, shaking his head. Cater came to attention. 'They don't call you the Dregs for nothing, do they?' The general chuckled, as did Manx and Jenever. Glum didn't seem to grasp it.

'Onwards!'

Task spared a quick glance for Sald and the others before dropping his shovels and falling in behind the general. They nodded in silent thanks. Sald even winked.

The corpse-crews had been busy all over the town. As they marched past the mouths of alleys and streets, Task caught a glimpse of the odd body, but the place was mostly rubble and blood. Stains painted every wall; rusty-brown after a day of sun. The rain would wash Purlegar clean by the sunrise. Maybe it would even purge the smell of flesh and firepowder, and keep those blood-red creatures away.

Task wondered how much of it he had caused. The memories were dim. Here and there he caught glimpses of things that stuck out like snagging nails: a shattered doorway, an obliterated market stall, a streak of dark blood that reached the length of a whole building. He ignored the visions, and studied the cannonball holes in the stained glass windows, or puncturing the sides of slate-roof houses.

Soon enough, they drew close to Purlegar's walls. In several places, they had been reduced to no more than a jagged mound of bricks. The gates still lay flat and trampled; splintered where Task's stone had met their wood and iron. He squashed them again now as he passed under the archway.

The lanterns had already been lit, although dusk had yet to fall. They marked the path: off the road and down into a hollow in the mound that Purlegar was built upon. Here, the remnant pieces of the camp were scattered, wide and far apart, each with their own sprouting of russet tents.

Lesky's—or rather Ganner's—stable was at the far edge, nestled between a tree and a rock shaped like a bell. A lantern glowed from one of the paddocks; the empty one. Task found himself smiling. Tiredness was not something he often felt, but the day had drained him. Corpses are weighty things; heavy in more ways than one.

The girl stood at the door; arms crossed like a scolding mother, face a picture of scorn for the golem's filthy appearance. She had the wisdom to hold her tongue.

The general rapped his hand on the gate, waking some of the sleeping fawls. They bleated in protest.

'Child,' said Huff, 'if you continue to stare at your commanding officer like that, I shall have words with your master. I'll have him show you what respect looks like. Need I find him? Wake him even?'

'No, sir!' Lesky came to attention, and slapped a hand over her eyes in salute. Huff basked in it, for all its brevity.

When her hand was down by her side, she flashed a wry smile and turned to face the golem. She saluted again, slower this time.

Task moved without thinking, his hand covering his face with a clunk. As he lowered the salute, he realised what he'd done. The look on Huff's face confirmed his mistake.

The general's skin flushed crimson around his cheekbones. He spent a moment dragging his lip back with his teeth.

'I have had a fantastic idea! I think this paddock is not befitting your status, Task.'

'My status?'

'Remember what I said about questions? There must be a change. Something more appropriate for the beast that you resembled today.' Huff came close to stare up at him. 'I warned you, Task, that you do not want to see my bad side. Well, *beast*, you have pushed your luck, and you have continued to disrespect me. Do you think yourself above all your masters, Task?'

'No, Master,' he said, between clenched teeth.

Huff snapped his fingers at Lesky. 'Girl, go inside, see to some duties. Tell Ganner his paddock is no longer needed. And yes, he will still be paid!'

Lesky peeled herself away from the door and disappeared.

The fingers snapped in Task's face. 'You are coming with me,' said Huff, striding deeper into the hollow.

'General?' Manx whispered as he caught up. It was that inane breed of whisper that was as loud as standard speech, just hoarser. 'What's in your mind?'

'Discipline, Captain!' Huff dropped his voice to a mutter. 'And humility, while I'm at it.'

Just a salute. One slip and he taken a tumble down a mountainside. Any surviving notions of Huff being the honourable and chivalrous master had been trodden into the grass. He truly was as vengeful as the rest. Every one of them, at some point during their reigns, had turned on him.

'Glum, go talk to the beast-master on three and see how big his jork-traps are.'

Task would have given a shard of himself to know what a jork-trap was, never mind a jork.

'Aye, General!' Glum lurched into a hobbling run towards the adjoining stable. He soon had men out, waving lanterns.

One in particular came rushing forwards, hands clasped as if in prayer and eyes avoiding Task at all cost. 'General Huff, sir! I thought we had discussed this—'

'So we have, and nothing changes. He measured Task with a hand. 'Your jork-traps. Would you have one big enough?'

The man's gaze crawled up Task's body. He began to nod. 'I think we've got one that might do it. Just the one, mind. If he breaks it—'

Huff led the man away, back to his stable. 'I will have the Council requisition another. Manx, make a note.'

The jork-trap, when it came, was a large iron cage with bolted joints and twisted spars for strength. Task almost laughed.

'Here we are, General. Biggest one we've got.' The man sounded proud.

Huff cast a sideways glance at the golem. 'Have it taken to the field, back near the gates, where he can protect them if needed.'

'Follow it, Task.'

'Yes, Master.'

The jork-trap was heavy, and therefore slow. Task walked beside it, listening to its creaks and rattles. If they thought this would hold him, they were mad. But he knew the virtue of obedience, even if he didn't exercise it as he should. It kept a master happy and calm. Task would sit in their iron cage, and let the good general think he'd won their battle. *Maybe it would lend him some spine.*

The jork-trap was pinned to the ground with iron rods, and lashed to tent-pegs further out. At least Huff had the decency to have it laid on its side, rather than upright as first considered. Whatever jorks were, Task had the impression they were as tall as him; possibly wider.

'In!'

Task was already bending down. 'Yes, Master.'

He sat with his legs out and his back against the bars. It was a position he had grown accustomed to over the centuries. The trap was slammed shut and locked with two cogs. Task hid a smirk.

'Do you see how you've brought this upon yourself, Task? Do you understand now why I warned you? Perhaps you will by morning. We'll see. I bid you a goodnight.'

'Good night...' Task paused, for just a moment longer than usual. 'Master.'

Huff left with a satisfied smile beneath his blonde moustache. Task watched him and his captains until they were swallowed by the lights of the road and the archway.

His chuckles rumbled to life, echoing across the field and rattling the metal bars at his back. Somewhere in the patchwork gloom he heard a firn snuffle, and he let his laughter die away.

Task couldn't care less whether it was a cage or a paddock they put him in. Stone has no need for comfort; blankets and pillows and such. Stone sleeps where and how it likes.

What mattered to him was the absence of the girl. Even though she was a musket-shot away, she was not there with a lantern, telling him off or distracting him with her dreams. He kept his eyes on the lights of her stable, and wondered whether she would be brave enough to venture out again.

Task waited as only stone can wait: motionless, silent as a cloud.

Further up the mound, Purlegar was ablaze with song and drunken cackling. The stone reflected the sound into the night, making it echo across the hollow and the fields beyond. The celebration was foolish, especially on the first night of claiming a town. He had seen many over-confident armies slaughtered mid-revelry by a counter-attack under darkness.

Task eyed the brewing clouds above. He found himself smiling at the anticipation of rain.

While a man may balance in the grip of a noose, or tiptoe along the edge of a cliff, for immortal stone it is more difficult to flirt with finality. Although there are still many ways it may perish: one is time, another is water.

Task had seen the world carved up and washed away by both, again and again. He had seen the great ocean shape shores and humble storms batter cities into submission. He had seen buildings crumble under nothing more than years, and people shrivel into shades of themselves.

Though a golem is sworn to never kill himself, and time alone holds no sway over its life, the elements will still do their worst. The patter and dribble of rain across his shards was the closest he could come to a sense of mortality. He taunted himself, and he knew it, but it brought him joy to feel his grains washed away. It felt as if he had skin instead of stone, and a beating heart in his chest that would one day hiccup, and fail him.

Better to live one life bold and bright, instead of flickering on for decade after decade, bearing too much along the way. Too many fools like Huff. Too many cages.

Immortality was a curse.

32ND REAPING, 3361 - THUNDERSHORES, CHANARK

The waters threw themselves against the smooth cliff-face, rising up to make a rainbow of the blinding sunlight, before the fall back to the rushing sea. The noise was a constant roar; an endless battle between rock and water.

The Thundershores were aptly named.

The Spinning Sea stretched for a league or two, maybe more; an unbroken half-moon of black rock spattered with orange where the iron seams had long rusted. Within it, the water spun like a balancing top, thrashing at the cliffs with unending venom.

Task stood at the southern arm of the curve, where the seawater rushed back into the great ocean; frothing green curdling with deep blue. Beyond it, the waters filled the horizon, as endless as the rocky desert, rolling away behind them.

'Do you see now, Task, how this world is slave to the Rent?' Belerod asked, his shouting voice quiet against the roar.

'I am beginning to, Master. Though I think it is something that needs to be seen to be believed.'

'But you can see it, Task! That dark smudge on the horizon is the Rent itself.'

The golem turned his head, regarding the faint shadow loitering in the far distance. It might as well have been a stray cloud.

He tried again to imagine it: the colossal whirlpool Belerod had described to him more than once; how its great dark eye churned in perpetuity, burrowing a column to the bottom of the ocean. Or to the centre of the earth for all the Realm's thinkers knew. He shook his head.

'I cannot understand why any god would curse the world with such a thing.'

Belerod thwacked him on the arm with his cane. 'To doubt Haspha's teachings is to scorn sense, Task. The ocean was split to let magic back into the world. To pave the way for the gods' return.'

'But the Lexicog tells of a time when this land was forest and field. The teachers say the Rent has turned this land to desert.'

'And I should have words with those teachers, for filling you with confusion. It is a price the Harmony has gladly paid, for what the wisdom of Haspha has taught us.'

Task looked up at the criss-crossed sky, where long streaks of vapour bent their heads toward the Rent, drawn by its pull.

'Is it not true, then?'

Belerod went to whack him again, but thought better of it. He shuffled forwards, standing at his golem's elbow.

'It is true, the Rent has seen fit to take the moisture from our lands, sending it north. But as I said, Task, it is a test. A necessary evil. Two thousand years, we Hasp have waited. And we will wait two thousand more if we must, even if the desert swallows us.'

Task nodded. A lie, really. His mind was still fogged. Their religion made no sense to him. The many gods did not speak. The Rent had sucked the Narwe Harmony dry, and yet they clung doggedly to their hope. That's all this religion thing seemed to be: blind hope.

There was a whistle behind them, and a soldier waved a spear.

'It is time.'

Task bowed and followed Belerod down the slope. The puke-yellow Chanark tents had been raised opposite the Hasp camp. Their owners milled in the sand, drawing figures and lines. Almost like a map. His curiosity grew.

'Tell them we're ready!' Belerod said to his men. Almost fifty of them had taken the trip to the Spinning Sea, not including soldiers. The Chanark had brought double that.

The Chanark had brought a golem too. A lesser thing, made of driftwood. It barely reached his shoulder as he came to a halt beside it, on the Hasp side of the line. Task looked down at its sun-bleached skin, its wonky jaw, and the listless glint in its stump-like skull. He narrowed his eyes. Wood golems can rot, and are therefore prone to madness. The old-magic always takes on the quality of the material it is given to bind.

'I bet you don't even speak.'

A creak of wood was his answer. Task looked away, lip curled and smug.

'Let us begin!' Belerod swept forward to the line drawn in the sand. He touched his forehead. 'Friends, trusted till otherwise, proud hunters. Thank you for your audience.'

A tall, skinny man stepped forwards; skin tanned a nut-brown, silk coat dragging behind him in the sand. His head was shaved and marked with streaks of paint. He didn't salute.

'Builders, Windtrickers, and, lately, thieves. We look for truth.'

'As do we,' said Belerod.

As the voices droned on, Task felt something lick his feet. Cold water, rushing around his ankles, frothing as it bubbled over the sand.

He looked to the golem by his side. The creature was enraptured by the talking, oblivious to the rising water.

Over his shoulder, the water was streaming down the hill towards them. Task tried to move, but the sand held him fast. He tried to speak, but water gargled in his throat.

The water washed across the meeting place, and still nobody else seemed to notice. It rose to their knees, sucking at them, and not a mention was made.

The waters began to turn, washing the tents from their spikes, drowning all as it filled the hollow. Where Belerod stood, a great eye opened at its centre, drilling down into the netherworld. His master was swallowed by the seawater before Task could even extend a hand.

The roar was deafening. The golem reached up to the light as the water engulfed him. He felt his stones being pulled apart, tugged away by the vicious currents. Then, darkness.

45TH FADING, 3782 - PURLEGAR

'Bloody spit on it! The beast dreams!'

Task heard the cackle through the fading remnants of his dream. As the spinning waters fell away, and reality began to bleed through the fantasy, he could have sworn he felt the patter of rain across his left arm and on his chest.

'Reckon it dreams of the Baroness, like we do?'

The laughter wrenched him from the final ties of sleep, and he jolted awake. There was a whoop and a round of cheers as he clanged his head on the roof of the trap, making the iron squeal in protest.

Task's head snapped to the side, catching sight of Taspin standing with his breeches around his arse-cheeks, genitals in the open air, pissing onto Task's arm. His riders were gathered in a half-circle; bottles in hand, grins plastered across their doltish faces.

The golem moved as though he were wading through battle, throwing out his other arm, quicker than a musketball. The spikes between the bars bent under his fist, and he let a single finger flick outwards.

He caught Taspin mid-stream, just as the man was hopping backwards, hands already scrabbling for his buttons.

There was a sound like a steak being hurled against a wall, and then a moment of deathly silence as Taspin hobbled backwards. He began to fold in two. His face was aghast, threatening to snap if his mouth opened any wider.

Task was enjoying every second of it.

The howling started; the kind only a man and his crushed manhood can make. It was a breathless, guttural screech, as if Taspin's lungs had shrivelled up and he was forced to scream with only the spit in his throat.

He collapsed to the ground. Half the riders scarpered, while the other half swarmed around him, trying to coax their leader up to his knees.

Task chuckled. 'There was a saying, in the camps of Yalazar. "You can only piss on a golem once." They learnt that very quickly. I expect you will, too. Now, go. Run away.'

Taspin waved his men aside. He brandished a trembling finger at Task as he summoned the air for words. His face was a mask of spit and snot.

'You'll pay for this, golem! I'll have Huff break that hand of yours!'

Task snorted. 'I'd like to see him try.'

Taspin made it to his knees. Task wasn't sure in the torchlight, but it looked as if he had turned a greenish-white. A grin was forming on his face.

'If I can't hurt you, then I'll just have to hurt something you're fond of.' Taspin's eyes edged along the path, down to Lesky's stable.

'Maybe I should pay her a visit tonight, while you're locked up in there?'

Task leant close to the bars. 'And I will break more than your balls, rider. I will start with your legs and work my way up to your neck.'

Taspin was helped to his feet. The glint in Task's eye made him pause for a moment. One of his men nudged him.

'He's locked up, Lancer. Isn't going nowhere.'

Task turned his eyes on the man, and he shrivelled up. Without breaking his gaze, Task reached up to the spikes his fist had burst through. One by one, using only the hook of his finger, he bent them back into place.

'I wouldn't be so sure,' he said, his voice cold as daggers.

That put the appropriate level of fear in the men. They began to peel away from the cage, back towards the road and the gates. It was a slow retreat, with Taspin hobbling all the way, taking tiny steps on turned-in feet.

The golem's face was grim. The Lancemaster's threat had not fallen on deaf ears.

'Hey!'

Task jumped at the sound of Lesky's voice. She had approached like a ghost once again, too quietly even for him to hear; a creature who could feel every slight vibration of the ground through his stone. The cage rattled with his surprise.

'Sorry,' she said, smiling. Task had always wondered why skinbags got so much pleasure at surprising others. For him, surprises usually came in the form of soldier-ranks looming out of mist, or assassin's knives flashing through curtains.

'What did they want?' She had brought no lantern; just a small basket which dangled in front of her knees.

'The usual,' said Task, looking down at his wet arm. 'To test me.'

Lesky moved around the cage to see, but her nose told her before her eyes did. 'Ew!' she said, waving a hand. 'That stinks of gutwine.'

'Gutwine?'

'Made from berries and left inside a fawl's stomach for months. It's foul.'

'While it's alive?'

Lesky chuckled. 'No, silly.'

Task smiled and watched her sit. With great care, she laid the basket on the grass and removed its cloth.'

'What's that?'

'Pinkies. Cakes made of pink sugar. Got a bit of torig in them, too.'

'Did you make them?'

Lesky snorted with laughter. 'People in this camp should be more careful where they leave their cakes to cool.'

'Thief!' said Task, not sure whether to chuckle or to chide her. He let the word hover between them.

Lesky shook her head. 'Hungry, is what it's called. Ganner's cut my rations for losing you.'

'Because of me?'

The girl talked around her mouthful, pink sugar dusting her lips and chin. 'Mm. He was getting ten extra tants a week for keeping you. He's been paid for now, but there's no more coming.'

Task bowed his head.

Lesky sighed. 'Stop worryin'. Ain't your fault. And that's what I told Ganner. Told him it was Huff and his ways, nothing more. But he wouldn't have any of it. You know why he's punishing you, right?'

Task had yet to tell Lesky of his "condition", as Ghoffi had called it. His battle-lust. He feared to scare her, so he avoided the subject.

'Because of the battle today. I went too far.'

'Yeah, I heard the gossip, but that ain't what put you in the cage.'

'I saluted you.'

Lesky nodded, stuffing another cake into her mouth. 'And quicker than you do for him, I'll bet.'

'He orders me to do it. As if getting me to cover my eyes for him is a sign he's conquered the beast, or something. What a proud man he must be, to be so worried by a little girl.' Task looked up at the gathering clouds as they rumbled once more. He could feel the energy in the air. 'Ellia said I'm to ignore his orders and do what I think is right. Do what I can to end this war, save people like you and the Dregs, and put people like Taspin out of a job. I'm starting to run out of reasons why it's not a good idea.'

'Who's Ellia?'

'Baroness Frayne. She spoke to me after the battle.'

Lesky pouted. 'I don't trust people, and I trust her the least. She wears furs like she's from the Mission. But she isn't, so it's weird. I can normally tell what somebody's like before they open their mouth. Mam says it's my special gift. But her? Can't read a thing. She's like a blank wall.'

'She says she works for the king.'

The girl shook her head. 'Mam says her sort of person always works for themselves. That means greed. "Judge not by what the bowl still has to give you, but what you've already taken from it." It's just like with Ganner. The deffer's already fat as it is. Don't need my bowl of stew. That's why I took the cakes.'

Task challenged her. 'So thieving is fine if it's for a good reason?'

'Yeah. Maybe. Just don't tell me mam when you meet her. She'd understand, but I'd still get a whack round the ear. You too, probably, for tellin' her.'

The golem nodded, wondering what ears he had to whack.

'In short, don't tell her.'

Task smiled. 'I won't, don't worry.'

They sat in silence for a while, listening to Lesky's contented chewing. When she was halfway through the basket, she rolled back on the grass and patted her stomach.

As he looked down at her, Task thought of Taspin's threat and of Huff's narrowed eyes. Yet there she lay, full of cake and not a bother in the world. Task wished he felt the same. He knew too much of threats, and how the majority are not made empty, like promises. Friendship was a dangerous thing for a golem.

It was then that the clouds burst. The rain started in patters and drips. Lesky bid him goodnight and scurried for shelter.

Task settled back in his cage as the downpour gathered momentum. The water trickled through his stones, and he closed his eyes, trying to savour the feeling as it washed away the dust, the blood, the lancer's piss, and the worry.

10

' "Dragon-slayer" (occupation)
One who hunts dragons in their forms, large and small, for the
purposes of meat, glory or pest control. One notable example is the
victory of Alabast Flint, Knight of Dawn, a swordsman of little
repute. He managed to overcome a notorious Destrix Sheen (see
"Dragons") plaguing the Kopen area. Readers should note:
becoming a dragon-slayer is not recommended, as it has been
widely agreed the Sheen was the last creature of its kind.'
FROM GOBBY'S COMPENDIOMICON OF THINGS

46TH FADING, 3782 - SAFFERON FORTRESS

Alabast knew all about tactics. He had read all the books; well, thumbed through all the books. He knew the importance of height, and how a dirty great distance between a person and the ground can do wonders for survival. He also knew—and this was something the books hadn't told him—that if one chooses to be based up high, choose a place with windows and a bloody roof.

He had considered dispensing this wisdom to Lord Lash on his previous visits. Every time he had opened his mouth to comment, Lash had filled the moment with glaring, or impertinent raving about some troop movement or other. Alabast had decided to hold his tongue and shiver in the breeze.

What made matters worse was that Lash was not a drinking man. There was no room for decanters and crystal upon his bookshelves, just musketball casts and rolls of records. There was no available tipple in the corner of his desk to coax some warmth into his bones; only maps and ink blotches. Alabast had wondered about the drawer, but it would probably be full of Truehard scalps.

He had come to the conclusion that Lord Lash was either a brilliant and committed soldier, or an old man desperately trying to look like one.

Lash had yet to acknowledge him. The Fading commander always liked to overlap. He would have his subjects arrive early so they could witness the fate of those in the previous slot. It was a trick Alabast had seen lords and ladies play many times.

The knight crossed and recrossed his legs, making his leather breeches squeak. He longed for Borian silks and Braaden furcloth, instead of this forsaken Hartlund-wear.

'And tell those halfwits that I wanted the east side shored up yesterday, not tomorrow.'

'Yes, Lord,' said the messenger, scurrying from the room with a handful of papers and a headful of notes. Alabast waited for the door to slam before slapping a hand on his knee.

'A fine morning to you—'

'Let's dispense with the pleasantries, Alabast. I think we're past them.' The man wheeled himself across the tower to settle by the big hole in the wall; Alabast refused to call it a window. Lord Lash surveyed the camp below, sprawled over the old ruins of the fortress.

'I don't see you in the training yards very often. In fact, come to think of it, I've never seen you set foot in them.'

Alabast had propped his head against his hand. 'That's most likely because I don't train with others. I train on my own schedule.'

Since his arrival, Alabast had floated about the camp, stuck somewhere between bored and tipsy. He had made a few friends of gamblers, drinkers and brawlers; the sort of people he liked to swindle. But no real connections. His only recreation had been napping, or loitering by the washer-huts, flirting with the gossips.

'What schedule is that exactly?'

'One that I have refined over years, Lord Lash. I'm an early riser. I do most of my training and exercise in the morning, before the camp stirs. That way I have peace. Then it's breakfast, getting to know the soldiers, the war, the camp, and so on. From there it's waiting until I'm needed by the Last Table, maybe even helping the workers with their embroidery. It is a skill a maid in Ralanaz taught me.' He sighed. 'Devilishly helpful, she was.'

The lord looked at him as if he was having trouble deciding the best way to remove faeces from his favourite rug. His slitted eyes and arched shoulders suggested a punch in the face might be coming, but his knuckles and bunched muscles made Alabast's gaze crawl to the pistol at the man's side.

'Early riser, you say?'

'Yes indeed, your Lordship.'

'Strange. Most of my men say they don't see you till the sun is at its peak, and that they can't get rid of you until the Mothers have gone to bed. I fail to see where that leaves room for training of any kind. Unless you classify "helping with embroidery" as training.'

Alabast smiled. 'Depends on how difficult it is, my Lord.'

Lash's fist came crashing down onto the desk, nearly popping out the nails. The pistol was wrenched free and tossed onto the wood with a clunk. Lash's muscular hand hovered beside it as his eyes bored into Alabast's.

'I know your kind very well. I came up with quite a few like you, in fact. When the war broke out, we had floods of them. Every one used to strut about like they were trying to attract a mate. Puffed up, chest out, shinier than a new shield. This wasn't a camp for them, it was a social club. Somewhere to drink and whore until there was a battle to be fought. Then they'd polish their armour, strut some more, and wade into the fight on a hunt for eternal glory.' His eyes had yet to blink. 'Do you know what happened to them?'

'No.'

'They died. Every last hero that has marched through my gates in the last nine years has ended up face-down in the mud. The true heroes are the ones I see down there every day, training until they sweat blood. The sort of heroes that fight tooth and nail with the best of them. Getting the job done. Not flouncing around looking for pats on the back and a free bottle of glugg at every tent. Am I making myself clear, Alabast?'

'If I see any of those sorts around, Lord Lash, I'll be sure to point them your way for a chat similar to this.'

Lash curled his lip. 'The Table paid a lot of tants for you, Alabast. As such, they want results. Who gets them results? I do. What does that mean? It means that the moment you agreed to this job, you belonged to me.'

Alabast's bravado wavered for a moment. 'Is that so?'

The lord let a grin spread across his face. He spoke slowly, and with a mock glee that only served to highlight the danger behind his words. 'It is most definitely so. You can ask your minder, Westin. Now listen close, Alabast, because this is the important part. Belonging to me makes you a soldier in my army, and being a soldier in my army means I have certain expectations of you. They are simple. You will rise at dawn. You will not be drunk and disorderly. You will do the tasks assigned to you. You will not gamble, you will certainly not interfere with the workers. And you will train until your blisters have blisters. I expect this of all my men, whether they're a peasant or a Graden prince.' Lash wheeled himself forwards. 'I don't care if you killed the Last Dragon with your bare hands and dragged it back to Kopen on a rope. You are no hero to me. You're just a washed-up knight with gutwine instead of blood, and a spine that's seen too many silk sheets. You've forgotten how to be a soldier, and I intend to damn well remind you.'

Alabast rose to standing, reaching just short of the lord's eyeline. His throat was clenched, and his temper rising, but he managed to keep himself composed. 'Like you say, you know my kind.' With that he stepped to the side and looked towards the door. 'Will there be anything else, Lord Lash?'

The old deffer had the audacity to look victorious. 'In fact, yes. We've just had a delivery from the Montish. I've had it sent to your room. Perhaps you should take a look, get reacquainted. I think the other soldiers may benefit from seeing some dragon-slaying moves. The Truehards are moving north across the mountains. There'll be battle for my soldiers soon and I want them ready.'

Alabast managed a weak smile. 'As you wish.' He bowed and made for the door.

He wanted to slam it. He wanted to rip it off its hinges and send it crashing to the floor. Instead, he closed it in a calm and controlled fashion, and then bared his teeth and spat curses, waving his arms wildly and imagining Lash's face within their arcs.

'Good meeting, Alabast?' Westin. Standing a few paces behind him.

'The very best, Carafor!' Alabast brushed past him.

Westin called after him. 'I always find that if you don't agree with Lash now, then you do later. Usually when you manage to calm down!'

Alabast yelled around the corner. 'Fine advice as always!'

The mouldy walls were a blur to his narrowed eyes. Every step was another mutter, another curse. In his head, he went about the bitter dissection of Lash's insults, over and over, hunting for ways to prove the man wasn't…

Alabast ground to a halt. 'Right,' he said aloud, through gritted teeth.

Usually he could not have cared dust for Lash's opinions. The lord was far from rich or famous, and therefore he should have been inconsequential. But his words had run Alabast through, quicker and deeper than any dagger.

Truth is a mirror, and Alabast had just been shown a reflection he had refused to look at for years. He was happier with the memories of the man he had created from nothing, and elevated to rub shoulders with the elite of the Realm.

His righteous march became a trudge as he was forced to account for the difference between that man and this half-hungover paragon of poor choices. The last event he had attended was the Twin Duchesses' Reaping Eve dinner. *Little over a year ago.* It hadn't exactly been his finest moment. Urinating in a count's soup after an argument over dragons and wyverns was the highlight of the evening, closely followed by his forcible defenestration at the hands of the duchesses' elder brother.

If he were brutally honest, he knew he was clinging to a fantasy. His high standing had sputtered out and died a long time ago. He'd once bowed to princes, not mobsters; courted nobles' wives instead of saucy dowagers. He used to entertain princes, not drunken old soldiers and cathouse whores. The only thing he had left was his legend, thank the Architect, but even that was crumbling.

Alabast sighed. All in all, it had been a shite year for the mighty Knight of Dawn, and his prospects were hardly gleaming. For here he was, a soldier once again, under the thumb of a vengeful storm of a man, and tasked to fight an unbeatable creature.

'Deff it, if I don't need some wine!'

His room was cold. Somebody had left the window open, and the curtains were casting shapes in the air. He shut them with a bang, growling to himself about privacy, and rifled through last night's clothes.

His hands pounced as a finger brushed it. He brought it into the weak sunlight and grinned as he made the liquid slosh. It was a small pocketsip, the good metal kind with the screwing lid. He had lifted it from a drowsy shield-man the night before, when all eyes had been on a big hand of judge. His cards had been worthless last night, but he had won this at least.

In three gulps the fiery torig was drained, and he threw the pocketsip down with a snarl. His eyes toured the room, looking for something else to occupy him. He spied his bag and sprang into action.

If there was one thing Alabast was good at, it was knowing when to part ways on a deal. He could always sense when things were souring, and judging by Lash's opinion of him, and his opponent, this job was already on the verge of rotting. He would bow and scrape to keep Lash occupied until nightfall, and when the watch changed, he would slip south to Caverill. He could hole up there for a while, try to get a whiff of some of the old work, then take a ship south. There were always people locked away in tall towers who needed saving. And if not, he could kidnap a few; get the cannonball rolling. Get the rumours flowing again.

Into the bag went all his clothes that didn't scream Last Fading. South and the city was Truehard territory, from what he knew. He didn't want to go inciting any riots. The pocketsip followed, along with some spare boots and a few of the books. Some people will pay a pretty price for literature. Alabast called those people idiots.

The knight looked around the room for anything else he could hawk. His eyes fell upon the dark-wood trunk sitting by the door, waiting like an assassin fallen asleep.

The delivery. The training. Alabast slapped himself in the face.

He saw to the huge latches, flicking them aside. The metal-lined lid was heavy, just like everything the Montish built, as if weight was somehow equivalent to worth. He thrust it open, taking a chunk out of the stone wall.

Inside there was a black cloth covering something uneven, and atop the cloth lay a sword. Alabast stared at it, not daring to touch it until he was sure.

The pommel-stone, the crallig-skin handle, even the silver stitching on the scabbard.

It was all as he remembered, better even. The rust had gone, for starters. Alabast yanked the sword free to smell the polishing oil.

Forged from folded Graden star-steel, with ribbons of silver running up the blade, the weapon had never notched in all the time he'd owned it, nearly six years before losing it in a game of judge to Prince Yovin. It had been a gift from Kopen for his glorious deed. He tutted to himself.

Yovin had brayed for months about how he had cheated the Knight of Dawn of his famous sword. Cheating was the only word for it. Yovin had known every card, every shuffle. A quickminder, a skullsearcher, if ever he'd seen one.

The knight let the sword drop back to the trunk with a clang. Losing his sword had been both the precipice and the push; the start of his slippery fall to the muck and mire of the forgotten. As such, it felt tainted, even if it was the finest sword he had ever laid eyes on.

Lash's orders were clear and cold as ice. He wanted to see what the knight was made of; whether their coins had been spent wisely. Therein lay the problem: Alabast hadn't fought anything but a hangover for almost three months. His once-famous sword arm was now used mainly for wine-pouring, and he doubted he could cut anything but a fart in the training yard. Lash either wanted to embarrass him or jolt him into life; more likely the former.

And yet, his eyes still edged to the blade, as if tugged by strings. Perhaps it was his need for practise, his fierce pride, or some last vestige of honour that pulled him to it, step by ponderous step. Or maybe it was simply the desire to put a deeper scowl on Lash's withered face. Alabast nodded. Few things are sweeter than proving somebody wrong.

The blade sang as he tugged it free of the sheath. He gave it an experimental whirl. It was heavier than he remembered, and on the second swing his finger slipped from the hilt. He froze as it slammed into the brick a hair from his boot, sending a spark flying.

One more day. He could survive that.

By the time he reached the training ground, the torig had sunk its hooks into his limbs. Fortunately, Westin had found him in the hallways and escorted him. Alabast had been glad for a back to follow, and offered only affirmative grunts in response to the executor's chatter.

All he could think of was the sword on his belt. It felt strange, foreign, as if he had slipped back five years in the shutting of a bedroom door, and it had all been a horrible, wine-fuelled dream. The weight of an old life hung at his belt.

As they emerged from a thick door, Alabast curved away from Westin to patrol the edge of the expansive training yard. The familiarity coaxed out some of his usual swagger; he had been raised in training yards like these. In warmer country, yes, but just as every tavern is the same from one corner of the Realm to another, so is every training yard. The faces change, but not the rules.

Alabast settled against a wall and watched the small group of soldiers jabbing at each other with long sticks and blunt swords. He had spent enough time with both in his hand to pick out the characters worth watching. He examined every parry and turn, every jab and strike. The clatter was almost soothing.

It didn't take long for the whispers to spread through the other watchers. Alabast could hear them hissing over the noise.

'Knight of Dawn! The Knight of Dawn is here!'

Soon enough, everybody was offering him polite nods and smiles. A few of the fools even saluted him, before their officers yelled them into silence. Alabast shrugged. He wasn't going to tell them to stop; an ego of his size enjoys the occasional salute.

But as the whispers built to voices, and fingers began to point, he found himself wishing for silence; even ignorance. He knew the bigger they built him, the more he could disappoint them. He longed to be just another Fading soldier, reporting for training.

A small group had gathered now. Fists waved back and forth, clutching tants. The clamour brought the training to a halt, and all eyes turned to Alabast.

'Knight Alabast!' came a shout from on high. It was Lash, leaning out of the window of his decrepit tower. His challenge came crashing down. 'Perhaps you'd like to run a few of these men through their paces? Show us the skills that brought down a dragon! Mr Westin, if you please.'

An excited murmur spread across the yard. Feet stamped. Alabast winced.

'Any takers?' yelled Westin. 'Make yourselves known!' A scattering of hands shot up. Alabast assessed their owners, and for a moment he was grateful. Just brawny lads puffing out their chests; he could best them in an instant.

Unimpressed with the number of volunteers, the trainers began to sift through the ranks, tugging at shirts and whacking elbows.

'You, and you!'

'Come forward. Flenda, you too!'

'All of you, form a line! One at a time!' said Westin.

The voice from on high spoke again. 'Unless you would prefer several combatants at once, Knight?'

Alabast pushed himself from the wall, throwing up a sour smile at Lash. He could barely see him with the sun behind the tower's roof, but he guessed the lord would be wearing a similar expression.

'We'll work up to that, if you please, Lord Lash. Some of us were up late winning hand after hand of judge last night. I believe we'll start with a group exercise.'

There came a round of sniggering from the soldiers. The trainers set about them with canes, catching ears and drawing yells.

As Alabast strolled into the centre of the yard, he swung the sword in an arc once more, testing its weight, making sure to keep all fingers firmly secured. The metal whined against the air.

He could feel the weight of many eyes upon the sword. Alabast couldn't blame them. Firstly, his blade was not blunted, which was cause enough for chatter. Second, its sheen and silver etching were a realm away from their plain steel weapons, stacked in a line against the far wall. Most of them didn't even sport a scabbard.

Alabast executed an old flourish and slammed the blade into the earth. He strode away, leaving it to wobble. An applause of stamping feet rose and fell.

Behind his cheery mask, Alabast was beginning to sweat. The torig was doing nothing for his nerves, and now he just wanted to throw up. As he made a show of stretching, he sifted through the blurry memories of his training days, trying to drag out some old routine or sword-dance that could buy him time.

One came to him, as he was handed a blunt sword. It was nothing more than a dirty trick; the kind a Kopen student learnt in tavern gardens rather than in the training yard. Alabast cleared his throat.

'As a knight I'm taught to uphold chivalry, honour, and above all, decency. But a good knight also knows when to put all that nonsense aside. Some people just don't like to fight fair. Especially in war.' He gave Lash another look before beckoning the first soldier forwards.

He was a fire-haired boy, scrawny but tall. The kind with a big reach. Alabast motioned for him to stand a few paces away. 'Come in for a low swing.'

The soldier did as he was told, bringing up his blunt blade in a wide, slow arc, aiming for just under the ribs. Alabast didn't bother to match his speed. He kicked dust at the boy, then charged, leading with his shoulder and elbow.

With a thud, Alabast sent the soldier flying, twisting his blade from his hand. The boy met the dust with a wheeze.

The yard erupted in laughter. Alabast grinned as he helped the boy to his feet. He felt the tug at his shoulder tendons as he held the soldier's weight, and hissed under his breath.

He addressed the group. 'You see how it works? You don't always have to fight with your blade.'

'Aye!' came the shout.

Alabast spotted an opportunity to take a rest. 'Pair off and try it out. Kick, barge, grab and twist!' He sought a nearby bench. Already his heart was pounding.

The chosen soldiers went to it with a will, like children with a new toy. Soon, bodies were toppling left and right. If Lash's eyes weren't still beating down on him, Alabast might have laughed.

The soldiers soon grew bored of the repetition, and the exercise only lasted a few minutes. One by one, they dusted themselves off and lined up for another lesson. Alabast scowled. He had been too busy watching their capers to think up something else.

Lash called down from the tower.

'I think what would be beneficial, instead of learning cheap tricks, would be to get some experience in one-on-one combat. Fancy taking on any of my soldiers in a fair fight, Alabast?'

Alabast gave another hollow smile, feeling the sweat dripping down the small of his back. 'Why not?' he said, throwing up his arms. There was at least the small mercy of being able to select his opponent.

His eyes roamed the line for the over-confident ones, or the ones with wider eyes of worry. So many young faces; some little more than boys. *That was good for him.*

'How about you?' He pointed at a young man with a mess of wispy hair around his cheeks and chin.

'Alright,' he said, in a cracking voice.

On the sidelines, hands began to move, swapping coins and slips of paper. Shouts of support for the man echoed across the yard.

'Go on, Gutcliff!'

'Keep your head up, lad!'

Alabast watched the boy prepare himself; settling into his legs, making sure his arms were curved and his sword at the perfect angle. He hadn't spent more than a few weeks with a blade, by the look of him. It hadn't yet grown into his arms.

Alabast mirrored him, feeling old muscles wake up as he tested his stance.

Architect, it felt like an epoch ago.

They circled each other, tapping their blades every now and then to taunt the other into striking first.

It was the boy who took the bait: a wild jumping stab to the chest, reaching in over Alabast's cover.

Reflexes alone saved him, sluggish as they were after three gulps of mulled torig. He slammed the blade aside with the flat of his own, turning it to tangle with Gutcliff's legs as he overreached. The soldier's face met the ground with a crunch.

There was a smear of blood beneath his nose when they hauled him up. S*erves him right for trying such a bold move*, Alabast told himself, as he paced back and forth, trying to wake up his legs and work out the sweat. Bold or not, the Knight of Dawn had almost been caught off-guard by a fluff-faced boy. That was unacceptable.

Alabast chose his next opponent quickly, eager to see this over and done with.

'You next!' He selected a short woman with close-cropped black hair and darting, nervous-looking eyes.

She stepped forward more eagerly than he would have liked. The knight chose a high stance this time, hoping to intimidate her with his size. The woman held her sword across her face, a classic defence.

'Keep your feet quick, Flenda!' came a shout from the others. Alabast flashed a mean look in its direction.

He chopped down, feigning a vicious strike. He had hoped her sword would flinch up to block it, but she side-stepped and countered with a swing at his ribs. Alabast stopped it with a quick block; but only just. He had to dance away to avoid losing his balance.

A low moan rose and fell among the onlookers. Somebody even chuckled to themselves. The flow of coins changed direction.

Alabast could feel the sweat pouring. It was as if he were teetering on the edge of a crumbling wall.

This Flenda was clearly trying to make a name for herself. She was creeping forward again, blade out straight and waggling like a wark's tail. Alabast matched her stance and batted her sword away. Again and again, she pressed him. Again and again, he knocked away her blade. His muscles reverberated with every clang.

The knight forced some strength in his next swing, aiming to batter the sword out of her hands. Annoyingly, she chose the same moment to press him. Flenda dropped her sword as he went for glory.

Alabast would have spun in a full circle had it not been for the shoulder that introduced itself to his ribs. He was off-balance, overstretched, and now falling to the earth. There was nothing Alabast could do to stop it. He watched the ground rise up, like a widening grin.

By the time he had pushed himself up from the dirt and coaxed some air back into his lungs, he found the cocky young girl had already withdrawn into the pack. Hands clapped her heartily on the shoulders, but not a word was said. A shocked silence had settled over the yard.

Alabast stood alone in its centre; a harlequin of dust and sweat. His sword tip hovered over the ground, searching back and forth. He felt the itchy heat of shame spread over his face.

'Again!' he yelled. 'You next!' His sword found a big man with a bigger smile. The man shrugged and sauntered out to meet the knight. The yard was alive with chatter now. The Knight of Dawn had been beaten. By a young soldier, no less. He could almost hear the last gasps of his legend as it crumbled away.

Spit on them all!

There was a clang as the two blades met in salute. Alabast charged immediately, bringing his sword down on the left, then the right, then up under the man's armpit. The soldier fended him off, back-stepping until he was pushed forward by the crowd.

Alabast took one too many steps and the man drove his pommel into the knight's stomach. The next two jabs hit their marks with ease, one in each shoulder. The man raised his sword and cheered, wading through the crowd as it surged forward, each soldier now eager for their taste of glory.

Alabast watched him with strained eyes and a rumbling gut. Bile sloshed behind his tongue. A vomit would have been the delightful sprinkle of gold on this turd of a morning.

He felt like the bruised and battered boy of old, kneeling in the heat-haze with a master yelling in his tear-stained face. There had been only one thing to do then, and there was only one thing to do now. Alabast grit his teeth and slapped the flat of sword on his leg over and over until silence came to the yard.

'Again!'

'Knight Alabast, perhaps my soldiers have seen enou—'

'Next!' Alabast cut Lash off. His nostrils flared like a fawl's. 'Two of you this time. Let's make it quick. I'm sure you all want your chance to tell the story of how you beat the last Dragon-slayer.'

Silence fell, and Alabast listened as his heart hammered out its laboured rhythm. He let it fill every inch of his body until he felt no sweat, no pain, no shiver of torig. Just his heartbeat. Old memories awakened between its pulses, filling his mind with a thousand different days.

'Come on! I said two! Keep them coming!'

A pair of soldiers were pushed forward. They patrolled around him, taking their time, winking at each other. Alabast didn't move. He stayed deep in his internal rhythm.

'Come on. Don't be scared. The others have done it!'

That goaded them. The two pounced together, bringing their swords down in great arcs, cries tearing from their throats.

Alabast's body wailed as he drove life into his forgotten muscles. A sword-dance found its way into his limbs and he let it lead.

Clang! One sword was batted away, torn from the soldier's grasp.

Clang! The other came to a shuddering halt, shaking the breath from its owner.

Alabast moved like a seed on the breeze, whirling to the side to swipe the first man's legs from under him, then driving his blade up under the chin of the other. Both were flat on their backs in seconds.

No cheering now. No stamping of feet or clapping of backs. Just the next two soldiers, pushed forwards against their will.

Alabast strode forward, sparing no time for guards or salutes. The concussions of their blades filled the yard. One, two, three, and then two sharp yelps. The soldiers clutched their backs as they hobbled back into the group, leaving their swords behind.

'Four!' he said, monotone and vacant.

Four men came forward, more confident in numbers. They spread around him, and challenged one at a time. Alabast dealt with each severely, cracking his blade off wrists or jabbing ribs, until they all charged at once.

His sword was a grey streak in his hands; unseen until it caught an arm, or a throat, or burst with sparks against another blade.

When the soldiers were all staring at the sky, rubbing their heads or blinking away stars, Alabast looked up at Lash's tower. The lord had disappeared.

He let the blunt sword fall from his grasp with a clatter and sauntered to collect his own, still wedged between the flagstones.

He spared a moment to meet the gathered eyes, all fixed on him. Some were narrow, nurturing suspicion, while others were wide and wriggling. Alabast didn't know whether they were shocked or impressed. For once, he didn't care, and for a man of infinite pride that was new, strange, and satisfying.

'Lesson's over!' he said, just loud enough for the yard and its overseer to hear.

He marched to the door and reached for the handle.

One more day.

11

*'My blending of glimpses and gazers, Holy Treyarch, has proven,
to be plain, disastrous. These "grims" of his are no better than wild
beasts. With barely any training, they can tear into minds or drive
a man to kill himself through madness. It is intolerable, Treyarch.
Architect spit on it.'*

NOTE LEFT BY MASTER FLATCH BEFORE AN UNFORTUNATE ACCIDENT

47TH FADING, 3782 - THE SIX SISTERS

His stone feet carved deep holes in the gathered snow. Ice flakes battered him like musketballs. All around, the murky sky crowded in, choking the air.

The soldiers had said it best: the Six Sisters were jealous bitches.

Task had never known a wind with sharper teeth. It howled through his stones, bending and pushing, testing all his edges to see which would give first. It was a murderous wind, resentful and bitter. Task could sense its intent as he raised a hand, daring it to try harder. It seemed to acknowledge him, pressing in from all sides, cutting with its cold claws.

The snap of the rope around his waist tore him from his private battle, and he grunted in acquiescence. Digging his powerful legs into the ground, he began to wade through the icy onslaught, tugging the wagons through the mush. He could feel the tremor from the soldiers' hands in the ropes. Was it the cold or fear? He didn't blame them, either way.

Fourteen had already taken the tumble that day. If the cold couldn't kill them, the wind plucked them from the mountainside and threw them to the scree and shale far below. Nobody walked away from a fall like that.

His glorious master hadn't spared a soul for a search party, not for any of them. One had been a sergeant, and a well-respected one at that, or so said the whispering through the howling gale.

130

There was a jerk in the rope and Task felt one of the wagons slip. The rope creaked around his waist. He heard the yelp of a fawl caught on the gale.

Task leaned against the weight, digging a foot into the snow. He felt the wet dirt and rock beneath. Task gave the soldiers time, to calm their nerves while they saw to the beasts, or the wheels, or the traces; whatever the wind and cold had been gnawing on.

Something thwacked the line, and he took another step, digging a trench in the snowdrifts as he powered forward. He felt the rattle of wheels and nodded.

There was something enjoyable and defiant about climbing a mountain. Every step upwards was a punch thrown in a fight, a jab parried in a duel. It was a test of the oldest, purest kind, where the closer one comes to death, the stronger the sense of being alive. Like the rain he let gnaw at his stones, it was the challenge of it all that made Task grin; the whiff of mortality that bewitched him.

The mountain and its weather was powerless against him. When he felt rocks in his path, he shoved them aside, clearing a path for the wagons. When the winds threw themselves against his chest— concentrated and rash, as if it were personal—Task made a blade of his hands, and shouldered them aside. He could have laughed; even at their fiercest, the Sisters were still no match for a Wind-Cut Golem.

Task couldn't say the same for the army below. The storm battered them. He could almost feel the soldiers' sour moods, floating up on the wind. Huff had refused to watch the weather, and the bravado of a few successful battles had muddied his mind.

The golem's thoughts turned to the girl. He wondered whether she had found any blankets for the journey; whether she was a warm ball of furs or a shivering wreck of blue skin. Oh, how these pink things could change colour! Green and yellow when sickly, red when angry or hot, pale and blue when cold. He had only one colour, despite the curtains of snow and ice-rain pelting him with every step. Grey was his only hue.

Something creaked around his waist. He paused, staring down at his ribs where the rope had been knotted. He heard a snap within the coil, and before he could snatch at it, the line began to unravel. Yells rose up from below.

Task turned and slammed his heel into the ground, settling down on his haunches. Whirling an arm in great arcs, he trapped the rope and wrapped it tightly around him. With the other arm, he caught the last lengths of rope as they flew from his waist. The golem clamped down hard and dragged his hands into his chest.

The rope steamed in his grip, but it remained still. He leaned into the weight and began to haul, working slowly, moving hand over hand with method and care. His stone muscles bunched and shivered, but he never faltered. He could have been hauling a sack of grain for all the effort he displayed.

A score more steps and he felt the ground level. Task quickened his pace, turning so he could march with the rope over his shoulder. The gale drove at him again, but it lacked its usual venom, as though the Sisters had grown complacent now they had been beaten.

The snow on the pass had gathered in great clumps and drifts. He drove a path through it and found a spur of rock to tie the rope around. Then he pulled, dragging the great wagon chain forward with ease.

The soldiers emerged from the white haze like ghosts, all hollow-eyed and wan. Task nodded to each of them, but they gazed through him; staring instead at the arch of rock that marked the centre of the mountain pass between Nelid and Lamanae, two of the shorter Sisters.

He shook his head at the shivering bodies as they clumped together to share their warmth. Task found himself wishing he had the power of an elemental, to glow brightly like a bonfire, and give these poor souls some flames to warm their hands.

He frowned. Since Purlegar, this war had been gifted a face, and it was the weathered, tired, and yet determined features of a Truehard soldier. Not a captain, not a general, and not a Lancemaster, but the man or woman who fought for their scrap of farmland, and nothing more. He saw the Dregs staring back at him through every curious glance.

The feeling was rare, and too unusual to be ignored. Hundreds of wars had washed over him, and never before had he found a *reason* to fight in them. Now, the inkling of a cause had burrowed into his head, planted by Ellia's words.

Do what you know is right.

He knew he could help these people; these strange creatures he had spent centuries loathing. It was why every step up the mountain had been taken not to please the almighty General Dartridge the Third, but to save the lowly soldiers' skins from the Sisters' fury.

'Right, you scrotums!' shouted Sergeant Collaver, rubbing his mail-clad hands together and wading onto the pass. 'I won't hear any grumbling out o' yer. You've done a fine job, but we got to press on. At least to the other side, when we can get some fresh limbs up here to relieve you. Understand?' He was rosy-cheeked, and his nose was so red it looked bloodied. Crooked veins struck out across his cheek like stranded seaweed.

The sergeant moved to the golem's side, and nudged him with an elbow. 'How are you farin', Task?'

'Cold.'

Collaver looked him up and down. 'You feel the cold?'

Task smiled. 'I feel everything.'

'Is that so?' The sergeant scratched his scarlet nose. 'Well, Architect spit on me. Stone that feels. Does it hurt? Bloody hurts my foot, I tell you that. I'll be surprised if I don't lose a toe.'

'Not as you would feel it.'

That was all Task gave him. It was true that he felt sensation: the touch of a fallen body, a tortured landscape, blades hacking chips from his legs. Sometimes those things were too raw to bear, and they stung him in a way that could be called "pain". But he had sensed the human version many times, and he knew it was not the same. He had little envy for it, but plenty of pity.

Collaver sniffed and spat in the snow. 'I'll take that as a good thing, I guess. You've done a fine job today, Task. Those wagons would've floundered without you. Too damn heavy, like I told 'em.'

'Told who?'

'Manx and the general. And did they listen? No.'

Task wanted to snort, but he held back. 'Is that a common occurrence?'

'Not being listened to?' Collaver laughed heartily. 'Daily, my stone friend. If not hourly.'

'Shite does roll downhill, so I hear,' said Task, echoing Cater's phrase.

The sergeant regarded him for a moment, then broke into a wheezing cackle.

'Then we'd better enjoy our time at the top of this deffing mountain, shouldn't we?' He slapped his thigh and swaggered away to look out over the churning masses below.

A squad of thirty or so soldiers had begun to form up. Task edged through their ranks. 'Away we go!' he grunted, and the soldiers began to trudge. His presence seemed to bolster them.

He led them under the long arch. Its stone was smooth, like his; wind-worn if not Wind-Cut. The ceiling was too high to reach, but that didn't stop Task from longing to know its life. Perhaps he would come back, when the war was done, and test the Sisters again.

Out from under the rock, and they came upon a gully of still air. The storm howled above them at the lip of the walls, and the rushing snow formed a roof. For a moment, they sucked in the cold mountain air and let their breath rise to mingle with the swirling canopy. Little pleasures, Task had found, were those humans enjoyed the most.

As the slope steepened, the rock fell away and left them bare to the elements once again. But while the wind still bit deep and the cold searched for every cranny, the northern slopes were more sheltered, and the storm was now an inconvenience rather than an enemy.

The going was still tougher than it should have been. Old landslides carved the path in jagged routes just wide enough for the wagons and beasts. Task tested every boulder and edge with his feet. If the path could hold his weight, it could hold an army.

Before long, the road found its way back to a steady track. The soldiers were strolling now; bodies relaxed without the worry of pitfalls and shale whisking them away to sharp and painful ends. Even the snow was thinning.

At the tips of the pine trees, they paused to look back up the slope. The head of the army was only half a league or so behind them; the rest were still trickling down the mountain. Through the haze of the storm above, the golem could see the dark smudges of wagons moving, and of bodies braving the chill.

'Well, would you look at that!' One of the soldiers pointed at a streak of blue in the clouds above. 'The bitches like us.'

'We passed their test,' said Task.

A few eyebrows hovered for a moment before a woman grunted.

'Aye, sounds about right. Just the Banished Gods, shaking in their mountain prisons.'

'Enough with that fawl-piss,' said the first man. 'Creeping Isle folklore, Jennia.'

'Always the same stories,' said another.

Jennia pinched her brow together. 'It's the right of my heritage, I've told you this.'

The first man sighed. 'Well, can't you heritage quietly or summat?'

Jennia spent a moment glaring about the group. Her lips were pursed, ready to spit out some vehement words. Task wondered whether he needed to step in, and put a stop to this little squabble.

The musketball did it for him, slamming into Jennia's temple and tearing out through her white lips. With the sound of ripped flesh and snapping bone, her corpse pitched forward into the frozen mud.

In that awful, speechless moment between confusion and surprise, more muskets crackled, hidden in the trees. One soldier was caught in the thigh, another in the gut. He fell onto his backside and spent his last moments staring at the new hole in his belly. The next volley saw a musketball cave in the skull between his eyes.

'Behind me!' said Task, spreading his arms and fingers, hunkering low. The soldiers rushed to obey, chased by the musket-fire, dragging their wounded. Another man was caught as he dove for the cover of the golem's leg. His neck burst open, revealing a ragged gash across his windpipe, spraying blood like fountain. Hands dragged him to shelter and clamped to his neck. Lips whispered encouragement. It was a useless sort of kindness, but one that all soldiers were due when the end is near.

The muskets turned their attention to Task, peppering his chest and face with lead as the volleys became a sputtering clatter. Sharp cracks filled the air as musketballs bounced like raindrops from his stone. He narrowed his eyes as one ricocheted from his brow, chipping him. He clamped his teeth with a crunch, keeping his tongue firmly behind their walls.

Horns had begun to blare on the mountainside behind them. The army had heard the guns. A quick look told Task that aid was surging forwards, but given the snow, it was still half an hour away at best.

His eyes roamed the trees, picking out muzzle flashes and flickering shadows between the bushes. Three-score, he guessed, with half of them high in the branches. He caught the stench of sweat and leaking latrines on the chill wind. They must have been waiting for days. He flared his nostrils. That would make them cold and tired, and above all, slow.

The golem edged forward. The soldiers stuck close behind; some even clung to his legs between steps. A few had dug out their pistols, but their firepowder was wet. Curses filled the spaces between musket-shots, and hands turned to knives and swords instead.

Task found them a boulder almost as big as he was, and walked them to it. They scrabbled for cover as musket-fire sprayed them with stone chips. Task was growing tired of the relentless impacts on his skin. He was beginning to feel the sharp edges of anger.

'Stay!' growled the golem.

He reached for a rock the size of his head and wrenched it from the ground. Drawing back his arm like a catapult, he hurled the rock into the treetops.

Cries rang out as it crashed through the foliage, making toothpicks out of branches. Task could have grinned when he heard an almighty thud.

Another stone was torn from the earth and sent flying. Task chased it into the woods, mud spraying from his heels. A snap and a cry came from above, and he looked up to see a Last Fading soldier dangling from a shattered branch. His tree, barely more than a sapling, swung like a flagpole in a gale.

Task hit the tree hard, shoulder-first, splintering its trunk. The soldier wailed all the way to the ground, where something crunched and silenced him.

'Mine now!' Task seized the trunk with both hands and hauled it over his knee. With his elbow, he snapped it to an oar's length and raised it like a sword.

Humans put far too much trust in their muskets. They wielded them like wizards' staffs, as if just pointing and praying could solve any problem.

Even an angry golem using half a tree as a club.

The Last Fading soldiers were no different, and Task found pleasure in re-educating them. Wherever they stood, frantically thumbing lead into barrels and filling the woods with clouds of smoke, he found them all.

Bodies flew like butchered meat. Armour snapped with branches and bones. Task tackled them one by one, like a desert twister sniffing out towns to ruin. If they ran, Task bounded through the icy loam to break their legs. If they climbed, he shook their trees and met their falling bodies with fists and fingers.

He was angry—vengeful, even—but his anger held no sway over him that day. This murder was methodical, delivered with the same lack of mercy offered by the Fading soldiers. They had played foul, and he would show them his version.

As it turned out, three-score was about right. Task hunted them down, almost to a man.

The soldiers scattered in all directions, knowing the golem couldn't chase them all. Task leapt after a few stragglers, but he let most of them leave. Lessons can't be passed on by dead men. The rest of the Fading needed to learn the consequences of playing dirty with golems.

He was turning back to the mountain when a flash of light and smoke caught his eye. Literally.

A musketball bounced from his eye-socket, causing him to stagger. When the sparks had left his vision, he saw the back of a man sprinting through the undergrowth, a pistol waving in his hand.

Task gave chase with a snarl, cutting an arrow-straight course through the trees and bushes, barging everything aside. Tree-trunks groaned at the touch of his stone. Shrubbery was crushed under his thrashing feet. Resin and leaves plastered him.

Pace by pace, he gained on the fleeing soldier. The man zig-zagged, desperately trying to shake off the charging golem. Each look he threw over his shoulder was more terrified than the last. As Task reached for him, he fired one last shot in panic, spitting lead into the dark canopy of the forest.

THE HEART OF STONE

A swat of the golem's hand sent the soldier hurtling into a pine. He slumped to the wet earth, tongue lolling, eyes rolling about their sockets. Task stood over him, marvelling at how quickly the bruises blossomed on the man's forehead. Sweat streamed down his face. Pine needles decorated his curled blond hair.

Usually, this was the moment that the begging began. Task may have been monstrous, but he was no monster. He usually gave in to pleading; even from soldiers who dealt in trickery and ambushes. It was a rule he had clung to over the years, like a hand clamped over a festering wound; a memory that refused to die.

But this man was in no mood to grovel. As his eyes focused on the hulking shadow above him, his terror turned to hatred and scorn. He wiped the snot from his nose and spat out a laugh.

'Your end is comin', stone demon!'

Task hadn't been called demon in centuries. But it wasn't the name that bothered him; he had been branded with every name in the Realm at one point or another. It was the man's crooked sneer and the venom in his voice.

He rested a foot on the man's breastplate, letting his weight descend ever so slowly. The armour began to buckle, and the soldier squirmed as he hammered his fist against Task's stone.

'How many more surprises can we expect?'

'I ain't tellin' you shite!'

Task pressed a little harder, bending the armour flat. The soldier gasped for breath, and yet he still spent it on curses.

'Deffing demon! You wait. You wait until the Knight of Dawn comes for you!'

Task brought his face low, watching the colour drain from the man's cheeks.

'Who?'

The soldier offered only cruel laughter. Task contemplated driving his foot down and showing him a swift end. For a moment, with stone teeth bared, he teetered between the choice of life and death. But no, it was not his nature. To crush the man, here and now, would have been too human; too close to the deeds he abhorred. Under the sweat and pine needles, Task saw just another soldier fighting for his scrap of field.

He removed his foot, allowing the man to scrabble for the buckles of his breastplate. The metal was still crushing him, and the golem stood aside while he gulped down mouthfuls of cold air., spitting and hawking in the pine needles. When some of his colour had returned, Task seized him by the neck and dragged him upright.

'You should just kill me. That's all they'll do with me, anyway. I ain't tellin' you nothin.' The words were followed by a gob of saliva, flecked with blood. It struck the golem in the chest.

Task shook his head, gripping him tighter. 'Not me, perhaps. But you will talk to the general.'

The soldier just sneered.

'That deffin' boy? He's no general to me.'

Task growled and carried the man off through the ruined woods, letting the empty eyes of the corpses remind him of the reasons to be silent.

When Task and his charge arrived at the edges of the pines, he found the Truehards in disarray. Those who had made it down the mountain slopes were trying to form lines across the narrow road. Orders ricocheted back and forth over their heads. Boots churned the ground to icy mud. Feet slipped and armour crashed against pebbles. Their faces were mottled red and white; marks of panic and cold.

Shouts greeted him, along with the clicking of muskets.

Collaver bellowed across the lines. 'It's the bloody golem, you festering bastards! Stow those weapons!'

The sergeant faced him. 'Who have you caught, Task?'

'A Fading soldier. No name given.'

'A prisoner?' said somebody in the front row.

'Yes, a prisoner.'

Collaver didn't look too happy. He rubbed his grimy chin and beckoned to one of his men. He whispered something in his ear and the soldier ran away, cutting through the ranks.

'Set him down, golem,' said the sergeant.

'On your knees!' said Task. The Fading soldier obeyed, but with a sour face. The front ranks began to hiss, quietly at first, then building like waves swelling. Others cursed to their neighbours. The rest spat over their shields, lips curled in disgust.

Task could feel the heat of their anger so acutely he had to take a step away from the man. He left him in a lonely vacuum; an object of hate. To the Truehards, he was the embodiment of today's bloody murder; the trigger-finger behind the fresh corpses still lying in the cold dirt.

The golem grew uncomfortable. An old and ugly memory reared its head, and he wondered whether he should have simply betrayed his training and let the man flee.

It wouldn't be the first time.

But it was too late now. He could see the commotion in the back ranks, higher up on the slope where the snows withered. General Dartridge had arrived.

The man looked like he had been swallowed by a huge black coat. Only his pink face remained, poking out from a hood ringed with fur. Even his hands were wrapped up in leather gloves. His captains, flanking him, were dressed to match. Between them, they carried not an ounce of baggage.

The general swaggered through the parting ranks, hands swinging by his sides. He performed a quick tour of the scene, taking in the corpses, the twigs plastered to Task's body, and finally the Fading soldier, still wearing that sour face.

The mighty general sighed as he removed a glove. He levelled a finger at the prisoner.

'Who is this scum?'

'He gave no name,' said the golem.

'Did you ask?'

Task shook his head.

'Well, then!' Huff threw up his hands, almost losing the other glove. Chuckling from the men. Collaver whacked his fist against a shield, drawing their silence. Huff bent down, bringing himself level with the soldier.

'Who are you?'

'Jin is my name. Musketman of the Fourth Spear. Under Captain Mascat. And I ain't tellin' you shite.'

'Sir!' Manx barked, nudging the man with the toe of his boot. '"I ain't telling you shite, *Sir*!"'

'He ain't no "sir" to me, and you ain't either.' Jin snorted and spat at them both. Some of the phlegm found its way onto the general's coat. 'Royalist pigs!'

A low growl rose up from the Truehard ranks. Sergeant Collaver shook his head, looking to the murky sky in disbelief.

Huff circled around to Task, arms crossed, his face wearing the expression Task was beginning to loathe. A tongue-lashing always seemed to follow.

'Have I ever told you to take prisoners?'

Task frowned. 'No.'

'Has Councillor Dast, Baroness Frayne, or any of my captains ever told you to take prisoners?'

He knew he should hold his tongue, but he had to ask.

'How do you learn an enemy's movements? Find out their secrets? It is a general practice in war to take prisoners for—'

'Not in Hartlund, it isn't! Truehards do not take prisoners. Neither do the Last Fading. We live, or we die. No mercy and no quarter. Do I make myself clear?'

A lone cheer from the soldiers. Sergeant Collaver pushed men and women aside, digging through the ranks for the culprit.

'Crystal,' said Task.

'Now, golem. As you brought him here, I order you to deal with this cur.'

Task looked down at the soldier. Jin stared back, defiantly daring him to go right ahead. There was a glimmer in his eye that spoke of something other than defiance. It was fear, and Task couldn't ignore it.

'I...'

The words stuck behind the golem's tongue. The magic was already tugging at his hand, bidding him to act.

Huff stepped forward. He glanced at the ranks and spoke in a low, dangerous tone. 'Are you disobeying me again, Task? We have talked about this, remember? Yet here you are, once again embarrassing me with disobedience. As my golem, you do what I tell you to do, and I am telling you to end this man. Or would you rather release him, to kill him another day?'

Task had no answer. He ground his teeth as he looked up and down, at the two pairs of eyes boring into him.

'As your master, I command you to kill him.'

'Get it done!' yelled a voice in the ranks.

Task could not move. All he could see was the pleading eyes of Sald, or Cater, as if they knelt in the muck instead of Jin. If he thought deeper, he saw a dozen more faces, sun-burnt and raw with fresh bruises, their jaws shivering despite the heat, and their eyes glistening with tears. Task remembered how they had all cowered when he had raised his arms.

'I...'

Huff clenched his bare fist so hard Task heard the knuckles pop. 'You continue to defy me, golem? Push me further, and I will have you broken into chunks, and left by the roadside!'

Task saw movement in the crowd behind them and spied the baroness and Dast standing there, as if Huff's mention had summoned them somehow. The councillor's eyes roved the scene, but Ellia's curious look was fixed on the golem.

Task let the words spill out of him, in a low growl.

'Empty threats do not fill me with worry... Master.'

'Kill him, Task. Or I shall.'

The magic seized him then. The golem reached out a mighty hand and let it hover over Jin's skull. His fingers rippled, a few skimming the blonde hairs of the man's head. Jin began to whimper.

Task did not squeeze. He tried his hardest not to. But the magic did the business for him, curling his fingers into a fist. He stared at Huff as the soldier's skull crumpled with a wet crunch. Not an eyelid was batted, even as the warm gore oozed through his fingers.

A few cheers went up from the soldiers. The rest stared on, satisfied, until Collaver ordered them into columns, ready for marching.

Huff only had a nod for Task. No words. His look said it all.

Good golem.

Task wanted to roar in his face.

He was left alone with the headless corpse; left with his thoughts and the mess in his palm. He stared down at it. What was once a world of ideas, memories and feelings was now just a muddle of grey and red, punctured by milky shards of bone.

He should have left him in the forest.

12

'Faith is not a mantle one can wear with ease. It is heavy work, and tiresome. The urge to take it off will be strong, but to reap the benefits, it must be worn at all times. There is no more righteous a path to greatness than absolute faith.'

BLESSED MANUAL OF THE ARCHITECT
BRESU, VERSE 24

47TH FADING, 3782 - THE SIX SISTERS

Evening found the Truehard camp on the edge of a wide river which coursed through the flatlands at the base of the Six Sisters, like the train of a long cloak. Only two of the Mothers had risen tonight. The river-waters caught their blueish glow on myriad ripples, swirling it with the fiery orange from the glowing camp.

Task had been tethered to an iron post, on Huff's order. The jork-cage was with the other half of the army. The golem had almost laughed when he saw the smith waiting, chain and hammer in hand. The general may have been making a point, but it was a blunt one, and harmless. Task had let them attach the chain, and chuckled to himself as they had scampered back to their bonfires and cheap wine.

The golem had been pitched on the far outskirts of the camp, down by the reed clumps that hugged the river's edge. He didn't mind in the least. He could listen to the waters burbling as they hurried past. It was peaceful, reminding him of the countless fountains of Lezembor. Even better, it drowned out the revelry of the camp.

His eyes kept themselves busy, switching from the river to the raucous camp, then to the buzzing things hovering over the reeds. Somehow, they always landed back on the stables, just a stone's throw away. There had been no sign of the girl that day, and it had brought back the worry.

Task caught the tremor of boots on the earth, and the tumble of quiet voices on the night breeze. His stones grated as he stiffened. His eyes scoured the darkness, looking for the cut of riders' uniforms, or the intolerable smirk of Lancemaster Taspin.

Instead, he spied slack shirts and old boots, easy smiles and hands grasping bottles of various liquids. And there was a square shape among them; something big and heavy enough to need two to carry.

'Mr Golem!'

It was old Sald, come to visit him, and with most of the Dregs in tow by the look of it. They were bathed in moonlight now, and Task looked at each of them in turn. All nodded.

'Sald. What are you doing here?'

'All the officers are having a private meeting in Huff's tent, so we thought we'd come and keep you company. Say thanks and all, for what you did today. A couple of our friends were in the ambush.' Sald grabbed the shoulder of the man next to him, who grinned and waggled a leg swathed in bandages. 'Guliber here is eternally grateful. He's just too drunk to form a sentence right now.'

Before the golem could say anything, Sald crooked a finger, and two soldiers brought forth a low table. They set it down beside Task, while the rest scattered ragged blankets around it. Cater held up a lantern for a moment before placing it square in the middle of the table, as if in preparation for some ritual.

Sald bent down to open the lantern, wincing at the same old pain in his back.

'You ever play judge?'

Task was still trying to understand what was going on. He cocked his head. 'I can't remember ever playing a game.'

'Then it's high time you did. Judge is the best of them all.' Cater watched on with a frown as Sald produced a small cloth bag from a trouser pocket. 'It's a maker of men.'

'And women,' said the soldier with the birthmark across her face.

Cater snorted. 'Yeah, but not you, Nerenna. You're as good at cards as Sald is at growing hair.' Nerenna rolled her eyes, seeking a blanket by the table.

Sald was done with the oil and wick. He sprinkled the contents of the bag into his palm. It looked like firepowder.

'I'm just surprised you've got some of that sorcerous dust left,' said Cater, leaning over the lantern.

'Use it sparingly, son. That's the trick.' Sald caught Task's narrowed eyes. 'Destrix flickerdust. Watch.'

Cater was still not impressed. 'Yeah, and mind your faces. Bloody dangerous stuff, golem.'

Task watched as Sald took a pinch of dust between finger and thumb and sprinkled it into the oil. His keen ears caught a soft fizzle before the soldier shut the oil-trap door and flicked its latch. He gave the lantern a gentle shake for good measure. 'Light?'

Iron struck flint, and a reed was set alight. With an impudent smirk, Sald lit the lantern's wick at arm's length, making the others shuffle backwards. As the flame took hold, it sputtered and sparked, then began to glow a bright red, then orange. Within moments, the lantern burnt a shimmering yellow, brighter than any candle Task had ever seen.

'Perfect,' said Sald , before finding a blanket of his own. 'Cater, you deal.'

The table was laid. First came the cards: nine to each of the dozen or so Dregs, and nine to Task. Then the drink: splashing from mouths of bottles into horn and bark cups. Finally the coins: not copper or silver, but wooden chips with symbols burnt into their faces. Sald flicked a few to the golem, and Task held them to the lantern-light.

'Gambling ain't allowed in the camp. And it ain't wise, either. Penniless men don't fight half as hard.'

Task thought about that for a moment. 'Or, they fight harder, with nothing left to lose.'

Sald's face broke into a wide smile. 'We got a philosopher in our midst, Dregs!'

Chips were knocked on the table as the smile spread around the circle.

'Do you drink, philosopher?' Nerenna raised a glass to the golem, but Task shook his head.

'Stone can't get drunk. Leaks right through me.'

Cater raised an eyebrow. 'You ever tried?'

Task threw him a jagged grin. 'I have.'

Sald clapped his hands. 'Let's begin. There're five houses, twenty cards in each house. Storm, Mountain, Tide, Ember and Snow. We turn over a card from the deck, and we all go 'round placing each of our cards down. When you get a match, such as three Magistrates of Ember, or two Knights of Tide, the winner gets the cards. If you can't go, or don't want to go, you can put some cards face down in the hope of convincing us you're not lying. If we doubt your truthfulness, we shout, 'Confess!' and you tell us something about yourself. We'll bet on you lying or telling the truth. We then confer. If you convince us, you get the pot and the cards. If we catch you out, you have to pay back the same amount in the pot. You win when you take everybody's money and their cards. Got it?'

Task opened his mouth, but no words came forth. He shrugged instead, making the Dregs laugh.

'You'll pick it up as we go along. It's all about watching your fellow card-players. You got to judge them, sniff out their lies.'

'To the Mothers, both risen and hiding!' toasted Sald, and the circle raised their drinks to the twin moons. There was a clatter and thud as the cups were banged on the table and drained. The bottles circled again, and the cups were refilled.

'Dealer.'

Cater took a card from the remainder of the pack and laid it face-up on the wood.

'First Magistrate of Ember.'

And so it began. Wooden coins rattled and cards flew. It was a rapid game, full of bravado, with the players taking great swigs from their cups and laying down their cards with flair. Within three moves, the hand was snatched up; three fiery-looking cards in a row.

Another was turned, and Task eyed the symbol as it landed, trying to match it with one of his own. The cards looked so small in his great fingers.

By the time the play reached him, he had chosen a card he thought looked appropriate. He was about to drop it when Sald held up a wooden token. 'You got to pay to play, Task. You got any coins? Cater can lend you some. He spends half his free time carving up sticks.'

Cater scowled. 'It's because I choose to play with thieves and robbers, not honest soldiers. You lot are always swindling me.'

'You're just shite is all, Cater,' said Nerenna. Cater mumbled something foul into his cup.

Sald was still looking at Task. The golem was about to shake his head when an idea came to him. Reaching to his shoulder, he found a small chip of stone and wrenched it free. It clattered across the table to mingle with the wooden coins.

Sald shrugged. 'Looks like somebody might win a golem tonight!' The Dregs cheered, throwing back their drinks once again.

'Go ahead, Task. Play your card.'

The golem laid it down. He looked around the circle, but nobody seemed to be complaining. Sald was waiting on the man to his left, Guliber. He wore a deep frown, eyes switching from the table to his cards.

'You're up, soldier,' said Sald.

'Deff it!' Guliber cast his chips into the pile. Nerenna pushed them across the table towards Task, and the golem found himself smiling. He had never won anything before. It was a strange but welcome feeling.

'Beginner's fortune,' said Cater, dealing the next card.

Task growled. 'We'll see.'

The game moved on, tumbling from player to player. Hands snatched at coins and cards as the conversation grew. Jibes and jabs began to fly across the table, with casual bets topping up the pile between cards. Task chuckled with the soldiers, and before long his ribs had grown hot from the constant heaving. He hadn't laughed like this for decades. *If not ever.*

It wasn't long before the first lie came forth. Cater puffed himself up as he laid three cards face down on the pile and threw in his coins.

'Twenty tants for the Storm royalty, in order.'

'Such a small bet, Cater,' said Nerenna. 'I'd expected more from someone of your rumoured prowess.' She nudged the player next to her; a straw-haired woman with a fiendish grin, whose name Task had learnt was Joley.

'Confess!' came the cheer.

Cater pinched his chin for a moment as he pondered. 'I've never thrown up before a battle.'

There was a moment of spluttering and cursing before the coins began to fly. The soldiers nudged the golem, and he threw a few of his stones on the pile, too.

'What do you reckon, Task?' asked Sald. 'Judge!'

The golem gave his verdict in a heartbeat. 'A lie.'

Sald looked over the piles of coins to check. 'The table has judged in favour of a lie.'

Cater looked around the circle. Slowly but surely, the smile grew. 'Truth.'

'Fawl-piss!' said Nerenna.

'Sald, come on!'

Sald rested his chin on his hand. He had a glaze of alcohol in his eyes. 'It's true. I never seen him chuck yet.'

Cater sniggered to himself as he grabbed the largest share. He split the rest of the winnings between Sald and another woman, both of whom had voted truth.

'Dealer.'

'The Second Knight of Tide.'

Task's eyes followed the card to the table. Its name bounced around his head, bothering him, but before he could dwell any longer on it, the game stole him back.

And so it went. The alcohol sank in, and the banter became a constant patter. Tongues began to slur and laughter filled every gap in conversation. Task laughed with them, even throwing in a few threats of his own. He could have been one of them, wearing a grimy shirt and swaying on his arse, knocking back torig and glugg. For a brief time, he felt human, and as Lesky had already shown him, it was an odd yet pleasurable thing. The world could be confined to a small circle of lanternlight, and the war could be shut out and laughed off, if only for a little while. Like the Dregs, Task found enjoyment in distraction.

'Forty tants for a run of Earth lords!' he said.

The table hummed. Every eye searched the golem's face, looking for a reason to doubt him. He gave them nothing.

'Confess!' said Sald, his face crinkled in a smile.

Task made a show of leaning back against his post and crossing his arms, mocking the others. 'I have never lost a battle.'

There was a round of thoughtful hissing and sucking of lips. The coins came in a stutter as each soldier made their bet.

Task gauged the piles. The table leaned heavily towards truth.

'A lie,' he said, grinning.

Hands thundered on the table. A few cheers, too. Task basked in it, sweeping the mass of coins and cards towards him. Those who remained in the game were looking short on both. As Sald was about to call for the next card, Cater held up a hand.

'You lost a battle?' He sounded quiet in the silence.

Task nodded. 'I've lost two.'

The young soldier looked confused. He wasn't alone. Half the table leant forwards.

'How?'

'Golems can be beaten, you know. Walls can be too high and too strong. Fires too hot. Moats too deep. Numbers too many.'

'What battles were they?' asked Nerenna.

Task thought for a moment, wondering if it might be better to stay quiet and leave it there.

'The first was in the Diamond Mountains. We were fighting against a Graden army. There were five golems with us. The Graden had taken a stronghold and made a home for themselves. We were sent in with the first wave, told to break the doors, smash the walls and root them out.'

'Sounds simple enough,' said Cater.

'Have you ever heard of the Icaria Cavada?'

'Nope.'

Task shook his head. 'The Icaria Cavada is a fortress so old that nobody remembers who built it. Imagine walls half a league high, with a black-mouthed canyon barely a musket-shot from the perimeter. Not much space for an army, let alone siege engines. Two golems were driven into it on the first day, taken by huge stones rolled down pipes in the walls. They cut through the lines like a knife through parchment. Arrows fell like rain.

Bombs of firepowder, too. Bursting through anything that stood in their way.'

'Sounds like the Destroyer's Furnace itself,' said Sald. The man's chin was slowly creeping closer to the table.

Task didn't know what that was, but he nodded all the same.

'And the second?' Cater was still curious.

The golem smiled. 'Let's just say, Wind-Cut Golems and ships don't mix too well. We tend to break them, especially in rough seas. It's all the ropes and complicated rigging, you see. My master soon changed his mind about ships after I had to march back across the seabed for a day.'

The Dregs cheered that for some reason, and Task had to laugh.

'I have a question,' he said. His story had jogged his memory of knights.

'Confess!' yelled the soldiers, breaking down into laughter again.

Sald waved a hand.

'Who is the Knight of Dawn?'

Cater slammed his cup down. He'd taken quite a gulp, but that didn't stop him trying to speak, dribbling words as well as wine. 'The Knight of Dawn is one of the finest swordsmen alive. A hero in his own right.'

'Why?'

'Because he slew the Last Dragon. Put a sword right through the beast's throat. Two days, they fought. It was a monstrous beast, by all accounts. It had spent the summer terrorising the villages. Taking fawls, warks, even people. It was golden, covered in spines. A Destrix Sheen, they called it. Some lone survivor of dragon-kind. It must have been older than you, golem. Kopen's mayor sent firns far and wide, calling for fighters, beast-hunters, anybody who could help. So, Alabast Flint, young champion of the Kopen Bladehall, decides to take matters into his own hands, and marches out to fight it one sunny morning. He told only one person before he left. Some tutor of his school. And he went straight to the mayor. Two days later, when he came back, with the dragon's head on a rickety wagon and looking like shite, the whole city was waiting for him. My age, he was.'

Sald had a smile on him. 'You tell it as if you were there, boy.'

Cater puffed his chest. 'I read all about it.'

'You can't read.'

'Somebody read it to me, is what I mean to say. I ain't the only one who's 'eard it.'

'I heard he's got a face like a jork's arsehole,' said Nerenna.

Cater wagged his finger. 'Not likely. They say half the ladies of Kopen queued at his door the night he came back with the dragon's head.'

Nerenna cackled. 'Shame it was the last one. I'd quite like a queue of ladies at my door.'

Task ignored their laughter, and worked away at his jaw, making it crunch.

'Not the answer you wanted, friend?' said Sald.

'The Fading soldier I caught...' There was a round of hissing before he could continue. 'He said the Knight of Dawn was on their side. That he'd come to kill me.'

The table fell silent. Cater's face was frozen in an odd mix of disappointment and deep confusion. Sald hummed into his fist. Nerenna was too busy pouring more wine into Joley's cup to react, and by the look of her, Joley was fast asleep, leant against Nerenna's shoulder. The rest just stared at their cards.

'In Hartlund?' Cater managed to squeak.

Task nodded. 'So it would seem.'

'What, you want your sword signed before he lops your head off with it?' said Nerenna.

'Have you told our illustrious leader?' asked Sald.

Task frowned at the mention of Huff. 'Not yet. It's why I had hoped Huff would keep the prisoner alive for questions.'

Sald blew a sigh. 'Don't tell him, Task. I'm not fond of the idea of being driven even harder on the morrow.'

The golem couldn't help but growl.

'Not a fan of Huff, are you?' asked the old man. 'Especially not after today, I imagine. With the prisoner and all? Partly why we came to see you.'

Task shook his head. 'He's the same as Lancer Taspin. Cruel. Brash. But in a different way. Not as loud-mouthed, but far more dangerous.'

The criticism came thick and fast from the Dregs.

'Only because he's the top wark. What he says, goes.'

'Not unless 'is father has anything to say 'bout it.'

'Bloody fool. Thinking we can march up a mountain and not have a rest.'

'Thinks we're beasts he can whip to get moving.'

'And if anybody steps out o' line, he has to prove his point, don't he just?'

Sald delivered the final blow. 'What General Huff Dartridge the Third doesn't get, Task, is that we respect a man for his deeds on the field. For getting his hands dirty. Not for which velvet-lined womb he fell out of. If he ever does get that, he could be a great soldier. A great leader, even. Not some spoilt brat who's been given an army, and thinks soldiery is all about swagger and loud voices.'

'And in any case,' said Nerenna, 'if you tell him about Dawn, he'll likely panic, and get even meaner.'

'What's there to panic about?' said Task, eyeing the concerned faces.

'He slew a dragon,' said Cater. 'Dragons are big.'

Nerenna waved a cup. 'Bigger than you, he means.'

Task had fought gritwyrms, deep in the Khandri Duneplains. Wingless, and lacking in fire they might have been, but they were big all the same. Humongous, in fact. Longer than a warship. And they had a penchant for spitting a sleeping poison before they bit.

Task nodded. 'I understand. You think he could beat me.'

'Huff won't want to see his precious golem in pieces,' said Sald. 'I'll bet my tent that's why the Fading have brought him here. To fight you.'

Perhaps Task should have been worried—fearful, even—of this new enemy. But all he felt was the urge to smile. He had caught the whiff of a challenge and was already lusting for it.

'I say let him come and try his luck,' said the golem. 'I've seen my fair share of heroes in my time, and every one of them met the dust with a surprised look on their faces.'

Cups were raised to that. Even Cater put his to the air, still looking confused. Task bowed his head.

'And that, ladies and gentlemen, is where I think we should call it a night,' said Sald. 'Follow the Mothers to bed.' He waved a hand at the speckled sky, where the moons were slipping below the distant ripple of hills.

A few moaned, eyeing their thick piles of wooden chips and stones, but Sald shook his head. 'No doubt we'll be up early, so let's not do it with gritty eyes and a sour stomach. Who knows what our grand general has in store for us tomorrow. Off with you all.'

'Before you go, I'll need my stones,' said Task.

Wine-smudged eyes narrowed as fingers tried to pick the stones from the piles.

Task shook his head. 'I have a faster way.' He laid his fists down on the table. The cups rattled as he tensed his limbs, pulling at the faint shiver of his pieces. They all returned to him, snapping into place with the stuttering of a musket-line.

Half of them grinned like fools, drumming fingers against the table, while the rest gawped, as if they had been slapped around the face.

'Move, Dregs!' Sald chivvied them. The golem gave him a hand as he levered himself up, still wincing.

'You should see to that.'

Sald scoffed. 'Jus' too many days spent marchin', is all, friend. Never you mind.'

Task nodded. He envied the man in that moment, with his papery skin and knots and gripes. The grave was not far from him, and yet he would find a peace there that Task could never have.

The table was dismantled at half the speed it had been arranged, even though the bottles were lighter and the bodies rested. The Dregs clumped together, half-leaning against each other for support as they readjusted to being upright. Task smirked at them.

Sald covered his eyes and flashed a last grin. 'We will return, Mr Task. Beginner's fortune, be damned! And don't you worry about the Knight of Dawn. He's just another bag of meat for the breakin'.'

It was a strange sentiment, but the golem bowed all the same, touching his head to his knee.

They shuffled off into the gloom between the torches. Task closed his eyes and followed their hushed voices until they reached the sprawling capillaries of the camp.

Only then did he shake his head, and let a smile reach across his face. He rested his back against the iron pole to watch the moons while he once again pondered the idea of friends, and how he suddenly seemed to have so many.

Task had never figured how friendships started; just that they happened every now and again, like one wandering path colliding with another on an otherwise barren plain.

'Stone does not need conversation,' Belerod had once said. 'It does not need to trade tales, to laugh and be merry with beaker in hand. Stone is not flesh.'

But these were lies. Somewhere within Task there was a shard of stone that needed all of those things. Over the years he had learnt to ignore the feeling, but this night had rekindled it.

His eyes kept edging to the stables, and his smile faded. The Dregs had been fine company and a good distraction, but now they were gone, and he was left alone to wonder once more.

'Let the hero come!' he said, and rested his head on the grass, closing his eyes on yet another day.

13

*'I've found more stimulating creatures under my fingernails than
in the towns and taverns of the Darens.'*

WORDS OF KING GARALD THE SIXTH

47TH FADING, 3782 - THE SIX SISTERS

Lesky wrenched herself from her sleeping bag, scowling into the
darkness. Sleep was avoiding her, prowling around the edges of her mind,
elusive as a thief. What little of it she'd managed to catch was full of
voices and strange thoughts. She had punched her straw pillow more than
once. She had tried her back, her sides, her front. She had even tried
counting fawls.

Shiver was the lucky one. She could hear him snuffling and
whining in his dreams, just a poke away from her head.

There was nothing else for it. She shoved herself from the bed and
padded across the rough blanket that was their floor for the evening. A
dull rumble rose from somewhere nearby, hidden behind curtains. It was
Ganner, sleeping off whatever reeking wine he had managed to pilfer.
Lesky tutted under her breath before seeking out her boots. That man
needed taking down a peg or two; but not tonight.

She took a scarf from her drawstring sack and wrapped it around
her neck until it smothered half her face. She took a moment at the
doorway, biting her lip in the darkness as she double-checked herself and
strode forwards.

The cold night made her shiver, and brought pimples to her bare
forearms. She thrashed through the long, dewy grass, soaking the legs of
her breeches.

The Mothers had sunk into the earth, and only the dusty stars cast
their light. Lesky traced a few of their patterns as she walked, following
their swirls and flickers. She saw Urdith, the snow-witch, reaching with

her candle to the hunter, Basilt. And the Broken Arch. They all looked down on her, lighting the way.

She heard the golem's stone grating before she saw him. He was breathing hard, shoulders crunching as he twitched in the grip of some dream, just like Shiver. A silver chain snaked around his neck and led out to a pole.

The starlight showed the rough cut of his features, and Lesky crouched down beside him, curious as ever. She found his face in a deep frown, his eyes locked behind puckered stone.

She sat there for a time, staring hard at his forehead, longing to know what dreams swirled beneath that granite dome. She felt if she could dig hard enough, she could see them. Lesky even tensed her jaw, making her head shake with effort, before a sharp pain in he temple made her stop.

'You are a strange one,' she said, stepping back. She perused the ranks of reeds poking out from the riverbank, looking for the longest one she could find. She snapped it off at the base, tugged away its remaining leaves and returned to the golem.

Lesky held her arm outstretched, reed wavering. It touched the golem on the lip, but he dreamt on. She poked again, whacking him on the cheek. Still no luck. She raised it once more.

41ST REAPING, 3361 - WIND-CUT, HASPIA

'Fourteen of the Chanark tribes have agreed to join us.' His master beamed over the stone table. Task watched the expressions of those who sat around it. Not all seemed pleased.

'Fourteen tribes is far from enough, Belerod,' said a woman. 'The Accord have amassed twice that many in under a week. A full Graden army has joined the great crusade. They crouch in Lezembor, waiting to cross into the mountains.'

'The Khandri must be supported,' said a man whose skin was fairer than the Hasp. His dark hair was knotted in complex braids, curly at the ends. A Khandri lord, according to the whispers.

Belerod fought back. 'And they shall, Ghaspa, but the Narwe Harmony is a fragile thing. You know that better than I.'

The Khandri had forged the peace between the southern Realm, Task remembered that from his lessons. His neverending lessons.

His master went on. 'The Hasp are with you. The Chanark are hesitant, but willing. Affela, too, is behind you. And Ifl, what little it can spare. The Harmony rises, Ghaspa. In time it will surge. While we wait, we have our golems and our war-engines.'

Ghaspa regarded the score of golems standing like fearsome decorations along the walls of the room. Each stood behind their master at the table: a Hasp lord; a Windtricker; a Narwe prince. Most were Wind-Cut, while others were crafted from lesser stone; steel-cut and silfrin-washed to give them a glitter.

Task spied a few bone golems behind the far pillars. An iron golem by the door. Even an ancient one made of clay.

Something disturbed the column of sunlight that pierced the dome above. All necks snapped backwards.

Task read the vibrations in his feet; he thought he could feel a feverish drumming. He realised it was their hearts.

The tension was a bowstring, stretching tighter each day. Task was still learning the liquid ways of their skin, how it would change and ripple through emotion after emotion.

Ghaspa seemed convinced for now. 'Then I ask you to the mountains. The Cavada could do with your numbers.'

A number of them scoffed, including Belerod. 'That fortress can be held by a hundred men.'

'Times have changed since we last fought, Lord Belerod. Walls weaken. Gates rust. The Icaria Cavada is not what it once was.'

'So you want us to help you repair it.'

Ghaspa looked again to the golems. The room bristled. 'As you Windtrickers are so proud of your craftsmanship, I assumed you would eagerly lend your expertise.'

Belerod held up his hands. 'If that is what it takes to preserve the Harmony. But our command is to be respected, our advice sought after, and we must be given the final say in decisions. Agreed?'

Ghaspa wriggled for a moment before slumping in his chair. He waved a hand in a cross-shape motion.

Rings clinked against glasses and silfrin cups. Backsides rose from seats.

Task raised his head as his master paid him a glance; with a wink.

The golems remained still as the wine was poured and the dignitaries came poking and prodding. Task had seen them do the same with their chariots and carry-boxes, comparing the coverage of gold-leaf, the origins of the wood.

Belerod had taught him to stay still. It had taken more time than it should have, he had said. Task retreated in on himself as a couple came to stare at his features and run their hands over his shards. There was something in their touch he did not like. It leaked into him. He felt... angry.

No. Jealous.

His eyes flicked to the iron golem standing across from him. He knew it was theirs, and although it was made of iron, it was a clumsy thing; a poor cousin to a Wind-Cut Golem.

Ghaspa came to prod him with tough fingers, testing his jawline. He was tall, but was still forced to stretch.

Task flinched away.

'My Lord Ghaspa...'

He heard his master's voice. And something else; a trickling of some sort. His feet felt cold.

'My lord! It's best not to antagonise them.'

But Ghaspa did not desist, prodding at the seams now. 'Merely testing this old-magic you're so proud of, Belerod. Merely testing.'

Task grimaced, eyes catching Belerod's in warning.

'Golems are built for war, Ghaspa. Not entertainment. They are dangerous.'

Prod.

'Mechanical.'

Prod.

'And dull.'

Prod.

'Especially this one.'

The cold had spread to his knees.

47TH FADING, 3782 - THE SIX SISTERS

'Architect's balls,' cursed Lesky, ducking his mighty swing, as he batted at something invisible.

The golem's white eyes flared, leaking trails of vapour. Lesky was mesmerised.

'You dream!'

Task took a while to speak. He sniffed at his arm, checking it for piss. Lesky pouted.

'Yes, I do.'

'How can stone dream?'

'The same way it walks and talks and fights. Magic.'

She sat cross-legged on the wet grass beside him. The waters burbled below the reeds.

'And what exactly does stone dream 'bout?'

'Isn't that rude to ask in your culture? The Hasp never share a dream.'

'Don't know 'bout culture, but it ain't rude to ask. It's just rude to bore people that 'aven't asked to hear your dreams. At least that's what Mam says. I always have the strangest dreams. They're so real, like I'm livin' other people's lives, or swimming in their thoughts. Places I never heard of. Things I never seen. Been havin' them for years now.'

Task stared out at the mist for a time.

'So?' she pressed.

'So what?'

'Your dreams, silly.'

Task huffed at her. 'Golems dream their own memories. At least I do.'

'Your memories?'

'We don't really have imaginations, so we dream everything we've ever done, over and over.'

'So you never forget things?'

'Never,' he said, eyes fixed on the grass.

Lesky ducked into his line of sight. 'And what else? Don't be gettin' grumpy on me now!'

Task held up his hands. 'Lately all my dreams end with water. Rushing water.'

Lesky thumbed her itching nose, thanking the Architect it wasn't Rising yet, when they'd be plagued by crawling, buzzing things.

'What do you think it means?' she said.

'You're the wise one. I was hoping you'd tell me.'

Lesky sniffed the cold air, and scrunched up her face. 'I think it means you need a wash. I can smell blood and worse on you.'

Task rolled his eyes, but it didn't hide the curve of his granite lips. The golem tugged the chain apart as if it were no more than a loose thread, and stomped towards the river. Lesky tucked her knees beneath her chin and watched, eyes so wide with intrigue they ached.

Ellia hovered behind a tent, breathless as a corpse. Her eyelids were clamped tight. She searched the darkness with her ears, sifting through the noises of the slumbering camp.

The distant clink of empty bottles. Something crying out in the wilds, beyond the mist. The crackle of writing paper and scratching of ink. The hiss of a lantern across the path. The snoring of a guard up ahead.

Her eyes snapped open, adjusting to the half-glow of the lantern, defying the darkness just a stone's throw away. She strode with confidence, lest she be spied creeping, and yet her steps fell as silently as two feathers tumbling over sand.

She did not stop or breathe until the fog-bank had swallowed her, leaving the camp as a dull glimmer over her shoulder. There was a faint starlight in the haze, rolling with its vapour and lighting her way. Ellia counted her every footfall, following the numbers Spiddle had placed in her head that afternoon.

'Four and two and six...'

She turned on her heel and followed the natural dip in the land.

Its shadow touched her before she saw it: a monolith sitting at an angle in the soil, shaped like a broken hand reaching for the Mothers. The epochs had weakened its resolve, worn away its joints, and sharpened its fingers to points. What ages it must have seen.

Ellia's hands wandered its smooth surface, feeling the deeper cold of the metal in its grains. She heard his intake of breath before he spoke.

'The locals say silfrin runs all through this rock.'

Ellia didn't doubt it. She could see its glint in the faint light. 'Then why haven't they ripped it up and melted it down?'

Spiddle shrugged, making the leather about his shoulders squeak. 'They think it's a gift from the Mothers. They cast it down here in a fiery trail one night, so the story goes. Crushed a warlord and half his army in the process. Funny thing was, the warlord had come to crush the town and all its villagers. Saved their necks, so now they don't dare touch it.'

Ellia tutted. 'Moon-worshippers and luck-spinners. All dullards. Their stories of old-magic and faeries have rotted their brains. Have you been spending so much time in their taverns, lapping up their doltish thoughts, that you've begun to rot, too?'

'They're grey lumps in a grey sea to me. But you, Ellia, you shine like a light. Your mind glows!' Spiddle shrugged and threw back his hood, baring his shaved head to the night. He was paler than porcelain.

Ellia began to pace around him. A spiked cog was tattooed on the back of the glimpse's head, sprawling across his white skull. 'All Zealots' minds do, I'm told, Spiddle, so spare me your mystic fawl-piss.'

Spiddle looked amused. 'You've come face to face with a golem and yet still you question magic, the Architect's richest craft. It almost sounds like heresy.'

She snorted. 'You'll be wanting me in the Howlings next, pouring hot lead down my ears.'

'Only if you have something worth the Foreman's time...' He let the sentence hover like a question. Her stony eyes told him she didn't.

'Report,' he said, turning serious with a jut of the chin. She faced him, letting the glimpse lock his eyes onto her. His pupils faded to white, and even though he stared her in the face, he seemed to look at all of her at once. It felt like being disrobed.

She held on tight to the feel of his mind on hers, as if he were a beast in her house. She shut doors here, shored up walls there, and let him prowl only the areas she dictated. She let him take only the memories that she had warped. *And lightly did it.* Spiddle could not feel her touch. He would sniff trouble, and she was saving that for later.

'Are you done?' she said, jolting him from her mind.

'Done,' he said, his eyes snapping back to colour. He shivered as he spoke. 'Good job. So far, at least.'

Ellia found herself wishing the man had balls. Then she could give them a good kick for his insolence. But sadly for her, all glimpses, gazers, and blinders are eunuchs, as the Blessed Manual orders. Those given the pleasure of wielding the Mission's power must also keep their genitals in a drawstring velvet bag instead of between their legs.

'I bet that if I could read your thoughts as you can mine, I would find doubt rotting away in that brain of yours. And why is that? Why do you expect me to fail so? Tell me, Spiddle, have I ever failed the Treyarch? The Mission?'

'There have been dalliances in the past, if I remember rightly,' said Spiddle, with a smile. Ellia flashed him a fierce look, and he held up his hands. 'But it is not your success rate that worries me. It is your motives. I wonder whether you are truly devoted to your task.'

'You wonder, or the Treyarch wonders?'

Spiddle looked away. She cackled. *Perfect.*

'Just you, then.' Ellia came close enough to touch noses. 'Read my thoughts again. Go as deep as you want, and tell me what you see.'

Again, the hands capitulated. 'There are more pressing concerns.'

'Such as?'

'Huff may be moving forwards, but still not fast enough for the Treyarch's liking.'

Ellia stepped back and folded her arms. 'You want more speed?'

'Speed is for the fool, they say. The wise man favours haste. We want a country left at the end of the war. Use the golem, Frayne. As you've been instructed.'

Ellia had other plans for the golem. She led Spiddle towards another idea; one she'd clung tightly to her for many months now, waiting for a chance to set it free. She broached it carefully.

'After the ambush today, Huff drove the army on another three leagues before calling halt, just out of spite. Outrage. Vengeance. It embittered the golem. He's feeling something for these Truehards. I say that's what we need. To make this more personal than it already is, for both of them.'

'How?'

'For Huff? Perhaps a spy.'

'Who?'

'Anybody. The general's far too preoccupied with controlling the golem and doing a good job. Spies are the last worry on the his mind. That's why uncovering one would kick him like a wild firn. He'll be furious, indignant, and want to strike back at the Fading. He'll take bigger risks and larger leaps. If we want to end the war on the Mission's schedule, that's the way to do it. Besides, with the whiff of spies in the air, it would give me an excuse to make an excursion. It's about time we paid a visit to our other friends.'

Spiddle cocked his head. 'True and all.' He spent a moment watching the mist tumble about them. 'A fair plan. Who did you have in mind?'

'A lowly shield-chief. A messenger boy. Maybe a lowly soldier. Who cares. Somebody from as northern a county as I can manage. The perfect suspect. I'll make it look like soldiers' justice.'

The glimpse gave a sickly smile. 'And for the golem, Task?'

'What could be better than pitting him against another golem?'

'The Treyarch has already made his feelings clear on that.'

'Then convince him. Raise the stakes. Give the Fading a real weapon, not this Knight of Dawn.'

Spiddle hummed. 'The hiring of the mercenary came as a surprise to us.'

'The Mission and I both, Spiddle. The Last Table played that close to the chest.' The subject was wandering. 'I say give them the bone creature. Let it rip through the Truehard camp. Nothing will change. It'll simply stoke Task into a fury that will see this war ended swiftly and brutally.'

Spiddle said nothing.

'Just ask him.'

The glimpse turned away. 'I will suggest it to the Treyarch.'

She called after him. 'I assume that's all, then?'

'For now, Zealot Frayne. For now.' He already sounded distant, as though a fog had consumed him. 'I will be in touch.'

When she reached the gate, she found the guard was no longer slumbering. He was walking off his stiff legs, trundling back and forth across the path. She crouched in the long grass, wondering what county he called home; whether he would make a good corpse. The excitement, the blood-lust as she called it, had begun to rise, tickling her heart to make it race. She wallowed in the thrill of it for a moment, her breath short, and her front teeth firmly embedded in her bottom lip.

Remembering the stables, she crept parallel to the tent-spikes, towards the far end of the camp, where the river muttered away to itself.

There were more guards here, though they'd had the clever idea of loitering below the lanterns, ruining their night-eyes. Ellia snuck easily around them, darting behind a paddock crammed with sleeping firns. The beasts' muscles heaved with their dream-laden breathing.

In the darkness behind the tall tents and fences, the fog was a careless artist, smudging the edges of every line, blunting every corner. All was shadow; nothing real. She could have been tiptoeing across clouds for all she knew, or sneaking through the dreams of the beasts in the pens. But there was no time for flights of imagination. She kept moving, heading along the river's arc and swinging back towards the camp.

She heard it as she reached the path: a muffled slosh of water, followed by a thud. Then, faint voices, and the rasping of something solid.

Ellia took a step back towards the river; standing straighter, shoulders back. She let herself fall into her confident, rolling pace, her hands tucked behind her back.

The shape of the golem was unmistakable. Task stretched to his full height. There was another shadow by his legs. *The girl.*

'Only me, Task,' said Ellia. 'Little girl.'

'Baroness Frayne. Ellia,' said Task, with a gentle rumble of stone. The waif curtseyed.

'I was just coming to check in on you.'

'Isn't it a little late for visits, Baroness?'

She stepped forward, looking around them for show. 'And a little late for a swim isn't it, Mr Golem? What would your master think, girl?'

Lesky shrugged. There was something unashamed about her that Ellia almost liked. *One to watch, this girl.*

'I wanted to make sure Huff was not aware of my coming here, you see. I knew it would be a sensitive issue, after today's events.' She caught the shift of the girl's gaze, curious as always. 'I saw how Huff treated you. No better than before, I'm ashamed to say.'

Task raised his voice to a rasp. 'Worse.'

Ellia nodded. 'I'll have another word in his ear, in that case.'

'It did no good last time.'

Ellia was taken aback by the growl in Task's tone. 'I'm trying to help you, Task. Do you not recall our conversation? I am a woman of my word. I'll speak to him again, sternly so. Huff is a brat, but he is capable of change. In the meantime, you need to push him, drag him along. Set your own pace and finish this war. If this means letting loose the demon inside you, so be it.'

'It would—'

'Not be a good idea, I know. Nor can you disobey your master. Fine. But if you don't give him a chance to issue an order...' She stepped back, hands in the air, letting the idea linger like a sweet scent. 'It's not disobedient, is it? In the meanwhile, I shall have another crack at that dullard's head for you. And I'll say not a word of late-night swims.'

Task creased his brow, but Ellia could tell she had hooked him. 'My thanks, Baroness.'

'Anything for a friend, Task. I bid you goodnight. And to you, little girl.'

Another curtsey. 'Baroness.'

Ellia left the strange pair to it, and faded back into the fog. She strode for the camp with a hint of a bounce in her step. She had found that unexpected pleasures were always the tastiest.

The guards waved her through at the first line of lanterns, assuming a late-night or early-morning walk. She didn't care which. They were sleepy-eyed and their chins were grizzled.

There was a stench of booze and over-boiled stew in the air. Ellia followed it from one campfire to the next, picking over empty bottles, discarded blankets and the unfortunate few who had foregone their beds in favour of fresh air, and likely a sore back in the morning.

She scrutinised every shield she passed, staring at jork-heads, or chevrons, or nets of stars. Most of them were simple things, pitted and battered. Others were beautifully painted, with barely a scratch on them. It spoke volumes about who carried them. Ellia bet herself she could place their owners in rank and file, just from the amount of battle-scars.

She followed a path between the poorer tents, which were dirtier and bore more patches than the others. Their shields had been mauled by spear and musket-shot. A few good kicks and they'd be splinters.

She began to look for a loner's tent; something small yet big enough for wicked deeds. She soon found it.

Lingering behind a circle of tents, snubbed by their huddle, a patchwork cone was leaning at an awkward angle. The shield was patterned with a wheatsheaf; a sign of the peasant folk of Norset, a county that had been split in half since the first whisper of war.

With a shiver of anticipation, Ellia slipped a long knife from a sheath tucked in the hollow of her back, and used it to poke aside the flaps of the tent, cutting the inner fastenings. She was as silent as a whisper; slower than the sun's shadow.

She slid into the darkness of the tent with the mist trailing about her boots. The spilled light illuminated the edges of a slumbering lump in the middle of the floor, tightly wrapped in a blanket. Ellia closed the flap behind her.

She stood over the sleeping soldier, feet spread wide. *Not yet*, she told herself. It had been a few moons since her last killing, and she wanted to savour that lingering moment before the strike. No drug nor wine, no man nor woman had ever delivered the same rush. It was a feeling to be revered; a moment to be respected.

It was a woman, a handful of years younger than her, with a face weathered by battle. A web of scars ran across her cheeks, below a pair of hollow eyes. She looked worn and tired. Perhaps Ellia would be putting her out of the misery of a long war.

It is the nature of sleeping things to rise when being watched. There is some knack of the mind that keeps watch while dreaming.

It was the same with this woman, though she took her precious time coming to.

Ellia greeted her with a smile. She sank to her knees and placed the knife across her throat. The woman had the sense to freeze, snapping awake in an instant.

'I ain't got many coins, but I'll give you whatever I have. Alright?' she whispered.

The baroness took an excitable breath. 'I am not here for your coins.'

The soldier began to quiver. 'What then?'

Ellia used her fist first, driving it again and again into the woman's face until her knuckles ached and the moaning had stopped. Then came the knife. The blade flashed no fewer than a dozen times, finding a new home every time. Lungs, heart, face, stomach; she counted them all as she struck.

It ended with her breath ragged and panting, her knife dripping, and her arms shaking. She let a faint smile hover on her lips before wrenching herself away from the body.

Running her fingers along the faces of her knife, she began to write with the soldier's blood, making it sloppy but legible.

On the canvas, the blanket, the ground, she wrote just one word.

'Take no chances, reap no failures,' she said to herself.

Her grim business concluded, she put an eye to the flap and found the night as empty and quiet as she had left it. Not a soul stirred.

Leaving the flap wide open, Ellia sauntered into the night, letting the shivers move from her arm to her body. There they lingered, until she had sequestered herself in her own tent, wrapped herself in her blankets, and let the murder flash over the dark backdrop of closed eyelids.

Ellia Frayne fell asleep with a crooked smile upon her face.

14

'I write to inform you, General Gorder, of your son's complete inability to soldier. I regret that we cannot allow him to continue his studies here in Normont. We look upon the stabbing of other students very seriously, no matter how accidental they may or may not be.'

FROM A MISSIVE TO GENERAL DARTRIDGE, FROM THE GERALL SCHOOL
OF SOLDIERY, NORMONT

48TH FADING, 3782 - TRUEHARD CAMP

General Dartridge was pretending to be asleep. To admit wakefulness, to crack open the eyes even a smidgeon, would have spelled the start of the day. That meant a lot of things.

Clothing himself.
Talking to Captain Glum.
Marching.
Dealing with the stone beast.

And generally dipping a toe into the human cesspool his army was turning into.

The general listed his duties off in his head, stacking them against the soft embrace of his imported olma-down Braaden blankets, which demanded nothing of him except to lie there, and be alone.

Alas, it was not to be. The more Huff tried to will himself back into the fuzzy void of sleep, the more it escaped him. It was as if the morning's noises and smells—even the very light itself—were chasing it away. Within a few short moments, he found himself thoroughly, and disappointingly, awake.

Huff sighed deeply and rolled onto his back.

The colour of the canvas roof told him there had been no rain, which was a small mercy at least. The Greenhammer moors were known for being wetter than a boat's backside, and yet they had been lucky so far. Good fortune, perhaps, in return for the hell the Six Sisters had showed them.

Huff pushed himself from his bed, feeling the cold air seep under his collar and sleeves as he left the safety of the covers and went to stand in his mirror's eye.

It was the damnable golem. He had decided it at some point in the morning hours, while he'd been chasing his cup across his desk. The beast was the root of his problems. The army saw Task's power and his recalcitrance, and they applauded him for it. He was turning Huff into a joke. The councillor and the charming baroness might not have seen it, but he did.

Huff raised a finger to his reflection and held it there. 'Not today. Not any more.'

The general swept away from himself and approached his desk.

'GLUM!'

The moronic captain normally hovered near his tent from sunrise, waiting for the general to call for him. Huff had often reminded him that there were better things he could be doing, but he always just nodded and smiled.

As reliable as a fat old fawl, in walked Captain Glum.

'Morning, General!'

Huff threw himself into his chair. 'Good morning, Captain. What news from the scouts?'

'They returned just an hour ago, sir.'

'And? What *news*?'

'They've found the battalion you were looking for, after Purlegar. They've holed up near the Lumps. Taken a hill. Pushes us a bit east maybe, but it gets us around the Greenhammer nicely. I looked on a map.'

Huff clapped mockingly. 'Well done for you, Glum. West, it is. Any cannon?'

'One or two, maybe. Hard to see, they said.'

The general ran a hand through his hair, as if kneading an idea. 'Riders it'll have to be. And the stone lump.'

'Taspin won't like that.'

'Spit on Taspin. Letters?'

'Just the three today.'

Huff's eyes rose to meet the captain's. 'There's four here, Glum.'

'Four! Yessir.'

The dark-red leather envelope was the one he had left unopened. Only his father used those colours and wrote in that silvery hand. He placed a finger on the seal; a dagger pressed to a heart.

'Glum, go make yourself useful.'

The captain began to look around for things to do in the tent. Huff raised a finger.

'*Outside.*'

Huff ripped open the thin leather and held the letter to the light. His father was scrimping on the paper, these days; the thinner kind that let the ink bleed. Perhaps coin was even tighter in the capital than he thought. After all, wars can bleed all who dabble in them; not just those who die on the battlefield.

He devoured the words.

General.

I must admit the casualty reports of Purlegar are unsettling. Despite the golem, you lost almost a thousand men. With these losses, there won't be a country left for our king to rule when this war is done. As such, I am sending you a thousand more men, including the Iron Eyes regiment. They will reach you by the borders of Saffin county.

Despite your lack of communication, I have heard word that the golem is undisciplined. Can you not control him? If that is the truth, then tell me you have not broken him. We depend on him, Huff, as we depend on you.

I fear you may disappoint me.

G

Huff's cheeks bunched as he tensed his jaw.

Not even signed with "father".

He pushed aside several half-written letters he had attempted in the early hours, while drunk, and took out a new scrap of parchment.

'Dear *Father*,' he mouthed, as he dipped a quill, put it to the page, and lied through every splotch of dark ink.

I hope this letter finds you in fine health. My apologies for the lack of reports. I trust in Councillor Dast and Baroness Frayne to be shrewd and clear in their accounts to the Council, and so I don't see the need for a third view of the matters.

As an instrument of war, the golem is nothing short of perfection, and far from "broken". He is destructive. Lethal. Unstoppable. And above all, obedient. The golem and I are kindred souls. Under my control, we will crush the Fading exactly as I promised you.

As I know how fond you are of snatching young men and women from the boats and alleyways, I must decline your offer of more troops. My men are now battle-hardened, fierce and ready to win this war. I do not need cannon fodder getting in their way. I will do this my way.

As for disappointment, I look forward to the day when you pin a medal on my chest.

Your son.

With a sigh he pushed the letter across the table, to sit with the other replies he'd yet to send to his father. His fingers lingered on the desktop, drumming. He would never have given him the satisfaction of putting it in ink, but his father was right. They did need more men, but not from the capital.

'GLUM!'

The man appeared once more, though this time there was a rare hop in his step. Huff ignored it for the moment.

'Yes, General?

'I want new recruits.'

'Where from, sir?'

'I don't care where, just as long as they can hold a sword or cock a musket. Any towns that we pass, send out riders to call for volunteers. Tell them the king provides food, fires, and who knows, maybe even some tants at the end of it. And glory! Don't forget glory.'

'And if any say no?'

Huff's eyes searched the ceiling. 'Then you'll remind them of their duty to the king, won't you? But gently, mind. They'll soon see which way the tide is flowing.'

Glum nodded his head, making his chin wobble. 'Yes, sir. Anything else?'

'Yes.' Huff snatched up the parchment, folded it and stuffed it into a fine leather envelope. 'I want this sent out with the reports on the next convoy.'

'Right you are.'

Glum looked between the door and the desk. Huff was growing bored of his fidgeting.

'What is it, Glum, for Architect's sake?'

The disturbing expression on Glum's face gave the general a sour feeling in his gut; something that was swiftly becoming a common occurrence. It was surprising he hadn't contracted an ulcer.

'Spit it out, man!'

'There's something you might want to see, sir.'

Glum panted as he cantered ahead, like a wark pining for its owner to chase it. The general refused to indulge him, and walked at his own pace.

He looked back and forth as they walked into the more tangled sections of the camp. Sleepy-eyed soldiers rose to salute him as he passed. Huff put on a warm smile, wishing them good morning and praising their fine work on the mountain.

'This way, General.'

Glum waved him over to where a small crowd had gathered, standing in a ring around a small tent.

'Move aside! General coming through! Get your unwashed arses out of his way!' The man may have been a dullard, but at least he knew how to soldier.

Huff stood tall as he stepped through the ranks. He wasn't surprised to see Frayne and Dast there, perched like bloodthirsty jabbers on the edge of the circle. Their faces wore looks of quiet concern.

Huff shoved the last few soldiers aside.

In the centre of the ring was a blood-soaked tent, torn aside to reveal its occupant, a woman still laying on her blanket.

At least, he *thought* it was a woman.

He stepped closer, feeling his gorge rise, gulping it back. Vomiting in front of subordinates is not something an officer does.

A bloody cavern had been made of her face. Her chest was littered with wounds, knife-made and vicious. There had been no mercy here, and Huff knew why. It was literally spelled out for him; on the tent rags, the ground, and the blood-smeared belongings.

"Spy".

The word was on everyone's lips; at the centre of every mind. The day had delivered its first punch; an almighty sock to the jaw.

And to think he had been worried about the rumours of a Fading dragon-slayer.

'Explain this to me!' yelled Huff as he turned away. 'Immediately!'

Sergeant Collaver stepped out of the ring, wearing a sheepish look. 'Name's Joley, sir. One of the Dregs. Just a shield-bearer.'

Before Huff could reply, there came a wail from behind the circle. A woman in leather armour burst through the ranks. The scene hit her like a wall. She stopped dead a few paces before the corpse, knees turning inwards as she sank to the floor, and let another howl rip from her throat.

More soldiers appeared, grabbing her by the arms and wrenching her away.

'Stop there!' Huff's shout cut the wailing short. He picked his way around the mess, Collaver nipping at his heels.

'This is them, General. Sald Asper, their chief, and this is...' said the sergeant.

'Shield-bearer Nerenna,' said Sald. Huff caught the look he flashed to Collaver; that cold glare of worry. Only guilty men showed fear near their crimes, Huff had found.

'What happened here? Explain yourself!'

'We just woke up, sir, and she was already dead. Murdered in the night. We had to open up the tent after an hour of nothin', despite us callin' her name, and we found that. We took apart her tent to make sure it was her.'

Huff levelled a finger at the man. 'You found her?'

'Young Cater here did.'

The vacant look in the other soldier's eyes told Huff that at least was true.

The general flashed another look at the broken body. It was starting to reek. 'You're telling me that this brutal attack happened without any of you hearing a thing?' Huff knew how closely soldiers pitched their tents, and how thin their fabric was.

'Yes, sir. We were all asleep.'

A murmur spread around the circle of soldiers.

'Quiet down or disperse!' said Collaver.

'Traitors the lot of them!' came a yell. 'This is what happens when you bring field-scum like these into a camp!' It was Taspin, barely making the effort to hide himself. Huff spied him between two of his men, and threw him a silencing look.

As the general looked around at the suspicious faces of the soldiers, it was easy to pick out the peasants; those who knew spades better than swords. Broader backs, a little extra mud in the creases, or even the tell-tale curves of poor bloodlines. His army was as much worker as it was warrior, but he had never yet doubted its loyalty. To him, perhaps, but not the Truehards. *Not to the king.*

Huff thought of the ambush. He had taken the mountain road to avoid the normal routes, and yet the Fading had been waiting for them in the treeline. His suspicions had been forgotten with the business of the prisoner, and that stubborn golem, but now they raged anew.

Huff leaned closer to the old soldier, examining his grey eyes. 'Did you kill this woman? Did her tongue slip over the campfire? Did you and the rest decide to butcher her for being a spy?'

Sald looked down at the snivelling woman, as if she were proof of their innocence. 'No, sir!' he said, alarmed. 'We did no such thing.'

'She was my friend!' sobbed the woman, Nerenna.

'An accomplice, then!' Taspin shouted.

The word ricocheted through the soldiers. Collaver opened his mouth to silence their murmurs, but the general shut it with a wave. An idea had come to him. He had to make an example of these Dregs. He would turn this army's head for good. *Their doubt would die today.*

Huff delivered his conclusions like a judge holding court, slicing his wisdom into morsels his crowd and jury could gobble up.

'There are so many possibilities here, Shield-chief Sald. None of them paint you in a good light. You could have been working with her, and killed her to cover a mistake. That is treason. You could have found her out yourselves, and acted outside my authority. That is grave disobedience. Or perhaps you murdered her for another reason, and blamed it on spies. That is murder. And, if somehow you are innocent of all these other crimes, at very least you allowed a fellow soldier to be murdered in the night through neglect, Chief. No doubt with booze to blame.'

Huff kicked a nearby bottle to illustrate his point. He let the clinking of its glass ring with the echoes of his words. The ring of soldiers held its tongue.

'Which is it to be?' Huff clasped his hands together.

'We...' The old soldier's face fell. His eyes tumbled back to the corpse. 'Neglect,' he said, prouder than Huff would have expected. 'But don't blame these, or any other Dreg. Blame me.'

Huff winced. 'You should have gone with disobedience. Then I might have pardoned you on the fact I have one less spy to worry about. Shame.'

'Sir...' Collaver stepped forwards, but Huff ignored him.

'Fetch the hobbles. He trails for the rest of the week. Then cast him loose.' Huff raised his voice to let it reach every sprawl of the crowd. 'This man didn't look after his own. Something I expect all of you to do, both on the battlefield and around the campfires. This spy,' he paused to point at the corpse, 'got what was coming to her. Do you understand me?'

They understood perfectly. He could see it in the firmness of their lips, the sharp glisten in their eyes. The example had been made. The bar had been set.

'Now let's move out! Break down the camp!'

Huff dragged Glum away as Collaver set his hands upon Sald. The old soldier submitted without a sound or shrug. He took his punishment like a wronged man. A few soldiers put their hands on his shoulder before the sergeant batted them away. Cater and the woman, Nerenna, stayed by the body.

Frayne weaved her way through the dispersing ranks, hunting him down. She even had the audacity to take Huff by the arm. She spoke low, but hoarsely, as if last night's shouting had worn her throat.

'Are you out of your mind? You've sparked a witch-hunt, General. Do you realise that? Anybody acting the least bit suspicious will be torn limb from limb before Collaver here can even clear his throat.'

Huff laughed her off. 'Maybe that's what this army needs. It'll do them some good. Walking on tiptoes, competing to be the finest Truehard there is.'

Frayne stopped him mid-stride, yanking him around. Her face was thunderous. 'Perhaps one would think now is a time for camaraderie and cohesion, rather than a chance to let doubt and suspicion run amok. By taking it out on your soldiers instead of the Fading you are endangering the plan, Dartridge.'

Huff stood tall and proud even under Frayne's wilting gaze, framed by her firebrand hair. 'I received enough "advice" from you yesterday evening, Baroness. I do not expect another day of it. Some of us have an army to run.'

Frayne shook her head. 'You can't make a single right decision, can you?'

Huff's reply was interrupted by the waddling arrival of Councillor Dast. He threw a mock salute over his glass eye as he joined them.

'Good show, young sir. Made quite the example of the soldiers. Tough justice will win them over.'

Huff gave a fake smile. 'Yes. Thank you, Councillor. Here's hoping. Now if you'll both excuse me…'

Frayne wasn't giving up. 'The King's Council will have to hear of this, General.'

'Absolutely!' exclaimed Dast. 'The discovery of spies in our midst? Grave news all around.'

'Quite!' said Huff, angling his head at Frayne. 'Surely a sign that we must proceed with all haste, wouldn't you agree, Baroness? That's what you want, is it not? To follow the plan?'

Frayne gave them both an empty smile. 'I'm needed in the capital. I will meet you in Saffin within a week. If your men haven't stabbed each other to death by then, that is.'

She snatched at the collars of her fur coat and strode away. Huff found himself puffing up. He was developing a keen taste for victory.

'A torig, Councillor?' Huff suggested with a wink. 'We can discuss our next steps. And your report to the Council.'

Dast looked as if he had just found a swollen coinpurse in the mud. He smacked his gums. 'Sun's over the spearhead. Why not?'

Huff pointed him in the direction of his tent. 'Make yourself at home, Councillor. I have one more… thing to deal with before I join you. Pour me a glass.'

He let the Councillor hurry away up the path and peeled away in the opposite direction. He was headed for the river.

The difference in the mood of the camp was palpable, and pleasurable at that. It was as if the springs had been wound a little tighter in the clockwork. The pace was a quick march, not an amble. Soldiers scuttled to pack up their meagre abodes. Campfires were stamped on as if they were enemy faces.

Huff wound his way down the slope and found the stables in a similar state. The riders were queuing for their firns, spreading across the field like questing roots.

The general spied the hunk of stone before it noticed him. It sat hunched over, half-turned away, gaze lost in the reeds. Huff shook his head, wondering what, if anything, rattled around in that stone dome of his. He pasted on his warmest smile; the one he liked to use at boring formal dinners.

'Good morning, Task. I trust you are rested?'

The golem took his time standing up, moving as if great ropes held him by the shoulders. Huff saw that his chain was broken, but decided not to ask why.

Task gave no answer, so Huff tried again. 'Are you willing to fight today? There is a battalion west of here that could bite at our tail. One thousand men.'

He could tell his tone was foxing the great lump. He pushed a fraction harder. 'Of course, if you would rather stay with the main army, then I can see to that instead.'

'I can fight,' said Task.

'Good. You will be first up the hill, with the riders.'

'Riders?'

'That's what I said.' Huff's smile was starting to hurt. 'Is that not agreeable?'

Task shrugged. 'What the Master wants, the Master gets.'

'Hear, hear!' said Huff, retracing his steps. 'One hour, Task. And my thanks.'

The general left the golem with a quizzical frown on his face, and found a little swagger in his gait as he headed back to his tent, and the glass of torig.

The sun was indeed over the spearhead.

15

'Taste no evil, lest it turn you,
witches' curse and trouble maul you.
Wizards' tricks and 'Stroyer charm,
magic beareth nought but harm.'

DESTRIX POEM OF UNKNOWN ORIGIN

50TH FADING, 3782 - SAFFERON FORTRESS
'Alabast!' said the fawl, speaking with human lips.

'Excuse me?'

'Get up!' Strands of grass were stuck to the beast's furry cheeks, moist with saliva.

Alabast looked around at the tumbling fields. His home. His childhood, spread about him like an endless carpet.

'But I'm already up…' His mouth stumbled over the words. His lips were numb, arms sluggish.

'ALABAST!'

Executor Westin's shout sliced through the dream like a sword through a curtain, snapping Alabast back to consciousness. He sprang up from his bed, scattering straw pillows, and blinked the sleep from his eyes.

Westin stood at the door, with his arms crossed. He seemed to have been waiting a while.

'Dawn?'

'Way off.'

'Two bells since?'

'Three. That makes two hours since you were expected in the yard, and one hour since Lash wanted you at his door.'

Alabast nodded, dragging his palm over his face. 'Three.'

THE HEART OF STONE

Westin poked his boot into the knight's discarded breeches and coat, hoping for a sloshing pocketsip or a forgotten bottle. 'Drinking, were we?'

For once, Alabast could slide out of his bed without a hangover. They had mocked him at the campfire, but he'd still taken their tants by the handful. Westin's boot only drew the jingling of coins; there was no chime of glass or rattle of a flask.

Alabast stretched, letting his hand dangle in the executor's face. Westin batted him away.

'Happy?' asked the knight.

'Impressed, actually. What's this, the first night sober?'

Alabast flexed in his mirror, feeling his sleepy tendons pop. 'Fourth, thank you very much. And by the Architect, I think it suits me.'

'Lord Lash will fall out of his chair in amazement.'

Alabast shrugged on a shirt. 'Maybe I've taken a shine to some of you Fading. Maybe I've found the old me. Or maybe Hartlund glugg just tastes likes piss, and I've had my fill of it.'

Westin rolled his eyes and made for the doorway.

'If only the Table knew they'd bought a prize actor as well as a prize drunk.'

'Four days!' Alabast snapped before the door slammed.

'Four minutes!' came the muffled reply. 'Before Lash comes down here himself, and flays you with his bare hands.'

Fine. It had been three days sober. Maybe two, but that was still one more day than his annual average. It was a start, he told himself as he set to his laces. Lash was lucky Alabast was still here at all.

His half-hearted escape attempt hadn't gone well, to say the least. The Fading engineers had plugged every hole in the rotting castle with either bricks or bodies. The guards hadn't fallen for his charms, nor for his insistence on checking the outer walls for signs of structural stability. In the end he'd tried climbing over a parapet where the torches had blown out. Rope, however, is a key ingredient for most climbing activities; especially when climbing down. Alabast had given up after one slip.

The knight took his time getting dressed. He aimed for casual: shirt untied down to the narrow of his chest, sleeves rolled and sword slung behind him, spreading its weight.

Thanks to the blade, Alabast had found his sword-grip once more. It had reminded him with every swing and parry. Its lessons were heavy and harsh, but in just a short while, he had come to feel like a swordsman again.

He had the Fading to thank for that. He had never seen soldiers so tired of war yet so passionate to see it done. It had kindled something in

175

him; a part he'd thought long-withered. Respect? Camaraderie? A distraction from the thought of the golem? Whatever it was, he had applied himself to the soldiers' training. And the good thing about training yards was that they frowned on alcohol. Alabast had always found it easier to resist temptation when there was nothing tempting in sight.

He stepped outside. Westin greeted him with a look of disgust, as if he'd just sniffed the arse of a passing soldier. Alabast patted him on the shoulder, and flashed his teeth.

'Calm down, old chap, as you Lundish say. I'll be worth every coin, in the end.'

Westin pushed him off and stormed down the corridor. 'You'll forgive me if I wait to see for myself.'

Alabast chuckled. He followed his minder through the warren of brick and slime. The castle crumbled a little more every day, and yet Lash clung to it like a mother to a dying child; as if he had some attachment to this skeleton of stone. Maybe Alabast would pull at that thread before he left.

Westin led him up a spiral of stairs. He felt the cold breeze on his nape, and thought of the dry heat of the Kopen Plains; how it chapped the lips but persisted through the night, keeping the cold starlight at bay. It never blew in any direction but east, always towards the distant vortex of the God's Rent.

The knight distracted himself with talk. 'I take it the lord isn't best pleased?'

'I think "livid" would be the word I'd use.'

'No change there, then.'

The look Westin gave him was positively acidic. Alabast wondered what had happened to dissolve the cheery, underling charm. Perhaps it was down to the persistent chatter of conceded land and Truehard victories. Trust his luck to be bought by the losing side.

At last they came to Lash's door. Westin strode right in, bowing stiffly. He waved Alabast forward with a grandiose gesture. The knight had to hold in his laugh.

'Lord Lash, I'm sorry. As Westin will confirm, there was no alcohol involved. Just a pure case of over-sleeping.' Alabast offered Lash a lavish bow; the kind he normally reserved for rich widows.

Lash was sitting still; elbow on the desk, chin propped on his fist. He looked over his knuckles and eyed the knight as one might regard a steaming turd on a pillow.

'Sit.'

Alabast sat, with no argument or witticism. *Better to grin and bear it.*

'Time is a precious thing,' said Lash, still unmoving. 'More precious then gems or silfrin, a crown or a thrown. More precious even than the embrace of a loved one. And we are running out it, Alabast.'

'I see.' The knight could guess where this was going.

Lash nodded. 'The Truehards are marching across the Darens as we speak. They should reach the Greenhammer any day now.'

Alabast squinted at a patchwork map hanging on the wall, trying to make sense of the scratches and dots the Lundish called writing. The only thing that resembled a hammer was a small lake, halfway up the country.

'I understand,' said Alabast, rising to his feet and patting his sword.

'You do?'

'Completely, my Lord. I'll get out in the yard immediately, get back to training these soldiers of ours.' He flashed a dutiful smile.

It sounded as if Lash was chuckling behind his fist. 'Westin, remind me. What was it we hired Knight Alabast here for? Was it to train our army?'

Westin smirked. 'Hardly, my Lord. I believe the correct term the Table used was "exterminator".'

Alabast felt the chill run through him again; a shiver that emerged whenever the golem came to mind.

As well as a swordsman, he was a betting man. Apart from his very first, he had never taken a job he knew he couldn't finish. That was his trick. But now here he was: flesh and steel pitted against stone and magic, and the odds had an ugly look to them. It was a fact made painfully clear only the night before, by a disgruntled and rather hammered corporal.

Lash templed his fingers. 'It's about time you earned your keep, Knight. You're marching out tonight. We'll meet the Truehards south of the Greenhammer, half a league outside Burrage.'

Alabast eyed the map again, still clueless. 'When?'

'Two days, if we're fortunate.' said Westin.

Alabast nodded. *Two days.* Thoughts of ropes and walls quickly resurfaced. 'Well then, I'd better get myself ready.'

'That you'd better,' said Lash. 'We have a visitor arriving shortly, with news of the golem. We'll call for you when she arrives.'

The Knight bowed. He had no droll remarks to make; no cheeky grins to flash. He glanced at Westin's smug face as he left.

By the Architect, was he thirsty.

The seasons died quickly in Hartlund, each one trampled by the next. The breeze had now turned warm, and it slapped Alabast in the face as he walked out into one of the inner courtyards, making the cold prickle in his spine all the more noticeable.

'Should have just legged it,' he said to himself. 'Instead of sticking around and showing off.'

He had two immediate goals. The first was simple: get something he could pour down his hatch. The second was to find a rope, an unguarded gate, an overlooked crack in the walls. Anything that promised an unobserved exit.

Alabast found a stairwell long worn by countless feet. He jogged to its peak, where the wall flattened into a crenellated walkway. He patted the humongous stones as he ambled past; each was the width of his reach and as high as his shoulders. Through their gaps he could see the concentric walls of the old fortress, tumbling down the rift in the mountainside like a rumpled carpet. Beyond, the rocky tors and grasslands stretched out into the haze of a distant bank of rain.

He turned to stare at the central keep. Towers sprouted from each corner and side. About half had survived the test of time. The others leaned in unsettling directions, or were peppered by holes.

The knight poked his head through the battlements and examined the height of the innermost wall. There must have been thirty feet between the ledge and the bustling courtyard below.

Alabast cursed under his breath and wound his way down to the lowest level where the thick outer walls were topped with jagged crenellations; half-broken, half-designed. The walls were shored up by earthen moulds, built by some predecessor of Lash's. But they lay too low, and brought him no closer to escape. Guards wandered back and forth at the battlements. He counted at least a dozen before he gave up.

He followed the curve of the walls under arches and through gates until he reached the rockface. A group of guards huddled around the base of a small watchtower, sharing a pipe. Alabast gave them a friendly smile and made a show of tying his bootlace before plodding on.

An hour brought him no luck; only sore feet and boredom. He found himself loitering by a smith's wheel, mesmerised by the whine of steel on stone and the flashing sparks. A queue of soldiers weaved about the yard, chattering. Most seemed excited. A handful wore serious faces, staring into the same space as Alabast.

The knight flinched at the sound of bottles clinking behind him. It was a sound his ears were constantly tuned to. A cart trundled past, laden with dark sacks. With each slip of its wheel, the sacks played their music.

He peeled himself from his leaning and followed the cart and its red-faced owner. The closer he got, the more he recognised him. Alabast put on a smile, and clapped the man on his shoulder.

'Yemmer! Fancy a hand, old chap?'

The man was momentarily startled. His eyes narrowed quickly. 'Knight Alabast,' he said, in a gruff tone. 'Back to crow some more about your winning hand?'

Alabast laughed that off. 'Old news! Past history, my friend. You were close, though. If you'd had a Zealot of Ember, you would have trounced me.'

'So you keep sayin'. As if I could magic one into my hands just like you do.'

'Let's just say I'm a lucky man.' Alabast stretched his cheeks a little wider as he picked up one of the cart's reins and began to pull. It was heavier than the man made it look.

'Where you headed, friend?'

'First Courtyard. To the wagons. Why?'

'Just trying to do my part. We're moving out, I hear.'

'Aye. You finally get your chance at the golem.'

'Looking forward to it! Say, are these bottles full or empty?'

Yemmer snorted. 'Why'd you ask? Run out of pocketsips to pinch?'

'Ha! You know me better than that. It's just bloody heavy, and if they're full... well, we could lighten the load a little.'

The soldier released his reins and put his hands to his hips. 'Nickin' glugg from the stores gets you a week in the dark. You seriously suggestin —'

Alabast held up his palms. 'No, no. It was a joke, old friend. No offence intended. Come on, let's get this done.'

They worked in silence for a time, manoeuvring the cart into a shortcut between a wall and an old armoury.

'Thinking about it,' said Alabast. 'Let's say you did get a week in the dark. It'd save you trotting out there and fighting the Truehards, wouldn't it? Good excuse, too. You'd get some peace and quiet while we're off losing limbs and dying and whatnot, eh?' He laughed, and nudged the man in the ribs.

This time Yemmer stopped, taut against the cart's reins. He ran his tongue about the inside of his lower lip. Alabast knew to wait. An idea was like an uppity door-guard. It should be coerced, not shoved.

'How much would you reckon a man'd have to take?' asked Yemmer.

'Couple of bottles at least. I could help with a few, make you look more of a thief. You'd get to sip a bit, of course.'

Yemmer straightened and Alabast heard his spine click. 'You tell anyone...'

'I'm no blabber. I know how to keep a secret.' It was probably the most truthful thing he had said all morning.

Yemmer sighed as he reached for the nearest sack. He wiggled out a bottle of glugg, then another, until they both held two each. Alabast slipped one into a pocket and held the other up to Yemmer. Together, they broke the wax seals from the bottles and knocked them back.

Yemmer shook his head as he reached for another bottle. 'You've got a silfrin tongue, Knight o' Dawn. Here's hopin' that golem has the ears for it, if you can't beat him with your sword.'

Alabast's smile held until the man had tugged his cart into the courtyard, a bottle down each leg of his breeches.

The knight wound his way back to the higher levels of the fortress. He walked slowly, savouring the tingle of glugg in his stomach and its taste on his breath. He felt it more fiercely, after only two days apart. It was no torig or gutwine, but it did the job. Before long, he was shrugging aside his fears, their chill drenched in spiced alcohol.

He spotted a woman in the corner of his eye, and made a show of forgetting something. He retraced his steps, conscious of the bottle weighing down his pocket.

She was drinking in the weak sunlight that trickled through the gaps in the hurrying clouds. She stood with her back to the wall; eyes closed, flame-hair flicking in the breeze. Her face was pale in the light, sharp in its angles. Her mottled, grey-black coat covered her from neck to ankle.

Alabast traced the edge of the wall, following a path that would lead him past her in a casual fashion. He stared straight ahead as if he hadn't noticed her. At the right time, he would stop, turn and improve her day no end. He shoved his shoulders back, propped up his chin, and strode like a king.

'The infamous dragon-slayer,' said the woman, before he was even level with her. She kept her eyes closed.

Alabast was so fixed on his tactics, he stumbled when she spoke. 'Apparently, my reputation precedes me,' he said in a low voice, standing before her.

'Not always a good thing, I find. Especially with a reputation as grimy as yours.'

The knight watched her slowly open her eyes, like a sword creeping from its scabbard. They certainly pierced like a blade. Alabast stood straighter and flashed his most winning smile.

'Grimy, you say? I find that everything that was once glorious grows grimy over time. You just have to scrape away a little to see it.'

The woman laughed, clear and loud. 'I imagine all the females of Kopen and Gurnigen swoon when they hear that.'

Alabast shook his head. 'Perhaps once. Less so, these days.'

The woman crossed her arms. Alabast had met her kind before; the sort of who liked to make a man work for her attention. *They were usually inordinately rich.*

'I see,' she said, with a sly curl to her lip. 'The proud warrior fallen on hard times.'

The knight nodded, feigning humility. 'Hard times, indeed. But you know what they say?'

'No. What do they say?'

'That hard times require hard work. That's why I'm here: to help the Last Fading with this war. It's the least I can do for such brave men and women.'

The woman nodded, digesting his words. That lip-curl spread as she thought. Her eyes had yet to leave his own.

'Strange. Such integrity for a man who's drank and deffed his way across the Realm. Lord Lash must be thrilled to have you here.'

Alabast had been skewered. He stood with his smile crumbling, racking his brains for what to say.

'He can barely contain his excitement.'

The woman laughed again, left her wall and walked past him on a tour of the courtyard. He was quickly at her side.

'I haven't seen you here before.'

'I've been busy.'

'Doing what, might I ask? You don't look like a soldier.'

'What do I look like?'

'Somebody important. Vital, even.'

'How nice of you. So the gutwine hasn't addled your mind after all.'

'Some would say "improved".'

'Would they, now?'

'You're a captain's wife, then. Or a general's mistress.'

'Neither.'

'Don't tell me you're related to Lash?'

'And what if I was?'

'Then I'd congratulate you on your fine lineage, and for being spared his moody features.'

'Fortunately for me, I'm not. Now, don't you have some washer-maids to follow around a courtyard?'

'They're all busy today.'

'Lucky me, then.'

'What's your name?'

The woman stopped in her tracks and fixed him with another of her sharp stares. 'And what would you do with it if I told you?'

Alabast stepped closer. He could feel her icy exterior melting. He threw her another grin. 'Shout it from the battlements. Write it into a ballad. Scratch it in the space over my heart.'

She tapped her chin. 'I do find scars so very romantic.'

'In that case, you'll find none more romantic than me.'

She sighed. 'Well, it seems I'm stuck with you. Whatever will we do?'

Alabast winked, stepping closer. 'How about we run away? Slip out while the army marches. Sail a ship to Lezembor and live like Kaid and Rala in paradise.'

'If I remember that poem correctly, Rala kills Kaid for breaking her heart.'

'Let's stick to the first eight verses, then.'

It was her turn to step closer.

She matched him for height. Her hair billowed around them in the breeze.

'Do you really want to run away? Is that why you walked the walls today, poking and prodding?' There was a hint of a smile on her painted lips. 'You look like a man who knows how to get what he wants. I'd wager that if you really wanted to escape, you would have found a way already.'

Alabast's mouth flapped, but no sound came forth.

'Lady Auger!'

He had never been happier to see Executor Westin. The man stood in a distant doorway, beckoning to the woman.

'You too, Alabast!' Westin hollered.

'How very interesting!' She brushed past him. 'I think we're being called in. If I were you, I'd lose that bottle in your breeches.'

Lady Auger's eyes had roamed every inch of his face; examining rather than admiring. Alabast had never been undressed like that by a woman in all his life, and he'd had more opportunities than most.

Once he'd managed to start breathing again, he turned and followed, trying not to feel like a dutiful lapdog.

The corridor was cooler than the courtyard; frigid, almost. And after the burst of sunlight, dim and unwelcoming. Alabast let Westin and Auger lead the way. It was partly to watch her move, and partly to let him deposit the glugg by the boots of a bored-looking guard. His face immediately brightened on following Alabast's wink down to his gift. Armour clanked as the man stood a little straighter.

'You can always buy friends with beer,' he said under his breath. Auger still flashed him a curious look over her shoulder. Alabast returned a wink.

He was bewildered—and bewitched—by her mystique. He hadn't the faintest idea who she was to the Fading, and how much trouble he had just put himself in. She could have been their queen for all he knew.

The executor guided them away from the stairs. 'This way.'

'Why not the tower this time?' asked Auger.

Westin sounded grave. 'Structurally unsound, say the engineers, for now at least.'

Alabast bit his lip.

'We'll be in Lash's quarters.'

He brought them to a door made of iron, like a Kopen fire-bunker. It moaned as Westin dragged it open.

'First room on the left.'

Alabast and Auger did as they were told, finding a dining room with a high ceiling. A dark wooden table filled the floor, with four chairs either side. The rest of the room was Lash's usual brand of stark and formal, cut and drafted with military precision. Alabast had never trusted a man who didn't take pride in his home, even if it was a stinking old castle.

'Welcome,' said Lash, gliding into the room. He sat himself at the head of the table, and bade them all to follow.

Alabast sat alone on his left, while Auger and Westin settled on his right, each with their fingers entwined on the tabletop. The knight adopted his usual casual lean. Some might have called it a slouch.

'Lady Auger,' said Lash. 'Glad you could make it at last.'

The woman bowed her head. 'It's been hard to get away.'

Lash grunted in agreement. 'I can understand.'

'Excuse me?' Alabast raised a hand. 'As I've been invited to this secret meeting, I assume you require some of my expertise. If I'm to help, I will need to know what it is you two are blabbering on about. As of right now, I haven't a clue.'

Auger had a smile on her. She looked to Lash. 'Why don't you put it in your own words, my Lord?'

Lash leaned back in his chair. 'Lady Auger here is the visitor I mentioned. She is not only a proud benefactor of the Last Fading's cause, but for the past few years she has been working as a spy in the Truehard camp and the King's Council. She has been instrumental in breaking down their armies, their territories, their resolve. Now that Huff is in charge and a golem is on the field, she proves invaluable. And long may that continue, Lady Auger! Or should I say, Baroness Frayne?'

She rolled her eyes. 'Ugh! That name. So unrefined. And your hopes are not in vain, Lash. I have good news for you, at last.'

Alabast had to admit he was impressed. In fact, he was having trouble fully closing his mouth. 'So you've seen the golem up close?'

Auger looked smug. 'I've spoken to it on a number of occasions.'

All three men inched forwards, chairs creaking. Alabast waved his hand. 'Please, don't keep us waiting.'

'Firstly, my apologies, Lord Lash. I realise the news of the golem must have come as a shock to you. I admit it was arranged without my involvement. An agreement between the Grand-Captain and the Mission.'

Lash snorted. 'The deffing Mission. Meddling bastards.'

'Don't they suspect you?' said Westin.

Auger smiled. 'Not in the slightest, Executor. Half the Council were unaware. However, in retaliation, I've been attempting to drive a wedge between the golem, or Task as he calls himself, and General Dartridge. The proud brat thinks the beast is a machine that he can just point at and say "go". But Task is… strange, for lack of a better term. More human than Huff knows. Emotional. Proud. Remorseful, even. Something went wrong in his past that still haunts him, holds him back. I can see it like a splinter in him. Huff berates him for it and there's hatred growing fast between them. That doesn't aid us, however, as they are still bound by magic. The golem has laws.

'As for the army's position, most of the soldiers seem to favour him. The peasant ranks love him, mainly because he wins them battles and saves their filthy necks. Though some do fear him. Resent him, even. Mostly the noble-born.'

'And how do they favour the General?' asked Lash. 'Still detest him, do they?'

Auger didn't look so convinced. 'Huff is finally gaining their trust, and he'll have it too if he keeps winning battles. The Council seem happy with his wins, all except his father, who never will be.'

Alabast blew out a long sigh. 'I can't believe it's got a name.' Lash and Westin both glowered at him.

'He still presses forwards,' said the lord.

Auger nodded, looking disappointed. 'Faster and faster every day. Despite my warnings to take it slow and steady.'

The knight saw something in her face; something twitching in her eyes. It piqued his interest even more. 'Tell me more about the golem. Does he have any weaknesses?'

Lash levelled a finger. 'This is precisely why I wanted you here, Alabast. To learn from Auger how you can defeat this monster.'

'Not for your "expertise",' said Westin, pleased with himself.

'His tongue,' she said. 'From the letters his previous master wrote, it's the source of his power. The last piece of a golem, he said. If you break it or take it out, he'll collapse. Break into his pieces. No more golem.'

'Right,' said Alabast. 'And would you like me to brush his teeth while I'm removing his tongue?'

'You slew a dragon,' she said. 'How difficult could a nine-foot golem be?'

'Very, Lady Auger. Very. Let me remind you that it's made of stone, not flesh.'

She fixed him with an iron gaze. 'And may I remind you, Knight of Dawn. You asked for weaknesses. I told you one.'

'If that is what Alabast must do, then I'm sure he will try his best,' said Lash, like a judge delivering a sentence. 'We proceed with the plan while time is short.'

Alabast tried to distract himself. 'Why are you lot so concerned with how fast you beat the Truehards? Surely the longer you stave them off, the longer Lady Auger here has to work her magic, to see if she can break this golem.'

Westin glared at him. 'What, did none of the whorehouses or taverns in Gurnigen have newspapers, Alabast? No gossip to glean while drinking yourself into oblivion?'

'That's enough, Westin,' said Lash. The executor fell silent.

'Believe it or not, Lundish civil wars aren't usually the hot gossip of Gurnigen. Braad and Begrad only care about themselves.'

Lash was unimpressed. 'This isn't just about Lundish wars, Knight. This is about a war of the Realm.'

Alabast's chin found his palm once more. 'I'm afraid I don't follow.'

Lash and Westin looked too angry to answer, so Auger replied on their behalf.

'The Narwe Harmony is itching for a fight, Alabast. The God's Rent is starving them out of their homelands. The Accord won't loosen the port taxes, and trade is dwindling. The Harmony has not come together like this since the Diamond Wars. The Hasp, the Chanark and the Khandri have dispatched an ambassador to the Accord to hear from each country separately, to see where they stand. Personally, I think it's a farce, a spying mission, and when she arrives in Caverill, she will see how ripe Hartlund is for the taking, how weak and fractured this county has become. If we don't claim it back soon, we will be the first to see the orange flags of Khandri ships on our horizons. It'll give the Harmony the foothold they never had in the wars.'

Alabast looked between them. 'How soon?'

'She is currently delayed in the Duelling Dozen, last I heard. Four weeks maybe.'

Alabast rose and wandered around the room. There was another map on the far wall; this one framed and painted.

'Both you and this Huff,' he said. 'Racing towards each other like ships caught in the Rent.' He stared at the blotch that he guessed marked Safferon fortress.

Lash's cleared his throat. 'With our main army now receding, we have time enough to pitch two more battles before Huff reaches us. Two chances to destroy this golem.'

Alabast tutted. 'Zero pressure on me, of course.'

Nobody in the room seemed impressed, least of all Lash. 'I'm starting to wonder how you managed to even face a dragon, let alone kill it.'

Alabast's eyes flicked to Auger's. He found them twinkling with mirth. He flashed his teeth.

'I will face your stone demon, Lash, and I *will* kill it. Just like I killed that dragon. Even if it's just to prove you wrong, my Lord, I'll see it done. Now if you'll excuse me, I believe I have some packing to do. Have your lap-wark of an executor fetch me when it's time to march.' He made for the door.

He heard Auger chuckling behind him, and turned. She threw him a parting glance. 'Now that the Knight of Dawn is escaping… we should talk of other things.'

Alabast slammed the door on her voice. He didn't know whether it was the glugg or their doubt or the twinkle in Auger's eye, but there was a fire in his belly he hadn't felt in years.

He would show her, he swore to himself. *He would show them all.*

'A petulant one, don't you think?' Ellia smiled. *Oh, how she enjoyed playing Auger.* Frayne was far too sour.

Westin growled. 'And a drunk.'

'And a coward. But a damn-fine swordsman,' said Lash, making Westin twitch.

She was truly curious of the knight. He was set a fraction to the left of what she had expected. The stories were true enough, but there was a streak in the man she couldn't place, and it intrigued her.

'How does a coward kill a dragon, I wonder?'

Westin rolled his eyes. 'Maybe he used his razor-sharp wit.'

'Jealous, Executor?'

'Preposterous!'

'In any case,' Lash said, holding up a hand. 'He is currently the best hope in the Six Islands of defeating the golem.'

'Then I would be on the lookout further afield,' said Ellia. Huff would have exploded in that situation, but the good Lord Lash knew when to keep his cool. 'If Alabast is as good as his legend, we may have a chance. But I'm afraid I don't see it.' She crossed her arms. 'I would rather raise our measure of warrior.'

Lash raised a curious eyebrow. 'I know what that glint in your eye means. What are you hiding, Auger?'

Ellia flashed him a wink. 'Task may be the last Wind-Cut Golem in the Realm, but he isn't the *last* golem. On my previous visit to Caverill I managed to procure some of the Grand-Captain's research into golems. I came across rumours of another that was accounted as "whole and possibly functional". It has quite the history. It is made of bone. Not quite the standard of Task, but it could be just what you need.'

Lash looked at Westin with an accusatory glare. 'It's a shame this didn't come up before.'

Ellia chuckled. 'Oh, it's not Westin's failing. He would have needed access to the Royal Library and months of spare time. Besides, even these lesser golems are far too expensive for the Fading, even without frittering tants on Alabast.'

Westin leaned forward. She could see the question etched in his face already.

How much?

'I trade in favours, as well as coins, and in that respect I'm rather rich.' She paused to try on a proud look. 'I might be able to have the bone golem in a week. As a loan.'

Lash ran a hand around his chin. His eyes were empty, turned inwards. *Always thinking.* Ellia kept her smile up and waited it out.

'We give Alabast his chance. Then we'll see about this golem of yours, Auger.'

Ellia nodded. It was the best she could hope for. 'And I'm sure you shall. I'll travel ahead, make sure Huff is in the right mood. In the meantime, I suggest you have somebody keep an eye on the good knight during the march. Both cowards and drunks have a habit of wandering off, I hear.'

16

'There will always be war. So long as man has more or less than his neighbour, there will be war.'

HASP PROVERB

53RD FADING, 3782 - THE DARENS

The rain fell with all the fury of a personal vendetta, punishing the thousands who had dared to gather under its rumbling clouds.

Task felt every rivulet coursing down his frame, every raindrop crashing against his stones. He inhaled the sodden air and tasted its pressure; his exhale was a contented growl.

It was a good day for a fight, if there was such a thing.

He stood like a forgotten column in the squelching ranks of men. The riders had still not settled; they shifted their lines to get the better of the mud. It was useless. The fenlands became a mire after the feet of one army, never mind two.

Task peered at the dark smudge beyond the curtain of rain. He eyed the centre of the enemy ranks, judging where he would break them. The Fading had stopped just short of cannon range, spreading in a crescent shape to make themselves harder to hit.

And giving the golem more work to do.

Task snorted. Work was all he knew.

Quickly and calmly. Quickly and calmly. He muttered his new mantra, to the din of raindrops and thunderous clouds. It helped to distract him from the anxiety creeping through his stones. He had slipped in Purlegar; come close to falling over the precipice, and it had worried him deeply since. Six days, three skirmishes, and he had yet to stumble a second time.

'Make a hole, ingrates!'

Task turned to see four shining cannons being dragged through the lines. The things were immense, with mouths as wide as his chest. Their sleek sides were punctuated with rivets and supported by great struts of black steel. Their backsides dragged grooves into the mud where the wheels held no purchase.

Task moved to lend a hand to the fawls dragging the weapons. The poor beasts' eyes were rolling madly with effort. He reached over them and yanked the harness forward. Mud sprayed with each dig of his heel as he hauled the cannons to the shield-line.

'Very well done!' Huff's shout rose above the rain. Task released the cannons and stood hunched between the great chunks of metal.

The general came forward on a green-and-brown mottled firn. Glum and Manx had the honour of walking at his side. 'Lash believes he can out-think me, you see, golem. He thinks I'll stick to the tactic of keeping my cannons at the rear.' Huff tapped his helmet meaningfully and grinned.

The golem shrugged. He didn't care for this new, cheerful Huff. His tone felt greasier than the usual anger; it confused him.

'Ready yourselves!' Huff's command was echoed down the lines by the sergeants and shield-chiefs.

There came a thunder-roll of feet and clanking armour, of slamming shields and of clicking muskets.

Gun-crews rushed forwards, tending to their steel beasts. Hands flew over gears; levers were wrenched; embers stoked into life; firepowder poured from hollowed horns into black mouths, perfectly circular.

Cannonballs tethered by vicious barbed chains were brought forth and loaded. The golem watched, fascinated as always by the skinbags' knack to bend the world's gifts to their will. Fascinated, and yet ashamed in the same moment. All that knowledge, and they chose to spend it building war-machines, instead of forging peace. He was living proof of the humans' unquenchable lust for violence, after all.

Across the fenland, the Fading's drums had begun to pound. Screeching horns floated on the wind like the wails of watching ghosts. The Truehards answered with their own, almost drowning out the roar of rain.

Around him, the soldiers began to thump their shields with spears or armoured fists. They started slowly, building up and up. The rain rose with them, beating harder as though rallying against their resolve.

The golem dropped to a knee, feeling the cold mud seep between his stones. He closed his eyes and let the vibrations of the ground run through him. The mass of beating hearts, the nervous shiver of countless feet, the crashing of drums and shields... He felt them all, and through them he felt more than just stone.

He felt the rumble of the Fading charge before the sergeants could even fill their lungs.

'Ready yourselves!' the Truehards cried as one. Hands pressed to shields. Spears slid into notches. Muskets found gaps between helmets.

Task stayed still, keeping his eyes closed, waiting for the inevitable.

'FIRE!' somebody screeched.

The concussion of the cannon-fire ripped the air. The shockwaves hammered against Task's body. Fire and smoke billowed over him.

At his back, muskets rattled like fierce applause. Iron zipped past his ears. Task didn't care; he was morbidly enraptured by the chained cannonballs, spinning like dust-devils as they soared over the battlefield. He burst forwards to chase them, his mighty feet pounding the mud.

The golem watched as the weapons collided with the Fading ranks. Heads and limbs flew like splinters from an axehead. Gore and shattered metal filled the deep holes they cut through the lines. The screams alone were enough to stagger the Fading charge. The sight of the golem barrelling towards them brought the soldiers to a wrenching, skidding halt.

Task spread his arms wide.

He hit them like a landslide. Bodies were catapulted high into the air, others crushed underfoot. Spears were turned to matchwood. Shields folded in half. Those lucky enough to be swept along hacked madly at his chest and shoulders before falling to join their trampled comrades.

Task retreated to his cold and silent place, far away from the precipice, where he let his work become mechanical and distant. Where he could watch it from the hollow of his mind, instead of revelling in it.

Quickly and calmly. Quickly and calmly.

Within minutes the golem had carved a line of carnage through the Fading ranks. He turned back on them, pausing to take in the crash of steel as the two armies met.

As a few straggling ranks fanned out around him, Task gazed up at the clouds and let the rain wash some of the blood and gore from his arms.

'You can run, you know,' he growled at them. 'Many have before.'

They swapped glances. One man started to edge away, but was whacked back into line with a spear-butt. Tentatively, the stragglers began to close in. Task shrugged.

The golem tensed, feeling for the stone-chips scattered like a trail behind him, lying among the broken armour and twitching fingers. With a flick of his wrist, they came to him, clattering against the soldiers like miniature musket-fire.

Task was upon them before they could flinch. He clapped his hands around the nearest man's head, obliterating his skull. The fountain of blood alone was enough to stun the others.

He moved in a circle, crippling where he could, knocking senseless those that had the sense to stay still. Only a few advanced, and they met swift and brutal ends.

He felt the footsteps in the mud before he heard them: slow, measured and heavy with armour.

Task smirked. He knew that swagger well. It was the sound of confidence; of somebody who thought themselves better than most with a sword. Of somebody hunting glory.

The man emerged from the rain, coming to a rest a few long bounds from Task. He was young for a knight. Handsome, if not a little harsh on the eyes, with a face and jaw chiselled out of tanned marble. He wore no helmet; just a grimace at the rain. His dark hair was shaved at the sides; slicked back and tightly bound with twine. His armour was of plain polished steel; simple yet solid, not like the clockwork suits of the Khandri. He had a long sword in his hand, held low and steady. There was no tremble in its point, nor quiver in its dark grey blade. The knight was as composed as a statue.

The name hovered on Task's lips, but he held on to it.

'Impressive!' said the man, nodding to the groaning bodies at the golem's feet.

'Thank you. I have had a lot of practice.'

At first the man seemed taken aback by the golem's grating voice, but he recovered himself and started to chuckle. 'I suppose you have, old beast. I suppose you have.'

Task flexed his shoulders. 'And you, I imagine?'

The knight spun his sword in his grip. 'More than most.'

'And now you fancy yourself a golem-slayer as well as a dragon-slayer, Knight of Dawn? Do you have a taste for killing things that are the last of their kind?'

Alabast Flint bowed, keeping his head up. 'Once again, my reputation precedes me.',

Task shrugged. 'I've met many like you in my time, hero. Your kind like to talk more than you like to fight. How about we dismiss the introductions and begin?'

Alabast's face twisted for a brief moment; the first sign of worry Task had seen.

'Very well, golem. Very well.'

They circled each other. Task extended his claw-like fingers and hunkered down. The knight brought up his sword and aimed it at the centre of the golem's chest.

Each footstep told Task more about his new enemy. A lot could be revealed by the placing of a foot, or the turn of a hip: a dodgy knee perhaps, or an old injury refusing to heal.

Alabast had the footwork of a man who had spent too long on his backside in recent years.

He wasn't a fan of subtlety, either. The knight danced forward, landing a cut across Task's forearm. The golem batted the blade away with a grinding chuckle. Alabast danced out of reach. He was grinning, too; winking at something Task had missed.

He looked down and saw the deep gash in his right arm.

'A starsteel blade.'

'You're deffing right,' said the knight, suddenly buoyed.

Task laughed, deep and rumbling, until Alabast's grin had retreated. 'The smiths who made that blade? They made me.'

It had been some time since he had fought starsteel. It was the sharpest and strongest metal in the Realm, and, like the rain that pounded him, it tantalised him with a whiff of mortality.

Task reached out with a fist. Alabast ducked it deftly. The knight rushed in close, hacking a chunk from Task's neck before darting away again. The golem lashed out with a kick and almost tripped him, but Alabast folded into a roll and came up smiling.

Task strode at him, claws crooked. He moved like a windmill, whirling his hands in a lethal pattern. Alabast backed away, holding his sword as if the world had tilted, and he was clinging on for dear life.

Once, twice, three times the blade met Task's fingers. Sparks flew like muskets firing. Task touched the knight only once, raking a fresh mark across his breastplate before Alabast made a mad dive between the golem's legs.

The knight was smeared with mud when he got up. Task raised his claws for another attack, but something held him fast. Half his fingers had been shorn away, with jagged stumps left in their place. Task's found himself stuck between grin and grimace.

'The dragon had the same look on his face, before I cut his throat.'

'You'll get no such satisfaction from me,' said Task. He surged forwards, hands ready to grapple. Alabast knocked him away with vicious swings, always striking the same spot. By the time the golem realised what he was aiming for, it was already happening. He felt the snapping of stones as his wrist and hand parted ways.

There was a thud and a squelch as his stone met the mud. Alabast switched his attention to Task's face and neck, landing two hits before he ducked away.

The golem punched with his stump, but wherever he aimed, Alabast was always just out of reach. Task knew to bide his time; the problem with flesh is that it can falter and tire. Stone is far more stubborn.

The mistake came quicker than expected. Alabast's foot caught on a tuft of grass, slowing him just enough for the golem's elbow to connect with his unprotected head.

Alabast went down, sprawling in the muck. The golem stood over him as he tried to scramble to his feet. He reached down to grab the knight by the neck, but before he could lay a hand upon him, the sword flashed, and Task felt the blade slice across his face, from eyebrow to lip. The starsteel bit deep, almost to his teeth, and he recoiled.

As Alabast lurched to his feet, the golem stood with his shoulders hunched, heaving with breath. His stones were hot. Raindrops hissed as they met his skin, turning to steam. Task hadn't fought so hard in decades.

Alabast wiped the blood from his forehead. He stood ready, also breathing hard, but in better shape. Task took a great leap and lashed out with his stump, catching the knight square in the chest and sending him spinning onto his face, several feet away.

Alabast dragged up his head, spitting out mud.

'I wonder if the dragon hit you that hard?' said Task.

'Much harder,' said the knight, wheezing.

Alabast looked at Task over his shoulder, his face now a dark mask of blood and grime. The golem stood tall, stretching out his battered extremities, clenching his remaining fingers. The shards on the ground began to shiver and Alabast watched in horror as the pieces snapped back into place, making Task whole again.

'Had enough, Knight of Dawn?'

He flexed his hand, noting the new scars across his puckered stone and blue veins. Through the grooves of his fingers, he saw the knight crawling away on hands and knees.

The golem was about to give chase when he felt a rumble through the ground. He turned to find swarms of Fading turning tail and running. They gave Task a wide berth as they scarpered.

Task turned back to Alabast. The knight had found his feet and was now standing a good distance away, half-hidden by rain.

The golem raised his hands in question, but the knight looked finished.

'Until next time!' he shouted, before turning his back and melting into the fleeing soldiers.

'Coward,' said the golem, but in truth he was secretly impressed. That had been a fine first dance. He looked forward to a second.

A shout punctuated the clatter and squelch of running feet.

'They're on the run, golem! Get them!'

It was Nerenna, painted in gore, waving her spear in the air. Some of the Dregs huddled around her. Cater, for one. No Sald.

'Let them run, I say,' replied the golem, as she speared a straggler who had tripped on a corpse.

'Why?' she demanded. There was a fire in her Task hadn't seen before.

'Because if they run now, they'll run again some other day. When it matters. An army made of cowards is a useful thing.' Task had seen the largest fortresses felled by the weakest hearts, time and time again.

Nerenna chewed the logic for a moment. She spat on the body she'd skewered. 'Fading scum! I hope you're right, golem.'

'Where's Sald?'

Nerenna shook her head, and for a moment Task felt cold.

'Nothing like that, Task. He's the lucky one today. Sort of.'

'What do you mean?'

'You haven't heard?'

The golem shook his head.

'Huff hobbled him. He spent the last few days trailing behind the army in fetters, tryin' to keep up.'

All thoughts of heroes and mortality had vanished. 'Why?'

'Took the blame for a murder, that's why. Like a bloody champion.' Nerenna choked something back as she tugged her spear free. 'Joley. She's dead. Huff called her a Fading spy. Blamed Sald for not knowing anything 'bout it.'

Task didn't know what to say. He stared back at the Truehard lines, emerging from the rain with bloody grins.

'Nobody gets shat on harder than Dregs, Task,' said Cater. He looked dreadful. There was a deep cut above his brow, and he was limping. 'It's a simple fact.'

Task thumbed rainwater from his face, feeling his new scar. He scowled. Huff had not changed; the man was still as vindictive as ever.

The golem started to march, leaving Nerenna and Cater clueless. He ground his teeth as he stepped over body after body. When he found one of the chained-ball weapons, he scooped it from the mud and snapped it in two.

Lesky was in a bad mood.

'Spit on him,' she hissed for the tenth time since marching out of the stables. She tugged on Shiver's lead, making him yelp.

'Sorry,' she said, before coming to a stop and blowing an oversize sigh.

The problem with Ganner was that he was Ganner. No escaping it. The man was a deffer through and through; a mean, rude, short-tempered, evil... Her master's words still rang in her ears.

Stupid girl! Useless girl! Idiot girl!

She knuckled her eyes with her fists. Mam had taught her how hollow the words of bullies were, and that's all Ganner was: a bully. She raised her chin and snorted at the world.

'Come on, Shiver,' she tutted, letting the little wark scamper on.

Lesky wandered along the winding paths between the tents. She weaved through the campfires, dodging cantankerous soldiers, still busy cooking after their long day of war. At least it had been a victory. She had spent two years dodging cuffing hands and bearing insults while the soldiers had been losing. A winning streak does wonders for an army's mood.

Shiver was beginning to tire by the time she had curved back to the smiths' and sharpeners' tents, near where the stables had been set up. Latrines were still being dug here and there. Queues had formed behind the diggers. Armoured riders hopped up and down, clutching their codpieces. Lesky would have just relieved herself in the long grass at the edge of the camp. *Trust the riders to be so prissy.*

She slowed her pace, finding distraction in the bustle. Bodies were carried past on stretchers. The walking wounded sat slumped by the edges of the paths, bandages tight and bloody about their heads. Some gazed at their new stumps, bottles of gutwine hovering beneath white lips. Others lay sprawled half-in, half-out of their tents. They might have been dead for all she knew. If it hadn't been for the snoring, she would have kicked a few boots to make sure.

A few of the luckier fighters were breaking out the bottles and pluckers: stringed instruments made of bowls and firn hair. Their stuttering tunes rose up above the chaos, joined by wailing voices. She mashed a palm against her itchy nose and tutted.

The smell of burning meat tickled her stomach. The pangs took command of her legs, guiding her off the path and towards a wispy column of smoke which rose above one of the larger stables. Scooping Shiver into her arms, Lesky edged around the small crowd of stable-boys, workers and masters.

A barrel was burning at their centre. A rack for turning meats sat over it. Two skinny karabins had been stretched across the flames on spits. Lesky watched them sizzle as she tried to keep from drowning in her own saliva.

'Look who it is,' said a woman. 'Ganner's girl.'

'I have a name, you know.'

A young lad, almost twice her height, snorted. 'Idiot? Deffer? Cur? Any of those that Ganner calls yer?'

Lesky scrunched up her face.

The woman poked blackened tongs at the young lad, giving him a sour look. 'Calm it, Lesk, we're just pullin' at you. We heard the row.'

'Bet that master of yours drank all through the battle, as usual,' said a voice.

'Man loves the glugg a bit too much.'

Lesky nodded. 'Makes him mean.'

There was a round of hums and grunts.

The girl watched avidly as the woman poked the karabins with her tongs, testing their wings and spindly legs. She caught the girl's eyes through the fire. Lesky clenched her teeth as she held her gaze, thinking nothing but hungry thoughts. Perhaps it was the whiteness of her pressed lips, or the loud pop of hot fat that accompanied the moment, but oddly, it worked. The woman gestured towards the spit.

'He feedin' you enough, Lesk? Getting your slop?'

Lesky shook her head. It was only a slight lie. Ganner was a greedy bastard, but she often got her two bowls a day. It didn't stop her stomach rumbling at night, though.

The woman nodded, feeling the eyes of the group on her. Karabins were delicious little things. Harder to catch than a ghost. Lesky knew that another mouth meant less for theirs, but her stomach didn't care.

With a crackling of skin and hissing of fat on flame, the woman pinched a thick scrap of meat from the hot bones and passed it to Lesky. She grabbed the meat in a flash, not caring about the heat. She gobbled it down, enjoying the grease spreading around her mouth. Her stomach grumbled for more.

The woman heard it. 'That's all we can spare, girly.'

'Thank you all the same.'

Lesky spared a few stringy morsels to the wark in her arms, shivering as usual. She barely got her fingers back whole.

For a time she watched them, eyeing the meat being traded between dirty plate and greasy finger. There was no talk, just the crackle of roasted skin and working of mouths.

Lesky's stomach muttered to itself. Her gaze shifted across the field to where her own stable stood in the darkness. A sole lantern stared back at her like a glowering eye.

You can't get anywhere when somebody's tied you down. Her mother's wisdom, echoing inside her again. She inwardly grumbled.

Ideas are sticky things. Once one sprouts, they cling to a mind with needle teeth; like a wark with a grudge. It was at that moment, watching the distant lantern flicker, Lesky felt herself bitten.

'I don't trust him.' Her voice was small and hesitant.

'Whassat?' said a youth around a leg-bone.

'Ganner, that is.'

'What you gettin' at, girly?'

Lesky started to shake her head and dismiss the question, but the grumbling of her stomach, the chomping, the sizzling fat dripping from the carcasses... They all conspired to convince her.

'He's shifty, if you ask me,' she said. Louder. Head up.

'Shifty?'

'It isn't just the glugg he spends his time on. He takes long walks once the firns are fed. Don't come back until late, either.' She saw the curious looks creep across the circle. They emboldened her. 'Heard him whispering to somebody a few nights ago. Outside the stable. All hushed, like.'

'Whisperin' to who?' said the woman. 'Did you see?'

Other voices were less convinced.

'Man's probably just drunk, talking to himself while he takes a piss.'

'He heads up to the north side a lot, plays judge with the Caverill crew.'

Lesky shrugged. She could see it in the crinkles of their brows; their own inklings beginning to bite. She wanted them to wonder, and wonder they did.

'Didn't know he was a city man?'

'Nah. Burdge, I think?'

'No. Torn-ways, he told me. That would make sense.'

Lesky shook her head. 'Surset, he's always said to me.'

'Man don't know where he's from.'

The suggestion hovered on her tongue, but she pushed it back down. When nothing but chewing came and went, she tutted.

Slow beasts looking after slower beasts. That was all these stablers were.

'Better go back, keep an eye on him, I s'pose. Duties.'

She could feel them watching her leave. She affected a little tiredness in her walk, bowed her head. Mam would have swiped her ear for such play-acting. She wondered what Task would think had he been there, standing like a mountain over her shoulder. It wasn't like her to be so mean, and yet the idea of Ganner's comeuppance had been almost as delicious as the karabin grease. An uncertain smile crept onto her face, and stuck there.

Back at the stable, Ganner hadn't slunk off to find a game of judge. He was now sprawled across his makeshift bed, boots off, feet propped high and reeking, and a half-empty bottle of glugg propped against his heaving chest. His snores whistled through his grubby nose.

Lesky tied Shiver outside and tip-toed across the ragged cloth that formed their carpet. The straw underneath crackled. It always betrayed her, no matter how lightly she trod.

Ganner awoke with a snuffle. His head may have been foggy, but his ears were sharp enough. Lesky flung herself to her sack before he'd had a chance to blink away the haze.

'Thatchyou, girl?'

Lesky thought a snore might keep him at bay, but she knew he hated her pretending.

'Speak, whelp!'

'I'm here, Ganner.'

'Master! *Master* Ganner. 'Ow many times I have t'tell you?'

'Sorry, Master.'

'You're damn right!'

He made it to his feet, and took a handful of unsteady steps. There was a rattling as he reached for a lantern, flint and tinder.

It took an age of wincing for him to strike a light. Weak as it was, it revealed a grinning face, still full of anger. She curled into a ball, sack-cloth drawn up to her chin.

'I said I'm sorry, Master.'

'Where is that little cur of yours? That damn whinin' wark?'

'In the paddocks,' she said, keeping her gaze from the doorway. 'Sleeping.'

'Should roast him. Make a bloody meal out of it. That'll teach you for helpin' yourself to my slop!'

'You can't!'

Ganner came stumbling forward, glugg bottle raised high. Lesky hid under the covers, feeling his boot dig into her ribs. Between his grunts, she could hear Shiver whimpering to the darkness.

'Givin' me lip, girl? I'll teach you!'

Lesky squeezed her eyes shut and thought of the golem. She strained, trying to drag him to her with her mind; to save her somehow. But there were no pounding strides; only the creaking of her clenched teeth and the thumping of Ganner's fists.

As she held her breath, she thought of her lies by the barrel, and prayed they would blossom. She hoped for a passing soldier, a wandering sergeant.

A blow caught her on the side of her head, and escorted her into a darkness filled with countless clamouring voices. Out of their howling, one alone rose above. The voice had a face; its contours shaped only by flashes of light in the endless distance, like stars bursting.

Lesky heard its words as loud as gunfire.

And who might you be?

17

'Glimpses are an integral part of our Mission. Without them, who would keep the zealots in check? How would we glean our secrets? Or carry messages long distances? Just as the zealots are vital for the furthering of the Architect's mission, the glimpses are vital for protecting it. One hundred less tants per quarter cripples my training. If the Treyarch demands it, so be it. But I shan't be blamed for the nosebleeds and broken minds. That's on the Blade.'

FROM A NOTE TO CONSECRATOR JEBBISH FROM HANIGAN CANE

53RD FADING, 3782 - THE DARENS

'I said,' growled the golem, 'I'm staying here.' He dug his finger into the ground. It made a resounding squelch.

Sald didn't seem happy, but he was at least silent on the matter.

Task withdrew his finger and settled deeper into the mud. Despite his stubbornness, something gnawed at him, as if he were meant to be somewhere else. He stared up at the clouds sprawling across the sky. Stars glowed in the gaps between them.

'Huff will have to come and answer to me at some point.'

'This is my punishment,' said Sald. 'Like I said, he doesn't have to.'

Sald had told the story of Joley's death twice, and yet Task could find no blame for the man. It surely lay with the General instead. Huff's sweetness had been proven sour.

'You don't get punished if you haven't done anything wrong,' he said, louder than he should have. It was quiet outside the camp. His voice echoed across the fields.

'Yeah. I'm innocent, too!' snarked a man behind the golem, inciting the others to join in. Task and Sald were not alone. Half a dozen other skinbags shared the mud with them. Their feet were fettered too, still hitched to the wagon they had been stumbling behind all day.

'Me too!' another crowed.

'I wouldn't even know how to spy.'

'Tear these chains off, golem. Let's be on our way nor— south!'

'Yeah! We're clearly not wanted!'

'Quiet!' Task met Sald's withered look and shrugged. The shouts died to sullen mumbles and clinking of chains.

They sat in silence for a time, while the golem waited for the other mud-smeared soldiers to drift off, or grow bored with eavesdropping.

'How went the battle?' said Sald at last, after a fit of wretched coughing.

Task wiggled his head. 'The Last Fading were routed once their lines had been broken.'

'Good news.'

Task lowered his voice. 'I saw Nerenna out there. Shortly after the Knight of Dawn ran away.'

There came a splutter from beside them. 'The Knight of Dawn? Be serious!'

'Trust me, Task doesn't know how to joke,' said Sald. 'You fought him off?'

Task nodded. 'Partially. Cowardice did the rest.'

'Well, I'll never. Knight of Dawn a runner. Just don't tell Cater. That's that problem sorted, then.'

The golem wasn't so sure. 'For now, at least.'

The soldiers got to talking again. Anything to distract from the boredom and shame of lying chained up in the mud, leg-sore and accused.

'The Last Fading bought themselves a coward?'

'Should have bought a golem, instead.'

A voice blared across the mud, behind a shaft of lantern-light.

'What in the name of the Architect's arsehole is going on here?'

Sergeant Collaver's face was so red with fury it looked as if his forehead might pop.

'General'd have me chained up, too, if he knew you were squatting in the mud with spies and miscreants.'

The spies and miscreants seemed happy with this idea.

'Come join us, Chief!'

'Mud's very soothing after a long day's walk.'

'Sir, am I a spy or a miscreant?'

Collaver was far from amused. 'Pipe down, the lot of you!'

One man put his hand up and the sergeant marched over to wallop it with a cane. 'Don't be a deffer! This isn't no classroom!'

Collaver turned to the golem, hands on hips. 'Task, up!'

Task flexed an arm. 'I'm afraid not, Sergeant. I am staying here until the master releases Mr Sald.'

The sergeant rested his brow between two fingers, as if massaging away a headache. 'Get up, Task. I'm here to fetch Sald. It's about time to cut him loose. At least I think that's why I'm came here. I'm so tired it's like there's a deffin' voice yelling in my head. Now come on!'

'Cut him loose?' Task echoed.

'Boo!'

'Cut *me* loose!

Collaver's cane cracked again. 'Loose. Cast aside. No longer a soldier. Disgraced.'

'Free, in other words,' said Task, looking to the old soldier with a grin.

Sald didn't seem too pleased at the prospect. 'Poor, in others.'

'No honour. No tants for his trouble,' said another soldier from behind a hand.

Sald and the golem got to their feet. Sald was slower, his sore back making him bare teeth. 'I want to talk to the General.'

'As do I,' said Task.

Collar sighed. 'I ain't waking him at this hour. No bloody way. He'll have my cock and balls for matching bookends.'

'You'd be a lot shriller, Sergeant.'

'I hope he's got small books!'

'SHUT UP!'

Collaver's bellow would have given a cannon a run for its coin. The soldiers fell silent, except for maybe a snigger or two.

'Come on. I'll walk you to your stable, Task. Then we'll put you out the north gate, soldier.'

Sald stiffened. 'North? I'm no spy, Sergeant.'

He held up his hands. 'Huff's orders, not mine. I know you Dregs ain't got no reason to spy, but he doesn't.'

Task growled at that.

Collaver unshackled Sald and helped him on to firmer ground, much to the grumbling of the score or so soldiers. Task looked back at them. He had never had a knack for whittling out spies, but he would have bet an arm he was staring at a few. The sergeant appeared to have his own suspicions. Task could see him mouthing names as he put a hand to Sald's shoulder, committing them to memory.

They headed through the gate and into the camp. Tonight, the lantern-speckled tents wrapped the stables, blacksmiths and other important organs of the war machine like a glowing crown. The brightest light was at the camp centre, amid the dark void of paddocks. Torches had gathered in a great group, and something about it made Task's shards rise. They soon heard raised voices, and Collaver spat in the mud.

'Oh, spit on it, what now?' He broke into a jog, and Task followed. When they arrived at the source of the voices, they found the large group of men and women silent and still. They must have heard the pounding of Task's steps, or the clink of armour. Their torches and lanterns still spat, but their tempers had been shackled.

Task looked around as Collaver barged his way into the centre. They were workers from the stables; perhaps a few armourers and sharpeners, washer-maids, even a soldier or two. Almost to a body, they carried weapons: clubs, staves, knotted rope, and small leather-knives curved like scythes.

The golem took a step forwards, and they parted for him. It was Ganner they'd surrounded. The man was on his knees, snivelling. A dark smudge brewed under one of his eyes, and a thin trickle of blood had escaped his lip.

'I'll tell you the same as I told them, golem. I ain't no damn spy! I've been nothing but loyal over the last five years. So quit your staring.'

'You said you'd been here four years, Ganner,' said a woman with a spike-hammer cradled in her crossed arms.

'Well, it feels like longer!'

'Spy, you say?' said Task.

'Ask the girl!' said a voice. Bodies shuffled aside to reveal Lesky, standing with her arms crossed and her face tight, covered in cuts and bruises. Blood encrusted her nostrils and lips. There was a sag to her stance that told Task that wasn't the extent of her injuries. His knuckles crunched.

The woman was explaining to the sergeant. 'And that's how we found her, once we'd dragged him outside. It's all him, sir!'

That was enough for Task. Before Ganner could so much as squeak, the golem seized him by the throat and lifted him as far as his arm could stretch. Stones rolled up his wrist to add to his height. Ganner's legs thrashed like banners in a gale. His fingers yanked at the stone around his neck, but Task only squeezed tighter.

'Did he hurt you, Lesky?'

She was fixated by her dangling master, her expression lopsided. Task had never seen that look on her face before.

'Girly?' said the woman.

'He's been acting suspicious for weeks,' said Lesky. 'After I told the other stablers, I came back to find him drunk, as always. I asked him whether he was a spy, and he beat me to shut me up.'

Task shook the man. 'Is that true?'

'It's a filthy lie!' Ganner looked on the verge of spewing, but the golem didn't care. He'd had worse splashed over his stone.

'I asked, is that true?'

Ganner's wild eyes cycled from the golem, to the girl, to the crowd, to the sergeant; but in none of them did he find help. Spy or not, any man accused of raising his hand to a child was bound to find himself short on friends. Task shook him again.

'I'm dead whichever way I answer!' said Ganner, falling limp. The golem dropped him on his backside, and Ganner slumped where he sat, like a bag of meat. Task loomed over him, bearing teeth.

'Fine!' said Ganner. 'I'm Saffin-born. Are you happy? You got me. And curse you all for it, you spine-stabbers! Go on, string me up to the wagon.'

There came a triumphant murmur from the crowd. Backs were clapped. Weapons slapped agains palms. Task looked down at Lesky, and found an expression of poorly hidden surprise on her face.

'Looks like there's another one for the hobbles, Sergeant,' said the woman with the hammer. 'Shame we ain't hanging them.'

Collaver seized Ganner's wrists and hauled him upright. 'Oh, but we are! Should they confess openly to treason 'gainst the king.'

Ganner began to struggle, and several workers wrestled him into submission.

The sergeant went on. 'Huff isn't about to kill a man unjustly. He gets to prove his worth. Those that have been trailing? They've had the smarts to keep their mouths shut so far. They know that when they break, they hang. You saved us some time, didn't you, stable-master?'

Ganner was pale and silent. Collaver led him away without struggle. 'Right, you lot. Disperse! Back to your billets, afore I find somebody else to string up.'

'Just doing our duty, Sergeant.' The woman bowed as her group broke apart. She tucked a finger under Lesky's chin before she left, and said something that made the girl nod.

The golem called out. 'Sergeant?'

'What now?'

'About the girl. With no master, what will happen to her?'

Collaver held Ganner against a post while he worked his tongue around his teeth. 'Prob'ly get folded into the rest of them. Oh, spit on it, this is just what I need.'

Lesky sprang forward, limping a little. 'No!' she yelped. 'I mean, maybe I could run the stable on my own?'

Collaver laughed. 'Bollocks, girl! You? Huff'd never allow it.'

Task heard a cough behind them. Sald was standing alone near a tuft of grass. 'He could help,' said the golem.

'I don't need no help!' said Lesky. 'I can run this stable blindfold. Watch me.'

Sald raised a hand. 'I don't doubt you can. Maybe you can teach me, then. I know how to follow orders. Huff won't let me soldier again, that's for sure.'

Lesky's bruised face softened, but she looked more wary than impressed; as if another Ganner might be hiding under Sald's muddy skin.

Collaver was still shaking his head, but as he mentally compared the paperwork to the prospect of having his genitals made into ornaments, his shaking slowed until he was staring at the sky. Task wondered if he was looking for his Architect to smite him down or to save him.

'Fine,' he said. 'I'll make sure the details are changed. But if Huff comes calling, Sald pretends to be a fawl or something. Or changes his hair, grows a beard. I don't care. Just don't deff this up for either of us. You better hope you win this war smartish, golem.'

'See, Task, we're not all bad,' said Sald, before saluting the sergeant. 'Thank you, sir. Very grateful.'

'I just hope the rest of you Dregs don't start getting ideas,' said Collaver as he left.

With the sergeant gone, the three of them stood like the points of an awkward triangle in the grass, nobody sure what to say next.

It was Task's curiosity that broke the quiet. 'What happened, Lesky?'

Lesky aimed herself toward the stable doorway and spoke over her shoulder. 'A story for another bedtime, as me mam always used to say. I'm tired.'

Sald drifted away. 'I'll go collect my things. Give you two some time.'

All too abruptly, Task was left alone in the gloom, faintly lit by a dying lantern sitting by the doorway. He shook his head, and moved to the stable door.

'Lesky?' he called into the gloom. The light from outside found only a handful of edges. One of them looked vaguely like a girl.

'I want to understand what happ—'

'You weren't here. You didn't come for me. I needed you.' Her voice was small, but sharp.

'I didn't know. How was I supposed to?' The excuse sounded hollow, no matter how much truth it had in it.

'I shouted for you.'

The golem's mouth flapped. 'How could I—'

'Goodnight, Task,' she said, in her firmest tone.

The golem backed away from the door, bemused. With a sigh, he resigned himself to an empty paddock, and let the night-noises and snuffling of the fawls distract him, lulling him into a deep sleep, and deeper dreams.

1st SOWING, 3362 - MALAR DORAH, KHANDRI

Ingenious, he called it; and he had called it that all the way to the front. It had taken two weeks to tread the flat plains between the jagged mountains. Two weeks of shuffling through the ash-fields. Two weeks of crunching pumice beneath the feet of thousands; hundreds of thousands.

It was the largest army the Harmony had ever mustered. And it marched on the Diamond Mountains with vengeful purpose in its step.

'Ingenious, I say!' Belerod swaggered between the lines with sheafs of paper covered with blotched scrawl.

Before he could congratulate himself further, the horns blew at the sight of the Malar Dorah, and her tabletop of stone; the shell of a dead volcano, long-silent. It sat alone amid the dusty brown peaks around them, slumped and broken as though it had died in turmoil.

'No time to waste!' His master yelled, as he ran down the ranks.

Task turned his gaze on the lofty turrets of the Dorah, at the end of their valley. She was the lesser sister of the Icaria Cavada, but still one of the toughest fortresses in the Diamond Mountains. The pealing of her bells was already tumbling over the cracked landscape; bells rung by foreign hands.

'They know we are here,' said a sharp voice beside and above him.

The other golem sounded eager. Task nodded. He too felt anticipation spreading across the stones of his chest. That was what he called it, at least; the strange shiver that pestered him before every clash.

He looked again at the fresh crack in his shoulder, where an Accord axe had bit too deep at the Ashen Shores. The blade had been edged with starsteel.

The war had grown bitter and desperate in the last year. The surge they had spoken of had come to pass; it just happened to be a surge in the wrong direction. The Accord had claimed a hundred leagues in twelve battles, each of them fiercer than the last, and each of them had claimed at least one of his kind.

It took them all morning to reach the plateau and wind along its torturous zig-zag of a road. The golems led them in single file to the rumpled summit of the volcano. There, they spread into a line, thudding across the landscape until the whole army had made the ascent. They stood firm and silent as the bodies formed up, and the machine-crews went to work.

The hammering gave rhythm to the bells of the fortress. Desert-wood beams were joined together to reach for the sky, skeletal in their grasping. Rope bound them. Metal wrapped them. Men crawled over them like dustmaggots on a Khandri cracker.

Within two short hours, the engines of war had spread across the plateau: siege-towers, gate and cullis-rams, heavy cannon, devil-throats. And yet Task still felt the eyes of the Accord fixed on his stone brethren.

He looked down the line. Each Wind-Cut Golem stood motionless, gaze fixed on the enormous gates, hands curled into fists. There wasn't a heave of breath in them.

Task turned to the giant beside him: Belerod's final creation. Black and quartz was the beast, fourteen foot-lengths high at a slouch. Its jaw hung low, mouth open, exposing the jagged teeth his master had carved. Next to this creature, he felt almost human.

'Assemble!' came Belerod's cry. He surged forward with fiendish glee in his eyes. 'We will not be storming those gates today, my creations. Belerod is smarter than that.' He tapped his head with a silver gauntlet. 'Bring them!'

The black rock underfoot shook as three heavy-set catapults were dragged forwards. Before he could explain, a cluster of deep booms rang out from within the Dorah, and all eyes snapped to the fortress.

A strange cloud of objects rose into the azure sky. They flew lazily, without the purpose of arrows.

'SHIELDS!'

Task raised his arm with the rest of them. The other golems simply watched.

The first projectile struck the ground by his foot, exploding into something wet and putrid. Fragments of it clung to his shin. Before he could look down, another collided with his chest. It glanced off and ricocheted to the dirt with a squelch.

It was a rotting head, still wedged into its spiked helmet; bloodshot eyes rolled up, nose missing. Its neck had been cut with a hot sword, judging by the dark colour of the flesh.

The heads rained down on the front lines in their hundreds. Some were putrid and unrecognisable, others fresh enough to still carry expressions. Chanark, Khandri, Hasp, men and women, young and old. They had all been executed without discrimination or mercy.

The soldiers roared in revulsion. The clang of axes and spears and swords against shields rose to a frenzy.

Task stared down at the face in the dirt, and wondered what the man's name had been.

Belerod was already giving orders before the last head fell. The golems took their positions as the catapults were cranked.

Task moved automatically, flowing with the commands. He felt the shiver spread from his chest as they bade him to sit in the hand of the catapult.

The wood groaned as the horns blared their battle cries. The soldiers were a rushing river around them by the time they had hammered out the pins.

The ropes crunched and weights jolted, and the golems took flight, soaring into the air with their limbs outstretched against the winds. For a moment Task thought he would never reach an apex, as though an unseen rope were hauling him into the heavens, away from the hatred and fury below him. Away from this world.

In that moment, he found peace; in the altitude and the sensation of rushing air. It was brief, but unforgettable.

But then he chose to look down, as the heavenly rope slackened and the earth called for him again.

In the courtyard of the Dorah, a mighty pool of water was spinning and yawning. He heard its howl over the wind, and though he flailed and thrashed, his course stayed fixed: the centre of the green-grey vortex.

The other golems crashed into the walls below him, causing havoc.

He sailed on, one hand half-outstretched in a futile grasping motion.

The roaring maw opened wide.

18

'The secrets of a golem's construction lie in the stone and the correlating spells used. Each stone has its own tune that the magic must sing also. Limestone, for instance, can suffer from weak binding. Basalt has a tendency to snap under complex spells. Sandstone will crumble at the faintest error. But granite not only holds the magic, it is sturdy to most bindings, even after collapse.'

FROM A HASP WINDTRICKER MANUAL

55TH FADING, 3782 - SAFFERON FORTRESS

'You failed, good and simple,' yelled Westin.

'I cut his damn arm off, twice!' *A little embellishment never hurt. The mist had been thick as fawl-shite.* 'Even dragons don't grow their limbs back when you hack them off!'

'And how would you know? I'd wager you've never even seen a dragon!'

Alabast didn't mean to slap the man; it came out of habit. It was a good slap, though; the sort that connects squarely and makes a classic sound. It was just a shame the knight happened to be wearing his gauntlet.

Westin reeled away from the desk and collided with the wall. When he turned back, blood was on his lip, and he was reaching for his dagger. Alabast's sword was already halfway out of its scabbard.

Lash brought a hand down on the desk so hard that even his pewter wine jug jumped. The sound of the slap didn't seem so impressive any more.

'Gentlemen! I will have you both skinned alive if you don't sit down, shut up, and act like adults.'

The two men followed orders, exchanging fierce gazes.

'Carafor. I expect better. I haven't brought you here to fight. I've brought you to be helpful. Shape up! And as for you, Alabast. Westin is right. The fact is, you failed to defeat the golem. No matter how close you came and how valiant your efforts may have been.'

The knight bowed his head, squashing the growl that was rising in his throat. 'You said I had two chances, Lord Lash. I can—' He stopped as a finger was raised.

'To tell the truth,' said Lash, 'I half-expected you to be short of a few limbs by now. Or dead. But I have to say I'm relieved you managed to survive. Fear not. You're still valuable to us, but you will not face the golem again. I'm afraid we were wrong about you, and now we must try other tactics.'

Alabast knew the matter was sealed. 'My lord.'

'Which brings me to Lady Auger. Please, tell them what you told me.'

All eyes switched to the fire-haired woman sat at the far end of the table. She was busy picking her nails.

'Oh, you're ready to listen, gentlemen? Finished squabbling, Knight? Executor?'

She swept from her chair, and stood behind it. 'I have been busy speaking to the Last Table, and they agreed that it is time to place our faith in something other than the Knight of Dawn. Something more... solid a prospect. Thanks to my connections in the Accord, I am thrilled to say the golem will be here in two days.'

'What golem?' said Alabast. 'Task?'

Auger smiled in a way that irritated him. His fascination with her had soured since their last meeting. He had always been fickle with people who traded in rumours and lies. He was looking forward to picking that bone with her later.

'Task is not the only golem left in the Realm,' said Auger. 'After you stormed from our last meeting, I explained to Lord Lash and Executor Westin that there was a slim chance of procuring one for the Last Fading. Well, I've pulled my strings, and one has been procured. We shall pitch old-magic against old-magic, while we focus on the Truehard forces.'

'You're serious?' said Alabast, leaning forward.

'As I said, I've been busy.' She flashed a wink.

'What kind of golem?' asked Westin.

'Bone. It's been living in a crate, hidden away in a Borian museum for the better part of thirty years.'

'And you think a dusty old antique can do better than me?' challenged Alabast.

Auger checked a scrap of parchment before flashing that smile again; thinner and sharper this time. 'Well, for a start, it's over twelve feet tall.'

Alabast dug his buttocks deeper into his chair and folded his arms.

Lash cleared his throat. 'The Last Table has made its decision. Whilst I don't like being overridden, I agree with Auger and Master Ebenez. It's time to fight fire with fire. There's still use for you, Knight Alabast, as I said. I could use a swordsman like you on the field, where it's going to matter.'

A foot-soldier. Alabast's retreat from the golem was like a splinter worming its way into his brain, constantly niggling him. Despite a few large and ugly bruises, he had faced the golem and lived. He ached for another try.

'You could always go back to Gurnigen and its whipsore-ridden whores,' said Westin.

'Have you ever even been with a woman, Westin? Or do you prefer to deff your dusty scrolls when the lanterns are all out?'

The hand sprang back to the knife. Alabast laughed.

Lash sighed. 'Architect's sake, Westin! Control yourself. We're all allies around this table.'

In the silence that followed, Auger rapped her rings against the chair-back. 'So it is agreed, then. We will show the Truehards how foul their own medicine tastes.'

Lash pushed himself from the table's edge. 'I believe we have no choice, Lady Auger.'

Outside, Alabast waited for Auger. As she walked past, he snatched at her arm. To his surprise, she bent his wrist in an ungodly angle and forced him against the grimy wall.

He wheezed, embarrassed. 'Well, there's a first time for everything I suppose!'

'I don't respond well to being touched without being asked. Especially by second-rate knights who are convinced their tongues are made of silfrin.'

Alabast thought for a moment, but deemed the obvious innuendo to risky to try. He rather liked his wrists unbroken.

'I apologise, Lady Auger.'

She released him with a snort, and adjusted the sleeves of her fur-trimmed coat. 'Accepted. Now, what is it? If it's about the golem. I'd love to trade more clever words, but I'm afraid I'm rather busy.'

'Deff the golem. I want to know why you advised Lash to keep an eye on me on the march. I had somebody practically breathing down my collar the entire way to Burrage.'

Auger looked surprised. 'Because you would have attempted to escape. I saw it in you. But you were worth a try, Knight. So I thought it best to keep you with us. I would have thought you'd be glad that I cared so much.'

Alabast scoffed. 'If you cared, you would not have sent me out against the golem when you had another trick waiting up your sleeve.'

'What does it matter? You're alive, aren't you? And now you get to spend the rest of this war out of harm's way. Well, for the most part. I'd say you've come out of this glowing, Alabast.'

Alabast stood his ground, refusing to let her glinting eyes melt him. 'I don't take kindly to those who trifle in the lives of men and women, no matter how debauched or worthless they may seem. I wonder if the Truehards treat their soldiers the same. You would know, of course. As a spy.'

That chipped a shard or two from her icy expression. Alabast had expected her to flare at the mention of the enemy, but she barely moved. *Curious.*

'Fine, your life was trifled with. You were a mad gamble. A risky hand to play. But you're a mercenary. Surely you're used to it?' She narrowed her eyes. 'Or is it instead about you having an excuse for why you failed? Does it make it easier to swallow, knowing that the golem was always an impossible task?'

'I want another chance at the golem.'

Auger tutted. 'It's a bit late for trying to salvage your reputation, isn't it, Alabast? Unless… Oh dear, you're not trying to impress me?'

'No. And it's not my reputation. It's a matter of honour.' Alabast knew there was no point in pretending. The woman had seen the measure of his heart the moment her eyes fell on his swagger. She knew the lies he told himself as well as he did, and that made him feel as thin as gossamer. Hollow. Glimpse-like, was Auger.

The knight raised his chin, hoping she would see a different kind of heart in him today. Auger shrugged.

'Fine. Have another go at Task. Here's hoping your luck can extend to another bout.'

While Alabast was thinking up a witty reply, she leaned to whisper in his ear. He caught her perfume on the air, mingled with the smell of furs and castle must.

'Though, if you really wanted to return some substance to the empty, pretty vase you call a life…' She let him hang for a moment.

'Perhaps you could *turn* the creature, instead of killing him. Or being killed.'

'What?'

'Turn the Truehard golem to our side. Change his mind.'

Alabast wondered if she was making a dig at his charm. 'Impossible.'

Auger waited for a soldier to pass. Her voice was barely a whisper. 'I would not dream of telling Lash or the Table, but the bone golem is nothing more than a stop-gap. It's no Wind-Cut Golem. Task is the pinnacle of his kind. I had harboured some hope, but that was before I had seen him go about his work. Now I am certain. Unless we can separate the Truehards from their golem, the Fading are doomed. You should know. You've fought him yourself. If you want to make your name mean something again, then turn the golem to the Last Fading's side.'

Alabast could still feel the reverberations in his knees from the monster's footsteps. He could see the mist steaming from his craggy joints, the strange white coals burning in his skull-face. The knight suppressed an involuntary shiver and laughed at the audacity of it all.

'Surely he is bound by rules or—'

'Yes, but there's a conscience in him, Knight. I've already seen him flinch more than once at General Huff's orders. Who knows? If he learned how this war started, he might just be swayed. Huff has been quiet on the truth of the matter, so I understand. And all the soldiers spew the same royalist fawl-piss.'

In all the time Alabast had spent wandering the castle, stealing soldiers' tants and conning them out of glugg, he'd never bothered to ask their stories. He'd only wanted to voice his own. Auger must have seen it in his face. She bared her teeth, mocking him.

'You don't know either, do you? Well maybe you should find out for yourself. See if you can stir something in that wine-addled brain of yours. Now, if you'll excuse me, I'm needed somewhere more important.' She leaned in, pressed her cold lips to his cheek and swept away, hair streaming like a banner behind her.

Mad. She was as mad as the Rent itself, but by the Architect did she know how to tempt him. He felt like a wild beast, staring at an open trap, knowing the nature of the sharp jaws, but still slavering at the bait.

Alabast ran a hand through his locks. He had always been one for spinning scenarios in his mind; dreaming up possible futures where he always came out inordinately rich and grew more handsome with age.

The knight who turned a golem. It had a pleasant ring to it. And besides, if anybody knew the unexpected virtue in talking to strange and monstrous creatures, it was Alabast Flint.

With that in mind, he strode for the nearest clump of tent-cloth, on the hunt for stories to tell a golem.

The east road out of Safferon fortress was treacherous; mostly scree and shale in the good parts, unexpected falls and sharp rocks in the bad.

Ellia's firn was unsteady at first, but its claws soon took to the ground, and before long she was trotting along at a good pace. The beast seemed grateful to be out of the gathering stink of the old fortress. As was she; if only for a while.

She travelled openly, watched by the hundred guards perched above and behind, where the fortress walls soared, black against the last glow of the dying sun and the shadow of the mountains.

Ellia wore suspicion as if it were a cape, trailing and flapping behind her. As a spy, she was a liar. *And once a liar, always a liar.* Lash, Westin, and maybe even Alabast would all harbour that minuscule worry that she might one day betray them, if she hadn't already. She smirked.

Her attention turned to Spiddle, and his insistence on meeting at strange landmarks. He could always be found lurking wherever the ground had performed some feat, or something had fallen from the sky, or where moody things had happened in moody places long, long ago. It was as if these places were connected, like lakes punctuating a river course, or veins clotting at junctions.

This time he had chosen what sounded like some boring old pit. This time, he hadn't bridged with her, left a message in her mind. He'd sent a dervish with a letter tied to its leg. It had been brief; no more than a direction. She knew she would feel him, when he was close. Always questing, that one. Always on the hunt for thoughts to glean.

She came to a straight section in the wiggly mountain path. The hills rose up on either side, cutting an eerie channel. A cold breeze seeped between her coat buttons. It smelled musty, ancient, and thankfully, it was brief.

The pit was at the centre of the small plateau. Black-lipped and grinning, the maw was an almost perfect circle. It stretched at least twenty foot-lengths at its widest, offering little ceremony before the sheer drop of its throat. She stared at its smoke-stained walls, and wondered how many travellers had been swallowed by it; too busy with a map to notice where they were treading.

Ellia slid from her firn and approached the edge, wary to keep the reins in her grip. As she was peering into its cheerless depths, she felt the familiar pressure between her ears.

'How deep is it, do you reckon?' she said, backing away from the pit as Spiddle slunk into view. He'd been hovering behind a rock like a crallig on the prowl. His bald head glowed pink in the receding daylight.

'The locals...' He paused while Ellia rolled her eyes. 'The locals say if you fall, you fall to the bottom of the God's Rent, where you can see the very faces of the old gods.'

'Let me guess. Nobody has ever returned to corroborate the story.'

Spiddle's face sloped, and Ellia chuckled.

'Another load of fetid, rustic fawl-shite.'

'Must you be so abrasive, Zealot? I only attempt to educate you.'

'When I want education, I'll ask for it. Now let's be quick. What news from the Blade?'

Spiddle shook his head. 'Not so fast, Frayne. The Treyarch wishes to speak to you himself.'

Ellia inwardly flinched. Bridge with the Blade would require a level of concentration she had not prepared for. She guarded herself, stowing her thoughts in the dark closets of her mind and locking them up tight.

The glimpse gestured away from the pit, where two rocks sat like footstools. Ellia took a seat opposite him, marvelling at the lack of mud on his boots and dark cloak. By any rights, a man who spends his time sleeping rough, walking endless roads, and daydreaming in other people's heads should be coated in filth. Spiddle had barely a spot on him. Maybe he was a spectre, and there was more to his pale skin than just odd breeding.

It took Spiddle a few moments to ready himself, and she was glad for the time to do the same. Bridging took some concentration. *All the better to keep him from prying*, Ellia thought.

The glimpse held his hands flat and blade-like, prompting her to do the same. He touched their fingers together, so lightly she wondered if she was imaging it. She felt the warmth of contact begin to build, even in his cold and clammy hands. His eyes turned milky as the bridging began.

She shored her defences one last time, and let him in. She felt the weight of his consciousness seeping up from her neck and into her skull. She could trace his roaming; it was like ponderous footsteps on floorboards above, dust falling wherever he pried.

'Stick to the bridging, Glimpse!'

'As you wish.'

The darkness behind her eyelids shivered, like something clawing behind a thick curtain. Light chewed away at its edges, and then roamed wherever it pleased, sparking and popping as it traced the lines of a room several hundred miles away. Columns came first; stark and grand. Then a floor of stone triangles with the light skittering around their points.

Three faces, old and stern, stared back at her. Only the curves and crags of their features were visible in the shadow. It was all she needed.

'Zealot Frayne,' came their voices, booming through the darkness, as hollow as a cave.

'Treyarch, may the Architect never blind you,' she said through foreign lips. Her words were hers in the void, but she heard them echo in the gruff voice of the other glimpse sitting in the Blade. Just as there were two shores to every river, it always took two glimpses to bridge.

Two others sat either side of Treyarch Daspar: Consecrators Lockyen and Vullen, as usual, sitting like jabbers over an open grave.

She felt a shudder in the bridge. Somewhere in the distance, somebody snorted.

'I have to admit, Sirs, I was not expecting an audience. Has Spiddle not been relaying my—'

Lockyen cut her off. 'He has been relaying your reports just fine, when he has them. Your information has been scant to say the least.'

'With all due respect, Lockyen, I can't simply wander off any time I feel like it. Especially now that we've sown the idea of spies in the Truehard camp.'

Their grumbling was audible through the void. Even though they were creatures of sketched light and outline, she still saw the frowns on their faces.

'We have given you a long leash, Zealot,' said Daspar. 'Forgive us if we feel the need to shake it from time to time, to make sure there's still a wark at the end.'

Ellia swallowed her irritation before Spiddle caught wind of it. 'Of course, Treyarch. Forgive me.'

Vullen butted in. 'The Ambassador will be here at the start of Rising. That is less than two weeks away, and a war still rages. Perhaps it's time to bring you home, Frayne, and let another zealot finish the job.'

Ellia's skin prickled. 'If you want to end the war by Rising, then you must leave me in charge. I am deeply embedded in both the Council and the Table. I have Lash's ear. I have Huff and his Truehards stoked into a frenzy. Victory is what you asked for, and that is what I've put in place. Trust me.'

'We did, once, and got our hands scalded,' said Vullen. She felt the furrow in her own brow; the glimpse in the Blade would be wearing the same.

'That's enough, Vullen!' Daspar held up a palm for silence. He delighted in playing the fair hand, the benevolent leader; and yet she had seen the blood dripping from his fingers more than once.

'What my esteemed colleagues are trying to say is that we need reassurance. A lot of tants and time have gone into this scheme of yours. Not to mention *two* golems, now.'

'Then consider yourselves reassured,' said Ellia, stonier than she perhaps intended. 'Task of Wind-Cut needs a push, and another golem is exactly what it will take. I haven't failed you yet, and I do not intend to start.'

Vullen looked as if he would correct her, but the master must have silenced him somehow.

'Then we shall leave this delicate situation in your hands, Zealot.'

'Two weeks, or I'll fall on a sword to save you the trouble of acting yourselves,' she said, pulling herself back from the bridge before Spiddle was ready to close it. Once the darkness and faces had evaporated, like a dream in the face of daylight, she found him gritting his teeth.

'I do wish you wouldn't do that,' he said, snatching his hands away. His whitened eyes slowly found their colour.

'As the Master said, time is of the essence.'

Spiddle relaxed his jaw, but the sour look lingered. 'The Grand-Captain has commanded almost all of his forces north, hot on the tail of his son.'

Ellia had been halfway to her feet. She paused in a squat. It seemed Gorder was not following his orders. 'Leaving Caverill unguarded? Why?'

'Seems Dartridge the Younger thinks he can do this all without reinforcements. That has made the Boy King and Dartridge the Elder nervous.'

Ellia shrugged as she straightened. She would just have to move quicker than them, and have words with Gorder when she saw him next. *This was not in the plan.* She made for her firn. 'Good. That means he is confident, and we'll have more men to throw into the fray if needed.'

'There is something else. Something I think will intrigue you.' Spiddle caught her before she could slide a foot into a stirrup.

'And that is?'

'There's a natural in the Truehard camp. She broke out a few days ago, realised her power.'

Spiddle was right; it was most intriguing. That irritated her.

'How do you know?'

'Felt somebody questing. Raw, untrained. Knows nothing of her skill, of course. Cane wants you to collect her.'

'Her? A she? Unusual.' Glimpses were almost always men. Gazers, however— those who dared to stare into the Architect's eye and look upon the plans of the future—were always women. She started to rack her brains.

'Very. She is young, that is all I could tell. She broke from me before I could see her thoughts.'

'I don't have time to sniff out a glimpse, Spiddle.'

'If Cane wants it done, you will do it.'

Ellia raised her hands. 'Fine.' It was all play; she was already nurturing a suspicion.

The glimpse gave her a sly look, questing for her mind once more. 'You seem distracted, Zealot. Perhaps this job is taking its toll, as the Treyarch thought? A lot on your mind, perhaps? I can help with that, you know.'

Ellia ignored him and climbed up onto the firn. She wrapped the reins around her wrists, and kicked the beast into a plod, flashing a smart grin at Spiddle before vanishing beyond the rise.

Only then did she let him in, let him slip through her walls. He ran through the corridors she had prepared for him, snatching at whatever he could grasp as he barrelled through her, desperate and merciless.

She showed him just a sliver of her thoughts before throwing him from her mind. Just enough to lay a worm of doubt; one that would wriggle back to the Treyarch.

Alabast's face.

The murmuring of his lips in the corridor.

His eyes, hungry.

His dashing looks.

Dashing. That thought should have made the glimpse twitch, she thought, if nothing else did.

Ellia was thankful for that quality, at least. It greased the wheels, made it easier to stomach the rest of the knight and play her role. The difference between him and the man of her memories was enough to make her nauseous. Alabast was a shadow of him.

'Techan,' she said to the dark, before kicking the firn into a canter.

19

'Bend the will of man to a false patriotism, and he will walk
blindly into the fires of war with a grin on his face.'

BARON EMPA, SCOURGE OF THE VUPIN FOREST

57TH FADING, 3782 - THE NALDISH LUMPS

Roads are like roots. Intrepid things, roaming the landscape in their thirst for use: for boots to grace their dirt or stones, or for weary paws and wheels to rattle over them. When they find it, they gorge themselves, swelling up and up until they tangle and knot, growing villages between their lattices. Then they must stretch out again, questing for grounds ever new. And so grows a country.

Task had trodden more roads than he had stones in his skeleton, but never had he walked any that insisted on knitting such infuriating loops and lackadaisical complications. It was as though the lot of them were drunk.

The golem wondered why Huff didn't cut straight across the land, bypassing the tracks. But, no: the thick, bustling column of soldiers weaved back and forth across the landscape like an army of madmen.

Over the course of the morning, they had swerved near to the edge of a long, murky lake that the soldiers called the Greenhammer. The water was still, besmirched with mats of algae that steamed in the cold air. Its shores were grey scree, as if the ground had been shattered by some great hammer-blow many millennia ago. Dirty scraps of snow lingered. There was an island sitting at its distant centre; a sharp, ugly thing with a single tree to its name.

Huff called a halt for water. The army milled about in their thousands. A few campfires were sparked, and they were nearly ready with the spits when the sergeants came to crack their heads with canes. As usual, Collaver's roar rose over all.

'Damn lazy bastards! Cursed good for nothings!'

After that, Huff had them on their feet sharpish.

Beyond the hook of the lake, the world rolled on ahead, in a wasteland of scrub and gorse; that sort of incessantly undulating wasteland that always put a puff in the skinbags. They stamped and cursed all the way up, and clutched their sides and wheezed all the way down. He soon discovered the name of the place: the Naldish Lumps.

Task fell into a slow lope at the rear of the army, where the wagons took their time thanks to the drag of the scrubland. As the army grew slower with each incline, the fawls and firns nibbled at will, snouts snuffling in every bush they padded by.

Lesky sat proud at the far end of the column. He waved, but stayed put; he could feel the weight of a gaze on him. He busied himself with the rippled horizon.

On the peaks of the hills he gazed across the wasteland, spying copses and rivers, scattered trees and blooms of weathered rock, and storms convulsing with lightning as they rolled across the distant plains. The smudges of rain between the clouds and the countryside looked like tethers, lashing them to the earth.

For ground to be spoiled by war, it doesn't need to play host to a battle. War sucks the life from a land like a raw rash creeping over skin. It tiptoes and creeps, league by league, until one day, all that's left is the rash, and the skin is long forgotten. Fields lie untended. Cottages squat, with their thatch caved in. A garden rots, strewn with bones.

Task remembered the endless quiet of Haggia, where countless slums lay bare and empty in the wake of a coup in a city more than thirty leagues away. They had found food on tables, cocooned in dust. Clothes still in bags. Not even a ghost would have felt comfortable in that place. It was in those streets, baking and choking as they were, that Task had first learned the meaning of a shiver.

He was on the cusp of dubbing this wet wilderness another Haggia when the mutters of a town came racing down the lines.

Soon enough, the army came to a crunching halt. The officers broke rank to trot to its head, and when Task saw Huff spurring his own beast forwards, he decided to amble after them. A ripple of grim nods followed him; something of a new habit among the men. He wasn't sure he liked it. Only his deeds could have earned the respect, and they were not pretty enough to earn anything but disappointment.

The town had a name, but Task couldn't read the squiggles on the sign. It was a stretch to call it a town, in any case. The settlement consisted of a dozen stone and plaster buildings, gathered around a well with a conical slate hat. The tallest of them looked like a tavern; a board sporting a grinning, harlequin-painted face hung over its door, squeaking with every moan of wind.

The golem hung back, hunched behind the spread of soldiers. Spears, pikes and crossbows bristled around him like a stripped forest.

Nervous eyes poked from doors held ajar. Fingers twitched at cloth curtains. Grubby noses pressed to grubbier windows. Task shrunk lower, not wishing to worry the inhabitants.

A man swaddled in a great mound of robes was bowing and scraping to Huff. To Task, it looked a lot like begging; he had seen enough of it to know.

Huff was his usual aloof self, twirling his hand at the man's pleas. If a soldier's head hadn't moved into his eyeline, he might have seen the man kiss the general's ring.

The conversation turned sour. Task saw the creases piling on the man's forehead, and the downward decline of his jaw.

'Bring up Task!' came the shout, ricocheting through the ranks.

With a grunt, the golem stretched to his full height as a channel quickly opened up for him. He came to a halt at the general's back.

'As I was saying, we have no doubt of victory, with this behemoth on our side. Task, break something for these gentlemen.'

Even though Huff reeked of duplicity, Task was enjoying the respite from being yelled at, not to mention being asked to crush men's skulls. That was a bonus.

He reached for a lump of stone that had been left near the well. Even as its life leapt down his arm, dashing past his eyes, he crumbled it between his fingers.

Huff was busy examining his nails. 'He does the same to armour. Spines. Skulls.'

'It's true,' said Captain Manx, receiving an acerbic look from his general.

'So, in summary, we'll gladly take any strapping lad or lady that you have to offer, and in return I won't have Task here take apart this town piece by piece.'

The golem bristled, stones rattling. The man took it as a show of dominance.

'We have no place in this war, my Lord,' he said.

Huff looked appalled. 'Are you not Naldish, born and bred?

'Yes.'

'And therefore, a proud Lundishman, I expect?'

The man built his chest. 'I am.'

'This is a *civil* war, my friend. It affects every single man and woman and babe in arms on the Six Islands! Even King Barrein himself would pick up a sword if he needed to! I ask you again, are you a Lundishman or not?'

This time, the man answered with a hint of outrage. 'I am!'

'Then it pays to pick a side.' Huff beckoned the man to lean closer. 'Preferably the winning one, hmm?'

'Of course, my Lord.' The man collapsed into a bow and scuttled away.

'Good man.'

Task was sent to stand by the tavern door and look big and imposing; something for the patrons to goggle at over the tankards, maybe. He did as he was told, retreating to a private space in his mind while the town was ransacked of its able-bodied.

The soldiers were gentle at least; some even cheered the new recruits as they paced down the ranks, on the way to the rear. A few got claps on the back. One or two smiled at least, and Task wondered how long that would last once they had felt the weight of a helmet and a sword instead of a cloth cap and a pitchfork.

Twenty-one in all. From fathers to first-borns: those who pined for adulthood and those still clinging to their youth. They drifted from their doorways one by one, eyeing Task with fear and wonder. He did his best to turn his craggy face into a smile, but the recruits' widening eyes told him it looked more like a snarl, and he switched to a good old fashioned nod.

'I want you up front for the rest of the day,' said Huff, before rejoining the ranks. 'This is enemy territory, and I want you sharp-eyed.'

'Yes...' Task let the word linger. 'Master.'

Huff flashed him a smile. 'There's a good golem.'

Task set out along the curve of buildings. A few doors slammed before his shadow reached them; others held weeping eyes and sorry looks.

He led the army at a reasonable pace; enough to keep his stones cool and air in the soldiers' lungs. The land flattened for them over the next rise, revealing a long plain of grasses and gorse. He spied a dozen solitary mountains spread far and wide. A few smudges in the hazy distance suggested more.

'The Naldish Watchmen,' called a voice. Task turned to find Lance-Captain Taspin had brought his firn up slow and quiet, while the golem's ears were busy with the clatter of mailed boots. He was accompanied by three other riders.

'Cousins of yours, perhaps? Old and dead by the looks of them. Is that how you'll turn out, golem?' A few snorts came from the others.

Both the rider's smile and armour gleamed in the scant sunlight. Taspin probably meant to embarrass him, but it only reminded him of the Knight of Dawn, and how he had slunk away.

Task gave the lancer a withering look. He spoke slowly to make sure every ear could catch him.

'Perhaps. But what I want to know is how you're managing a saddle, what with the recent damage to your crotch? You could barely breathe, let alone walk.'

Taspin smile persisted but his lips stretched whiter. There were sniggers around him.

'Let's form up! Yah!' he said, kicking his firn into a gallop. He and his cohorts tore down the lines. Task was left chuckling.

As the roads finally began to behave, stretching out along the borders of old farmland, they found more scars of war; two—maybe three—years old, by Task's reckoning.

Great gashes striped the earth, dug by cannon-fire. Rusted contraptions lay about between the creeping bushes. Burial mounds squatted here and there, tufted by thick green grass; greener than anything else the Lumps could offer. It was as if the corpses beneath still strived to live in some way.

Where boots had trampled, the ground had died; too churned to be of use. Beneath its cracked crust, sun-bleached bones poked into the light.

Task made sure to step over them; it was a small respect to pay. The crunching sounds from behind told him the soldiers carried no such veneration. He wondered who lay in the unmarked mounds; who had been turned to dust and splinters. Had the Truehards or the Last Fading won here?

Around the curve of a large mound, the road delivered them a surprise. Task stopped dead, raising a fist so the soldiers didn't crash against his legs and back.

The young woman's hands were firm around the old musket. No shake in them. Her head was already bent to its sights, and Task could see one angry eye glaring through the thread of smoke from the slow-match.

He held his arms out wide and empty, holding her aim while he studied the peripheries. A flock of waddling, feathered creatures were gathered on the road behind her. Three more shapes stood steady among their flow. They too were young, and held muskets against their shoulders.

'TO ARMS!' came the bellow, many-voiced.

The front ranks dropped to their knees with a loud clank. Spears were leaned on their shoulders, muskets on the other. There was a wave of noise as a hundred flints were primed. The riders were summoned.

Task took a step forward. The feathered creatures scattered, and like ships beached by receding waters, the three challengers were left bare and open.

Taspin held his riders in an arc, their lance-points forming a sharp wall. His puffed posture dared the youngsters to try themselves against it. Task would have none of that. These youngsters were stupid, but brave. Task could imagine their story: maybe their father went to war for the Fading, left them with a few muskets and promises. Maybe he never wrote back, and now a fierce resentment had grown in the place of love.

'Hold on!' he said, making the young woman flinch. He could see in her eyes she was having trouble taking all of him in: the size, the voice, the impossibility of stone walking and talking.

'Put down your muskets and you'll be done no harm.'

'Stone liar!' She switched her aim from rider to rider. Task took a slow step forward to reduce her options. Now he was closer, he could make sense of her. She was barely a few years older than Lesky. She looked well fed, with rosy cheeks and bright eyes behind curls of black hair. She was far from a desperate soul. She was deadly serious.

'The war is coming to an end, miss. And the king will win. Put down your weapons,' said Taspin.

'Spit on the Boy King!' she said, making the riders bristle.

'Do you want to die, girl? Put it down!'

'Spit on the king! And all the landed gentry that piss on the poorest without care.' It sounded like she was preaching from some heavenly gospel. 'Down with those who deny freedom and opportunity!'

'Traitorous capitalists!' yelled a soldier.

Task wasn't sure what the word meant, but it was the flame that lit the firepowder. Literally. The girl's musket puffed smoke and a clang rang out behind Task. The golem turned to see one of the riders topple from his whinnying firn, a new hole in his breastplate and a shocked look on his face.

Task turned to receive his own musketball. It glanced from his brow with a crack. It would have been a fine shot on flesh. A third shot caught a firn in the leg, sending it crashing to the dirt with a warbling scream.

The golem tried to step in, but the riders surged past him. The lances went about their sharp work in the space of a blink. Before Task could say a word, three skewered bodies slumped to the earth; a few more notches to be added to the tally of war.

'Drag the filthy creatures aside, golem,' said Taspin, trotting his firn in a circle around the slaughter. 'They're in the way.'

He galloped back through the lines; no doubt to inform Huff of their swift victory against three children. Task clamped his jaw shut, and did as the man had told him; not out of obedience, but because he could show the dead some final respect, as he carted each of their bodies to the roadside.

He touched their skin, and felt their brief span flash through him.

Three more settlements had the pleasure of a visit from the Truehards before the sun sank into the earth, and three more lines of confused-looking men and women were welcomed into the war with cheering.

Huff gave the third town the honour of hosting the entire army for the evening. The townspeople did their best to look thrilled at the opportunity, even when the tents began to encroach on their doorsteps, and the cooking fires and bawdy singing burst into life. Behind bolted doors, faces peered from windows; curious more than fearful. Task imagined they didn't often get fifteen thousand soldiers and a golem camping on their doorsteps.

Once Huff had issued his decrees to the townsfolk, he spoke to Task. 'I want you to stand right here for the whole evening. To keep them in check.'

'Who? Them or us?'

'Both! The road riled the soldiers today. Who knows how many more muskets point at us from these windows, or how many spies might take their chances to sneak into our camp tonight. Like parasites hitching rides on warks.'

'Yes, Master.'

Lesky ducked behind the canvas doorway and listened for the sounds of an axe being introduced to wood.

Salt, as she had taken to calling him, was not a bad man to have around, and not a bad man altogether. He had nothing but polite smiles and plenty of questions. She liked those; they made her feel smart.

Now she'd ordered him to chop logs, and chop logs he did. Slower than her, but stronger by the sounds of it.

Needing no lantern, she went to her sleeping sack and sat cross-legged on top of it. She had no idea if this was the correct position, but it was the best she could think of.

She had tried in the wagon earlier that day, when Salt had gone to check on the train of fawls. But the shaking and constant natter from the next wagon made it impossible to concentrate.

The question had burned within her since Ganner had been taken.

Who might you be?

She didn't yearn to answer it, but instead to ask the same of… him.

Him. It had to be a him. A man who had reached inside her mind from somewhere else in the world. She snorted. Of course she was going to try and reach back. *What curious, stubborn little Darens whelp wouldn't?*

Lesky clamped her eyes shut, hooking onto the rhythm of splitting logs. She thought of a big, dark space, and tried to fill it with muttering, as she'd heard before. She held it for almost a minute before she gave up with a humph, and slumped to her straw pillow.

Her fingers wandered her ribs, finding bruises and cuts to poke at. Maybe if she was in pain, like she had been before, it would work better. Wincing and gritting her teeth, she prodded, harder and harder, until she could see the pain at the corner of her eyes. She latched onto it, imagining it as a thread she could use to haul herself into that cavern of voices.

Somehow, she broke through. It was like stumbling through a doorway into a rowdy party. She felt her body go rigid as all of her consciousness retreated to her mind.

Snatches of conversation. Flashes of emotion. Stories never voiced. It all tugged at her attention.

She clenched her fists and waited for the right one to snag her. She waited and waited; a bobbing boat on an angry sea of darkness.

And then, there it was. It just appeared, where there had been nothing before. They had found each other.

Lesky strained as the weight of him pressed her flat. She felt her body convulse, but she held on. Something was sifting through her thoughts. She recoiled, and it stopped. A hollow voice spoke in her mind.

Who are you?

She pondered. *I came to ask you that.*

Why?

Why should I tell my name to a stranger?

You're a brave one.

What is this place?

Two questions now!

And I don't have no answers to either.

Then I must ask you two.

Fine.

There was a pause as the man thought. He offered no ghostly face this time. He was just a voice that floated about her, like a crallig circling in the dark.

Spiddle. And this place has no name. It is what you create for yourself to understand the bridges your mind can build.

What bridges?

Three now! That was not our bargain. Who are you?

I'm not telling you.

Another pause. The silence was heavier this time. She felt something stir in her mind. She pushed him away.

What's your other question?

Have you heard the Architect's call yet, child?

Lesky reeled back, tearing herself from his clutches and grappling for daylight. She felt her back arch, almost folding her double. Something dragged her down again, and she lashed out with her fingers. She railed against him but felt nothing but a brick wall. She pushed again and again, but nothing budged. Her screams made it only halfway from her mind to her mouth, emerging as wretched gasps. She could hear them over her panic. Blood poured from her nose, filling her mouth.

Lesky felt her nails grate against rough stone, and something in that physical connection broke the hold. Her eyes snapped open to find a concerned-looking Task staring down through a ripped canvas, holding her legs and arms with his two great hands. The relief was enough to keep her conscious for a few seconds. Then she drifted back into the darkness; though this time it was a kinder, quieter sort.

The golem stood like a statue on the edge of the town, where a few huts clumped together around a small orchard of low-lying vines. To his left, the camp sprawled into the night, a dishevelled blanket sprinkled with hot coals. A hundred different songs blared into the night sky. Somewhere close, a drum was being battered, and a pipe and stringed instrument duelled to its frantic beat. Task didn't know what they were celebrating: the new recruits, their victory over three angry children, or the fact they'd made it through another day without dying.

He looked down at the youngster who had refused to leave his side for more than half an hour now.

Dizzy-eyed, mouth agape, he was glued to the spot, swaying back and forth as if swinging from a rope. His expression had gradually cycled from disbelief to utter confusion, and was now stuck somewhere around utter wonder.

His ill-fitting clothes suggested he was a fresh recruit. He was drunk enough for a recruit, that was for sure. There were new Truehards to baptise tonight, and it had to be done right. He had seen it in every army he had ever fought with. "Done right" meant trying to drown the poor souls in liquor.

The youth swayed a bit too far and caught himself. 'Wha... whayou eat?' he said, slurring. It was good to know the man had a voice. The golem decided he might as well have some fun with his visitor.

'Children.'

The lad's eyes rolled around their sockets. 'Chilren?'

'Yes. The younger the better. Don't you have anywhere to be?'

'Ah'm not a chile.'

'Trying your best, though.'

The lad raised a hand. 'They sayou dream. When you sleep.'

Task tilted his head. Taspin's wagging tongue, no doubt.

'Whayou dream 'bout?'

The golem reached out and turned the youth to the side. With a gentle pat on the back, he moved him along. 'Nothing,' he said, but the lad was tenacious.

'Can't dream bout nothin,' he said, hiccuping. He looked around to see where the noise had come from. 'Whayoudream, golem?'

Task narrowed his eyes, though not at him. 'Water. Rushing, swirling water.'

The lad nodded as if he'd heard it all before. 'Gossren,' he said.

'Huh?'

'Godsren.'

'God's Rent?'

'Thassaone. They say you dream of the Godrent, it means y'going to die. Know that?'

Task felt something inside him skip. 'Who's they?'

The man turned his dazed look upon the town, and threw his hand in an arc. The meaning was lost on Task, but the lad, clearly feeling he had dispensed enough advice for the evening, trod a jittery path back to a circle of tents, throwing up over a vine along the way.

Task hunkered down, not caring for Huff's instruction to stand. Even perched on his heels and backside, he was as tall as any guard, so he didn't see how it mattered. He pondered the lad's words.

Captain Manx came strolling out of the flickering shadows, with a few guards forming a tail.

'Up, golem,' he said, almost cheerily. Perhaps he too had been at the gutwine. 'General's changed his mind. Back to your stable, or wherever it is you sleep now.'

'Why?' Task enquired.

Manx went to say something, but thought better of it. He just shrugged and waved him aside. Task didn't complain; he was happy to be relieved. His thoughts had turned again and again to Lesky as he had stood watch. She had barely offered two words to him since the night Ganner had been taken away.

He set off between the tents, ignoring the random cheers and applause that sprang from the clumps of soldiers. He had apparently graduated from hate figure to hero. All it had taken was the murder of a few hundred enemies. He acknowledged them with a wave. Cups and bottles clinked all around.

'Task!' came the cry, from a shadow hobbling up the path towards him. Task broke into a jog, face chiselled with concern. It sounded like Sald.

'Now if there's one thing that I can do, it's light a damn fire. And that's just what you need, miss.'

Task looked down at the girl. Despite the warmth, she was still shivering. She had to clamp her mouth shut just to keep her teeth from smashing together.

With a knuckle-crack of stone, he threw another blanket over her and settled by her side. Lesky thanked him with a juddering look, and went back to her staring. The flames were beginning to lick at the wood.

'Magic,' said Task. It was the first word he'd said to her in days. 'That was old-magic, what you were doing.'

They had found her fitting and foaming at the mouth, blood streaming from her nose. She had almost ripped her fingernails off scratching at the golem's stone. Her eyes had been a pure white, as though she were blind to the world.

Sald hunkered down on the grass on Lesky's other side, and nibbled at some seeds from a pouch. He was hooked now.

Lesky shook her head, as if Task had just accused her of being able to fly. 'I don't think so—'

'That face!' said the golem, pointing a finger. 'You're making it again.' She had flashed it the night Ganner had dangled from Task's fist.

Lesky frowned. She took a stick and poked the fire. 'Don't know what you mean.'

229

He shuffled forward, grinding. 'I thought friends shared.'

The girl spat some blood in the dirt. 'Usin' my own words against me! That's not what friends do. Mam'd rap your hands, she would.'

She dug herself deeper beneath the blankets. 'When Ganner was beatin' me senseless, I tried callin' for help. Not with this!' She dabbed a finger to her tongue. 'But this!' The finger moved to her temple. 'I don't know why, so don't ask. I thought of you, Task, but it didn't work. You didn't come. So I thought of anybody. A soldier, an officer. Even the general 'imself.'

'Collaver,' said Sald, face full of half-eaten seeds. 'He came to fetch us. Seemed all foggy-like. Reckon you reached him by accident?'

Task remembered well enough; he had felt a pull in his mind. 'And today?'

Lesky squirmed. 'When I first called out, a man found me in the dark places. He asked me who I was. I didn't tell him. I think I got hit too many times in the head before I could. I thought I'd try again, see what he wanted, who he was.'

'Curiosity killed the crallig, miss,' said Sald. Lesky stuck out her tongue.

Task didn't bother to ask what a crallig was. 'He found you, I'm guessing.'

The nod was quick and sorrowful. The golem ran his tongue over his teeth, like a sword on a grindstone. Magic twitched inside his mouth.

'Heard him right between my ears. I could feel him crawling about my head. He told me the Architect was calling for me, and let me ask him two questions. His name was Spiddle, and he talked about a mind buildin' bridges.'

Sald clicked his fingers. 'She's a bloody skullsearcher!'

'No, I ain't!'

The golem cleared his throat and the two died down. 'A what?'

Sald mimed as he spoke. 'A searcher of skulls, Task. Reader of thoughts. A thinkpicker, or a glimpser as the Mission calls them.'

'Glimpse,' said Task, wondering where he had heard it before.

'They're a feared bunch 'round these parts. Six crowns ago there was a glimpse on the throne. Knew the minds of every king and queen and prince in the Accord. Built Hartlund into what it... was. Then he went mad and killed half the court before they brought him down. His son was executed and his cousin put on the throne. It caused a small war, but that's Hartlund. Since then all such magics have been banned. When I was a boy they burnt a glimpse on a stake in the square. I don't think I ever got the stink out my nose.'

'I don't want you to do it again, Lesky. Sald found you spitting and screaming,' said Task. 'Don't toy with magic.'

Lesky huffed. 'I'm not a glimpse!'

'Well, it's ether that or you've got a malady of the head,' said Sald.

'I don't have no malady!'

Task fixed Lesky with a deep stare. 'There it is again! That face you keep making.'

Sald sensed the mood shifting, and made himself scarce. 'I think I'll see to the ripped canvas,' he said, hawking up some phlegm.

Lesky ignored the golem's eyes, and kept her gaze fixed on the fire. 'It's my face. That's that.'

Task bent forwards. 'Happiness is an easy one to spot. The smile gives it away. Sadness? The wailing, the tears. But you have none of those. Just a flat line of a mouth and still eyes. Lies always look different for each human, and they come wrapped up in all sorts. I never catch them at first, but after two or three, I start to catch on.'

Lesky's eyes were beginning to glisten. Task had never understood this leaking. It took a while for her to speak.

'I lied about Ganner,' she croaked.

'Lied? How so?'

'He beat me, but he weren't a spy. I made that up. Or at least I thought I did. Told the other stable-hands and got them all wound up enough to come knocking. It's them who saved me. They came running as soon as they heard him yelling. S'pose it was a good enough excuse.'

How did the Borians put it?

'You framed him?'

'If that means got him in trouble, then yes.' Lesky looked stuck between proud and guilty.

'You lied to me.'

'I lied to everyone.'

Task shook his head. 'But you lied to *me.*'

Lesky squirmed again, the movement made all the more pathetic by her shivering. 'But it was a good lie! Like if Huff asked you if you hated him, you'd lie, right?'

Task could remember the general doing almost exactly that; asking whether he doubted him. He recalled his lies clear as crystal, but that had been to keep a master calm. He growled. 'That is not the same as sending a man to the rope!'

'He did confess!' said Sald, from further inside the stable. 'And he did beat up a little girl.'

Task opened his mouth to argue, but he couldn't find the words. 'Still… You… You shouldn't lie to me.' After all of Lesky's smiles and kindness, she was the same as the rest of the skinbags. He ground his teeth in disappointment.

'But everybody lies, Task,' said a voice.

Baroness Frayne was leaning over the fall paddock. Task had no idea how long she had been there. His ears had been too busy with the girl's excuses. He was halfway to his feet when she motioned for him to stop, and to remain seated. Even the girl was told to stay.

Ellia picked a spot on the other side of their fire. She stayed standing, looking for all the Realm as if she were rising out of the flames. Her hair was the colour of the embers.

She had been absent for several days. On business in the capital, so the rumours said.

'A little one here and there, or big ones every now and again. To a wife, husband, comrade, brother or sister. For politicians, it's practically our job. For everyone else, it's just part of being human.'

Task squinted. *And people wondered why he didn't trust skinbags.*

'I pride myself on integrity, Task. As I know you do. But I am a politician, and so...' she countered. 'Tell me, why do you hate lying so much? Did someone important once lie to you?'

The ponderous look came over the baroness' face once again; the same one she had worn in Purlegar, when she had asked a similar question.

Always digging, this one. She should have sought a career in mining instead of politics.

Task lingered long enough in his answer to draw Lesky's attention. The young could always sniff out a story.

He broke her gaze and rose to his feet. 'I am not sure what you mean, Baroness. I'm just a servant, sworn to serve.'

Ellia snorted, most unlike the lady she was supposed to be. She checked a pocket-watch and wandered back towards the path. 'A likely story, golem. But I digress. I had an order to convey, as it happens. You're wanted at the north gate. The spies are being sent home and our good leader would like you to make sure they do as they're told.'

Task shrugged his shoulders. 'As you wish.'

Ellia spun as she walked, making her fur coat twirl. 'I do hope that in time you'll learn to find trust, Task. There are some of us who have your best interests at heart. Isn't that right, girl?' She looked at Lesky. 'We are not all the same—'

A detonation of breaking timber ripped through the baroness' sentence. Task sprang out to the path, his head snapping in the direction of the noise.

On the edge of camp, half a wagon was descending from the sky, like a meteor without the flames. It landed with an almighty crash.

As the screams rose and horns howled, Task shot a finger at Ellia. 'See that Lesky is kept safe!'

'You can trust me on that,' said the baroness, her voice firm. There was barely a trace of surprise or fear in her face. The golem snarled as he burst into a run.

Flames leapt to the night sky as lanterns were dashed aside in the chaos. In the glare, he caught the shape of an unexpected foe. Something roaring in the darkness. Something large.

It was a golem.

Task's heart, if he truly had one, didn't know whether to sink or to leap.

20

'*Love can drive a man to murder just as easy as hate.*'

HASP PROVERB

57TH FADING, 3782 - THE NALDISH LUMPS

Each step was a fearsome lunge, each arc of his arms a catapult swing to drive him forwards. Speed was all; he had no time for courtesy. The fleeing soldiers who didn't dive from his path were thrown aside.

The specimen was huge. Stick-legged for the most part, with low-slung arms and curved, scythe-like claws.

Another lantern exploded against its skin, and Task saw what it was made of.

Bone. From the ribcage of some giant beast to the broken skulls adorning its kneecaps and shoulders.

He grinned as he piled yet more speed into his charge. Bone and stone had clashed before, on sandy Chanark plains too hot for man or magic. He had faced their bone creations then, and he had broken them into splinters.

Task aimed for its closest knee. He became a cannonball, tucking his legs into his stomach. He tensed for the impact. If any soldier had been brave enough to stand by and watch, they might have glimpsed the confident smile on his face. And they would have seen the smile fade as the stone golem collided only with the ground, tearing up a cluster of tents.

Bone might be brittler, but it's lighter. Task had remembered his teaching a little to late. The bone golem was a nimble thing, and now, with its attention fully earned, it turned its tricky ways on him.

It staggered forwards. A screech tore from the grinning hole at the centre of its face: three enormous skulls mashed together between two curved horns.

Its hands swept back and forth like pendulums, scraping at the ground with its claws. It lashed left and right, shredding tents and slashing the unfortunates not quick enough to duck or run. Screams joined the clamour.

The bone golem seemed fixated on him. Task knew orders when he saw them; the dogged stare, that singular direction.

Task studied its gait, analysing its construction for a limp, a lean, a loose bone or two.

He ducked a slash of a claw and caught the next on his fist. There was an audible crack from both sides. Task slid back again, noting the glowing seams in his wrist.

Bone had fared worse. A great chunk was missing from the tip of one of the golem's claws. It stopped to stare at the injury, and with great, grinding heaves of its cavernous chest, it stoked itself into a rage.

It came at him again, with another ear-splitting screech. Task seized the nearest lantern pole and swung it like an axe. One leg was swept away, but the other stayed firm.

Before Task could swing again, the golem reached out and scored a mark across his chest. It was enough to throw him off-balance, and the next strike caught him square in the face.

He must have flown at least a dozen foot-lengths. As he smashed through tents, wagons and a lean-to, he felt the bodies break beneath him, heard the wails accompany every wet thud.

Task lifted his nose from the dirt, staring down the gruesome new path his stone had carved. At least six bodies lay moaning amongst the wreckage of canvas and wood. At the far end, the golem heaved with satisfaction.

It leapt to close the distance. Task charged with him, ducking under its claws, seizing the golem's ribs and prising them apart.

The bones cracked like gunshots. Task felt the fire within him flare. He was digging deep for power, walking that fine edge. It was only the retaliation that stopped him.

The golem clawed at Task's back, wrenching him away and tossing him to the earth. He only collided with dirt this time, but the blow had driven the fight far too close to the stables for his liking.

Task threw himself once more at the beast, aiming high on its shoulder. His sharp fingers fell upon any crack they could find; any seam or join. He gripped hard, as a glacier seizes a boulder, and heaved.

It took all his weight and a vicious twist, but the bone golem's arm came free of its dusty socket in an explosion of bone fragments. Task landed hard, snapping the forearm beneath his knee. He knew it would still feel the pain; the magic bound the bones tightly.

The bone golem wailed; a keening, burbling howl of pain and outrage. Task could hear the drums beating riders to arms, and gun crews to their cannons. He snarled. Huff was a fool if he thought that was the answer.

This was Task's battle, and his alone.

He struck again, aiming for the knotted wrist; a mass of pitted shoulder-blades. He was rewarded with another crack, but no snap. Another claw came swinging, and he beat it aside with two clasped fists.

Once more, he ducked in under the bone golem's claws and gripped its thick spine. Stones crunched as they flowed up his back, like an inverted landslide. His shoulders and arms bulged. The stacked bones were packed tightly, thick as a tree-trunk; but he could hear them beginning to splinter.

Once, twice, three times he yanked, twisting his direction each time. On the fourth pull, the spine burst, just as the claws plucked him away. Perhaps the golem's blind fury had finished the work. Task crashed to the ground, showered by bone-splinters.

Task saw her flickering shadow first. Taller than usual. Bulkier. She was carrying something heavy. He saw the nose of a great crossbow poke into the light, then her straining arms, and finally her bruised but determined face. Sald was trying to pull her away, but she resisted.

Task felt a keen wind blow through him.

'No, Lesky!'

'Get back!' she yelled at the top of her lungs. With a snatch she cranked the bow to its full strength, and levelled it at the broken beast just a stone's toss away.

Crossbows could often rival muskets for volume, and Lesky's shot unleashed a great whoosh and thud of pressure. The hit was even louder: a shuddering collision of steel and bone. The bolt punched a jagged hole in the bone golem's throat and stuck there.

Task saw it immediately. *The switch,* his masters had called it. The moment a golem changes from cold construct to vengeful beast. Pain could bring it on; or the awareness of impending destruction.

With another screech, the golem wrenched itself free of its wreckage and began to claw itself forward, trailing its ruptured spine. It was as if necromancy, not golem-magic, was pulling its strings.

'Get her out of here, Sald!' Task darted to finish it off. As his feet pounded the earth, his gaze fell upon the bolt jutting from the bone golem's neck, and he was struck by an idea.

There was a crash from behind as the bone golem's claws reached out. Sald's cry almost stopped him, but Task had too much momentum now. He flew into a slide, aiming under its awkward elbow and colliding square with its jaw. He wrapped one arm around its head and punched, again and again, until its teeth and cheek crumbled away like old china. He thrust his fingers into the golem's mouth, grabbing for the hot lump of stone at the back of its throat. He roared as he yanked it free, showing it to the night sky before casting it to the earth. The bone golem slumped, joints and bindings cracking.

Task's breath came ragged, and only then did he realise how far he'd slipped. He pressed the anger back down as he stumbled backwards over the motionless corpse. He half-fell, half-leapt to the crumpled figures lying on the edge of the path. Beside them, the stable had been rent in two. Broken spars and ripped canvas sprawled in all directions. The fawls had scarpered through the hole in their pens. Somewhere among the wreckage, a lantern crackled, threatening to spark a fire.

'Lesky! Sald!' Task barked their names as he knelt in the grass beside them.

Task had never been the praying sort. Religion was reserved for flesh, not for creatures of stone and old-magic. And since the prayers of the flesh went largely unanswered, he had never seen the point of calling on a deity who had no fondness for listening, never mind reaching out to fend off a storm, lift a plague, or smite a thief.

But at that moment, he prayed like a lifelong sinner at the wrong end of a knife-blade. The pleas that filled his mind were wordless and singular, but they were certainly prayers, offered to any god who might be listening.

The old soldier wasn't moving, but the smaller lump half-covered by his arm stirred with a moan at the touch of Task's heavy hands. He could feel the weak patter running through Lesky's bones, but sensed nothing similar in Sald.

The man's chest had no rise or fall, and the golem could feel no tremor in him. Task pressed his knuckle to the centre of his chest and tapped, as lightly as he dared. He had seen humans do it in the aftermath of a battle, when they weren't slitting throats or poking in pockets.

Three more times, he tried, but Sald's heart remained still. Blood leaked from his mouth. Task bared his teeth, feeling his chest begin to swell and burn.

He turned back to Lesky, lifting her head.

'Stay awake, girl.'

The rumble of his voice stirred her, and she opened a bloodshot eye to stare up at him. Dark red trickled from one nostril. Her breaths came heavy and rasping.

Task looked around at the shapes fighting the lantern-fires or poking their heads around wrecked tents, all wary of the horrifying corpse spread over a hundred foot-lengths.

'I need help! I need a surgeon!'

The urgency in his voice brought a handful of them running. The rest scattered as the riders burst through the smoke and dust. Their firns reared at the sight of the golem's bones. Huff and his entourage arrived, barging solders aside as they galloped up the path towards the broken stable.

Task let them see to old Sald. He held on to Lesky while a man with a white scarf tied to each arm poked at her limbs, then her head. She moaned as if trapped in a nightmare. Her eyes had rolled up to the white.

'Up, golem!' said Huff, bringing his firn to a skidding halt. 'The Fading are out there!'

That stoked the fire in Task; not the prospect of paying revenge, but the terrible need to see Lesky fixed. He had already let her down once tonight. He refused to make it twice.

'The girl, General...' His breath was short and shallow now. He could feel the prickle in his temples.

Huff practically flew from his mount, striding through the crowd of soldiers to stare down at the body cradled in Task's hands. No smiles or simpers now; just pure, unfiltered rage.

'I don't care about the girl! I care about the bastards that loosed a golem on my camp! Now get out there, and kill every Last Fading you see!' He looked around at the others. 'As you should all be doing! MOVE, damn you!'

Only a handful of soldiers shifted. Task lifted himself to his feet, his anger rising with him. He wanted to tower over the man, to show him how small and pathetic he was. They stared at each other for a moment, watching the firelight play on the other's face.

The golem ground out the words as though he were milling flour.

'I will see her safe, General. Then I will slaughter every last one of them. Have no fear of that.' He did not move. He tensed every grain in his body, trying not to tumble off the precipice. Every part of him wanted to explode.

Huff lurched forward to push the healers and soldiers away. He stood over Lesky, his lip curling.

'Damn the girl, I say!' He puckered, and spat, right on her chest. 'Now get out there and do what you were m—'

Task seized him, encircling the general's collar. In a blink, he had lifted him bodily and driven him into the churned mud with an almighty roar.

The golem did not stop himself. He couldn't have. The rage had gripped him as tightly as he held Huff.

Task drove his fingers deep into the earth, leaving Huff nothing but breathing room between the mud and his stone. His magic held him from pushing further.

He heard the pistols clicking in the captains' hands, felt the whoosh of air as lances were lowered. Everyone froze.

The look in Huff's eyes was a muddle. Cold shock, mostly; then utter terror. In that moment Task saw to his core, and met the coward that huddled there.

'You can't!' he gasped, laying hands to the golem's stone like a criminal to bars. 'It's against your rules!'

Task inwardly recoiled at his touch, but the fury kept him steady. As the crimson ate away the edges of his vision, he brought his face close to Huff's. The general's eyes switched from glowing pit to glowing pit. A tremble had taken over his lip, and yet his own fury still bubbled away somewhere; an audacity bred into him.

Task spoke slow and steady, as if his words were spare stones to be dropped onto Huff's face.

'I am surrounded. Beset on all sides by cowards and villains. I don't understand your mind, but I understand your emotions, and they paint for me the sort of man you are. I am tired of working for masters like you. Masters who prey on glory, no matter how many skulls they must pile to reach it. You want this war finished?'

Task caught movement in his periphery. Baroness Frayne had crawled out of her hiding place. She hovered nearby, watching wide-eyed. He looked to the nervous soldiers, their pistol barrels shaking. He wanted to laugh.

'Then I shall finish it,' growled Task. 'Without you, if I need to. Take what glory you can from that. But I will not move a pebble until the girl is seen to.'

'You do not make demands of me, beast!' whispered Huff. The terror had solidified to outrage.

Ellia opened her mouth. 'Decency is not a demand, Huff. The golem knows the difference between right and wrong. And you, General, in this moment, are wrong.'

Huff glowered at her over Task's knotted knuckles.

Ellia came closer to lay a gloved hand on the golem's arm. Task felt nothing of her life. She was like a moon-shadow. 'I will take the girl to the healers. Trust me, Task.'

The golem did not move. Every stone in his arm wanted to press down, to steal the breath from the general's throat. Just a quick shift of weight, and Huff would have been buried in two parts. But the magic held him fast, sitting like an immovable collar around the man's skin.

He peeled himself away from Huff's neck, smeared now by mud and bone splinters. The general stayed put, until the golem was standing full and tall over him.

The two held each other's eyes. Huff slapped away the proffered hands of his captains and hauled himself to his feet. Task saw the quiver in his hands. The general's eyes found Sald on the floor, and a fresh anger flooded his face. Behind him, Collaver melted into the crowd.

Task turned to watch as the girl was carried between the tents, beyond the lantern-fire and bone-wreckage. The night still held yelling voices and clashing swords. The Fading had not sent their golem alone.

His steps started sluggish, dragging through the whorls of mud. Then the prickle in his skull spread down across his chest and sides, igniting his stones into action. The crooked veins of mica began to glow, sparking as he bounded through the tents.

The simplicity of rage pulled him; nothing more. The yawning precipice in his mind had claimed him. He allowed himself to fall, to feel its depths, powerless against its dark charms. He felt the anger rise within him like the boiling of a forgotten pot: the lust to break and destroy things, to spill their pieces on the grass; the urge to crush and shatter; the desire to see every unfriendly face battered and choking in the bloody dirt.

The golem's sharp eyes adjusted to the darkness beyond the flames. Men sprinted alongside him. He roared to them, and a battle-cry of many voices rose into the night.

Sputters of flame betrayed their paltry numbers; just a squad of Fading marauders smeared across the landscape. He heard the petty clatter of their crossbow bolts. Tails of fire streaked over his head, and there were squawks behind him. *Fire was a coward's tactic.*

He met their lines with a ferocity that would have shamed the Destroyer. Swords, many with limbs still attached, were strewn into the night. Armour was reduced to jagged shreds, screams cut short by vengeful swipes.

He whittled their numbers down to two pathetic men. Both tried to run, but Task seized them by the heels and gave each a vicious flick. He felt the crackle of their spines in his fingers. *Mere twigs.*

The golem met the second wave with his smile wide and his fingers searching. The first soldier was run right through, the second torn in two. He wanted to laugh. He wanted to roar like an avalanche and burn fear into their hearts. He wanted to quench the heat in his stones with their blood.

Then, he saw the hero; the one who had fled him before. He was sitting astride a firn behind a group of bowmen. He held his head high, showing none of the previous fear. His sword glinted in the far-flung flames. The light painted the hot breath as it escaped from his lips.

A deep chuckle built in the golem. He felt the soldiers' shivering through the ground; the drone of their hearts and shuffling feet.

In two short steps, the knight whirled his firn in a tight circle. Three steps and he was already fleeing, dirt spraying from the beast's claws.

The sun will shine at night before a coward changes his ways.

The golem howled at the weakness of it. His feet made thunder as he gave chase, masking the cry of, "Fire!"

A dozen crossbow bolts bounced off him; as pointless as the men who had fired them. Task broke through their line like a weak door. He snagged a handful of them before he raced on, pulling their wriggling forms tight into his chest and squeezing, snuffing their pathetic cries. *One, two, three.* He cast their broken bodies to the mud, where they belonged.

Golem and knight galloped across the rolling grassland. Mists of morning had crept into the gullies between the hills, and Task kept losing the hero to a frenzied shadow, only to catch sight of his full form again on the soft slopes. Each time, the golem cut a fraction from the distance between them.

Ruins loomed out of the mist, and crested the hills they sped over: a few moss-bitten pillars; then the ridges of a wall at the edge of an old battlefield, sticking up like vertebrae. Task barged through in his mad hurtle, breaking a spur of stone into bricks. Flashes of fire popped behind his eyes; images of molten stone pouring, bubbling.

He wrenched himself from the flashback, and found the knight gone. The mist filled the spaces between the shadows, taking the shape of the old ruins. It was as though the walls had not rotted and rusted away, but evaporated into vapour.

He forced himself to stop, digging troughs with his heels. He strained for the sound of galloping, but there was nothing but the distant clatter of battle. Steam rose from his hot stones, wrapping him in a mist of his own making. His bright eyes bored into the shadows, his breath coming in gruff snorts; angry and impatient.

A scrape of grass, and the golem turned, driving a fist into a nearby pillar. The rock crumbled, leaving a swirl of dust.

He moved on, pacing from ruin to ruin. Had he the time or calm, he might have been fascinated by the bones of the building that had once stood here. Now, he saw them as bothersome; barriers between him and his cowardly prey.

'I wish to talk, golem!' The cry was muffled by mist.

Task pivoted towards the voice, snarling. 'Last words?'

'Hopefully the first of many!'

Behind him now! *Infuriating.* The golem growled as he turned. The rage still held him tight; his fingers twitched for something to crush.

'I had no part in tonight's attack.'

Even in his heightened state, Task had the sense to stand still, to let the hero grow curious. He clenched his stone teeth and waited.

'I had no part in any of this. This isn't my war, as I know it's not yours.'

'Let us talk, then. And absolve your guilt.' *With blood and anger.*

'And we'll have no fighting?'

Coward's talk. This hero was just another fool with a sword. The golem would show him his grave.

'Step forward, Knight. And meet your Architect.'

'I need your word.'

Task bent his mouth into a grin. Every grain of stone was screaming for retribution. He whispered to the mist.

'Of course.'

The hero took his time to emerge, sword drawn, with a face as stony as the golem's skin. He hovered, barely visible, half-stolen by the mists. The golem started forwards, fingers reaching.

'Task!'

He tried to back away but stone was faster than flesh. He stretched out a hand and seized the human's arm. A blade hacked him away, but there was nowhere to run. The knight scrabbled backwards, his sword spinning in intricate loops. Several of them carved out stone chunks, but the golem's rage was all-consuming. He seized the knight's leg, and received a blade across the face, cutting across his eye and lip. That stoked him hotter.

'Listen to me, beast! You've been lied to!' The knight spun away from the golem. 'You think you fight for the honourable side? The right side? It's all a lie.'

'I fight for my master.'

'Even if what he asks you to do is wrong?'

'No right. No wrong. Only war.'

Swing. *Clang.* Another portion of himself lay in the dirt. It mattered not.

'I heard from a reliable source that you had a conscience!' The knight kept moving, winding a path between arch and column, anything to keep out of the golem's reach. 'I heard you had thoughts, feelings, needs.'

Another clang as sword met fist. This time the golem snatched away the blade, turning the knight sideways and tossing him against a pillar. In seconds, he had him pinned. Stone squeaked against the metal of his collar. Thumbs and fingers dug into the dirt around his neck. *Just like Huff.*

Fear ruled the man. Task could feel his heart trying to beat a path out of his body. There was anger, too; perhaps at such an inglorious end. Yet the Knight of Dawn did not panic. He didn't grapple for breath nor space. He simply lay there, locked into the glowing eyes of his executioner.

'I heard that you had a heart.'

Task snarled, pressing harder until the knight gasped. Blood dribbled from his nose, and the golem thought of the girl; how her eyes had been nothing but dazed slits, how the blood had run a path to her lips. These creatures were so frail.

It was like being dragged from a dream he had mistaken for reality. As the rage faded, the night grew lighter around them. The ruins seemed marble now, rather than granite; the grass a shade of charcoal, instead of black. The crimson tinge had faded. He felt the cold, laden air brush against his hot stones.

He looked down at the knight, whose face was whiter than chalkstone.

'Well?' said the mortal.

Task took a long, slow breath, purging his rage. He did not know how long it would stay suppressed. Once it pounced, it was hard to wrestle it back into the pit. The knight's babbling might distract him.

'Speak, and speak quickly, before I fall back. Before I change my mind. My maker gave me ears as well as claws. I may as well try to use both.'

The words were snarled, but the man breathed an enormous sigh of relief. His head lolled back against the pillar. 'Architect spit on it. I thought that was it.'

Task tensed his arm. 'And it will be, if you don't start—'

'Alabast Flint.' A hand poked over Task's wrist. 'We haven't been formally introduced.'

Task showed his teeth. Alabast grimaced.

'I'm here to tell you that you're fighting for the wrong side, golem.'

'I have no side.'

'Task. The fact of the matter is that you have no idea what you're doing.'

'I am obeying my master, as I am made to do. I have no choice.'

'And at what cost?'

Task thought for a second. 'None, besides my own.'

'I know several corpses out there who would disagree. This feral dump of an island is dying, golem.'

Task studied the man's shade of skin, the cut of his jaw. 'You're not Lundish. Why would you care about this country and its war? Its people?'

'Because they pay me to. And... they have a certain fire.' A clever look came over the knight's face. 'Why would you?'

'I do not care.'

'Like I said, I've heard differently.' Alabast smiled. Task eased his grip and lowered the knight to the ground. He stood hunched, rubbing his throat.

'I come bearing a proposition.'

Task did not usually deal in propositions. He worked with do or do not, nothing more. Yet tonight, curiosity pulled him in a different direction. Part of him still searched for an excuse to kill the Knight of Dawn. As much as he tried to stamp it out, the urge lingered.

'What is it?'

'Come with me,' said the knight. 'Meet with the Last Fading, with Lord Lash and Lady Auger. Hear our story and judge for yourself whether you fight for the right master. It sounds as though I've a malady of the brain, I'm well aware. But I implore you. You say you have no side. Perhaps it is time you chose one, golem.'

Task was surprised. Others had tried to tempt him before, usually with gold or promises of freedom; even with a palace, in the case of one particular Borian prince. But Task had no need for human trinkets. An appeal to his morality, however, was at least original.

'And why would I do such a thing, if I could?'

'Because if you didn't care, you would have dug down with those hands of yours, decapitated me, and disappointed a great many ladies of the Realm. I can recognise bloodlust when I see it. Battle-rage. I have something of the same. Yet you chose to listen, and that tells me you are more than just a machine. That you, against all odds, might have the capacity to care.'

They stared at each other for a long time. It was only when Alabast's eyes wandered to his sword, lying a good leap away, that the golem spoke.

'I will be missed.'

'You? Really? Who would notice you gone?' Alabast sniggered, growing bold now he wasn't on the cusp of being crushed. 'The night is young, golem.'

Task looked back at the glow of the camp and found it had been lost to the mist and ruin. He could hear not a single clank of sword. He was alone, unwatched, unshackled, and itching with curiosity.

Alabast coughed. Task sighed.

'How far?'

'At our pace? Two days' march.'

'No. Impossible!'

The knight paced back and forth, hands tucked under his armpits. 'What were your orders before you left?'

'To kill every last Fading I see.'

'And did you agree?'

'Naturally.'

'Did you make any promises of any kind?'

Task remembered his bitter words. 'That I would end this war.'

The knight clicked his fingers. 'Well then, what better way to do it than being personally escorted to Safferon Fortress?'

Task's face furrowed. That had his attention.

'Give us a day or two of your time. If at the end, you haven't changed your mind, then go wild. Tear the place apart from the inside. I don't care. I'll be long gone.'

Lesky. Ellia. Huff. The truth. An end to the war.

All the elements batted around his weary mind like insects in a jar. He pressed his fingers to his temples, hard enough to make the stone squeak. The golem was used to orders, not choices.

But you can bend the rules.

Ellia's words came to him, from the day in Purlegar.

Don't give him a chance to issue an order.

Damn that woman and her sugary words!

'A day, Knight. You will have one day. And believe me when I swear I will carry out my orders if I am not convinced. Impress me, Alabast, or suffer me.'

Alabast gave him a wild look. He sucked his lips. 'Right!'

'Lash is going to love this,' Alabast muttered.

As the knight fetched his sword, Task turned back to the mist-wrapped ruins, listening again for sounds of feet or voices. The night bore nothing for him; just the chill of a graveyard.

'North then, golem!' said the knight, once he'd found his firn, still breathless. The beast's amber eyes were narrowed on the golem, and there was a stiffness to its stocky frame. Its scales stood on end. Alabast stroked them gently.

'North it is,' replied Task. He moved forwards, feeling something snap underfoot. He looked down, peeled away his stone, and found a broken skull hidden in the grass. A few straps of flesh still clung to its shards.

In the light, it was plain to see: it was a child's skull, with a sword-blade gash across the forehead. Task picked up a fragment and stared at the wound.

He had felt it the moment his feet had kissed the black Lundish sand: there was something sick and rotten about this country. He would find out what it was, and if he couldn't, then he would finish this war in one bloody swoop. He might even have the pleasure of meeting the glorious end he longed for.

The girl moaned. Her eyes were puckered knots of clammy skin, her grey lips a constant tremble. Fingers scratched at the cloth of the carriage seats.

'Do something about her noise, surgeon,' said Ellia, ducking her head inside.

The man's gnarled hands hovered over Lesky, unsure. 'I cannot, my lady. If I give her any more lauendi, she's likely to fall into a sleep of months, years even.'

'Then do something else, grey-beard, or find me another who can!'

'Yes, Baroness.'

Ellia slammed the door on them, and strode to check on the firns, muttering curses. She could still feel the girl questing with her mind, lashing out; not searching and gleaning, but crying out. Five times now, the wailing had flashed through her thoughts, making her retch. The girl was stronger than Spiddle even knew.

Ellia held her mind strong, keeping focus on a solitary thought: a location, a crossroads. She penned it in extreme detail—tufts of grass and all—and held it until she heard the rattle of chainmail on the path.

Her gaze snapped to the sound, finding a lone figure in the mist. The driver had returned.

'My 'pologies, Baroness. The battle—'

'Never mind. Onwards!'

He looked back over his shoulder. 'But, Milady, there's a few—'

A raised hand shut him up. More armour on the path, plate as well as chain this time. She bit down on a curse and shoved the driver towards the carriage.

'Baroness!' Sergeant Collaver called, emerging out of the haze with a trumpet-shaped musket on his shoulder. Half a dozen soldiers accompanied him. Ellia stepped forwards.

'Sergeant. To what do I owe this interruption?'

'You can owe that to the general, Ma'am. Given tonight's… shambles, he wants extra protection for you. He says if you insist on leaving for the capital, then we shall have to accompany you.'

Ellia smelled resentment. 'He would spare one of his best for a journey to Caverill? I imagine it's something to do with that spy still being in the camp? Salt, wasn't it?'

The man looked uncomfortable. 'Apparently so.'

'Well then, what choice do I have?' She bade them towards the carriage.

Collaver was confused. 'Now, Milady? Surely the morning would be safer?'

'The Fading are busy fighting, not watching the roads. What better time than now, Sergeant?' She rested a hand on the carriage door. 'I will need privacy, if you please. I suggest riding with the driver. I've told him the directions already.'

'Aye, Baroness.'

Ellia waited for them to all clamber aboard before she slipped through the door. At least she'd had the foresight to close its curtains. She shoved a finger against the surgeon's mouth until the whip cracked and they had lurched into the night.

'I want you silent, surgeon. And I want the girl the same way. Do you understand?'

A nod was all she needed. Ellia waved a hand and settled back against the carriage-cloth. She half-closed her eyes, letting her gaze rest on the girl, while in her mind she held tight to thoughts of crossroads.

Half an hour of rattling came and went, and by the time the driver slowed, the girl was deathly-still, but breathing. Ellia threw the doctor a look before cracking open the door.

'I suggest we stop here, Sergeant, and survey the road ahead.'

'As you wish.'

She reached down into the surgeon's case and plucked a copper scalpel from its hollow. She admired its sheen in the lantern-light.

'Baroness…' The surgeon's eyes widened.

'Fear not. This is not for you.' She bent close to him. 'Remember what we agreed about silence?'

He went back to his healing.

The carriage juddered to a halt. Ellia pressed herself to the door, scalpel gripped in her fist, and waited. She could hear the soldiers clearing their throats and shrugging on their metal, but she stayed put.

She felt the weight of another mind creeping into her own. At first she expected another wave of crying, but this touch was softer, skilled.

Spiddle.

'About time.'

A wet thud emanated from above her, and moments later, there was a crash as a body met the road. Another followed not two blinks afterwards.

She burst from the door as the third arrow glanced from the carriage roof and came spinning down at her feet. The night was thick with mist, and the soldiers were too panicked to see her coming. Two went down with their throats wide open, blood spraying.

Another arrow flew from the murk, pinning a soldier by the arm. Ellia gave him another reason to stick around, dragging his mail up his chest and slashing him across the belly. All a man can really do in that situation is affix a ghostly look of horror onto his face, and try to gather up what he can before the shock sets in. Ellia left him to it.

The driver sat as still and upright as a nail; eyes forward, reins battling the skittering firns. She let him be for the moment, and slipped under the carriage as Collaver dragged his musket from the seat. She caught the barrel under her arm and drove her copper blade up into his neck. The blood trickled over her knuckles and wrist, staining her coat dark in the faint light from the carriage door.

Collaver wore the usual look of surprise she liked from her victims; but there was also relief there too, bordering on gratitude. She twisted the knife and let him slump to the dirt. He died staring up at the swirling mist.

'I see you haven't lost your zealot's edge, Ellia,' said Spiddle, creeping up behind.

'And I see you've been practising,' she said, nodding to the bow in his hand.

'Firepowder and guns are barbaric to me.'

Ellia rolled her eyes.

Spiddle's wistful look grew serious. 'Why the sudden change in plan? What happened with the bone golem?'

'It performed just as expected. It sent Task into a rage. He tore off after the Fading forces. All we do now is wait.'

'Fine work. Now what of the glimpse?'

'She was injured in the attack.'

Spiddle stepped closer, his eyes half-closing. She felt him pick at her mind, and once again steeled herself. He cast a look at the carriage, and she made a show of giving in. 'I can use her. She has secrets.'

'Then I will take them from her, before I bring her to Cane.'

'No. She is important to the golem.'

Spiddle tilted his head.

'And in the hands of the Last Fading, she will be bait to him.'

'Cane will not be pleased,' said Spiddle. 'The Treyarch will wonder —'

'Let him wonder!'

The glimpse threw back his shoulders. 'Careful, Zealot. You speak too freely for my liking.'

'With all the thoughts you wade through, it's a wonder you have an original opinion left in that tattooed head of yours! I'm tired of climbing this wall of doubt. Piece by piece, I have built this scheme, nurtured it, sweated over it, pushed it into being. And now, just as I am about to succeed, you damn me for improvising. I refuse to let this fail because of your obstinance. Take that back to Cane and the Treyarch, if you must take something. Otherwise, leave me alone to do my job.'

Ellia barged past him and wrenched open the carriage door.

'North, driver, if you please.'

The driver stammered his consent, then cracked his whip with the alacrity of a gallows victim being blessed by a second chance. Spiddle was left standing in the circle of corpses, bow in hand, looking stern and confused.

Ellia closed the window with a smile.

Perfect.

21

'The question of whether the golems were creatures of their own thought, as we are, is a difficult one. They are slaves to their magic, but at the same time, they are capable of limited conversation, plans, decisions. With some, one gets the impression of a soul. Particularly the Hasp creations.'

FROM TREATISES OF THE NARWE HARMONY 3012

58TH FADING, 3782 - TRUEHARD CAMP

'What do you mean, you've lost him?'

Taspin looked to Manx. Manx turned to Jenever. Jenever tried to find success in Glum, but the man was staring at something on the floor.

'I ASKED YOU A QUESTION!' Huff pounded his desk with his fists. The captains shuffled backwards, cringing. 'Where is my golem?'

Taspin tried his luck. 'If I may, General. The last we saw of him, he was chasing down Fading bowmen. He might be tracking them down, one by one? Taking his time?'

'I did not order him to take his time. I ordered him to kill a battalion of Fading!'

'Maybe he's lost. Ran so far, the mist turned him around.' Manx, this time.

'Any other bright ideas?'

The question stirred Glum into life. 'Perhaps he's doin' exactly what you ordered, General. He's gone after the enemy, lonesome like.'

Huff hunched over his desk. Glum kept his eyes up, confident in his reasoning, as always. For a change, his reasoning was not the rambling of a fool, but that didn't mean Huff had to like it.

'Unacceptable, Captain. Absolutely unacceptable!' Huff cast a sheaf of documents from his desk with a vicious swipe.

Before the last paper had floated to the dirty rug, Huff had already grabbed his coat from a hangar, and barged the gaggle of idiots aside.

'Follow!'

Striding fast, Huff led them to the shattered section of the camp, where burnt tents and stables still smouldered, where bodies lay broken in rough clusters.

A large pile of bones lay off to the side, smeared with mud and blood. No form or shape could be spied in the muddle, and no two bones clung together. Set apart from the bundle was a small object, surrounded by a group of wary soldiers. The bone golem's tongue.

Councillor Dast roamed the tortured ground where the beast's claws had dug deep furrows. He tutted to himself, shaking his head. His monocle was missing.

It was an unusual sight for many a reason, but mainly because Dast had not been seen up before noon in almost a week. The good councillor had been putting the general's considerable stash of torig to good use, even taking to sleeping in his carriage so he could be moved along when needed.

'Councillor,' said Huff. 'What plagues your mind so that it has dragged you from your bed barely an hour after dawn?'

'Your father, Huff. Your father won't be pleased with this. Not pleased at all.'

Huff threw a guiding arm around the man, and steered him away from the bodies and bones. He motioned to Glum. 'Take the good councillor back to his tent, and get him some torig to calm his nerves.'

Dast began to protest, but Huff pushed him into Glum's meaty arms, and let that particular problem walk away. *Next.*

'Where is Collaver? Corporal, do you know?

The woman shook her head.

'Shield-chief?'

'No, sir.'

'You sent him to look after Baroness Frayne's carriage, sir,' said Taspin.

'Yes, but she cannot have left already?'

Shrugs.

Huff snarled. 'Then find me the girl.'

'The girl?'

'The bitch who has put a spell upon my golem. The one Task protected. The dirty wretch who...' Huff pulled at his collar, careful to avoid the bruised skin. 'The stable-girl that Frayne took away. Manx! Jenever! Find me a surgeon.'

The two captains looked around the wreckage, as if searching for a man wearing a "surgeon" sign.

'Go!'

They scurried away. Only Taspin remained, squirming.

'You, Taspin, will gather your riders and start to sweep the countryside for the golem.'

'But the mist, General—'

'You will have to contend with it! Have you never seen a Naldish mist before, man?'

'As it happens, no.'

Huff offered his darkest look. He was tired of fighting for respect, of screaming for compliance. If they thought they had seen the limit of his cruelty, they were mistaken.

'Rally your riders, Lancer. Unless you wish to be flayed.'

Taspin left, and at last, Huff Dartridge the Third stood alone; not harried by cretins, nor beset by vicious tongues. He took a breath and held it, while his weary eyes roamed the camp. He gave up counting the dead at fifty, and with plenty more to go.

The bones stole his attention. It looked like the ceremonial pile of some heathen cult, and yet his gaze was fixed upon it, intent on knowing every one of its jagged, ghoulish angles. It was as if there were a message hidden in the muddle; a pattern to be drawn out and learned.

Huff took a step closer. And another. And another, until he stood at the foot of the mound, eyeing a long, curling rib. It was too big to be human, or jork, for that matter; and they were the largest beast to roam Lundish soil.

He reached out to feel the rib's pitted surface. He recoiled at its touch; colder and smoother than it looked. It had the texture of cut glass.

'Who made you?' he said aloud, daring to reach again.

Growing bolder, he began to pick through the pile. He found a knuckle-bone as big as his fist, a clavicle that could have been used as a shield, and the bony tail of a spine; decidedly human.

This golem was of an ungodly design; something thrown and stuck together rather than shaped by a creator's hand. Unrefined, perhaps, but still effective. The stinking piles around him were evidence of that.

Huff withdrew from the mound and retreated to the cloth-covered tongue. With a wave, he dismissed the soldiers. He flicked aside the covering and stared down at the bright gem. Bronze swirled inside yellow and clear stone. It had been carved into a lozenge about the length of his arm, and then polished smooth. The general could see his own face in its sheen, warped and flattened.

Huff found his fingers reaching once more, and as he caressed the gem's surface he felt a numbness in his fingers. Something wriggled under his nails, and he snatched back his hand. *The spell still lingered.*

Noting the stares from his men, he replaced the cloth, and walked back towards the bone-mass. He found himself stuck halfway, unable to break from the pull of the tongue. The tingle of old-magic filled his mind.

Before he could retrace his steps, he spotted Manx weaving his way back through the soldiers. He looked more hurried than usual.

'Good news I hope, Manx? For your sake.'

The captain winced. 'The surgeon helping the Baroness has disappeared. So has the girl.'

Huff pieced it together in an instant. 'She has taken the whelp with her. To Caverill.'

'You don't think the golem went after her?'

Huff strode away. 'I do not, as it happens, Manx! He is simply lost, or eagerly fulfilling my orders. Wreaking havoc, I'd wager. Lancer Taspin will track him down soon enough.'

Lies. All for show. He knew soldiers liked to prick their ears when the boss was around. A dark horror had formed in his mind, of a web spun by Frayne and the girl. Of the golem betraying his oaths. *Of losing his edge.*

Huff dismissed the thoughts of failure, and turned to face the pile of bones.

'Gather it all up, and place it in my tent.'

'General?'

'Every fragment, every splinter. In crates, trunks, sacks. Whatever it takes.' He reached down and claimed the tongue for himself, sliding it under the folds of his coat.

Manx was rooted to the mud. Huff brought his face a whisker from the captain's.

'Was I not clear?'

'No, sir.'

'Then why are you not screaming at these soldiers?'

Manx stepped aside, taking an enormous breath. 'FORM UP, INGRATES!'

'Much better, Captain.' Huff strode away at speed. He could already feel the tingle of the gem creeping through his shirt.

The knight had called them the Bastard Marshes, and he was not wrong.

They had some other grand name, apparently. Something that sounded like "squatch". He hadn't managed to catch it.

The maze of bog and grass mounds were infuriating enough. There was no need for the sulphurous stench, nor the buzzing things that infested the place. That was just malicious.

Task waved the winged creatures away from his face. They seemed to have a lust to explore every one of his crevices. They crawled over every inch of stone, and it was all he could do not to roar whenever one found his eye-socket.

But what bothered him most was the fact that he endured the cruelties of the marshes alone. Alabast looked as though he were on an afternoon ride.

Not only could his nimble firn skip between the patches of solid ground, something about its musk kept the dreaded insects at bay. Task slogged through the muck, while the knight watched the world go by like a prince in a carry-box.

It had barely been ten hours since he'd snapped. The golem still felt the precipice calling like a fresh wound. The longer he watched the knight, the more it began to ache.

'Comfortable up there, Knight?'

Alabast was nibbling on something from a pouch at his belt. 'Very much so.'

Task let his stones rattle.

'Apologies again,' said Alabast. 'This is the quickest route, as the olma flies.'

Task looked up to see if he could spot any of the fat, feathery creatures, but the sky was painted a wash of fetid yellow with the marsh vapours. Nothing lived here but insects.

The golem clenched his face and felt the squish of many miniature bodies. He doused his head in the bog-water and shook himself, managing to spray the knight.

'Oi!' he cried, wiping the slime from his face.

Task echoed him. 'Apologies!'

Alabast muttered a curse. 'Midges bothering you?'

'Evidently.'

'Here.' The knight reined in the firn and wiped a handkerchief along its bronze scales and fur. 'Wrap this around your head.'

Task snatched the cloth. It smelled horrific up close, even with his nostrils full of sulphur. He tied it about his thick neck, and waited.

Alabast was playing no trick. The buzzing things retreated from his crags, and even had the decency to steer clear of him. He cracked a grin;

not for Alabast, but for himself. Like a victim of torture being handed a key to the chains.

Alabast reclined once more, using his pack as a seat. 'See? I'm not so bad, am I? I've been called generous before. Kindly, even.'

'Personally, I'd call you a coward.'

The brought Alabast's head snapping around. 'I faced you last night, didn't I, golem?'

Task flashed him the remnants of his grin. 'Doesn't mean you didn't run on our previous meeting.'

'Lady Auger was right. You're a strange beast.'

'Who is this Lady Auger?'

Alabast chuckled to himself. He was as quick to mirth as he was anger. 'You'll see.'

'The only thing I see is a man immensely pleased with himself. Relieved, even. Almost as though he had just won the war singlehandedly.'

'I'm glad to be alive. What can I say?'

'No. You skinbags are numb to being alive. You see it as your divine right.' His tone had turned to a growl, and he pulled himself back.

'Perhaps I'm happy you put those ears to good use, and gave us a chance to tell our story.'

The golem snorted.

Alabast slowed his firn so he could ride alongside Task, to show him the firmer ground. 'What's so funny?'

'It appears to me that you're more excited about your own story. I'd wager you couldn't care less about the Fading or their war. Let me guess. The dragon-killing dried up, so you needed a new monster to slay? But you couldn't, so you had to find another to make a name. "Knight of Dawn, Golem-Whisperer". I'm just another dragon to you, aren't I? Another coin-purse.'

'You're smarter than you look, golem. But, trust me. If I could, I would be far, far away from here, drowning in Braaden women and gutwine. This wasn't my bright idea. It was Auger's.'

'Hmm.'

'What now?'

Task took a moment to stretch as the firn lined itself up for a jump, haunches wiggling. 'I've been getting good at spotting lies recently.'

Alabast put so much effort into his scowl he almost tipped from his firn upon landing.

'What about "Knight of Dawn, Betrayer". Or "Turncoat". I always liked that word.'

Alabast halted. 'What do you mean?'

'Perhaps I've convinced you to take me straight to Safferon and your Lord Lash. It would look like you turned sides, and escorted the Truehards' greatest weapon through the gates of the Fading's last bastion.'

Alabast's expression turned fearful. Task couldn't help but enjoy himself at the expense of the so-called hero. It was distracting. The golem gave him a wink before pressing on through the filth.

Alabast's hand crept to his sword-handle, but he was smart enough to leave it there.

'You said—'

'Unlike you people, I know how to keep a promise.'

Task heard the sigh, then the trusty trot of paws.

It was some time before the knight spoke up again. The ground was gradually becoming firmer, though it still had a squelch to it. Yet the golem still waded: he had traded noxious bog-water for a sea of marsh grass.

'Tell me, golem, what brings about your curse? What makes you snap?'

The golem rumbled. 'It is not something I like to discuss.'

'Go on. Just a clue.'

'Many things that humans do, like asking questions when they haven't been invited.'

Alabast was ambitious. 'So it's never based on your own behaviour?'

Task counted a few examples in his head. 'Never.'

'Curious. My anger is the opposite. It always feeds on my failure. And it brings a clarity. Not a calm, but a...' His words failed him, so he jabbed the air. 'Like a shard of ice hunting down everyone who comes against me. Does that makes sense?'

It did, but it was upside-down to Task. 'Mine brings nothing but death.'

The words hung between them for a few moments, as bothersome as the sulphurous vapours.

Alabast took the opportunity to clear his throat. 'Naturally.'

'Do you expect me to talk the entire trip? What is this need to know me?'

Alabast shrugged the comment aside. 'I find it's always nice having somebody to chat to on the road.'

Task heard the twang of another lie. 'You're either curious, trying to save your backside, or trying to root out a weakness.'

'Do we all start out as villains in your mind, or is your hatred something that we earn over time?'

The golem couldn't help but hear Lesky's voice in the question. It brought out a flicker of anger. 'I have seen more wars than you've seen seasons, Knight. I've been sold from master to master for four hundred years, and each was more a beast of war than I am. I've been shot at, hacked at, pummelled with catapult-stones, doused in flaming oil, tipped into drowning-pits, even covered by a landslide. I've seen every kind of violence humans know how to wreak, and I have learnt that you are creatures beyond cruel, beyond vengeful, beyond dishonest. So, yes, Knight. You are all villains in my mind.'

Alabast nodded. 'As something of a hero myself, I know the correlation between a long life and the amount of villains one encounters.'

Silence again, as Task strived to overcome his seething.

'With so many enemies, golem, do you not have any friends?'

Task found his answer strangely comforting. 'More than usual, recently.' And then the feeling was gone. 'Though fewer every day, it seems.'

Task looked back along the marsh, scanning the mists and rugged landscape for any sign of followers. The Naldish Lumps glowed green far beyond, where they gave way to the wetland.

'You and I seem to be rather alike, Task. Perhaps we could be friends.'

The golem thought of the girl once more, and flashed him a wicked smile. 'Best friends.'

By sunset they had broken free of the marshes, and were galloping across the plains of Norset county. Along their flanks, small mountains sprang up from the tail of the Naldish Lumps, but they were far from the spectacle of their southern cousins, the Six Sisters.

Here the farmland stretched for miles; field after field, all untended but plenty haunted by the ghostly remains of lives once lived. Through the lengthening dusk, they passed broken crofts, empty swings on trees, and the bones of long-dead animals.

The same question lay in every one of those relics. *How did they get there?* The thought kept pulling Task north, despite all the longing gazes over his shoulder.

The night fell with a bitter chill. Steam curled from the golem's joints and hot breath plumed from both firn and rider.

Around a spur of the mountain range, they found a haven of humanity hiding in the narrow cleft between two cliffs. The city was a cone of yellow lights, clinging to the rock. It was too far away for Task's thunder to be heard.

'What is that?'

'Gillish!' said Alabast.

'Hiding from the war?'

'There's no hiding! Most of the city fled to Safferon and Dinwint weeks ago.'

Task knew that was his doing. Every battle he'd won, he'd put the fear into these people.

On, they ran and rode. They made short work of the miles now that darkness had fallen, and the roads were clear.

Beyond Gillish, not a single light pierced the darkness. With only one Mother to light the evening, Task had to imagine the endless procession of fields and homesteads waiting for morning.

Another league past the city, and a watchtower greeted them with its lofty flame. It perched like a splinter on a huge knuckle of rock the size of a palace. Lanterns lit the ground for foot-lengths around it. Alabast paid it no heed, and Task guessed it was a Fading outpost.

As the mountains curved towards the northwest, the landscape opened wide into a flat plain that stretched on for hundreds of leagues, to the east, west and north. Dotted across the plain were gigantic trees, the colour of milk and silver-leaf in the dim moonlight. A few gathered in clumps of three or four, but most stood alone and aloof, reaching towards the sky with tendril fingers. Between them was thick brown vegetation, claiming every foot-length. Here and there, patches of snow still glittered, reminding them that Fading still held sway for now.

Task felt the knight's pace falter. He slowed with him, wary, but as it turned out, Alabast and his firn were both on the edge of breathless. When they came to a halt, he wrenched himself from the saddle, and entered a heap-like state in the deep grass. The firn followed suit, its legs splaying in all directions. It rattled its scales as it took deep lungfuls. They undulated like an ocean wave.

'What are you doing?'

Task crossed his arms, though he was secretly glad for the halt. His stones had grown hot and heavy over the past hour. He supposed he could have called it tiredness.

'It's called resting.'

Task looked around at the expanse of grass 'Here?'

'Good a place as any. Won't be no campfire. Long grass. You can keep watch.'

Task would tackle the subject of sleep later. 'What about under one of these trees?'

'No, no,' said Alabast, amused.

'Why not?'

The knight sighed. 'Roamwillows like to, hmm, how shall I put it, *roam.*'

'They move?'

A nod. 'A little every night. There are many stories of travellers camping under them, only to be crushed in their sleep. They're a willow in reverse. They point up instead of down, and they won't stay still after you plant them. Plenty of Norset folk can tell you more. Save your questions for Safferon.'

Task stared at the nearest behemoth, stretching far up into the night. Its leaves almost sparkled in the Mother's light. *Roamwillows.* He ached to touch one.

'Where do they go?'

Alabast shrugged, a feat of some effort by the look of it. 'Anywhere they want. Lately, away from the war. Away from here.'

It did look as if the trees had a lean to them. Some pointed left, some right. There was a faint divide between the two.

'But they're still here.'

'I said they roam. I didn't say they did it quickly. By the time they change their minds, there'll be another war on.'

Task could understand that, and it fascinated him. Not all old-magic could turn the materials of the world into walking, talking life. Some of it was subtle, or, as Belerod would see it, weak. If these trees had magic in them, he wanted to feel it. Maybe it would give him some peace.

Alabast noticed his longing, and waved a hand. 'You go. Look at them all you want. I'm going to feed me and this girl. I take it you don't eat?'

'No.'

'Sleep?'

'When I can.'

Alabast pulled a face. 'Why?'

Task shrugged. 'Gives me some peace and quiet away from you skinbags for a while, that's why. That, and my stone gets hot after a long day. Itchy.'

'How odd.'

Task took that as the end of the matter, and strode out towards the nearest of the trees, one aimed west. He took his time to get there, transfixed by the slivers of wood sprouting from its head. They seemed a cliff's height away. He could have been twice as large as the biggest golem ever built, and he wouldn't have reached halfway up the trunk.

As he got closer, he finally understood the magic of it, and how these things went about their roaming. Half the roots were above-ground, thick and gnarled like the tentacles of a sea leviathan. They penetrated the half-frozen dirt; some pulling, some pushing, all creaking in constant, almost imperceptible movement. Task could feel the changing in his stones easily enough, but he had to stand still, and look closely to see it.

The tree even had a footprint: a long trail of churned mud between the grass, hidden until now. Task stepped around it and chose a spot between the roots where he could place his hand. The wood was white as unmarked flesh, fine-grained to the point of seamless.

The old-magic was stronger than it looked. It grabbed him almost immediately, wrapping around his arm like a noose to a thief's neck. He held tight, letting its fragmented past flash before him. As much as he drew from the wood, he felt double bleed from him.

The plant's history blended with his, painting pictures of trees burning like bonfires, of children's smiles, of birds pecking his shoulders, cannon-fire ripping through drystone walls, of creatures gnawing roots, and fields of corpses, swallowed over decades by a grinding forest.

Task wrenched himself away from the wood, pulling a piece of bark with him. He lifted up his claw to shake it off, but it crumbled before he could do so.

'Bred for war. Or at the least the dregs of it,' he said to himself.

Whatever good and wholesome thing this tree had been raised for, centuries upon centuries ago, had been perverted by violence. Whether the souls of the dead, or their memories, the magic had absorbed a little of them each time. A hundred voices yelled within that trunk. It was tired of them.

Tired of war.

Task found himself saluting the tree, there in the dark, alone. It was a sign of respect. It was comforting that another creature knew his pain. Perhaps far more keenly than he did.

The golem took a breath before retreating back to Alabast. Sleep was calling.

He found the knight snoring against the slumbering firn, both deep in their dreams already. He chose a spot away from them, turning his back on the plains and the forest so he could look south. For a time he watched for lights. And, as the darkness stole him, he thought of Lesky.

29TH SOWING, 3362 - WIND-CUT, HASPIA

'Tie him down. Lash him, for Rent's sake!'

The men stepped forth, dangling ropes from blood-soaked hands, wincing every time the golem shifted.

The black and silver one. Again. Belerod had been whispering for weeks about it being too big for its mind. The madness came too easily to it, he said.

Task was still dealing with his own madness, or rather the lack of it. The lack of anything at all, in fact, besides revulsion. He had tried, over and over, to feel what the other Wind-Cuts felt, and yet he was finding he had no joy for the business of ending lives. He looked again at the crooked forms on the floor, the ones he had cleaved through with cold calculation not too long ago.

Dead bodies were only grotesque when compared with the living; if they are their own creatures, then they are meant to be bloody and torn, and the sight of them can be managed.

Task let his gaze roam over the sea of dead which had flooded the courtyard. Elbows and feet poked from heaps. Torsos groped for their legs. Not a glint came from the scattered armour and blades, no matter how hard the mountain sun beat down. There was nothing pristine or shining in this fortress any longer. All that remained was filth and decay; and under the clouded but watchful eyes of the dead, Task felt no cleaner.

'Task! Pay attention!'

'Yes Master.'

'Hold him!'

Task paused far too long for Belerod's liking. He had a ghastly cut across one eye. The golem wondered if he would ever see again.

'You useless creation!' Belerod whipped him with the flat of his sword. *'Do as I say and hold on to your brother!'*

'Aye, Master.' Slow and steady, Task reached out for the giant golem's arm. It was almost as thick as his waist.

As stone met stone, Task felt the jolt of old-magic meeting. His fingers clamped down, as faces and shapes burst in front of his eyes. Red. All red. His vision was drenched with it.

'Task!'

The arm wrenched away, and came swiftly back, walloping him in the chest. Task was thrown backwards, crushing a soldier who had been too slow on the uptake. He felt the crunch beneath his spine and the flagstones.

'ROPES!'

With great difficulty, they reined in the golem until he had calmed. Task had risen to his feet, staying beside his newest corpse with an apologetic look on his face.

His master marched to him, standing so close that Task had to tuck in his chin to meet Belerod's furious eyes.

'Him! Him I can understand! Bloodlust is all he has, and that's a good thing in a golem. But you, Task. You are a liability! I watched you today, and what I saw disgusted me. You hesitate, golem, and that is as despicable as betraying your orders. There is no anger in you, no lust of any kind!' Belerod moved to strike Task in the ribs but thought better of it.

'You are broken, golem! Get out of my sight!'

Task obliged him, melting into a side-street with a head full of angst and blood-soaked images of another life.

Task looked down at his stained hands, pressing them together with no effect. He ran them across the nearest wall, but in his muddle he couldn't feel anything. Was this just another product of his brokenness? Or just old-magic meeting old-magic? He wondered whether he had ever touched another golem before.

He was halted by a corpse in his path, lying half-in, half-out of a doorway. Inside the building a shattered lantern smouldered.

Task knelt and pressed a hand to the woman's neck, just to the side of the gaping wound in her breast-bone. He managed to feel the warmth of her skin before the magic pounced once more. He had no choice but to endure as her last moments were played for him, as if he had been the one pressed up against a door when the axes had broken through.

The golem recoiled, falling to the flagstones. His hand had crushed her neck. The stones of his fist shook with a vigour he knew not.

'Rain's comin'!'

The voice was so small it seemed like a trick of the mind.

'Not today, but soonish.'

It was a girl, sun-dark and hair shaved to a faint fuzz. Task could see the notches of her skull through her papery skin. The street waif had nothing to wear but sackcloth.

'Go away!'

The girl made as if to do so, but got stuck halfway. Her eyes were so dark-brown they seemed black in the shade, and they held no fear of him.

'Do you like the rain?'

He had no feelings for it, save that it served to cool him, and wash some of the dust away. With a shrug, the golem headed for the camp, away from the little creature.

'See you soon, you big lump.'

Task's head snapped around with a crunch.

Lesky stood in place of the girl. Calm smile, hands clasped in front of her. She seemed oblivious to the horror of the scene.

Bubbling water seeped through the flagstones beneath her feet. An ugly grin of bloody flesh and white bone spread across her neck and shoulder, bloodless but still as raw. She smiled as if it were a mere scratch.

Task felt his feet slipping in the water as he backed away.

22

'Nobody knows where the God's Rent came from. The Harmony
believes it released magic back into the world. The Mission say it
came to swallow evil. The Destrix think it as a god itself,
demanding sacrifice. One thing is for sure: it is the most
breathtaking, and yet terrifying sight this author has laid eyes
upon.'

FROM REACHES OF THE REALM, BY HORDFIN

59TH FADING, 3782 - NORSET PLAINS

There was no doubt the thing was dreaming. He snuffled. He creaked. Had
the golem eyelids of skin, Alabast was sure he would have seen his
glowing eyeballs roaming wildly.

In the dawnlight, he took the chance to let his gaze roam, tracing
the mica veins that ran through the golem's slate-grey, blueish stone. He
was full of cracks and pebbles, all carved into a hulking forgery of a man.
Somehow, he looked even bigger lying down.

It dreamed. What in the Realm did a piece of rock have to dream
about? He was no stranger to the quirks of old-magic, but this was nothing
short of bizarre. A stone with dreams. Alabast scratched at his forehead.
The longer he watched, the more it seemed like he was witnessing a
nightmare, and the deeper it disturbed him.

The knight put away his road-crackers, brushed his hands and got to
standing. He looked for something to poke the golem with, but
only laid eyes on his sword. He fetched it with a shrug.

Careful to keep the blade in its scabbard, Alabast held it at arm's
length and began to poke the beast in his broad chest. Softly at first, then
bolder, until he was practically thwacking him.

Task came to life with a roar, sending the blade spinning and taking Alabast's legs from under him. He dropped like a puppet with the strings cut, head bouncing from the hard ground. The pain of it momentarily blinded him.

When he recovered, he found the grimacing face of a golem hovering over him, so close he could have licked his stone.

'Explain yourself!'

Alabast couldn't do anything besides wheeze for a moment, but he soon found his words. A hand reached in the direction of the sword. 'You were... having a nightmare.'

Task gave him some space, retreating to the patch he'd worn in the grass overnight. He took some time to stare at the risen sun, teetering on a distant smudge of hills. Then at the trees, noting how different they looked in the light.

'Just a dream.'

Alabast pushed himself to sitting. 'Look, I've slept beside enough bodies to know the difference between a dream and a nightmare. You, golem, were maring, as they say in Gurnigen.' He winced as he adjusted his knee. The golem had almost snapped his leg clean off.

'Though usually when I wake someone from a nightmare, I get a kiss, or more.'

'Call that a golem's kiss, then. Shouldn't have woken me.'

'And leave you to whatever darkness hides in that stone dome of yours? Your choice.'

'Like you care.'

It was true. Alabast didn't really care, but he was curious, and that could give the illusion of compassion. The only thing he truly cared about was keeping the golem on his good side, long enough to ride his stony coat-tails out of this country.

'I want to know what you dream about.'

Task was a beast with no time for fawl-shite. He sniffed it out as easily as a wark with a sausage. Alabast had realised that quickly enough.

'Another question with a private answer,' said the golem.

'I am simply curious.'

It took some time for Task to answer. 'Memories. And water, recently. Though for what reason I don't know.'

'Water?'

'Yes. Water. A great ocean of it that tries to drown me. Now, should we not be moving?'

'As you wish, golem. As you wish.'

Alabast calmed the firn and readied it for another long day of riding. He expected the beast to collapse at the shadow of the gatehouse. He had driven her too hard already.

The previous day's aches returned the moment he climbed into the saddle, mostly around his buttocks and crotch. He reached for his usual remedy of liquid medicine, but caught himself with a smile. It had been ten days since a drop had passed his lips.

Did he feel different? He had asked himself every day. Overall, the longer he went sober, the more he felt, dare he say it, *responsible.* He was not sure if he liked that.

Alabast kicked his heels and the firn sprung to life. He let her warm up for the first league or two, but soon the golem was pushing to go faster. Before long, they were tearing through the grass like fugitives, racing time itself. The firn slavered and panted, but its rippling muscles kept pace.

The day stayed cold, but pleasant, with the exception of a lone shower that rolled in across the plain. Alabast took the opportunity to call for a rest, and let the firn drink. They chose a spot under a wizened roamwillow, and stood hunched and staring at the rain.

'How does one kill a dragon, then?' said Task.

He was poking fun again, perhaps, but Alabast was glad of the conversation. His tongue always felt restless if it was asked to stay still.

'With great difficulty, to cut a story short. To cut it long, it's a matter of getting somewhere high, so you can come down onto the back of its neck, where its armour is weak. There's a reason a sheen, that's the—'

'A Destrix Sheen.'

'That's the bugger. The weak armour is the reason they have such great horns, all curling backwards. But if you can get under there with something like starsteel...' He patted his sword. '...you've got a chance.'

'Two days, I hear you fought,' said Task, raising an eyebrow.

Alabast flashed an easy smile. 'You know how stories grow with every telling. It was a long day, I can tell you that. I crept in at dawn, just as the creature was settling to sleep. Night-hunters, they are, and deathly quiet thanks to the feathers on the edges of their wings. They snatch fawls from their pens, riders from saddles, even guards from watchtowers. Black and grey, like a Motherless night. A beast so big, even the God's Rent would have struggled to swallow it.

'I caught it a blow across the chin before it woke. The rest is a blur of being chased around its cavern, with its spit melting through my shield piece by piece. Then my armour. Before long it was just me and the starsteel. He made the mistake of turning his back on me, and that's when I struck. Straight down and sword first. Right through the vertebrae with a crack so loud I was deafened for an hour. And just like that, he was dead, leaving me halfway between life and death.' Alabast sighed for effect. It was a story long rehearsed. 'Then came the gruesome task of taking its head, and dragging it back to Kopen. Its skull now sits in the palace grounds, with my name on the pedestal.'

Task looked at him for a long time. 'And you enjoyed killing the dragon? The last of its kind?'

Alabast nodded. It was an unusual question; one he hadn't ever prepared an answer for. 'It was terrorising the city and the countryside. No hunter could come close. I fancied myself a worthy opponent. I trained at the Kopen Bladehall, after all.'

'I understand that,' said the golem. 'I hunted down gritwyrms doing the same thing in the Duneplains. They are as long as a tower is tall, all made of segments with armour thick as a fencepost. They swim through the sand as if it were water, bursting up underneath caravans or campfires. The trick is to grab them by the jaws and break them, or let them eat you so you can snap their spines from the inside.'

Alabast threw a sideways look at the golem, and Task shrugged. 'Not that it's a competition, or anything. Difference is, with you, they adored you for it. I didn't even get a pat on the back.'

'If I were your idiot general, I'd be thanking you every day. The man's making a career out of you.'

'Isn't that what you're doing?' said Task, with a smile. It was a curious thing; so foreign on a face of stone.

'Erm...'

'Relax, Knight of Dawn. We each do whatever we have to do to survive. I understand that necessity, and in that we do have something in common.'

'And here I was thinking you were just a disgruntled war-machine. But Auger was right again. You do have a soul to you. Something human.'

The stone smile disappeared. Task turned to the north.

'The rain has lessened.'

With no further talk, they set off once more, on the final leg. There were only twenty or so leagues left to travel before they reached the gates of Safferon. Task seemed to sense it, and without words, it drove them faster. Clawed feet and stone toes beat out a merciless rhythm on the hard ground, trampling snow and grass.

They kept their silence, even when they raced past a line of refugees coming from the west. Most ditched their belongings and scarpered at the sight of the golem. The remainder cowered on the trail, hands raised in prayer. Task ignored them all and kept running. Alabast felt the need to mouth an apology as he passed.

The distant smudges of rock soon solidified, turning to imposing mountains that dominated the edges of the landscape. These were the Cairns. One half of the range ran northeast to southwest. The other ran in the opposite direction, so that they met far in the distance, putting an end to the mighty plain.

The sun was slipping to dusk, and it painted the mountains with a glow Alabast had never seen before. It turned one side to black, and the other to fire. Natural features never intrigued him until he had to fight or trudge across them; but now, with time and a wandering mind, the Cairns held his full attention.

Snow capped the mightiest of the crooked peaks. The few plants that found foothold on their charcoal rocks were scrawny and brittle in the Fading cold. Alabast realised how wild they were compared to their serene, gorse-covered cousins in the south. In the light, their jagged outlines were harsh and irregular, as if they had once been whole, but had shattered somehow. Or perhaps they were young, in mountain terms, and yet to be worn by storm and season.

The road led straight for the crook of the mountain range, where Safferon Fortress could already be spied between the lengthening shadows. It was just a thumbnail's width at this point, with a few early lanterns and straight lines to betray it.

Alabast watched the fortress grow with every stride. Perspective made the mountains shrink behind it, and its broken towers rise higher.

At two leagues from its gate, where a brick watchtower stood guard, Alabast opened his mouth to give the golem some advice. But the blaring of a horn came forth, and for a moment he found himself confused.

It took moments for the call to be picked up by another, further down the road. Then the fortress spoke, its great horn rumbling deep within, as if the Realm itself were sighing.

The golem had fixed him with a glare. 'Are they not expecting us, Knight?'

'Of course they are! That's the good kind of horn.'

Alabast could hear the growl over the thunder of their feet.

He looked back at the fortress and squeezed his jaw tight. He wondered of Auger and the intent behind this challenge of hers. Was she tricking him again? *What if she meant to ruin him?* The golem's word came back to haunt him. He spoke it through thin lips.

'Turncoat.'

The mighty gates opened, and Lash was revealed, sitting in the middle of a row of musketmen. They all sported mighty bags under their aiming eyes. Even Lash's were heavier than usual.

'Lady Auger! Your arrival is as unexpected as it is poorly timed. You grace us on the eve of bad news.'

Ellia was in no mood to play games of formality.

'We lost. The bone golem is destroyed.'

'You have heard?'

'I was there.'

'You must have travelled quickly, Auger.'

'Non-stop, Milord.' She gestured to the wheezing firns.

'And who is your new friend?' Lash levelled a finger at the young driver, who was frozen solid on his seat.

'A driver. One of three, actually.'

'Drivers?'

'New friends.' Ellia whistled through her fingers. Most unladylike, of course, but she was past caring.

The musketmen switched aim as the door to the carriage popped open. Out came the surgeon, still soiled in blood and sweat. He looked on the verge of collapse. Even with a dozen guns trained on him, his eyes still drooped.

'I'll need this one for a while. There is a girl in the carriage who must be carried to my room. Carefully. She is very important.'

Lash looked confused.

'The driver you can do with as you wish. I shan't be needing him any more.'

'Am I to assume this means you've cut your losses?'

The Lady Auger sighed. 'And ran. Huff has disgusted me too many times. I cannot be Baroness Frayne any longer. Besides, I have what I need. Huff has been stoked into a frenzy. As has our Wind-Cut friend. Even without the bone golem, I can still win you this war, Lash. If you'll permit me, that is.' She extended a hand full of rings. 'I will tell you all, momentarily.'

Beneath bushy eyebrows and a curious grimace, Lash placed a kiss on the back of her hand.

Ellia smiled. 'Out of interest, what's become of our good Knight of Dawn?'

The lord looked disappointed. 'Yet to return. But he is one of many. We lost far too many good soldiers. We shall give them one more day…' Lash lowered his voice for the sake of his men. '…before we move on without them.'

Ellia nodded, grasping the edge of his chair. She felt a chill of sadness at the news; for her plan, of course, but for the knight as well. In another life, in another Realm, there might have been a future for him.

'A wise tactic, as usual, my Lord. Come, let me help you to your room.'

'I am more than capable, Ellia. I'm not dead yet,' Lash pushed himself out of her reach.

'As you wish,' she said, hanging back to watch as the men carried the girl from the carriage. 'Careful with her! Treat her as if she were your own daughter. Or sister. Or finest porcelain, for all I care.'

Ellia was about to berate them further when she heard a distant horn. The soldiers around her flinched, looking to the skies, then to each other.

Within minutes, the fortress sounded its own horns, buried deep in the surrounding rock. The ground shook as they moaned.

'To arms!' said Lash. Bodies exploded into action. 'Long-lookers! Tell me what you see!'

A shout came down from the gatehouse. 'We're just looking, Milord!'

'Now, damn it!'

'Yes, Milord! Erm…' The voice trailed away. There was a frantic squeaking noise.

'It's the golem, sir!'

'Ours?'

Ellia watched Lash as he gritted his teeth and waited, cheeks raised and brow pinched. His face tumbled as the answer came, and she saw a flash of fear run through him.

'No, sir. The Truehards' golem! And he has the Knight of Dawn with him!'

Ellia felt her own smug expression collapse, replaced by an open mouth of shock. And strangely, relief. *The lucky swine had done it.* Her gamble had paid off.

Lash swallowed something. 'To arms! To bloody arms!'

Ellia stood still in the seething mass of soldiers.

'Lash! I need to speak to you!'

Safferon was one mighty fortress, no doubt about it. Broken, but mighty. Task stopped to stare up at its heights, vying with the dark rockface for dominance. Each concentric wall was taller than a siege ladder, and thick, judging by the number of spears that bristled on the outer brickwork.

The fighter in him was already figuring out its weaknesses. It may have been mighty, but he had broken mightier. He could already see the opportunities. There was one issue with building a fortress up against a mountain: there's always a higher point of vantage. That's how they had broken the Cavada.

Most curious was the fact that it wasn't Lundish-built. A golem could always be trusted to know masonry. He didn't even have to touch it; it felt older, grander than anything he had seen so far in Hartlund.

As they walked a road lined with stake-pits, towards the mighty gatehouse, Task grew sure their greeting was not going to be warm. He had seen the dull gleam of muskets on the wall-tops, and the smoke of matches for the cannons.

'You lied.' he said to the knight. 'This was your idea, wasn't it? And yours alone, by the looks of it.'

Alabast flashed him an honest look for once. 'It was not. It was Lady Auger's, and with any luck she's here to help me explain it.'

'And if not?'

The knight thought about that. 'Then you're about to witness the infamous bargaining skills of Alabast Flint up close.'

Task snorted. 'I imagined a man gets a lot of practice, when he has to bargain for his life so frequently.'

Alabast slid from his firn and let her wander back down the path. Worry was etched into his face. 'What will you do, golem? Have you made your decision?'

Task stared at the bristling gates. Would he trust in the knight and the hospitality of the Fading, or take the head start, and reduce them all to meat? In the end he let his curiosity sway him towards trust. He could always change his mind. *At least he wouldn't have to break the walls from the inside.*

He let the knight lead, hands wide and open, as they walked to within a musket-shot of the walls. A loud voice, brassy and metallic, bade them to go no further. Task came to a halt with crossed arms.

'Explain yourself, Knight!'

Task picked out a man poking from the gatehouse. He had a large cone in front of his mouth.

'I know how this looks!' Alabast began. Task rolled his eyes. 'But hear me out. The golem is here with good intentions.'

Silence reigned on the wall-top. There seemed to be some unseen discussion going on below. Task could hear heated voices behind the stone.

'What intentions?'

'He is here to listen to us, to find out why we fight. He is giving us a chance to change his mind.'

Somebody barked something behind the wall, and there was a clank of turning locks. Muskets clicked in unison to orders. Task clenched himself.

With great slowness, the gates crept open. Two shadows stood in its gap: one short and one tall, sinuous.

As they stepped into the light, Task saw a grizzled man with a russet face in a wheeled chair, and a woman he recognised immediately.

'Ellia Frayne!'

'Or as we know her, Lady Auger,' said Alabast. Task pushed past him and began to stride across the cracked ground.

A cannon fired at once, spitting fire from a hole in the walls. The shot bounced from the earth a foot-length or two in front of him. Dirt sprayed him. Task stood still, letting Alabast advance and stand with him once more.

'There was a reason I was staying by your side,' said the knight. 'The soldiers won't shoot me. They love me.'

The man in the chair spoke. 'I'll order them to shoot you, too, if you choose to stand with him, Alabast!' He pushed himself over the potholes and ruts.

Ellia, or Auger, had a blank look on her face. Task ignored Alabast and the man, and looked only at her. She met his eyes without hesitation, and held them.

'Baroness. Where is Lesky?'

'Alive. And safe. I kept my promise to you.'

He wanted so much more from her, but he knew it had to wait.

'You don't talk at her, you talk to me, sir.' The grizzled man got straight to business. 'I am Lord Lash, and you will tell me what you are doing here. Now! Before I order another volley.'

'I am here at the behest of Knight Alabast. He told me you have some truths to tell me. I wish to hear them.'

'Did he now?' Lash looked to Ellia. *There was truth in that, then.*

'As I said before, I never expected him to pull it off. A wild gamble. That was all. The impetuous Alabast Flint has proved us wrong.'

Alabast crossed his arms at that, looking furious.

'No, he proved *you* wrong, Ellia. He proved us idiots for trusting him. You've brought our biggest enemy right to our doorstep!' His hand didn't know whether to signal for cannon-fire or slap his leg with rage.

'I am here to listen, Lord Lash,' said Task. 'I promised Alabast my time, that I would try to understand you.'

'And then what?'

'I will make my decision on what should be done about this war.'

Lord Lash was turning from red to purple. 'Auger! You've gone too far!'

Alabast shrugged. 'That's what I said.'

Now it was Ellia's turn to be furious. She glared at him.

Lash looked utterly cornered. 'Where is Dartridge on this?'

'He does not know.'

'I lured the golem away from the battle,' said Alabast, looking proud.

'I was given no specific orders to destroy, just to hunt you down. I have done that. That leaves time enough for Huff to get here and claim me. I have agreed to give you that time.' He grunted. 'Not that you deserve it, given your cowardly tricks.'

Lash curled his fists. 'And when Huff gets here, he'll give it some new orders, and our stories won't make a blind bit of difference. No! This is madness. This is worse than madness! It's treachery, Auger! You as well, Alabast! Did you think this would help? Architect piss on both of you!'

Ellia sighed, gesturing for them to move it along. 'The golem was always going to stand at these gates, whether you liked it or not. This way, you have more time. I've bought you a few days at least. And who knows, maybe we'll find this golem has more heart than we give him credit for. Remember what I told you? He's his own beast. He's capable of realising what needs to be done. Perhaps he will.' She winked at the golem as if they shared a private joke. Task kept his mouth shut and his face impassive.

'And if what it decides to kill us all?'

Ellia shrugged. 'You had better tell him a good story, my lord.'

The golem stepped forward, rearing tall. 'It is not as if you have much of a choice.'

Lash took his time to ponder. His eyes flicked back and forth between Task's, no doubt wondering how to pick a lie from a stone face. He was clearly a man unused to being circumvented.

'Well, it appears I don't! If we are to play out this pointless charade, then we may as well get it over with. You, sir, will stay outside the walls. I will erect a tent. One cross word. One dark look. One quick movement, and I will have you destroyed.'

Task let him have that, and nodded. 'You have my word.'

With that, Lash turned and pushed himself away, leaving Task alone with Alabast and Ellia.

'*You* have some explaining to do,' Task snapped at Ellia. *Was that even her real name?*

'Doesn't she just,' said Alabast. 'Trickster.'

'Where is Lesky?' said the golem.

'Safe, like I told you. I brought her with me, out of Huff's clutches.' Her smile was infuriating, but before they could interrogate her further, she waved her hand and stepped after Lash, leaving the two of them out on the road.

'All in good time, gentlemen. All in good time. As his lordship said, we have a pointless charade to play out.'

Task's knuckles crunched.

23

'Gazers and glimpses shall never mix their seeds.
Should offspring come from this union it shall be struck dead in
the womb.
Should it survive, it shall be burnt upon birth.
The grim is an abomination in the eyes of the great Architect.'

FROM THE UPDATED MISSION STATUTES

59TH FADING, 3782 - SAFFERON FORTRESS

The work of assembling the tent was completed in a hush, as if the soldiers were worried that a stray shout might trigger the guns, or the golem.

Task spent the time with his arms crossed and his eyes on the overlooking musketmen, wondering if they sweated in the gleam of the winter sun, or shivered in the cold breeze.

When the tent was done, the soldiers picked up their pikes and formed a ring around it. Three chairs and a table were brought out, and set beneath the grey canvas. Task stayed where he was, wearing a look of boredom. Alabast hung by his side, also cross-armed, and with a similar pout on his face.

Finally, Lash came forth, Ellia once more by his side. He had his pistol on him, but his face had softened. A look of calm and patience had replaced the deep furrows of anger.

Another man walked with them, dressed in smart attire and with a gleam of sweat on his brow. He was carrying a satchel so stuffed with papers, they leaked from its edges.

The skinbags took to the chairs. Task bent down to his knees, rested on his heels and folded his hands on his lap. Like the Borian monks, ready for meditation.

Lash began loud and clear.

'If we are going to pursue this farcical conversation, I first wish to understand it better. Why does a beast bound by his master's whim want to know more about the enemy he fights? What does it matter to you, sir, when you cannot disobey Dartridge?'

Task let him see the brightness of his eyes. 'Because golems were built not to care, Lord Lash. It comes easy to us. I've spent three centuries not caring, and I've gotten rather good at it. I can wade through battle without a thought in my mind, every face just another blur. But here, in Hartlund, instead of blurs, I see desperation. I see people fighting for homes, fighting for a quiet life, fighting for *something*. Perhaps I am growing old or mad with the years, but somehow I find myself caring about them. I know it's true of the Truehards. I am here to find out whether the Fading are deserving or not. Believe me, it would be easier to shut my eyes and crush every skull in this land. I know the downsides of caring. I know its dangers.' As he paused to let Lash think, he caught Ellia cocking her head. 'I don't need to make this life of mine any harder than it is, but I am willing to, if necessary.'

The sweating man spoke up. 'And if we're not deserving? You didn't quite answer the Lord's question.'

'Then this war will be over swiftly, and with any luck, it'll be the end of me as well. I can have peace.'

Lash threw up his hands. 'See? A farce, as I said. There is no point to entertaining this idea.'

Ellia was staring at Task, something hard at work behind her eyes. 'Did you listen to nothing I just told you, Lash? You should have seen him pin Huff to the ground when he threatened his stable-girl. There is more than just stone in him. I can see it. There is a chance for redemption here, for all of us.'

The word sounded as alluring as it did unreachable. Ellia was right; he had snapped against his master, but he had also felt the pressure of the magic holding him back.

Lash pushed himself away from the table and paused for thought. He seemed the type of man who liked to test and feel every word before it was spoken. 'Earlier, you mentioned cowardly tricks?'

Task nodded. 'The bone golem, for one. And in our first encounter, you turned your cannon on your own lines just to get at me.'

Lash's chin found his his palm, and stuck there. 'Our first encounter. Westin?'

Westin rifled through his papers. 'Beyond the Arnidge fields, south of Purlegar.'

'And you say the cannons fired on our own troops?'

276

Task could still remember the weight of the cannon in his hands. 'I am sure of it.'

Lash beckoned for Westin. The man got up swiftly, bent an ear to Lash's mouth, then scurried off back to the gates. Silence reigned over their table as the minutes slid by.

When the executor reappeared, he had a soldier in tow; one with officer's bars on his arm. The man's eyes widened with every step, in both fear and recognition. Perhaps if he'd been fleeing in the opposite direction, Task might have recognised him too.

'Cannon-chief Lunist,' said Lash, beckoning him to stand between his lord and the golem. Lunist did so with a quiver in his step.

'Have you met our guest before?'

'Aye, sir. In battle. Several weeks ago.'

'He informs me that you ordered your battery to fire on our own lines, during the midst of engagement.'

Lunist turned a pale shade of grey. 'You'd take the word of this beast over mine, sir?'

'I am merely asking, Lunist.'

'Well, spit on it! It's not true!'

'It is,' said Task.

The chief looked from the golem to his leader, back and forth, until an excuse bubbled up. 'They were all doomed, sir. Every one of them. The beast was cutting through us like a knife through old cheese. I had to do something!'

Lash cut the fat from his words. 'So you admit to firing on your own?'

'Well, yes. But I had to—'

Lunist got no further. Lash whipped his pistol from its holster and blasted a musketball right into the man's forehead. The chief collapsed to the dirt, cross-eyed and mouth frozen agape.

Alabast was almost grinning. He bent a hand to whisper to Task over the howling. 'Friendly fire. Not so fun when you're on the wrong end of the firing.'

Task ignored him. He was too busy being surprised. Impressed, even. The punishment seemed fair to a beast like him. Brutal, but fairly so. Lash had not drawn in anger, nor cruelty, but with calculated calm and justification. It was almost refreshing.

'That will be all, Chief.' said Lash, as he blew the soot from the pistol's muzzle. Two men dragged the body away.

The lord turned his attention back to the table. 'May we consider that matter settled, and move on?'

'We may,' said Task, looking once more to Ellia. 'But the matter of the girl remains outstanding.'

Lash sighed. 'The girl, yes. Auger has told me. We will give her our best care. Unlike the Truehards, we keep prisoners alive.'

Task nodded. 'A step in the right direction.'

'I'm pleased,' said Lash, though his face suggested quite the opposite. 'Let us continue, then.'

'What have you been told so far?' said Ellia.

'That you Fading are responsible for the war. That you made a grab for power, marched on the city, and since then you've opposed the crown at every turn, for nine long years. All because of taxes and greed. It's a story I've heard a dozen times before.'

Ellia chuckled. Westin flipped through his papers, fuming. Even Alabast looked indignant, if Task looked closely. It seemed that they both hid beneath their exteriors. *Another thing in common.*

Lash was working on that red tinge again. 'Well, it's the *wrong* story.'

'Care to tell the right one?' said Alabast.

Lash waved his hand. 'Executor Westin is far more used to telling stories than I, and he has a better voice for it.'

Westin cleared his throat and spread the contents of his satchel on the table. He spoke as if delivering a report, picking up bits of parchment and clippings to emphasise his points.

'Before the Boy King, Barrein the Fourteenth, to give him his proper title, his father ruled Hartlund. King Raspier the Sixth.'

'My friend,' growled Lash.

Alabast nodded. 'And Lord Lash does not make choices of friendship lightly, as you can imagine. I've been trying for weeks.'

'I regret to say that Knight Alabast has a point,' said Westin. 'Raspier thoroughly deserved that friendship, and many others. He was possibly one of the greatest rulers ever to sit on the throne. He united the old seats of power with the guilds of traders and merchants, lowering taxes for the first time in half a century. He gave bursaries to crafts and arts. He filled his Council with men and women who deserved their seats on merit, not by birthright.

'Raspier died of a flux in the Reaping of three and seven and seventy-two, ten years ago now. His son was four, and while Castle Sliver's bells tolled out the death of the king, the horns also sounded for Barrein. He was crowned the very next day. Hartlund has never gone more than a week without a ruler.'

Westin tapped a diagram that looked like a tree.

'The problem with a king with four years under his belt is that he needs advisors, wards, people to issue commands on his behalf. This of course led to some power struggles. A boy king or girl queen is no more than a puppet, easy to manipulate, easy to shape as he or she grows. Within a month, half the councillors had made their move, while the others desperately hung on to Raspier's legacy, like Lord Lash here. They watched as those around them were declared bankrupt, heretical, mad, sordid, or treacherous. Others filled their place, eager supporters of the new rulers of Hartlund, the men and women who saw opportunity in having a king as a pet. Lord Lash was one of the last to be thrown out.

'The majority of this new Council were noble-born, and eager to begin the reversal of all that Raspier had strived for. While they kept the Boy King distracted with toys and Khandri chocolates, they raised taxes, cut the bursaries, stripped land and property from any who objected, imposed tough levies on businesses, even passed rules to allow scurrilous employers to cut pay and increase hours. Within six months, Hartlund had regressed a decade. It was also becoming very, very angry.

'Pamphlets and rumours started to spread, telling of what the King's Council were doing. Ejected councillors began to speak up. Then they were swiftly silenced in the night. For a month or so, Hartlund limped on. Then a plague began to spread. The rich locked up their doors while the poor died in their beds and in their streets. That's when the riots started.'

Ellia spoke up. 'I still remember the cracks of firepowder, still smell the smoke. I watched it all from the Sliver's balconies. Four days it lasted. Barrein wailed all through it.'

Westin produced a paper with a sketch of a smoking city. 'The fires put an end to the plague, at least, but not to the discontent. At the time, we were nothing more than a group of business owners, traders and new-lords, as they had been dubbed. Nobility "bought" with coin, or capitalists, for want of a better word. We knew where Hartlund was heading. We had seen it happen to the Duelling Dozen, and those principalities had already been at each other's throats for several years, with no signs of abating. We needed to end this cycle of royal rule and create a true meritocracy. At the very least, we needed to make each man and woman free to chose their own life again. So, we planned a peaceful march on Caverill, on the day of Fading's Eve. There was even a rule of no weapons, only banners. And no shouting, only the calm demand for an audience with the king and his Council, and a chance for change.

'They waited until we stood at the gates of the Sliver before firing. They even brought out the Boy King himself, whispering in his ear to make him laugh at us. When we implored him and his councillors, he giggled before running back inside. We had thousands with us, all pressed together and nowhere to go. At least one thousand died in that initial attack, hundreds more as they escaped into the streets. Half made it out alive. Black Fading's Eve, they called it. That's when we formed the Last Fading, so called because we swore it would be the last Fading we would have to endure the noble-born.

'As the Council struck back at the country, levelling a few villages, razing farms, and executing merchants, we took to the north. We found the largest merchant vessel we could and created our own Council. The Last Table. We made a pact there and then to dismantle the ruling class, using our combined resources and contacts in the Realm.

'It was only when we were sold out by a member of our own, a certain Gorder Dartridge, that we went to war. Yes, Huff's father. He informed Lord Baragad, the king's newest and closest advisor, of the location of our fleet. They sent a dozen ships for us, but we had spies of our own, and managed to slip to Braad and gather support. We returned a week later to join the war that the Council had started.'

'That was nine years before the day you came to Hartlund, Task,' said Ellia.

'Indeed.' Lash now. 'And since then it's been a bloody mess. It took four years for us to start winning. Not a corner of this land hasn't seen war in some form. We've fought north and east, south and west for this country, even over the Creeping Isles. Hartlund is war-torn and covered in bones, Task, but we're not about to give in yet. We've driven ourselves to bankruptcy to see the job done, and the damn crown is not far behind. If they didn't have the Mission behind them, we would have won already. We were on the cusp when you showed up.'

Task had a question. 'Do you not all follow the same religion?'

Lash drummed his nails on the table-top. Telling the story had eroded some of his patience. 'It's called a civil war, sir. We're pitted against our own countrymen, our own flesh and blood. We share many things besides religion.'

'I understand war perfectly, Lord Lash, but I am confused why a church would choose a side at all.'

'Because the crown and the Mission have been closely tied for years. Raspier, for all his qualities, entertained the Mission far too much. He let them build churches all over, let them construct their Blade in our capital. They feel entitled to this land. We're children of the Architect, but we don't recognise their church.'

'And how does the Baroness, or her ladyship, fit into this?'

Ellia spoke again. 'It all began—'

'I want to hear it from Lord Lash, if you please,' said Task.

'Lady Ellia Auger came to us three years into the war. She gave us troop movements, numbers, weaknesses, the lot. In three weeks, we'd taken Kenmire and Broad, then Soakmarsh. The Table immediately appointed Milady as an advisor and spy. She had always been a quiet supporter of the Fading, and as a member of the new Council, she was perfectly placed. Our luckiest strike was her being appointed to watch Huff.'

She nodded. 'Lucky indeed, Lord Lash. But our fortune ran out the day the Truehards started their search for you, Task. An idea of the Mission's, did you know that?'

'I did not.'

'They funded you, Task, along with Grand-Captain Gorder Dartridge and Baragad.' Ellia paused to examine her nails. 'In part, they are your masters.'

Alabast shivered. 'I've always refused to work with the Mission.'

'How noble,' said Westin, making Task frown.

'And what of Huff?' he asked, more in curiosity than an attempt to poke holes in their stories.

'The boy is trying to prove his worth to his treacherous father, any way he can. He just so happens to think cruelty is the way to do it. And he was given a toy to do it with. You.' Lash looked the golem straight in the eye. 'Had it been another general, maybe even Gorder himself, things would have been different for you. We might not be sitting here, trying to convince stone to change its mind. Though I am glad for the chance to do so.'

'All my masters have been cruel. I doubt another would have been any different.'

'Then maybe it's you,' said Lash. 'I had not expected more than simple words from you, if any at all. Yet here you are, curious at the very least. Auger is right. The difference is in you, and that gives me hope.'

Task rose to standing, making the soldiers flinch. A few primed their muskets, ready to fire. While they had been speaking, the sun had fallen behind the jagged peaks. Evening was reaching out from the east.

'Stow it!' said Lash to his men. 'Have I offended you, golem?'

'No. I have heard enough for now. Or to put it another way, enough from you.'

The lord's face was stuck somewhere between anger, disappointment, and confusion. 'Go on.'

'I find that those with less to lose have the least to lie about. I am not saying you were lying, but I want to speak to your soldiers. The dregs of your army, as it were.'

'I could arrange a few to come to you.'

Task shook his head. 'Inside would be better.'

Lash drummed his nails again. 'Why?'

It was Ellia who answered for him. 'Because out here, Lord Lash, it feels like a siege is being discussed. If you wish to change his mind, then show him what he should be changing it for.'

Task rumbled in agreement. She had guessed his thoughts perfectly except for one: that inside, Task could touch the stone, the metal, even flesh, and know the truth of this place. *Its people.*

More drumming, until Lash pressed his palm flat to the table.

'You will respect our rules. And you will have an escort. Young Alabast and the Executor here.'

Westin sweated some more. The knight nodded.

As they got to their feet, Task asked for one more thing.

'First, I wish to see the stable-girl.'

Lash gestured broadly towards the fortress. 'Suit yourself.'

Task wasn't used to suiting anybody but a master, but it was warmly welcomed. He felt watched and aimed at, but at least he was loose, set free to wander. And that was rare.

He crunched his heels together and lifted a hand to cover his face. It was a thank-you and a mark of respect rolled into one.

He heard the silence behind his palm, and when he took his hand down, Lash was also saluting. Task could have sworn there was an upward curve to the lord's wrinkled mouth.

Voices. She head them clear as day. Not muffled, just quieter in places. Unhindered by distance or stone.

It felt like stone. It was cold enough. She felt the prickle of her skin even without touching. A tautness.

Where was she? The voices had accents, and they were not of the south or the Creeping Isles. She heard no familiar snuffling of fawls, no grind of snoring stone, no Sergeant Collaver hollering.

This was not home.

In her half-asleep state, with her body heavy, aching and refusing to move, she listened to the words that echoed around her.

Can't believe it's here, already.

I need a drink. If this is going to be my last night, I'm having a bloody drink.

Rint getting wall duty's a bit of a luck. Shows what you get when you mouth off to the chief.

They're letting it in? Just like that?

Just look at the deffing thing!

A scrape wrenched her alert, to a place beyond that echoing void. Somewhere with blotches of light between the shadows. Somewhere that reeked of mould.

Wood met stone beside her and she heard the pant of quick breathing. Perfume mixed with a musty smell; one she'd smelled before.

Her eyelids took a while to move, cracking open a sliver, then wider, until finally she could make sense of the shapes and surroundings.

It was stone. A room made of grey brick and mortar and slime. A chipped and dented lantern burned in each corner. She was lying on a wide bed. A woman was sitting beside her, arms and legs crossed, with a friendly smile.

Baroness Frayne looked pleased about something.

'Where am I?'

At least that was what she meant to say. It came out more like a croak.

A glass of water was pressed against her lips, and a hand behind her head helped her drink.

'Where am I?' Clearer this time.

'You are safe, young lady.'

'And what are you doin' here? I know this ain't the camp.'

'Questing again, I see, even in your condition. You're a strong one.'

Lesky felt like shifting away, but her body was still not keen on the idea of moving. If she couldn't have felt her limbs, she would have thought her back broken.

'This is Safferon Fortress, Lesky.'

'…Pardon?'

'Safferon Fortress. I'm afraid the surgeon dosed you pretty liberally with lauendi. You'll be able to move in an hour or so.'

'Your accent's different.'

The baroness got up from the chair and went to stand at the end of the bed. She sighed. 'I haven't been honest with you or Task.'

'Spy! You're the spy.'

'Guilty as charged,' said Frayne, still holding her smile. 'But I've come to think of it as a job. One that I'm forced to do to get where I want. Just like you and your stable.'

The stable. The last she saw of it was a bone claw renting it in two, scattering the fawls.

'Task asked me to save you and so I did. I brought you here to be safe, away from Huff. He spat on you. Task threatened him.'

Lesky blinked, trying to take it in. She could feel the pull of the voices calling. She struggled to move.

'What happened to Task. Is he okay?'

'More than okay, my dear. In fact, through a stroke of fortune, we are not the only ones who fled the camp that night. Our favourite golem is right here, in Safferon.'

Lesky managed to raise her head as she tried desperately to move herself to the door.

'You can go and see him soon. He's waiting for you in the main courtyard.'

It was useless. She was like a sack of hay without the hands to lift it. She resigned herself to the pillow and stared long and hard at the ceiling.

'I don't trust you. Never did.'

'And that's why you're a very smart girl. But you're also something else, Lesky, and I think you already know that.'

'Don't know what you're talkin' about.'

'Let me guess. You usually know what somebody is thinking?'

'Usually.'

'And you always have the most vivid of dreams, but you can't quite remember them?'

'Mm.'

'And you're pretty good at convincing people. And sneaking up on them, too.'

Lesky said nothing.

'It seems pretty plain to me.'

'I ain't no thinkpicker.'

'There's nothing wrong with it, Lesky. Trust me. I should know. I've known enough glimpses in my time.'

'You?'

There was that grin again. 'I have plenty to tell you, Lesky. Plenty indeed. What's more, I can help you. But for now, you rest. Then go see your golem, and we'll talk in the morning.'

Lesky was about to complain when she heard raised voices and a familiar rumble.

This time she managed to raise a hand.

'These corridors were not meant for somebody of his size! *That's* why I'm concerned, deff it!'

'He's barely touching the ceiling, look!' said Alabast, right at the moment the golem chose to head-butt a section of old plaster. It fell at their feet.

'You see?' said Westin.

'I will be careful, Executor,' said Task as he crouched lower. He shuffled onwards, with Alabast, Westin and a gaggle of soldiers in tow. They were still as twitchy as new recruits.

Task didn't want to wait for the medicine to wear off. That's what he had told them, several times, before taking matters into his own hands. Lord Lash had bade him wander, and so he wandered. They had just not expected him to enter the fortress.

'Take a left, Mr Golem.'

'Mr Golem,' said Alabast, tittering.

Task looked at them over his shoulder. 'I get that more than you might think.'

The left turn took them past a set of doors.

'Fourth along.'

Ellia opened the door as they reached it. She stood in its frame for a moment, before moving aside, and letting the golem duck his head and shoulder into the room.

'Task!' said Lesky.

'Are you injured?'

'Stitches in her head where she took a heavy blow,' said Ellia. 'A deep gash to her ribs, and a broken wrist.'

'I'll live,' said Lesky. 'I'm sorry for lying.' She threw him that wry grin of hers, although this time it had a gap in it. She had lost one of her teeth in the attack.

'I'll forget it if you won't lie again.'

'And I'm sorry, too,' said Ellia. 'I told them to attack from the north, but they didn't listen.'

Task's eyes pierced her.

'Conveniently.'

'If I didn't care, I would have left her in Huff's charge, wouldn't I?'

Task didn't have an answer for that, so he let the matter lie for now. 'If you don't mind, I want a moment alone with her. I will find you later.'

'How ominous, Task. Really.' Ellia snickered as she gave them the room. She hung back with the other soldiers, still watchful but chatting amongst themselves.

'I'm starving,' said Lesky.

'We'll have your new best friend get you some food.'

'Why are you here, Task? Did they catch you?'

The golem laughed. 'I came here with the Knight of Dawn. They want to change my mind. I'm letting them try to prove themselves.'

'But they're the enemy!'

'How much do you know about the war, girl?'

'That they started it?'

'Then you should come join me by the fire, when I talk to the soldiers tonight. The Fading tell a different story, and I want to know why.'

'What for? You're bound to Huff, aren't you?'

This was true. He was still torn. 'I don't know yet. We'll see.'

She sniffed at the mouldy air as she looked around. 'So we've switched sides, then?'

Task worked his jaw. 'I thought we should give them a chance, find out the truth. This war is different for me, Lesky. You people are different. This Lash, he's no Huff. He's a rare breed.'

'Rarer'n you?'

Task flashed his teeth. 'Hardly.'

Lesky managed to prop herself up in a series of pained movements. 'This is all upside down.'

'I know, but I'm going with it. What I want to know is what her ladyship wants with you.'

'She thinks I'm a glimpse.'

Task looked back down the corridor. Ellia had gone. 'Does she now?'

Lesky squirmed. 'An' I believe her. I heard their voices, Task. Not like I'm mad, but real thoughts. Other thoughts outside this room.'

Task grumbled to himself.

'Look, if you don't like me messing with old-magic, then maybe I should learn how to control it like you do. She said she can help, and I want to learn. Maybe I just go with it, like you are. And guess what, if we're both magic, now that's four things in common!' She flashed him a smile.

'Fine. I wonder how she knew?'

'She could have heard us talkin' before the—' Lesky shuddered violently. 'Before the bone thing came.'

'It's dead, Lesky. Ripped apart.' Task bowed his head. 'It got Sald, but it couldn't kill you. Now rest, girl. Be careful with that woman.' He turned to go, but caught himself halfway.

'I'm glad you're safe.'

'Takes more than a golem to finish me.'

'Toughest little skinbag I've ever known.'

With that, Task extricated himself from the door, and headed out to find a fire or two.

♛

'I was right about you,' said the voice, catching her halfway out of the door.

'Right about what, Alabast?'

It could have been the glow of the Mothers, but Alabast had a gleam in his eye tonight; fiercer than the usual glint he called charm.

'You care nothing for the lives of others. You sent me out on a wild gamble, not caring whether I lived or died. I was just a side-bet to you.'

Ellia pulled a face of innocence. 'I asked you to impress me, and lo and behold, you have, Knight. It's not often that happens. You should be pleased with yourself, instead of angry at me.'

'Flattery will get you nowhere.'

She stepped closer, playing coy. 'It's got me pretty far already.'

Alabast moved away, smirking without humour. 'One day your games will catch you, Ellia, just like they have caught me. Let's hope you have the guts to take a gamble on your own life, hmm? Enjoy your evening.'

She was normally impervious to the shrapnel from sharp words, but Alabast's had nicked her. She watched him leave, cheek twitching. Worse, she had nothing acerbic to throw back at him.

Ellia cursed at the darkness before storming away.

The guards at the main gates gave her no trouble. They were accustomed to seeing her come and go as she pleased, and they were too preoccupied with the golem's presence. She could hear their nervous chattering on the wall-tops and in the guardhouse. With the gate ajar, she slipped into the night, beyond the walls of the fortress.

Ellia paused for a moment to bleed the torchlight from her eyes, and then set off on foot. Spiddle had followed her carriage closely. He had left a thought in her head, demanding a rendezvous tonight. Somewhere close to the fortress. It was a sign that his concerns were overcoming his love of intrigue and theatre. A good sign indeed.

She readied her mind. Every thought she'd tagged and nurtured over the past week had been bundled up into a neat little package and locked away; not too deep, but not too shallow either.

The night was not a dark one; all three Mothers had risen, and they had brought their bright entourage of stars. Ellia trod confidently as her eyes roamed over the plain and its trees.

In the distance the watchtowers burned bright, guarding the road. They could have rested easy, built up their strength; Huff was still two or three days away.

It was a thin margin, even for her. The Treyarch made decisions at the same pace as a vineyard produces wine. Her hopes were pinned on the assumption that the circumstances called for quick action.

The meeting spot tonight was an overhang in the black rock, a quarter of a league east from the fortress. Spiddle had given her nothing besides that, and yet she still found it without trouble. It was hard to miss: a dark wedge of stone, maybe three foot-lengths thick, jutting from the side of a sloping wall.

In the silver light of the Mothers, Spiddle's white face seemed to glow. She spotted him instantly, in his shrouds of black and grey. He stood solemn beneath the overhang, hands clasped in his sleeves. He looked more like a Mission cleric than a glimpse.

She walked with her hands up and open.

'I come in peace,' she said, once she was close enough. 'I must apologise for my behaviour the last time we met. I imagine that's why you've called me here tonight.'

Spiddle came forwards to meet her. 'Intuitive as always, Zealot.' His voice was flat and emotionless. He held out in a hand. 'Report.'

'No stories, tonight, Glimpse? No anecdotes about this particular landmark?'

'Report, Ellia.'

She tossed her hair. 'As you wish.'

Ellia steeled her thoughts as his eyes faded to a clouded white. For a moment, with his shaved head and weathered features, he looked like the golem.

She felt the grope of his mind, more purposeful than usual. Rawer. Ellia held as firm as she dared without arousing suspicion. It had to look like an accident.

Bit by bit, he prowled around. Ellia diverted him as best she could, but he was strong, and it took some time to get him where she wanted.

She felt the surge as he leapt at the thoughts she had gathered for him. Every facet of her conspiracy was there for his taking: her pushing of Task to break, her theft of the girl, the moment with Alabast in the corridor, the promise to Lash. He did not sift or rummage, but tore at them like a predator, devouring it all. Ellia submitted, giving him everything the Treyarch desired.

He broke the connection without care, and she was left reeling. In the afterglow of his touch, she could feel his indignation. His face had grown tauter.

'If that will be all, Spiddle?'

'For now,' he said, before bowing low and deep. It was a goodbye, in Mission tongue. She made sure to look confused as they parted ways.

It was only once she was hidden behind a shoulder of rock that she smiled, and broadly so.

He had admired the pile of bones for far too long, it seemed. It was dark when he went to the doorway and looked out over his camp.

Some might have referred to the rumpled carpet of sparkling lanterns and cooking fires as beautiful. Mesmerising, even. Huff Dartridge, though, would have called it disgusting. A mire of human filth. *Useless human filth.*

Almost two days had passed since the golem had left, and still they had not found him.

Huff listened to the dying clatter of the camp. They had marched hard today, past the ruins of old Nurren and onto the Gillish plains. The soldiers had little energy for revelry, and they were retreating to bed.

The general could feel their doubt emanating across the hillside. If he listened closely, he could hear the combined murmur of voices, all grumbling.

He scowled and went back to the pile, and the rib he'd been nudging with the toe of his boot. The infernal wreckage still taunted him with its puzzle. The macabre pieces made shapes and spelled half-words for him, no matter where he stood or how he looked. It was old-magic.

Boots scurried up the path and along the tent. Then, the wheezing of breath at the entrance. Huff didn't even have to turn.

'Captain Glum.'

The others were too afraid to face him now. Not after he had shot off Jenever's toe during a rage. The general still claimed it was an accident. He'd even sent his pistol to be checked by the gunsmith.

'Sir!'

'What news?'

'None, I'm afraid, General. The last of the riders have just got in. No sign.'

Huff turned on him. 'Then we must assume three things.'

'Yessir,' said Glum, sweat trickling down his round cheeks. 'What, sir?'

'One, the golem has been destroyed. Though I fail to see how that's possible. Two, in his rage he has gone ahead to destroy Safferon, and we shall arrive to a smoking ruin and a smiling golem. Or three, he has defected. Betrayed us.'

'And which do you think it is, sir?'

'We'll find out on the road to Lash's last stand, won't we, Captain?'

Glum didn't know whether to nod or shake his head, so he did both.

'What about your father, General? The King's Council? Won't they need to be told? I imagine they're sending reinforcements.'

'That's enough imagining from you, Glum!' Huff turned back to his bones. 'Go make sure Dast is comfortable and drunk in his tent. And I want the troops up both bright and early tomorrow. We march before dawn. You're dismissed, Captain. Close the tent on your way out.'

'Aye, sir.'

When the boots had receded, and Huff knew he was alone, he crouched down on his heels and massaged his moustache in thought. A hand snaked out for the nearest fragment; a jawbone of some foreign creature. Huff could feel the tingling in his fingertips, but he held on, learning how to savour the taste of old-magic. His eyes roamed the sockets of lost teeth, the symbols carved in the hinges, even the raking butcher's marks.

It took an age for him to reach for the next bone. He could barely tear his eyes away to find it. His fingers spidered over one, two, and then three. The jawbone pulsated in his hand.

Huff saw the pattern, then; like tendrils tying all the bones together. All he had to do was unravel it. He snatched up a new bone—a kneecap—and raised both to the lantern-light.

The bones shivered as they came together, like two halves of a broken pendant.

24

'Safferon was built before the line of Raspier. It has survived a hundred sieges and will survive a hundred more. Scoff at me as you please, Master, but this castle has magic in its stones.'

LETTER FROM LORD LASH TO MASTER EBENEZ, HEAD OF THE LAST TABLE

60TH FADING, 3782 - SAFFERON FORTRESS

Task would have awoken bewildered even without all the shouting. Something about smoke on the horizon.

His sleep had been broken. One moment he had dreamt of crashing water, the next he was trapped in waking thoughts of the soldiers' stories; what few of them he had gleaned. Carafor's histories had been proven true at least.

It irked him. Sleep had once been a sanctuary. Now it had turned on him.

The golem pushed himself from the ground and stretched his cold limbs. The northern air was frigid at night. He was used to desert sands and baking steppes.

'What is it?' he heard a corporal yell.

'Smoke from Gillish!' answered a woman, mid-sprint.

Like an avalanche, the Fading soldiers flowed down to the main wall, where the pastel colours of the morning sky had been rudely interrupted with black columns. They rose at an angle from the south, dragged by the revert breeze.

He heard the voices chatter.

'How many were left there?'

'Couple thou', last I heard. Stubborn lot. Didn't want to leave their homes.'

'Fat lot it's done 'em now.'

'Could have been some strong legs and shield arms in that bunch, too.'

'Right you are.'

Task joined in, making them flinch. 'Maybe they fought for what they believed in.'

'Well...' ventured one, then bit his lip and shuffled away. They were still wary of his presence, as though he were a keg of firepowder with a temper and an undetermined length of fuse.

Task took to the steps of the main wall to see more clearly. He was relieved he had escaped another battle between streets and squares, but felt guilty for it. He wondered at how merciless Huff had been, without his golem to end it all swiftly. Perhaps the slaughter still raged on under those columns of smoke.

The golem guessed it would be a day, maybe a day and a half, depending on how long they languished in Gillish. Huff would be desperate without his stony beast, and no doubt angry as a boiling pot at his loss.

Task turned away and stomped back across the courtyard, where Lash had emerged to look at the smoke. Judging by his grim face, they might as well have been enemy banners.

'Two days, sir,' said Lash, causing Task to raise an eyebrow. 'That's my bet. He'll attack at dawn, ready for Rising Day.'

The golem snorted. 'Just like he promised when I first arrived.'

'If Huff was a woman then I'd say he was a gazer.' Lash caught Task's quizzical expression. 'Fortune-teller. Soothsayer.'

Task had never trusted their type. The future was best left where it was: in the future, unknown and unknowable. Show a man his future and he would either barrel towards it like a drunkard, or flee as a madman would from a waking nightmare. No good could come from it.

Lash marshalled his men. 'OFFICERS! To me! Preparations must be made! If you'll excuse us, sir, I must speak to my men and women in private. I hope you understand why.'

Task nodded. 'I do.'

Lash headed for the nearest doorway, one far too small for a golem. Task was left standing in a scattered sea of soldiers. Many milled about, picking at their beards or stray scales on their armour. Others remained transfixed by the distant smoke. The rest talked in hushed tones between themselves. Task caught several pairs of eyes sneaking in his direction.

'Not invited to the gathering either, Task?' asked a voice. It was Alabast, awake far earlier than Task had expected for a man of his nature. He didn't even seem to have a hangover. The previous evening, he had floated between the fires with Task for a time, simply listening, before escaping to his room.

'They don't want to give their secrets away too easily.'

'Don't blame them. Whatever helps them sleep at night, eh?'

Task nodded at that.

'Must be tough, being indestructible.'

'Nearly.'

'*Nearly* indestructible. Sorry. Must be so difficult.'

'I sense sarcasm. In all my years, that's never grown on me.'

'Cheapest form of humour, they say. I say cheap is a good bargain.'

'How does the Knight of Dawn spend his days in the fortress?'

'Thank you for not saying last days.' Alabast scratched the patch of stubble he'd been working on. 'Training, mostly, or annoying Westin.'

'I will watch you train. I doubt any of the men will wish to spar.'

Alabast winked. 'I'm sure they won't. Though I might.'

Task half-growled, half-chuckled. 'Itching to make it three defeats, are we?' He wondered what in the Realm was wrong with him. He was even growing to like the Knight of Dawn. *Damn these Lundish skinbags. And the Graden ones too.*

'Have you seen Lesky?'

'The stable-girl? Not since yesterday. Why?'

'I also haven't seen Ellia'

'Is that even her name?'

'I don't care. It confuses me less.'

Alabast blew a low whistle as they set off. 'Take it from me, you've got it backwards. It's much better when that siren isn't around.'

'You don't trust her?'

'Not after she gambled with my life, and sent me on a fool's errand. The woman's a spy. A crafty liar. She's incapable of the truth. However, that makes me glad she's on our side. As far as I can tell, at least.'

Task looked up at the crumbling keep, spread across the inner three walls. Its towers looked even more crooked in the early shadows, and long in the low sun. The bridges running between swarmed with soldiers, all gawping at the smoke in the south.

'"Glad" is a strong word for a golem.'

'How was the breakfast?'

Lesky could do nothing but mumble around her mouthful of fawl-bacon and oat bread. It was delicious; slathered in butter and meat-grease, and with some fishy sauce on the side. She had wolfed it down in under a minute.

Ellia beamed. 'Good. You're too skinny for my liking.'

'Mam always says skinny or fat, it don't matter as long as you're happy.'

'A wise woman.'

'People say that.' Lesky stared at Ellia, testing those eyes to see what lay behind them. All she found was that same old blank wall. It was most confusing; like when she had tried to grasp at Task's mind. Stone, and nothing else.

Ellia edged closer, along the bed. Lesky's legs were still wobbly from the lauendi, and it had been a while since she had slept on a real mattress, with real pillows.

'I can tell you don't trust me.'

Lesky wiped the last of the crumbs away, still digging out stray oats with her tongue. 'Not really. But Task told me I should.'

'Did he now?'

'He says you could help me with…' Lesky tapped her head.

'That I can.'

'How?'

Ellia took a breath, eyes on the ceiling. 'Well, I've known a lot of glimpses in my time. You pick up a few things.'

'How? Mam always told me they were outlawed. After some king.'

'Wise, indeed. It was King Dawtre the Third, the Glimpse-King. He went mad from power. Glimpses were outlawed after he was hunted down and executed. All except those belonging to the Mission. The Treyarch drafted the ones who escaped, and still keeps close watch for the natural-born. Like you. Since then, the Mission has always been involved in the King's Council, Lesky. Their glimpses have always been more useful than worrying, I suppose. I once worked with one, and he showed me a great many things.'

Lesky was eager to know what Ellia knew about banned magic. The unknown was alluring, and this woman was dripping with it. Lesky ached to be able to sift through her mind.

The girl spent a moment in deep thought, chin on knuckles to help the juices flow.

'I don't want to be a glimpse. Just like I don't want to be a stable-girl. But if I have to be one, then I better learn how. My mam warned me about a man that would one day come to take me away, for the calling of the Architect.' She wrinkled her brow. 'And I think I met him already.'

Ellia nodded. 'In your thoughts?'

Lesky wished the room had a window, so she could stare out, keep watch. She had never liked to be enclosed. 'Feels like he's nearby, somehow. All slippery like, as if he's a hole in the night sky. You can only see the lack of something.'

She felt the void begin to tug at her. It was getting easier to slip back into it, even without pain. Perhaps it was the lingering drowsiness of the herbs.

The woman put her hand on the girl's shoulder and shook her. 'No, no! We don't want to go there just yet. Easy does it. If you want help, then first you need to know how to shield yourself, like I do.' It was her turn to tap her head.

'I'm not going to let him take me.'

Ellia withdrew, a serious look falling over her face.

'What would you say if I said I knew this man? The one who spoke to you.'

Lesky tensed in the space between a blink. Had she not been so dizzy, she would have probably scrambled from the bed.

'You're working with him.'

Ellia held out her hands, trying to calm her. Lesky edged away. 'It isn't just the Truehards I've been deceiving, Lesky. I've worked for the Mission longer than I have the Council. Or the Fading. He's asked me to deliver you, so he can take you to Caverill. I said no. Now he knows who and what I am, that I'm no Mission zealot, and well, he's angry. You think he's nearby? He is, Lesky. Closer than you think and waiting to pounce on the both of us. He'll kill me and take you.'

Lesky watched her for a moment, trying to read her steady eyes, her ever-so-slight expression of worry. She could see parts of her mind now; just a few shapes at least. She saw a man with a shaved head and gaunt cheeks, white as Fading snow. A cog drawn in ink and needle across his skull. He wore a great grey cloak. Lesky could hear the memory of his voice.

Cane wants you to collect her.

She pulled back as the world began to tumble.

'His name is Spiddle!'

Ellia pressed her to the bed. 'You're still weak, Lesky. You must be patient before you start trying to glimpse like that. You have it, though. Your eyes went milky, as we call it.'

'If he's comin', then we have to be ready for him. I'll go get Task!' She reared up, but Ellia held her down again.

'No! Task has other worries. This would only distract him and risk everyone in this fortress. You and I can deal with Spiddle alone if we work together.'

'Deal with him? You mean kill him.'

'No. We use him to send a message, right to the Treyarch himself.' Ellia leant closer. 'That, my dear girl, is how we make sure the Mission never comes after you again.'

'What message?'

Ellia chuckled. 'You have much to learn, stable-girl.'

'Let's get started, then!' Lesky shifted into a sitting position, then pushed herself to her feet. It took more effort than she would have admitted.

Ellia looked impressed. 'My my. What fire! This mam of yours must be a proud woman. Is this how they raise all small girls in... where were you born?'

'The Darens, miss. A village called Witt.'

Ellia's serious face came back. 'Witt?'

'Just west of Dunsta.'

'I know it. From a long time ago.' Ellia stared long and hard at the girl. 'Tell me, what was you mother's name?'

'Milla, after my grandmam.'

Ellia's eyes were now boring into her. 'And your father's?'

The name felt dusty in Lesky's mouth. She had not said it in years. 'Techan.'

The baroness caught herself, shaking off her reverie and rubbing her hands.

'If you'll excuse me for a moment,' she said, heading out, 'then we'll get started.'

Lesky nodded, brow creased long after the door had closed behind Ellia.

One thing was for sure: the woman was as odd as a polka-dot wark. But there was use in her. All Lesky had to do was take what she needed, and not get too close.

Feelings are the enemy. Ellia recited her mantra as she pushed her way through the groups of soldiers and out into the daylight. She paused to catch her breath, conscious of the stares.

It was at times like these she felt the need to kill something; to remind herself that these beings around her were just flesh and blood. *Weak.* Cattle for the slaughter. If she felt too much for them, then they were harder to control, and she was as inadequate as they were.

Her feelings for Techan were the only ones she allowed herself to accept. They were the ones that drove her forwards, that underpinned everything she had worked for.

It was why Alabast's success at turning the golem had niggled her. She was relieved, impressed even: both unwanted emotions. Now the girl was drawing out others.

Techan's daughter. It was as unexpected as it was welcome.

She remembered the way he spoke about her; his fears for her, his hopes. Lesky had been a babe barely out of arms when Ellia had met Techan, in the courtyard of the Blade. He had never been like the other glimpses. He was what Cane had called a rogue.

Ellia snarled at herself, locking all of it away in the recesses of her mind, safe behind shadow and key.

She stared around for an opportunity to work her knife. An isolated guard, perhaps. One of the injured, hobbling through the dark spaces of the fortress. Maybe one of the workers, high up in the towers. *It would be so easy.*

No. She was already pulling at far too many threads to start on something new. She had control, and she exercised it. Floating on the breeze were the sounds of blades clashing, and cries of exertion from the training yard. It was a poor substitute, just a distraction, but it would do. Perhaps she would even flex her muscles. The girl could wait and wonder for now.

Ellia stormed up the steps and ducked under the arch of an inner wall, one of the spokes of the defences. The noise of training grew louder. Her keen ears picked out another sound: crunching, rumbling. *The golem.*

She halted at the edge of the training yard and watched the masses moving through their dances of death. Some she wanted to laugh at; others she studied closely, admiring their strokes and form. On the far side, the huge hulk of golem was gently pawing at some brave soul.

Ellia was no stranger to this scene. Hanigan Cane had been a ruthless trainer. She had endured him for four long years before they'd given her the rank. She was slyer than most with a blade, favouring the knife over the sword. It was more satisfying up close.

As the breeze threw her hair around her face, she busied herself with the business of distraction, as her mind chanted about the connection between feelings and enemies.

Alabast noticed her on his rounds.

'Lady Auger! Care to join in?'

'No, thank you. I'm simply admiring.'

'Suit yourself.'

Ellia moved away, beginning a tour of her own around the back of the yard. Some soldiers were drilling blocks and parries; others hacked at each other with bucklers and axes. A small number wiggled spears about, though they seemed to be prone to whacking each other about the head or legs. In truth, they could hardly help it; the yard was fit to bursting. The smoke on the horizon had sparked a renewed interest in training.

Now the golem noticed her. He was working some drill with a shaven-headed woman, with pockmarks on her cheeks. The golem was moving as if he were wading along the seabed, letting the soldier strike him repeatedly on the wrists and knees.

The more they practised, the faster Task moved, until they were almost at fighting speed. Ellia listened to the clangs of steel on stone, letting their motions blur in front of her eyes.

'Baroness. Or is it Milady? I still can't tell.'

Task was looking down at her.

'Lesky, where is she?'

Ellia cleared her throat. 'Asleep for now. Still a little woozy, I'm afraid. I'll have Lash whip that Truehard surgeon.'

'No need for a whipping. Just tell her to come find me.'

'As you wish, Task.'

Alabast weaved through the ranks. 'You're hovering, Ellia. Why don't you stop pretending and join in?'

'As I said, I'm watching, Alabast. I have no desire to train.'

He shrugged. 'Should the Truehards come tearing through the gates, don't say I didn't try. A lady such as yourself may suddenly find herself wishing she knew a bit more about swordwork.'

A low hum rose and fell among the soldiers, who had caught wind of Alabast's challenge.

She knew he was goading her, but she bit anyway. In a fluid movement, she slipped off her fur-lined coat and threw it to the cold dirt. Then she pointed at the nearest soldier; a short, lithe woman.

'You! Give me your sword.'

The woman obliged. She held her weapon out in her palms, handle first.

Ellia took it, whirling it in a figure-of-eight, making sure to look cumbersome.

Alabast raised an eyebrow. 'Thank the Architect it's blunted.' He was rewarded with a smattering of laughter.

'You, or the golem?' demanded Ellia.

'Me,' said Alabast. 'Let's start with the basics.'

'Probably for the best,' added Task, getting a few chuckles of his own.

A space cleared for them, and Alabast began to march around it, circling her. Ellia stayed where she was, waiting for him to make the first move.

He obliged soon enough, once he was done with his prancing. He came in with a low jab. Ellia batted it away.

'Good!'

Alabast brought his sword down in an arc. Once again, she knocked it aside, though this time she drove her knee up between his thighs. The Knight of Dawn sagged to his knees, wheezing like an old wine-skin.

She got the most laughter out of all.

'A good trick!' said Alabast, as he struggled to his feet. Ellia forgot that he must have received a fair number of knees to the balls in his time. He had apparently grown accustomed to it.

'Let's move on, shall we?'

Alabast swung again, faster this time. She blocked, moving in close to barge him with her shoulder. The knight had seen it coming from a league away. He rolled with her until she was tumbling on her own, landing flat in the dust.

She was upright in seconds, surging at him with a flurry of blows. He parried them all, making her work for it. When he sent her spinning for a second time, she came back fiercer, lunging at him, sword high over her head.

In a shower of sparks, the blade met black stone. The golem had closed his palm around it and was holding it firm.

'I think the lady knows her swordwork just fine, Alabast.'

'That she does,' said Alabast, wiping a smear of dirt across his sweaty brow.

Ellia let go of the sword and retrieved her fur coat.

'Your weakness, Alabast, is that you underestimate your foe,' said Ellia, straining to keep her voice from sounding breathless. Her eyes moved back to the sword in the golem's grip. 'Let that be a lesson to all of you.'

'Somehow it always seems to work out,' said Alabast, grinning, and shifting the mood from awkward to light-hearted. Spectacle over, the soldiers went back to their training.

'If you'll excuse me, I have some business to attend to,' said Ellia as she walked away, back to the keep.

Flustered she may have been, but it was temporary. The thump of blood in her head had done wonders. Sure, it would have felt better to slit the man's throat, but she could always look forward to that later. There would be time enough for bloodshed.

Ellia walked into the musty cool of the fortress with a fresh purpose in her step. She had taken Alabast's words in her stride, and dwelt on her own.

Never underestimate your foe. Even if it's a small stable-girl.

Ellia knew one thing for sure.

She had work to do.

The soldiers had been reticent to speak, so far. Mumble-mouthed, closed off. They had seen him as the enemy; a lurking presence, the rumble of stone they had dreaded for weeks. He knew he was the waking embodiment of a fear normally reserved for nightmares. And here he was: wandering around their camp as if the Table had bought him and not the King's Council.

Task kept this at the front of his mind while he tried for a second time to coax some stories out of their worried faces. The first night had excited only a smattering of talk; nothing that Task wanted to hear. He craved Sald's crackling voice. He wanted to hear Collaver's gruffness, countering the truth he thought he'd been fighting for.

The golem was in a state of flux. His thoughts refused to stay still long enough to analyse them. It was like trying to grab at fine desert sand. He was far more confused than he had expected to be, more torn than was acceptable. Lash and Executor Westin had already weaved quite a tale, and it had stuck in his mind like a bramble in a wark's hide.

At least the training had done him some good. Scattered amongst the usual blank or fear-stricken expressions, he saw polite nods, or quick glances. As with the Truehards, all it took to change their minds was a bit of brawn, and not killing them in their sleep. Task wished he had more than another night in this fortress.

He walked the edges of the walls, outer to inner, until he was lingering in the darker shadows. Two Mothers cast them tonight; one had not deigned to rise.

A campfire glowed from behind a ring of stone that might have once been a wall. Task lumbered towards it, making his feet soft upon the grass.

He heard voices laughing, and a familiar chant of, 'Confess!'. Task found a hopeful smile spreading across his face as he walked towards the huddle of bodies.

The sparkle of his mica must have taken their eyes from the cards, and they sprang up, hands to blades in an instant. Task held out his hands.

'I came to see if you wanted another player.'

The skinbags looked between themselves, silently calculating. One of them bowed his head. It was the young lad from the training yard: the one with a shaven head, and scars of the pox on his face.

'As you wish.'

Task settled for the dirt, shuffling up to the edge of the table. 'Tell me of yourselves,' he said as the lad dealt him his cards. The others stayed quiet, only looking when they thought he was distracted. There were three women and two men, all biting their lips. One of the men was clearly uncomfortable. Their stories were not forthcoming.

Task tried a smile. 'Let's just play.'

They went about it. The first dozen or so cards had nothing to offer; far too random to match with. When it was Task's turn, he found a run of two Servants of Storm, and decided to hook them. He laid a card face-down.

'Three Servants.'

A few mumbled. 'Confess!'

'I didn't want to come here,' said Task.

The coins shuffled to the centre, followed by verdicts.

'Lie.'

'Lyin'.'

Task flashed his teeth. 'Truth,' he said, as he cupped a hand around the small pile of coins.

'Why'd you come, then?' said the lad.

'Curiosity.'

The lad had gone from reticent to ruffled in the space of a word. He drew himself up. 'I don't believe you. You ain't curious.'

Task tilted his head. He was curious about this boy, that was for sure.

One of the women spoke up now. 'You don't seem a mindless beast, like they said. You must have more thought in you besides just being curious.'

Task nodded. He laid it bare, as he'd planned. 'I came here to find out if you were worth caring about. Worth doing something about. Your Lord Lash has made a good argument, but I want more. I was hoping you might be able to give me a reason or two.'

'Like what?' asked the lad.

'Tell me who you are.'

The soldiers took to silent council once more, swapping bewildered looks. It took a while for them to come to some decision. They seemed to be paying particular attention to the awkward-looking soldier, whose face was darkening in the lanternlight.

The lad cleared his throat. 'Name's Beert. Got seventeen Sowings under my belt. Fisherman's son from a place called Heckspit. Not the best name, grant you, but it was home.'

'Why do you fight?'

'My father fought for Lash. And died for him all the same.' It was said with a stoniness that the golem could respect; well-practised but artful, as a painter covers a mistake. Something half-finished and raw lay beneath his face.

'How long?'

'Three Sowings and a half now.'

The golem nodded and looked to the next soldier. She wore a thick scarf around her neck, and her eyes had a darting nature. She looked inscrutable for a moment, but then relented.

'Well, I suppose I'm Dispress, daughter to a factory-owner. I ain't tellin' you how many years I've got under me belt. I'm here because I want to be, for what the royalists did to my town and my friends.' She shuffled on the ground for a moment. 'Never told anyone this, but I was in Gillish the first time it fell.'

There was muttering from the group. Only Beert stayed quiet, pouting and confused.

'What's that mean?'

'First siege of the war, lad.'

'Weren't no siege,' said Dispress. 'It was a dirty trick. About a hundred refugees from the south came knocking on the gates one night. The moment the last one was through the door...' She clapped her hands. 'All over in an hour. The Truehards had been filterin' in for weeks, we found out. Out of the whole town only fifty escaped that night.'

'What about the rest?'

Dispress squirmed again. 'Labour, mostly. Building wagons, making shot and firepowder. The rest were left to rot in the gaols.'

'*Slave* labour,' hissed another woman. She dragged back her sleeves to show ragged scars encircling her wrists.

'The Truehards?'

The woman spoke through gritted teeth. 'Oh, yes. Service to the King, they call it. Royal rights!'

Task tapped his fingers on his knees, drawing their eyes. He thought of the towns Huff had visited along the road, and the way he'd swollen his ranks.

'Reason enough for you, golem?' said Dispress.

The golem looked to the silent soldier, whose eyes were now downturned, fixated on the soil. 'And what about you?'

With a scrape of armour, the man rose to his feet. His eyes flashed with hatred.

'What's all this for, golem?' he yelled.

'I—' But the man wasn't interested in an answer.

'To alleviate some of your guilt, or wallow in somebody else's pity for a change? And for what? From what I heard, it's not like you can do anything about it. You're a slave yourself, so what's the deffing point, I ask you? Architect spit on all your kind!' The man threw up his hands and marched into the darkness.

Task turned back to the others, eyebrows raised.

The woman with the scars winced. 'That's Arral Hanes. You... killed his son.'

Something sank inside the golem's chest. He had no words for it, nor for anything else. His jaw hung slack.

'It was Purlegar, or so I hear,' said Dispress. 'Story goes you snapped him in two.'

Task's memories of Purlegar were fractured at best, stowed away and ignored. *Just like so many of his thoughts.*

He stood and strode after Hanes, but the soldiers waved him back.

'No, golem. Hanes is right. You can't fix any of this. Especially that. What's done is done.'

Task weaved backwards and forwards, conflicted. He found himself wanting the soldiers to be wrong, but their case was solid. Time has a knack for permanence, and as mighty as Task was, he could not change the past. He felt his stones prickle with anger.

'Thank you for the game.'

He marched away, making for the lower levels. From the corner of his eye he saw Hanes standing alone, glinting slightly in the torchlight from the walls and keep. He seemed to be shaking.

Task grimaced. He had come here for clarity, and found only confusion and unease. He thought of sleep, but then of his dreams, and the tricks they played on him. Sleep had abandoned him, and hope looked to be close on its tail.

An hour's wandering found him no less agitated. The evening was late, and the fortress mostly asleep. As he wandered between the tents and lean-tos, he heard the proud snores of the handful who were lucky enough to sleep soundly. The rest were fidgety and moaning, stuck in harrowing dreams. At least the golem was not alone in that respect. It gave him a scrap of comfort.

Task sighed, pressing a hand against the cold stone of an inner wall. It gave up its secrets quickly enough, distracting him with flashes of quarries and carts, and more battles than even he could boast.

He withdrew his hand and sought a secluded spot between the wall and the rockface; somewhere he could blend in with the stone, perhaps. With any luck, sleep would be kind to him, and he'd wake when all of this was over.

Or, easier still, never wake at all.

46TH SOWING, 3362 - MALAR DORAH, KHANDRI

Orina. Nothing again. Not a scrape of bare feet running across rooftiles. Not a whisper.

Orina.

The golem wound deeper into the city.

Orina.

'Golem!' It was the call he had been dreading. 'You're needed.'

Task followed. He snuck looks down alleys as he went, hoping to catch a glimpse.

Nothing.

The city square had been clear for days now. A clamour of soldiers stood at its centre, around the spiky monument. They were hissing and jostling something. Task began to overtake his minder. Two other golems stood, statues compared to the crowd.

The bodies parted. His master beckoned to him.

'Task, I have work for you.'

The golem knew the meaning of work, and he knew how Belerod never tired of it. He enjoyed it far too much. Before he could wonder what the monster had dreamt up now, he stumbled onto it.

A score of beggars and strays were formed up in a trembling line, chained together like a slave gang. Twenty and seven, if he was right.

Rags hung from their bones. Dirt had replaced skin. Some wore signs of mortplague. His eyes rested on the figure directly in front of him.

Orina.

Belerod had found her before he had. This was a lesson.

'Execute them,' ordered his Master, wasting no time. He stood with his arms crossed, smiling, despite the new cracks in his face, and the deep shadows of tiredness beneath his eyes. 'Execute them all, starting with this one. A friend of yours, I believe? What have I told you about making friends with the enemy?'

Low boos came from the soldiers. Some spat at his feet. Task tried to retreat into himself. Belerod grabbed him by the arm. Unwanted images burst before his eyes. 'Kill her, and regain our trust,' said Belerod.

Then, quieter. 'You are not above reproach.'

'I cannot. Please, Master. You promised you would spare them.'

It was Belerod's turn to spit. *'A golem that begs! I should have your tongue ripped out for such insolence. I lied. Now kill her.'*

Orina was crying. She shivered in the unnaturally cold breeze that whipped up the dust of the square. Soldiers cursed and blinked.

'Kill her, I order you!'

'She... they mean you no harm.'

'Parasites! Vermin! Sub-humans! End their suffering, Task! Kill her! Crush her skull!'

Task turned his head away as he reached out a hand, the magic pulling him against his will. *'Don't! Please.'*

Orina's hair was matted beneath his hand. He felt her quivering, and in a moment, he knew her short story, full of cold nights and hunger.

She whispered to him. *'Told you it would rain.'*

She was right. The drops landed on his arm, bouncing then soaking into his dry stone. They covered him like a pox, and for a moment, the magic released its hold, and the chilling patter of the desert rain carried him away.

25

'When the warlord and mass murderer Belerod was buried, not a single back bowed, nor a hand rose to honour him. Silence was the only eulogy that man received.'

FROM HISTORIES OF HASPIA, BY RASAH AMION

61ST FADING, 3782 - SAFFERON FORTRESS

Ellia prowled around, flicking Lesky with drips from her glass. The girl flinched and cursed beneath her breath, but held on.

'What's the point of all this?'

'You won't often get a nice quiet place to glimpse, my dear. There will be distractions, danger, or times you can't concentrate, just like this. Our man Spiddle isn't going to come quietly.' Another flick, another flinch.

Ellia's mind sneaked from her grasp then, like an egg-yolk slipping through fingers. She grabbed at it, squeezing too tightly, and ruined the link.

'Try again.'

Lesky let her eyes fade to pale orbs; open but unseeing. Ellia's footsteps circled her. She followed the feet to her hips, then shoulders, and finally her mind. She imagined it like Ellia had shown her; as if she were squeezing into her mind through the seams of her skull.

Gently. She had to be light. She had to creep. It was more than just following her mind; she couldn't be felt pawing.

Water splashed her. 'It's like I'm wearing a lead hat, girl!'

'Alright!'

She pulled back, finding a corner in the dark cavern of the woman's mind. Shapes lingered in the darkness. They looked like crates and boxes piled into towers; fuzzy-edged and ghostly, constantly disappearing. Lesky tiptoed forwards until one of them grew solid and still; a giant box

306

the size of a cottage. It towered over her, and yet somehow she knew height had no meaning in this place.

A drop of water struck her in the chin, and the box's surface jittered. Lesky said nothing. She reached out and caressed it with the lightest of touches. It had no heat or cold; it wasn't smooth or rough. It was simply there.

Images of a dining room flickered through her head. It was a room grander than she'd ever seen or heard fireside tales about. It dripped with gold and yellow velvet. The wood was so varnished it was mirror-like. Guests young and old gurgled wine and filled their faces from dozens of overflowing dishes. A young girl with flame-red hair sat at the end of the table, quiet and alone, watching it all with a clever look in her green eyes.

'It's you!'

Lesky tried to dive deeper, as if she could push herself into the room and stand by the girl at the table. She wanted to smell the food, taste the juices, hear the gobbling of the rich. Just for a moment.

There was a sickening moment of as she lost her footing somehow, like climbing a staircase in the dark and imagining there's one more step than there is. The images broke free, and she burst out of the darkness and into the blinding light of day.

She hobbled to the corner, and hurled her guts into a pail. Sharp pain lanced through her skull with every heave.

'That happens,' said Ellia behind her.

When the last retch had come and gone, and she had wiped her mouth with the bandage on her wrist, Lesky sought the nearest chair and slumped into it. If there was one thing she despised in all this world, it was failure. She was not good at this.

When she looked up, she found that Ellia was wincing slightly. 'Did it hurt?'

A shake of the head. 'Not so much *hurt*. It was just... sudden. Dizzying.'

'It deffin' hurt for me. Like a hot poker in my ear.'

'That will happen until you learn to control it. Though I must say, you'd give some of the Mission acolytes a run for their tants. You're a born natural.'

Lesky bit her lip. 'Can I hurt people?'

Ellia's wince turned into a peculiar smile. 'Most glimpses can hold a person, almost separating their mind from their body. Some of the masters can make you forget they're in the room. I suppose you could get up to all sorts of mischievous things when you're invisible. Gazers can show your future to torture you. But physically hurting with the mind?

No. That's for grims only, and there are few, if any, of those left in the Realm.'

'I've 'eard of those. Nightmares and fairytales, Mam says.'

'Your mam was wrong there, unfortunately. They did exist. Another great idea of the Mission's. A man called Master Flatch. They bred glimpses with gazers to see what happened, and the results were catastrophic. They could put a thought into people's heads that would drive them to do things. Or they'd make you witness memories so terrifying that something would burst inside you. That's what you get when you toy with nature.'

Lesky didn't like being told her mam was wrong, but the gruesome details were too distracting. 'Did they all die?'

Ellia nodded. 'After Flatch threw himself from the top of the Blade, the Mission killed them all, one by one.'

'Did you know any?'

'No. Just glimpses.'

'Because you were a spy.'

Ellia half-smiled, half-sighed. 'We keep coming back to that, don't we?'

Lesky shrugged. Spies were liars by nature. Lies came easy to them, even when there was no need for lying. It became a habit, and habits can always be trusted in.

She matched Ellia's gaze, trying to skim her thoughts as she had before. She went too fast, and it was like grasping at steam. Ellia shook her head.

'Trying to gauge whether I'm lying, girl? Well, you're trying too hard. I can feel you prodding and poking like a corpse-looter picking at bodies. Why do you doubt me? Can you not see I'm trying to help?'

Lesky squinted. 'It's *why* you're helpin' that bothers me.'

'Because of Spiddle.'

'I'm thinkin' there's more.'

'Well, I'd like to think it's because we could be friends, you and I. Maybe we could even work together when this war is done.'

'Why?'

Ellia hung her head. She looked to be thinking hard, almost fighting with herself. Lesky ached to try and grope once more, but she refrained. She watched as the woman murmured and sighed and scratched her forehead. At last she looked up to the ceiling, as if praying for support.

'Fine,' she said. 'I'll show you.'

'Show me?'

Ellia tapped her head. 'You want to know why? Then I'll guide you. You can see for yourself, and save my mouth getting dry with talking.'

Ellia snatched the girl's hand from her lap and put it to her face. Lesky found it warm against her clammy skin. 'No distractions this time, and no worrying about being gentle. Just look.'

Once more, the girl felt her pupils fading. Her concentration flew straight down her arm and into the woman's head, like rainwater channeled through a pipe. Within moments, she was standing in the void.

Beneath her fingers, Lesky felt Ellia tense as she moved deeper into her mind. She did not have to go far. A wall reared out of the darkness, featureless and grey. It spanned as far as he could see or sense. She pressed both her hands against it and Ellia gave up her thoughts. They came at her like a flood.

Fading, Sowing, Reaping... Hartlund rotated through its costumes. A face with a yellowed grin, but kind enough, smiled at her. Fingers clutched at chainmail as a long embrace was broken. A tall building jabbed at the heavens, soil-brown and glittering with myriad lanterns. Feet tiptoed, doors slid open, then shut again. A flash of a cottage from afar; more familiar than it should have been. Night ate it, but still a lone light remained in its window.

A knife came on a silver tray, and Lesky knew it was for murder. She felt herself struggling in the memory, as Ellia must have. A nobbled hand reached out of the darkness for its handle, and she saw the man with the yellow-toothed grin. He no longer smiled, but bled from his neck. It was his face that lingered behind her eyes after Lesky pulled back, and snatched away her hand.

Their eyes were locked together. Lesky tried to push the memories back into Ellia's head before the connection faded. She did not want them. For a decade, she had thought of her father as lost, but lost is still a long jump from dead. The little hope she had harboured, that one day he might return for her, sputtered and died there and then.

'You knew him!'

Ellia nodded, no longer the swaggering baroness with pocketfuls of secrets. She was calm, expressionless and honest. 'Yes, I knew your father.'

'You *knew him*, knew him?'

'Yes, we had a relationship. For many years.'

Lesky's tone was turning bitter. 'So did my mam.'

Ellia winced again, but not as Lesky had seen before. This time, it was something that resembled regret. 'It was never my intention to hurt you.'

'Did she ever meet you? Did I?' Lesky wracked her brains for a fire-haired woman at the cottage doorstep.

'No. He was adamant about that.'

'But...' She knew she was running out of easy questions. 'How? How did you know him?'

'He was the glimpse I mentioned. We met after you were born, in the Blade of the Architect. It was... something at first sight.'

Lesky pushed herself to her feet and hobbled in angry, confused circles. She remembered the words thrown back and forth across her cottage, but none of them were of glimpses and missions.

'My mother must've known. She warned me 'bout them.'

'She did. She knew exactly what Techan was and who he worked for. Your mother wasn't a stranger to old-magic herself. He always said she got it from her mother, and so on. That was why you, Lesky, had to be kept secret.'

The girl was too much in flux to ask her to go on, but Ellia did so anyway.

'When a glimpse has a child, they're normally promised to the Mission. When two glimpses have a child, that's when you experience... complications. They aren't allowed to live, at least as far as I know. Your mother knew too much of old-magic for Techan's liking. That was why he hid you and her in the Darens.'

Ellia took a wavering breath. 'They never found out, and yet they killed him. For some imagined treachery he didn't commit. Not because of you, not because of me, but because they did not like him. That's why I hate the Mission, as you should. I asked for your help because you were a glimpse, but now I ask as somebody who loved your father, and wants revenge. Will you still help me, Lesky?'

There was much thinking to be done, that was for certain.

'I need some time. I need to talk to Task.'

Ellia nodded, but there was something frantic in her look. 'I understand,' she said. 'If it helps, Lesky, I had no idea about your parents. This was no spy's ruse, I promise you.'

Lesky hummed as she hobbled towards the door. Her body still ached in a dozen irritating places. She just hoped the golem was not far.

'Remember, however, we do not have much time. Spiddle is a strong glimpse. You'll be stronger, if you can learn how.'

'Whatever you say,' said Lesky, before shutting the door. She had to admit, there was a certain amount of appeal to the idea of thinkpicking.

It seemed that wood whispered just as well as bone.

Huff Dartridge listened to the incessant muttering of the roots. There were words in the crunching and gnawing. He strained hard to pick them out, but caught only senseless babble.

He stepped closer, eager to touch; he found old-magic worked better through touch. With a wriggle he removed his glove and reached out a clammy hand to feel a root.

He waited for the voices to grow louder, more sensible, but they continued to clamour. Death was the word he heard the most.

The general spurned the tree, flapping the tails of his cloak as he turned away. The things were clearly mad, hauling themselves across the plain as though possessed. He had no patience for them.

Jenever was loitering ahead of the ranks. 'General?'

'Take the riders. Give them pitch and torches. Send them out ahead of us.'

'To do what, sir?'

'To burn them,' said Huff. 'Burn the trees from our path.'

'Surely we can go around…'

'We do not "go around" evil, Captain. We scourge it. The trees are old-magic. Not of the Architect nor the Crown. Most likely allied with the Fading.'

'Allied, sir?'

'Did I misspeak, Captain? Did I falter in my words? No. Burn them down! Unless you want to lose the other toe.'

'Yessir!' Jenever saluted, limping away as quickly as she could and hollering for Taspin. It had been her own fault for standing too close to the desk.

Manx was the next to bother him, creeping out from the waiting lines with worry on his face.

'What is it, Captain?'

'Your… project, sir. It's worrying some of the soldiers.'

Huff snorted, staring out across the plain. If he looked hard enough, he thought he could spy Safferon between the distant mountains. 'Then let them worry. A bit of fear will do them good.'

'How did you manage to—'

'Ingenuity and drive, Manx. Two words my father once accused me of lacking. I have surely shown him now. Will that be all?'

'Yes, sir.'

Huff's eyes followed the captain's retreat back to the ranks, and watched him shrug to the soldiers. They rose to the lump of tarpaulin sitting two-score ranks behind, spread across two wagons and just as tall.

He smiled, something that seemed to be happening more often; the closer he got to the walls of Safferon.

♛

Task had not moved all morning. Cross-legged, back straight, he'd sat watching the frantic preparations of the fortress. Every hour that passed had left the soldiers more agitated. He was a stubborn boulder on the borders of a whirling stream.

Even as more smoke began to rise from the south, he stayed put. With a finger, he poked the embers, stirring them to sparks. He needed more wood, but the piles had been moved to feed the hunger of the defences. Probably for boiling oil.

He looked up to see the sun still obscured by a blanket of cloud, and the grey smoke, spreading on the breezes.

'Corporal!' he said.

The armoured woman froze mid-step. 'I'm Shield-chief Junes.'

'Whatever you are. What is the smoke from?'

'The roamwillows,' she said, relaxing enough to face him. 'Did you see them?'

Task nodded.

'Then, you know?' She drifted off.

Task knew a lot of things. He knew it meant the Truehards were barely a day's march away. He knew it made Huff more of a monster than he already was.

'Know what?'

'What they are. Not just strange old trees. Deeper'n that.'

Another nod from Task, more solemn than the last. 'That's what makes it sadder.' Then again, he also knew the trees might have been happy for the fiery release. He knew he would have been, if he were wood instead of stone.

Junes began to edge away. 'I thought the Blues were lying about you. You are different.'

'In a good way?' He'd been wondering the same all night, between his dreams of death.

'Not yet,' the woman said, as she slipped away to the archway.

The golem went back to his sky-gazing, watching the clouds wash over the hazy ball of light. It was as though the sun was reluctant to witness the next few days.

He snarled at himself, for what was possibly the dozenth time that morning. He hated the gloom that had descended on him. He had grown used to it, before Hartlund. But now it bored him.

The problem was, it wouldn't shut up. A lifetime of horrors and disappointment had a knack of entrenching doubt. Every time he felt an inkling of hope, it was quickly silenced. It was so easy to give in; to blame duty and magic for all the defeatist talk swirling round his head.

Broken. Belerod's words. He certainly felt broken that morning.

He heard the familiar tones of a comradely voice; half noble-born, half swaggering soldier. Alabast Flint had come out to see the smoke.

'Bastards, eh? Tree-burning bastards.' His insults rallied a few cheers, but he was largely ignored as he made his way across the courtyard. Only one soldier paid attention to him: a walking slab of meat following at his heel. The man was more than a head taller than the knight, and about twice as wide. A broad moustache covered his lip and cheeks, while a permanent squint was etched below his broad forehead. Task met his tiny eyes with curiosity.

'Golem!' Alabast greeted him with a bow. 'Staying out of trouble, I see?'

'Seems the smart thing to do.'

'Doesn't it just.'

'Who's the big skinbag?'

The man flexed as Alabast jabbed a thumb at him. 'My new personal guard. Olf. Lash has the cheek to think I'll run away the first chance I get. Put this shite-bowl behind me.'

Task raised an eyebrow, and Alabast shrugged.

'I mean, he's probably right.'

Olf decided to do some wandering nearby, so the knight took a seat on the dirt and stretched his arm out to the flames.

'When do you think they'll arrive?'

'Morning, maybe. Depends how hungry Huff is to reclaim me.'

'And will you be reclaimed, my stone friend?'

'You call me friend, yet as we both know, I simply served as a tool to you. Something to renew your career with.'

'Are you still upset about that? I thought we'd cleared it up. I was following orders, and you were as curious as a farmboy in a whorehouse. Simple.'

'Maybe I shouldn't have come.'

'Aren't you the melancholy one this morning? We can all blab about what we shouldn't have done, Task. I shouldn't have let that deffer Carafor pay my debts to Bally the Grin, for one. But here I am. It's what you do now you're here that counts.'

'Like run away?'

'Just one of many options.'

'I only see two. And one...' Task fell silent.

'One what, damn it?'

Task bowed his head. 'No, I was wrong. Both are impossible.'

'Deff it!' Alabast threw up his hands. 'Give me something, golem! Should I be pelting for the gates, finding a crawlspace? What?'

The golem snorted. He didn't know why, but that had amused him, cheered him even. Perhaps he admired the knight's singular purpose. *Save his skin.* All else bowed before that.

He winked. 'Whatever happens, it'll be quick and painless, I promise.'

'Charming.'

A new voice spoke up. 'What'll be quick and painless?'

Lesky had managed to sneak up on them, even while hobbling. The little ghost hovered by the rock face.

Task smiled at her. 'You look better,' he lied. She looked wretched. There was a dried smear of blood across her cheek, and her eyes hollow with tiredness. Her bandages were stained a dubious colour, and he swore he could smell old vomit.

'No I deffin' don't.' She limped over to the fire and threw herself in the dirt and cold grass. 'I've got a thumpin' hammer in my skull.'

'So this your pet stable-girl, Task?' said Alabast, through a yawn.

'I'm no pet, posh-breeches.'

The knight smirked. 'Got a bite though, don't you?'

'You ain't got no idea.' Lesky flashed him a look that Task had never seen before; one that blazed with confidence. It practically melted the smile right off Alabast's face. He went back to starring at the flames.

'How goes the story hunt? Found some reasons to like these Fading yet?' Lesky looked around at the soldiers, her face blank.

'Not so fast. Where's Ellia?'

'She's in my room.'

Task looked down his nose. 'And what have you two been up to?'

'Trainin',' she said, a little pride brightening her face. He did not like it.

'Hmm.'

Alabast looked curious. 'Training for what?'

'I'm a glimpse,' said the girl.

'For Architect's sake. Ridiculous fables, miss. You're not a glimpse. They died out before your mother was born.'

Lesky tilted her head. 'You're the dragon-slayer, right?'

He puffed up. 'Indeed I am! But that doesn't show you can read minds, I'm afraid. I'm famous.'

'More like *in*-famous,' muttered Task.

Alabast tried to flash a sour look, but he found himself trapped by Lesky's eyes, now narrowed and fixated on him. He curled his lip with mirth, clearly amused by the girl's efforts. Then he twitched, scratching madly at his neck. 'What was that?'

'The Knight of Dawn.' She spoke in a whisper. 'Interestin'.'

'What are you doing?'

'Lesky…' Task was growing uncomfortable. Her eyes were taking on a milky quality.

Alabast shuffled around the fire to sit nearer to Task. He eyed Lesky, massaging his temples. 'You've got witch-eyes, girl. In the Duelling Dozen they'd take a poker to your sockets. But you are no glimpse. Sorry.'

Lesky's eyes restored themselves, and she winced, massaging her head.

'Oh no? What if I told you I know a deep secret of yours?'

For a moment, the hollowness showed beneath Alabast's buoyant exterior. He leaned forwards, eyes wide and full of firelight. 'You don't know a thing about me. Nobody does.'

'Have you told Task about the dragon?'

Alabast sneered. 'Course I did. Everybody in the Realm knows about the dragon.'

'But did you tell him the truth?'

His mouth flapped. 'Of course!'

'Great battle, or summin like that, wasn't it?'

'It was.' The knight's tone had become fierce. 'You weren't there.'

Lesky simply grinned.

'I don't have to listen to this brat. Olf! We're leaving!'

With that, Alabast jumped to his feet and stormed over to his hulking minder. After some wild gesticulation, they marched towards the keep.

Task poked at the fire for a time, adding the rest of the remaining sticks while Lesky picked at stray threads. The silence was persistent.

'That was pretty funny.'

'Magic isn't supposed to be used for fun.' He looked at her twinkling eyes and began to smile. 'But that was pretty funny. You know what he's hiding?'

Lesky looked back over her shoulder, watching the knight barge his way through the crowds. 'No, I was just windin' him up. Ain't that good at glimpsing' yet. I thought you knew. Maybe he'll tell us one day. So. Your stories. Found any good ones yet?'

'What, can't read my mind?'

She pursed her lips. 'Nope. Can't read you at all.'

'Maybe it's the stone. Maybe it's better that way.' Task tapped his head, dreading the horrific things she could find in his skull. 'And the stories?' He ran his tongue along the back of his teeth. The magic tingled.

Even if she couldn't read him, Lesky was still intuitive. 'Not helping?'

Even now, alone with the girl, Task felt his lips clamping shut through habit. He knew it was pointless; she would claw it out of him. She might have been distracted by this glimpsing business, but she was still Lundish. It was why her gaze snuck over to the smoke now and again.

'I thought coming here would help clear my mind, but it's only made it foggier. On one hand, I know the truth of what happened. The Fading have changed my mind, like they said they would. My loathing of Huff and all my fears of him, they have been justified. But none of it changes the magic that binds me, nor that I know the cost of caring. That's why I pushed you away, and got angry at your lies. Every time I dare to think something different, I get reminded what you humans are capable of.'

Lesky looked hurt. 'The cost of carin'? What we're capable of? What are you sayin', Task? I thought you'd changed?'

Task scrunched his face. 'I have. I've got you to thank for it. You've made me wonder how many other campfires I should have sat around, how many causes had a shred of truth to them. There is nothing I can do about that, now, but I can't shake the feeling I can do something here.'

'I don't know what the Fading have said about the war. I don't really care. I just want you to be free, like you said all them weeks ago. That's been stuck in my head like a splinter in my thumb. That's what friends want for the other. The best. If that's your best, then so be it.'

'Perhaps we could just run away. Like Alabast. Nothing could stop us.' Task gave the distant gatehouse a sidelong stare. *Then again...* He had tried that once, but Belerod had found him and ordered him back. Golems aren't good at blending in.

Lesky stood up, hobbled to within a foot-length of his knee and folded her arms. 'You big lump. Mam always says if you run once, then you don't stop runnin'. Look at that knight. Where's runnin' got him now? Stop wriggling and figure it out.'

'I've tried.' His tone was more growl than he would have liked. Lesky didn't bat an eye.

'The old-magic. Can't you break it?'

'It's as unbreakable as I am.'

'Yeah but if I pull out your tongue, what then? Everythin's got a weakness. Ellia said you almost broke the magic when you strangled the general.'

Task shook his head. 'But I couldn't do it. It held me back.'

'Don't let it hold you. Push it aside.'

'This, coming from the girl who's known magic for about a day.'

'Fine. What's all this about carin', then? Why's that so dangerous all of a sudden?'

'Look at what happened with the bone golem.'

Lesky suppressed a shiver. 'That was just dumb chance. Ellia said as much. And look...' She pulled at the skin of her arm. 'Still alive because of your carin', see? Otherwise I'd be sitting with the Architect right now instead of here, arguin' with you.'

'If I didn't care, I wouldn't have snapped.'

'And you'd probably be standin' at Huff's side, watchin' those trees burn with him.'

'You wouldn't understand.'

'Then tell me, anyway. There's medicine in tellin' things.'

Task was inclined to agree with her. 'Your mam's wisdom again?'

Lesky took to the dirt again with a pained wince. 'No, that's just me for once.'

The golem relented once more. 'There was a Khandri fable about a sopher... a wise man, told me. One night, an old man, down on his luck and living in the gutters, cried out to the stars for change and mercy. Instead of the goddess answering his call, the Destroyer came to him instead, in the guise of a shining lord. He gifted the beggar a simple bell, just brass and wood, but with a ring as clear and sharp as broken glass. The Destroyer told the man that should he ring the bell, he would find his pockets full of coin. However, every time he rang it, somebody in the city would die. Just like that.' Task crunched his fingers. 'For a week the man didn't touch the bell, stuffing it with rags to keep it from ringing. But when he became so hungry he was wracked with pain, he reached for the bell and rang once. He waited and waited for a cry or shout but none came. True enough, he found his pockets full of coin.

'With the coin he bought clothes, food, and a room over an inn. Within a month, the coin was gone, and the innkeeper threatened to throw him back to the gutter. Once again, he reached for the bell, this time ringing it two times, and once again, no cries or shouts.

'Every time he rang the bell, it became easier. Even when news started to spread of a vicious plague that killed without mercy, he continued to ring it, every day, until he was lord of the city, drowning in coin and silks and women.

'One morning, hungry to break his fast, the man called for his servants, but none came. He struggled up from his chair, fat with wealth, to find them, but he found his tower empty except for bodies, both fresh and old. He went to the streets, but found them empty too. More bodies lay on the stone. He shouted for hours until he found the last person alive: an old beggar, sitting in the gutter, eating a loaf of bread. Hearing the man's stomach rumble, the beggar was about to offer some of his loaf when the rich man pulled the bell from his pocket, held it up, and rang it. As the beggar keeled over, dead as dirt, something fell from his rags. The rich man recognised it immediately. It was a bell, just brass and wood, stuffed with cloth so it could not ring.

'The point is as long as somebody on this earth has more than his neighbour, even a loaf of bread, then there will be cruelty and war and injustice. The weak and the true still suffer. Even if I could stop this war, there would be a next. Ellia has already told me it is coming. It's pointless.'

'I may not be able to read you, but I can tell that's not it. It's a good story, but it's not the real story.'

Task's gaze avoiding her searching eyes and stuck to the flames. Dreams played over in the swirl of red and orange.

'He made me kill them. For no more reason than simple inconvenience. She was younger than you, more of a waif, but she had the same odd fire as you. Orina. No more than a Dorah street rat. He had me crush her skull. At first I refused, begged for her life and for him to keep his promise. But he lied to me. He kept ordering me, over and over. Kill her. Kill her. He called me broken, called me a freak of magic, a mistake. In the end I snapped, but not at him. I became the golem he wanted me to be: a machine, a monster. I killed every one in that line. Twenty and seven by the time the rain started to pour. I could not disobey him, nor could I save her. I could only save myself. That's why I know the futility of caring. That's how I know I'm cursed to not be able to stop or change anything. That's how I know I made a mistake in coming here. Huff won't listen, no more than Belerod did. That smoke tells me everything.'

Lesky was silent. He could almost hear her brain working over the muted crackle of flames.

'I feel sorry for you, Task.'

'Don't bother.'

'No, not because you've suffered, or you're cursed, but because you don't realise.'

He threw her a quizzical look.

Lesky reached out a hand and placed it on his stone. He tensed, but felt nothing, just the warmth of her skin.

'You don't realise how human you are. All of us. Alabast, Ellia, me, Huff, even you, with a mind made out of stone. We all walk around pretendin' we're not broken in some way. Most spend their lives hiding it.

But we *are* broken. And you know what? That's fine. In fact, it's perfect because it's imperfect. Each crack, each blemish, each scar, whether of the skin or in the mind, they make us whole. We're made through livin', not by bein' born. What we learn is what shapes us. Some choose a friendly shape, others somethin' more jagged and sharp. That is what it means to be human, Task. We can choose. You say your master made a mistake? Made you broken? I think he made the finest golem there is. One who's more than stone, not just some mindless machine. One who can make a choice for himself. One who's got a conscience. A heart.'

Task had known silence most of his life, but he had never experienced speechlessness. He found himself too dumbstruck to form a reply, never mind an argument.

'You've got a choice, Task. You don't think you do, but you 'ave. You'll figure it out.' She threw him a coy smirk. 'Anyways! I know you won't let the same happen to me. You almost broke Huff's neck, Ellia says, and that was only for spittin' on me.'

'Where are you going?'

She pushed herself to her feet and limped back towards the keep. 'While you're figurin', I've got business.'

Task could only nod and watch her leave. Once again, his gaze drifted to the smoke of the burning trees, and lingered there.

26

'Glimpsing is like trying to peek through a dirty window.
Sometimes, you just have to smash the glass.'

FROM THE TEACHINGS OF HANIGAN CANE, UNPUBLISHED

61st FADING, 3782 - SAFFERON FORTRESS

Silence reigned over Safferon that night. An invisible tension built with
every scrap of dying light.

Sleep evaded most. Soldiers crouched on wall-tops and battlements,
or huddled around campfires, cramming in as much human contact as
possible before the morning could snatch it from them.

Ellia's gaze roved over the sprawl of concentric circles. She heard
nothing but the breeze and the occasional clank of armour. There was no
sign of the golem around any of the campfires. She pursed her lips,
wondering about his state of mind.

She swept from the railing and entered the tower. The room had
been procured earlier in the day, under the pretence of training. Lash was
so very fond of training.

It was high, yet not unreachable, and private. Most importantly, it
was one of the sturdier structures at Safferon.

In the candlelit room, the girl looked no more convinced than she
had an hour ago. She sat on the bed, picking at her bandages, that
obstinate look still twisting her face.

'I don't know why you doubt me.'

'We're in a fortress. Jus' seems unlikely.'

'Spiddle is an expert. He's been sneaking into fortresses for half his
life.'

Lesky huffed. Ellia moved to rest a hand on her shoulder. 'You
should be getting ready, not grousing over details.'

Lesky tried to rise, but Ellia held her. 'Promise me one thing.'

'What's that?'

'You don't hold back tonight. Pour all your fear and hate into this. Spiddle is strong, so you need to be stronger. He's a lesser breed than you.'

That poked at something inside the waif. 'Alright,' she said, manoeuvring herself off the bed and crawling under it, fingers gripping onto the rusted springs.

'All you need to do is hold him. And when we bridge—'

'Yes, Ellia. I know.'

'Fine, then.'

The room was plunged into darkness with a puff of breath. Ellia stood at the foot of the bed, at the very centre of the half-moon of space. Two doors and one window broke the walls. Above, there was nothing but nailed slats for a roof. Only the door to the balcony stayed open.

She let her ears do the work. Spiddle thought he was quiet, bless him, but Ellia could always catch his ponderous padding. Eyes closed, she listened to the night and its silence, waiting for the gentle scuff of feet.

Two hours passed that way, and by the dull clang of the second bell, Ellia's head had begun to give in to its own weight. Twice, she caught herself and jerked awake, glaring about the room. The tiredness came again. Waves of exhaustion washed over her, making her head roll about her shoulders. *The bed.* It was just behind her. *Spiddle would wake her. He would want a last word or two. It would be alright...*

'No!' Ellia tore herself from the haze, whirling around as Spiddle struck from behind. As his clasped fists bounced from the iron bed-rail, her elbow collided with his jaw. It gave her the perfect amount of time to slide a knife from her sleeve.

The blade cut him across the back of the arm. He spun away, reaching out a hand as if grasping for her throat. Ellia felt the pressure against her skull as he slammed into her mind, clawing at her thoughts. She grit her teeth against the onslaught, fighting not to shout Lesky's name.

'A neat trick.' She strained to speak. 'New?'

Spiddle had the nerve to bow. The dim light from outside caught on his white skull. 'One I keep up my sleeve for rogue zealots.'

He threw a punch, forcing Ellia's weight onto her back foot. When his kick came, it knocked her to her knees. She barely ducked the other fist, and while Spiddle was wrestling with momentum, she dragged the blade across the back of his leg. He hissed as he skipped away. He had been too bold, too personal for his own good.

Ellia forced a smile. She still needed him held for this to work.

'Ah, the coveted rank of the rogue. Just like Techan.'

That would jog the little brat.

'To business, if you please,' said Spiddle.

'Do go on.'

'The Treyarch and the Holy Consecrators have found you guilty of heretical ideals and questionable allegiances. Therefore, he has deemed you unfit to continue the Architect's work, and has requested that your soul be liberated from its mortal trappings. You shall be judged accordingly at the Forge Gates. By these words your fate is sealed.'

'I bet you say that to all the heretics,' said Ellia, waving the blade in a figure-of-eight.

'It is a shame I don't get to see what the Howlings and the Foreman could make of you. Pain is so purifying. The Architect might have forgiven you at the Forge Gates.'

'It's my pleasure to deny you the satisfaction.'

'Stubborn as always. When will you zealots learn? Again, Spiddle threw out a crooked hand, trying to stun her before he could advance with his own blade, no doubt concealed in the hollow of his back. *An old trick.*

He came again, feigning a jab, but cutting left with his free hand, striking her square in the face. Ellia staggered, but stood her ground, knife weaving to keep him at bay. She snorted and spat blood on the mouldy carpet.

He came at her again, kneeing her in the ribs before dropping her to the ground. The knife came flashing down, but her boots found his gut. He doubled up with a wheeze, retching as he retreated.

Spiddle tried to stand straight, but was having trouble moving. He looked around, eyes wide, confused. His body went rigid.

She seized her moment, barrelling forwards and driving a shoulder into his gut. The wind burst from him. There was a crack of ribs as he met the hard floor. They grappled, her arm clenched around his throat. Her weight forced his face to the carpet, making him breath its dust. She hauled him up, and slammed down again. Blood sprayed from his nose.

The knife was quickly at his throat. Ellia nicked him, making him bleed enough to understand. He soon grew still. Angry, spit dribbling from his bared teeth, but still. Risking the blade, he turned his head until he was staring at the girl under the bed.

'There you are!'

Ellia hauled him up and introduced him to the seat of a chair. Lesky scrambled out from under the bed, but hung back, watching from a distance as Ellia tied him up.

The glimpse's eyes ignored Ellia, staring instead at the girl. Lesky glared right back, battling him in the spaces between their minds.

Ellia slapped Spiddle in the face, good and hard, making him sprawl in his bonds. '"Your overconfidence will be the death of you". You remember telling me that in Caverill? Care to rethink?'

'Kill me and Daspar will send a dozen more. He will not stand for your treachery. He will see to it that you, your golem, your Knight of Dawn, your Fading, will find unexpected and painful ends. Go on, kill me.'

'I don't want to kill you,' she lied. 'I want you to bridge with the Blade for me.'

Spiddle smeared snot and blood across his shoulder, and painted a lopsided grin across his cheek, black against his white skin.

'Don't you recognise Techan's daughter, Spiddle? The resemblance is striking, once you see it. Got his powers, too. And her mother's.'

'Abomination!'

'Well, this abomination can keep this up all night,' said Lesky, spitting words through pursed lips.

'As can I,' said Ellia. 'Knife-work, of course. Not mind-games.'

Spiddle regarded the blade in her hand with a fresh reverence.

'A finger first? Ear? Or perhaps just go straight to the tongue. I have always hated your slithering voice.'

'Heretic bitch.'

'Opportunist, actually. I've been waiting for this moment for a very long time. Now that it's here, I'm going to enjoy it.' Ellia smiled. She could feel him scraping at her thoughts, but failing to get any purchase. The girl, and a broken rib or two, were doing a great job of weakening him. She leaned to whisper in his ear.

'Now, seeing as you aren't getting your hands on me or the girl, not tonight, nor ever, how about you bridge with the Blade like I asked?'

Spiddle spent far too long thinking for her liking. She grabbed the ear and began to cut. He wailed as soon as the knife bit. Ellia tutted as she released him.

'By the Rent, Spiddle, I thought you'd last longer than that. Not used to being caught, are you?' She turned to Lesky. 'I knew he was a coward.' The girl ignored her. She was beginning to sweat, and tremble. Her white eyes were teary.

Ellia returned to Spiddle, pressing the knife against his windpipe.

'Bridge, or die. I still may let you live.'

'No.'

Ellia seized his ear again, and this time she was not merciful. With one slice, it came away in her fingers, and she dropped it onto his lap, making him howl even louder.

'They're not expecting me!'

'I don't care.'

'The other glimpse will fight it!'

'I know how it works! Now get on with it!'

Spiddle hissed, stamping his feet on the boards to combat the pain. It took some time, and about another pint of blood for him to realise that resistance was pointless. He lifted his gaze to hers.

'Relax a bit, Lesky,' said Ellia.

Spiddle spat again, catching her shoe this time. 'Yes. Relax a bit, Lesky.'

Another slap silenced him. Ellia watched his eyes whiten as he grasped her mind, holding far too tight. She felt him and all his rage simmering away, but she also felt Lesky, standing between them. The girl was more like a hammer than a fine sword, but somehow she was doing the job. As the dark tower faded away, the bridge began to form.

The miles surged past her eyes as Spiddle reached south. The city flashed once, before she found a room lit by a quiet fire. Books were spread over a table. One sat in her hands, page half-turned and waiting.

Ellia felt her body jerk violently. The connection was unexpected, unwilling, and the glimpse in the Blade knew it.

'Lesky!' She heard her distant cry.

The girl surged in, swelling up inside the void, leaving no room for the Blade glimpse to think. There was another jerk, and another, before the glimpse fell still and submissive. Lesky was struggling. She could feel her trembles echoing in the bridge. She would need to be quick.

Ellia ignored the mirror. She could tell by her hands that she was a man, and that was all she cared to know.

She found herself in the lower half of the Blade, far from where she wanted to be. Echoes of Spiddle's sniggering floated along the bridge.

She found the nearest crank-lift, and bade the servant to take it as far up as the thing could go. The servant went to it with a will, hands flying over the cogs and wheels. Floor after floor passed beyond the iron grate, slowly enough to frustrate her, making her twitch. She could feel the tattoo plastered across the back of her skull growing hotter.

'You alright, sir?'

'Shut up. Keep cranking,' she said, in a gruff voice.

At long last the floors began to sparkle with filigree and marble. Ellia edged towards the grate until she was practically poking her nose through it.

When the lift finally reached its height, Ellia strode into the hallway, following it left then right, steered by years of practice. She had planned for this very night since Cane had slit Techan's throat.

Two guards in steel armour stood by the door to the atrium, where Daspar would be reclining, reflecting. He was famed for his lack of sleep. His pillows often went months without seeing his head.

'I need to see the Treyarch,' said Ellia, with a smile. She felt a moustache prickle her nose.

The bigger guard looked her up and down. 'On what grounds?'

'Important news from the north. It's me, Spiddle.'

The guard sighed, as if this glimpsing business was far too exhausting, and put a hand to the door.

'My lord Treyarch. A visitor from the north. Glimpse Spiddle in other form.'

'Allow him.'

Ellia was guided through the doors and into the bright light of the atrium. A fire roared on both sides of the room, and lanterns ringed every pillar. The rows of guards glittered.

'Spiddle,' Daspar intoned. He had left his throne for the evening, and was sat instead at a stone table in the centre of the atrium. A half-dozen scrolls were stacked before him.

'Treyarch. I bring good news,' said Ellia, looking around for the consecrators, but there was no sign of them. She walked towards him.

'She's dead?'

'Neck broken, throat cut.'

'Efficient.'

Ellia bowed. 'I have other news that I believe Consecrators Lockyen and Vullen would benefit from hearing. And Master Cane for that matter. About the golem and the battle tomorrow.'

'Tomorrow?'

'Yes, my Lord. Dartridge has made good time. Ellia did her job, despite her heresy.' Ellia twitched, shrugging her shoulder to her ear.

'Problems, Glimpse?'

'A little injured, my Lord.'

Daspar sucked at his front teeth. 'I see.'

'Shall I fetch them for you, Treyarch?'

'The hour is late.'

'I apologise, but the news is most important.'

Daspar shooed him away with a flick of his hand.

'I'll return momentarily, my Lord.'

Lockyen and Vullen practically shared their chambers across a thick wedge of the Blade's spire. Ellia knocked on both their doors at the same time. Vullen, quick on his gangly legs, emerged first, his face flushed with anger. Ellia caught thin shadows moving around in the candlelight behind him. He was sweaty, wrapped in a robe.

'What is the meaning of this interruption?'

Lockyen appeared at his door, bleary-eyed but just as furious. 'I second that! What's going on?'

'Important news from the north. The Treyarch has summoned you.'

They groaned and slammed their doors.

Ellia spared not a second. She jogged down a dozen levels to her own quarters. Tapping a brick free from the door-frame, she picked out a key hiding in its hollow and jammed it into the door. Seizing the blanket and sheets with both hands, she tossed them aside, and moved the moss mattress beneath. With her borrowed, but thankfully, strong hands, she prised away the boxes.

She jolted as all those in the bridge realised her secret; her longest game. She held fast to Spiddle's touch as Lesky gave another push.

Six containers of firepowder had been arranged beneath the bed-frame, gathered over years. Fuse-wire poked from a small hole in each box, twirling to form a meandering path around the bed. She fetched a leather pouch from a nearby chest, and with finger and thumb, plucked the end of the fuse from the bed. From the pouch came Destrix flickerdust, sprinkled on the end of the fuse until it was buried in a pile. Then, with the signet ring on her little finger, she struck it hard—once, twice—until a spark flew on the third. The orange dust exploded into life, and the fuse began to run. As did she, snapping the key in the lock before sprinting back the way she had come.

Going up the stairs was not so easy as barreling down them. This body was not up to her standards of fitness, and by the seventh level, it was snorting and sighing.

'Come on, you bastard!' Ellia shouted at herself.

Hanigan Cane was not in his chambers. His servants had not seen him. A guard had, however, and sent Ellia four levels down, to a spare room the master had, typically, turned into his own training room.

Cane was more suspicious than blustery. He stared sidelong at the glimpse in his doorway while he absently hacked at a dummy with a hooked axe. The twitching wasn't helping her. It was becoming more frequent with every passing moment.

'Glimpse?' he asked.

'Spiddle, sir. Treyarch wants you in the atrium, with the consecrators. I've got important news from the north.'

'I'm busy.'

'Treyarch's orders, sir. The war ends tomorrow.'

Hanigan dug his axe into the dummy with an exasperated grunt. *'Alright, for Rent's sake.'*

'Shall I escort you, sir.'

'What's in your mind, Spiddle? You don't seem yourself.'

'Injured in the fight with Frayne, unfortunately.'

'Tut tut, Glimpse.'

Ellia flinched again.

'You're slipping, man!'

'I'm fine, sir.'

She heard Cane rumbling behind her as they walked. Bizarrely, she wondered at how well he and the golem would get on.

The guards admitted them without fuss, and Ellia strode into the atrium to find Lockyen and Vullen already buzzing around Daspar's ears, spitting their complaints.

'All shall now be revealed!' he snapped, sending them cowering to their seats. Cane chose to stand beside Ellia as she took up the head of the table.

'Speak, Glimpse!' said Vullen. *'Tell us what is so deffing important at this hour.'*

'Well, I thought we'd have a bit of a chat.'

Cane growled in her ear. *'Explain yourself, Spiddle!'*

'It's been so long since we were alone like this, the four of us. Though we are missing one person. Techan.'

Daspar took to his feet. *'What is the meaning of this?'*

'All it took was two golems, a knight and some clever, clever lies to gather us here.'

'Spiddle!' Cane grabbed Ellia by the arm, wrenching her around to face him. Her smirk told him everything he needed to know. *'You are not him!'*

'And you thought you could kill me.'

'Frayne!' The consecrators had caught on. The guards peeled from their rows, and came to form a ring of spear-points. The Treyarch crept forwards, wary and smart as ever.

'Your child's life was ours to take. We spared it the indecency of being born.'

'You speak of it as a gift. I see it as a curse. A curse on you and all you stand for. The moment you ended their lives, you set this all in motion. As soon as the war started, I found my opportunity for revenge. I have been working to bring this Mission to its knees for almost a decade, Daspar. And its beloved Hartlund along with it..'

'Curse you!' Cane backhanded her across the face, sending her glimpse sprawling. The bridge shook violently. 'You dare to come here to gloat?'

'I thought you might want an explanation, before you realise.'

It was Daspar's turn to grab her. 'Realise what? What have you done?'

'Before you realise the depths of your ineptitude. You fell for your own tricks. I gave you the thoughts you needed to prove me a traitor. A kiss here, a question there. Spiddle once told me a Hasp phrase. Etara swarne. Compartmentalisation. *Just like how you caught Techan and I. Revenge is a strange thing. Bitter and yet sweet at heart. It feels...'* Ellia smacked her lips. *'Worthwhile.'*

'Spiddle! I command you to take control!' Cane pressed his fingers against her face and leant his own mind to the fray.

The bridge began to crumble. She felt Spiddle escape Lesky's clutches, and drive a wedge between Ellia and her glimpse. The man began to thrash and flail. He took control of his vocal chords and screamed at the top of his voice.

'Firepowder!'

Cane besieged her mind, driving against her with all the force he could muster, sending her spinning to the floor. She felt the glimpse go limp. All she could do was watch through his eyes as Cane ripped apart every one of her thoughts, tearing at the truth. Lesky was tied to it, scrabbling to be free of the barrage. Ellia felt her rally once, momentarily beating Cane back, but the master returned with a vengeance, pushing the girl from the bridge and pinning Ellia with his mind. Daspar joined the bridge through Cane, pouring his thoughts into the mix.

'How does it feel to be out of control?' thought Ellia.

'By dooming us, you doom more than just the Mission!' boomed Cane. *'The entire Accord. All of it. You give the Khandri their foothold.'*

Ellia made sure her thought was clear as crystal.

'That is precisely my intention. Chaos, Cane. Order has had its day.'

Daspar began to throttle her as an almighty explosion engulfed the room.

As Ellia began to withdraw from the glimpse's mind, she felt the Blade begin to lean, and heard the wrenching crack of stone beneath them.

Her last sight was of Daspar's face, cold and confused until the very last second, before the atrium turned upon its head. Before the walls came to crush him to paste.

'Yah!'

Ellia sliced the blade across Spiddle's throat and fell back onto the floor of the bedroom. Through a hammering headache, she watched the glimpse bleed out; the ragged gash across his windpipe gurgling and pulsing. It took him some time to pass, and she lapped up every moment of it. It was good to feel her own smile again.

'You're a monster!'

She turned to find Lesky also sprawled on the floor, her eyes bloodshot and tearful, vomit adorning her mouth.

'I saw it all,' she rasped through her obvious pain. 'Everything you are. Everything you've done. You're worse than Huff, worse than... everyone. I can't believe I deffin' trusted you!'

'Guilty as they come,' said Ellia, gasping for breath. 'But I'm the best kind of monster. The one who wins. And you can win with me, if you have the sense to follow me.'

'I saw the vial. The poison they made you drink. Not a knife on a silver dish. My da was killed because of *you*, not the Mission!'

'Lies!' Ellia jabbed the bloody knife at her. 'The Treyarch killed him!'

'You're the liar, and the murderer. I'd rather be eaten alive by jorks than follow you.'

With a huge effort, Ellia dragged herself back to her feet, and stumbled for the door-handle. She considered stabbing the girl, but she wondered if she still had a use for her; whether she could temper that hatred, those vitriolic eyes. 'I could make you rich, powerful.'

'Evil.'

'I am whatever I need to be to win, girl. There is no compromise, nothing I will not do to get what I want. What I *deserve*. That is why you and that golem will fail. You have boundaries. Limits. Feelings.' She scoffed, and grasped the cold handle.

Before Lesky could stand, Ellia had shut and locked the door. Several moments later, fists pounded against the wood. Screeches of frustration joined them.

'There's no use, Lesky! You'll stay here until I say so.'

'Let me out, you witch!'

Ellia whispered to the grain. 'You'll learn to like me. You'll see.'

27

'A soldier does not charge for his own anger. A soldier charges because other soldiers are charging.'

HASP PROVERB

62ND FADING, 3782 - SAFFERON FORTRESS

Dawn brought a smoky orange glow, and a cautious mist whose tendrils washed against the walls of the fortress.

That, and fifteen thousand Truehard soldiers.

They spread in a wedge between the mountains, twice the cannon-range away. No trenches had been dug, no spikes set. They just waited there, with their shields dug deep.

They sat in smart squares and columns, muskets balanced and spears waving in the front lines. Groups of bowmen punctuated the rows. Cannons bookended each regiment. The flanks bristled with riders, waiting with lances low. At the rear, a large tent had been erected, with pennants bearing the crown hanging in the dead air.

Task glimpsed it all from the stairs, through a gap in the crenellations. After a few moments of observation, he ducked back down. He had no wish to antagonise Huff, who was no doubt still slumbering, or busy waxing his moustache.

He thought of the Dregs, and Collaver, and wondered where they stood in the lines. He blew a sigh, startling a few nearby musketmen. The night's silence had yet to break.

'Sorry,' he said, and they raised hands.

He retreated to the churned courtyard and wandered through the fractured ranks until he found a clearing.

He had not slept. He had stayed alert, listening to the hushed whispers of the camp; to the heartbeats skipping every time a creature of the night screeched or another tree went up in flames, closer than the last.

Task had built himself no fire, nor pondered anything but Lesky's words. They had stuck to him like molten metal, fizzing all night long.

Task had thought he felt her in the early hours; something clashing against his mind. As quickly as it came, it was gone, and he resorted to staring up at the pinpricks of light and swirls of heavenly dust. The skinbags proclaimed the night sky told stories. All he saw were badly drawn shapes.

The golem wandered between the walls until he approached the mighty keep. Its stone bristled with the scars of cannon, musket and arrow. In the dim dawn light, the stone glowed as if aflame.

The Khandri say good news has quick wings. If that's true, then bad news must be fired from a cannon. Lash burst through a gate, captains and sergeants in tow, jogging to keep up. Carafor Westin and Alabast Flint followed on either side, each wrapped in armour and watching the general with worried eyes. Lash carried an urgency that Task had not seen before. Deadlines could drive a man to madness, and Lash was already his customary red hue. His powerful arms drove his wheels to skid on the gravel. He stopped at the sight of the golem.

'Just the man! To arms!'

Task felt the whoosh of spearheads, the sliding of feet. Three-score muskets clicked. He looked around at the circle of soldiers. A few gulped as he caught their aim.

He understood completely. Lash was protecting his interests. A feeble, yet powerful gesture. He wondered how many cannons were secretly trained on him.

'I had hoped to hear from you last evening. I trust you have heard what you need to hear from my men.' Lash paused, afraid to ask his question. When he did speak, his voice was so low Task almost didn't hear him.

'Have you come to a decision?'

Task knelt, both for comfort and respect. The general tensed as the golem leaned close.

'I have.'

'And?'

'I need you to open the gates.'

'Why?' said Westin.

Task looked at him solemnly. 'I wish to talk to Huff.'

'For what purpose?'

'To talk.'

Lash grunted. 'Then we shall all go to meet him. I've waited far too long to stare this brat in the face.'

'Just think what that face'll look like when he sees Task walking out with us,' said Alabast.

'Alabast!' Lash glared at him. The knight fell quiet, and dropped his visor with a clang. 'To the gate!'

Task knew that he was stone through and through, and yet he could not deny the sensation in his chest. That phantom organ of his was beating a nervous rhythm. He could feel it hammering between his steps.

'My Lord!' said a female voice. Ellia came bounding down a flight of steps to join their huddle. Despite the paint she'd daubed on her face, the dark circles of a rough night showed through. Her eyes were pink with burst veins. Task could smell magic on her.

'Auger? You should be in the keep. I thought that was what—'

'I was watching, and once I realised Task was not going to slaughter us all, I decided I would accompany you to the Truehards. I would rather enjoy seeing the look on Huff's face. I assume that is where you are going?'

Alabast chuckled to himself. 'Your assumptions are correct.'

'Fine,' said Lash, letting her walk at his side.

Ellia caught the golem's stare, and smiled. 'Lesky is safe, Task. Safer than you or I.'

The golem nodded.

Hundreds of Fading formed up behind them, taking up the march to the gates. By the time the gatehouse loomed over them, they numbered thousands, filling the first two rings of stone. Spears stood like spines.

They all looked at Task. Though many still aimed their weapons at him, he felt the weight of their hope like a mountain on his back.

Lash took a breath.

'Open the gates!'

General Huff Dartridge stood with his arms crossed and his eyes narrow. Safferon filled his mind as well as his view. His gaze crawled over its features; every patch of old stone, every overhanging crag, every yawning black cannon-hole.

'Well?'

Manx lowered his spyglass. 'Not a sign of him, sir. Not a peep.'

'Per'aps he was destroyed after all,' suggested Glum.

Huff backhanded the oaf, making him stagger. The captains fell silent as he turned back to the fortress. Dartridge didn't know what he thought. It was almost inconceivable that Task could have been killed. They had seen no stones along the path. And yet, it seemed equally impossible that he could betray his magic. Still, Huff knew now how golems could be coerced, and bent to purpose. Perhaps the Fading bastards were not beyond such cunning. He snorted to himself. If that were the case, Huff would bend Task back.

'Gates are opening, sir! Just a crack, but I see shields and spears.'

'Give!' Huff held out a hand. He jammed the spyglass against his eye and twisted its brass. The blurry shapes cleared. He could almost see their faces under their ash-white helmets.

As fluid as water, they flowed into two thick wedges, pointed directly at the Truehard lines. They had no riders, no artillery. Their shields glowed orange in the early sun; the shadows were still too long for them to sparkle.

'Two thousand, by my count, sir.'

Glum shook his head. 'Five.'

'Four, actually,' Huff corrected them, with a humourless chuckle. 'And no sign of any surrender or parleying. Slaughter, it is!' He handed the spyglass back to Manx. 'Tell the gun-crews to get ready—'

'General!' hissed Manx.

'What?'

The soldier could only flap his hand; he was too enraptured by what he was seeing. Huff squinted at the gates. Although his stomach had hardened, he snatched the spyglass from Manx.

Task walked by the side of a man in a wheeled chair; presumably Lash. On the lord's other other side walked Baroness Frayne, her hair fiery in the light and her face as smug as he'd ever seen it. Huff couldn't decide which betrayal disturbed him more.

He held the spyglass by its ends and smashed it over his armoured knee. He threw the shards at Manx and Glum.

'Bring up the wagon! It's time for a little chat with old friends.'

'What by the Rent is that?' asked Alabast, pointing a finger past Task's arm.

'A wagon,' said Westin, in a tired voice. He looked uncomfortable in his armour. Sweaty.

'Yes, but for what?'

'Something big.'

'Cannon.'

'Too misshapen.'

Task stared at the tarpaulin with his keen eyes. Nothing moved beneath it, but it made him uneasy. Perhaps it was the familiarity of being carried on wagons and under tarpaulins for a significant portion of his life.

'There's our good general,' said Ellia.

Huff walked like a king striding to greet his loyal subjects. Two captains, Glum and Manx, flanked him, plus a phalanx of guards. The general's head was tilted so far back he seemed to be staring at the sky. He wore russet armour, polished to mirrored plates. His shoulders were draped in a flowing cloak of red, and the crest of a crown was emblazoned on his breastplate. Task found himself clenching his fists at the sight of it.

Of course, the rage came calling. It was like a thug lighting a match in a dark doorway; letting him know it was there, waiting for a chance to drag him down. Task shrugged it away with a crunch.

'Twitchy, golem?' said Alabast. There was a nervous crack in the question.

'I'm perfectly fine,' grunted Task, stepping out ahead to stay level with Lash. He rested his gaze on Huff and didn't move it until the two parties stood within a stone's toss from each other. Truehards and Last Fading. King's men and rebels.

Huff wore a disdainful look, angled along the slope of his nose. It moved from Lash to Alabast and Carafor, then to Ellia and finally to the golem. Task matched his expression.

'We will accept complete surrender,' he said.

Lash snorted. 'We do not give it. And in situations such as these, *General*, it is traditional for introductions to come first, then terms.'

'Tradition!' Huff looked as if he were mustering spit, but he refrained. He cleared his throat.

'So be it. I am General Huff Dartridge the Third, Earl of Gulliger, and commander of the king's northern army. As far as you are concerned, His Majesty's own voice and right hand. These are my officers, captains Manx and Glum.'

Lord Lash looked at each for a long time before replying. 'An honour to finally stand face to face with my foe.'

'Stand?' Huff regarded the lord's chair with contempt. 'Strange. My father spoke many times about you, and he never mentioned a cripple.'

Lash did not blink.

'I am Lord Terralt Lash, supreme commander of the Last Fading forces, master of Safferon Fortress, Duke of Massin, once envoy and ambassador to the King Raspier. And as far as you are concerned, I am the Fading. My captains...' Lash gestured to the soldiers behind him.

'Executor Carafor Westin of the Last Table.'

'Alabast Flint, Knight of Dawn. You will have heard of me.'

'Lady Ellia Auger of the Last Table.'

It was Ellia's title that broke Huff. His haughty face had been cracking since Lash had started to talk. Now it collapsed into hatred.

'At last we see the true colour of your skin, Milady. You've played a fine game, Ellia. I had my suspicions, but nothing more. My father will be most disappointed when I tell him of your treachery.'

Ellia smiled. 'I wouldn't be so confident.'

'Enough formalities.' Task stepped forwards, eager to end this farce. 'To terms.'

Spittle flew from Huff's mouth. 'And Task of Wind-Cut! The biggest traitor of them all!'

The golem held out open hands. 'I wish you to see reason, General. This battle need not happen today.'

'So you've turned him into a coward as well as your pet, Lash? Tell me, what spells did you use? What trickery? What do you know of old-magic?'

'We have done nothing but tell him the truth, General.'

'Fawl-shite!'

Task tried again. 'This war can end on peaceful terms. Save your men's lives, Huff, and let us find a solution instead of fighting. You are the king's voice, no? Speak the words he cannot.'

Huff looked aghast at the suggestion, as though Task had just suggested he chew his own arm off.

The golem continued. 'You can make a name for yourself as a merciful, wise general, one who brokered the end of the war…'

'Task, I will not surrender,' said Lash, behind him.

'…a general who will be celebrated for saving Hartlund, not butchering it. Think, Huff. Think of how you want to be remembered. Think of what you could achieve here, with words instead of musket and cannonballs. You are not Fading and Truehard. You are all Lundish. These are your countrymen standing behind these walls. Not your enemy.'

'They are nothing but capitalists and traitors to the crown!' snapped Huff.

'General, Master, I ask you to—'

'Shut up!' said Huff.

Habit clamped his mouth shut. Four centuries of taking orders would do that. The loud clack of stone made the two parties flinch. Task stared down into Huff's eyes. He could almost see the workings behind their glass: cogs spinning, levers twanging.

'You are still bound to me.'

Lash and the others tensed. All eyes watched Huff's face begin to change, like a storm dissipating before blue skies.

'You are still bound to me.' He began to chortle; first at Lash, then at Ellia, then at Task. The only sound to be heard across the dirt was his laughter; harsh and mocking. Every breath of it made Task tighter, tenser.

'My, my, golem! I underestimated you! What a perfect ploy, I must say.'

Lash and Task met eyes. The golem shook his head.

'To pretend you have had a change of heart, have them welcome you with open arms, then when the time is right...' Huff clapped his palms. 'You lure Lord Lash and his captains out here.'

Carafor spoke up. 'Those are not the rules.'

'There are no rules! None besides kill or be killed. That is why I stand at *your* gates, and not the other way around. Isn't that right, golem?'

Task could feel the frustration building inside him. *The anger.* His stones began to rattle.

'You have to see sense, Huff. You must.'

'You are no soldier, sir!' said Lash. 'You are a disgrace to your uniform!'

Huff turned to Task, a pleasurable look on him. 'Golem, kill Lord Lash.'

Alabast's sword rang as it was yanked free. Westin brought up a pistol. The guards slid forward their spears. Manx and Glum both drew their sabres. Shouts from both armies rang across the battlefield. Ellia folded her arms.

Task felt the magic push him, as it always did; though this time it seemed to be personal. A maleficent force. Unnatural. Like a shoving hand instead of the blow of the wind. He resisted.

Huff stood his ground. 'Now, Task! Kill him, I said.'

Task looked to Lash. The lord had put hands to wheels but he had not moved. Spears surrounded him like a crown.

Task felt the force increase, commanding him to spill blood. He bared his teeth.

He took one step towards Lash, making the dirt tremble. Lash still didn't move. He regarded the golem with a calm and knowing look, silently willing him to break his master's bonds.

Another step, and he was within arm's reach of the lord. Still they locked eyes.

'Steady,' said Lash, either to his guards or the golem.

'END HIM!'

Manx and Glum tried to drag Huff back to the lines.

Task willed his hand to stay still, even though it shook to be free, to reach out and complete the order. *It would be so simple*, his insides sang. *So easy and natural.*

'I know you won't,' said Lash, quiet over the noise of feet and armour. The armies had begun to move. Orders ricocheted along the battlements.

Task snarled. 'I can't.'

Lash tilted his head as the claws inched closer.

Ellia sighed. 'Oh, for deffing's sake. I'm tired of this farce.' She dragged Lash back into the soldiers' ranks and stood in his place.

'Task, I command you! You will obey me!' bellowed Huff. He had broken free of his captains, and was now striding towards the golem.

'I'll make this simple for you, Task,' said Ellia. 'You break the magic, or the girl dies. And it won't be at the hands of the Truehards.'

Task reined himself back a foot-length.

Ellia's face was as stony as his. 'I will kill her, Task, if you do not follow *my* orders. I will kill her without hesitation.'

Confusion staggered him. 'Orders?'

She shrugged. 'Kill them all.'

'Ellia!' said Lash.

'Silence, you old fool. Look at you.' She sneered at the lord and the general. 'Both of you pushing on opposite sides of the same stubborn wall. Pathetic. It's time that this war came to an end, and you both with it. Truehards and Last Fading alike. I'd call that a fresh start, wouldn't you? That's what this cursed Realm needs.'

'What are you doing?' said Alabast, striding forwards. She threw a hand to his throat, under the visor.

'More lies, Frayne?' Huff now, as confused and angry as the rest.

She ignored them all. 'That's your choice, golem. Kill them all, or kill the girl. Is she worth it, Task? Only you know.'

The golem saw it painted across her face. 'You're enjoying this!'

She spared a moment to look at the lightening sky, fading to dusty-blue now the sun had begun its climb. 'It's been a long time coming, Task. What's not to enjoy about a plan falling into place? Now kill them, or you'll never see her again. I have a Mission glimpse ready with a knife to her throat. If he doesn't see blood soon, he will spill hers. Simple, really. Much easier than all your soul-searching and stories, than trying to figure out whether there's a heart amidst all that granite. Which, of course, there is. You're just too stupid and damaged to realise it. That's why I've made this an easy choice for you. The girl, or your friends.'

Every grain in his body fought with itself. He felt as if his very insides were at war, like the country around him. He was frozen at the centre of their battle, no other choice but murder. He shouted inside his head, desperate to overcome the wordless roar to obey. To forge a different path.

He looked once more to Lash, but found Belerod sat in that wheeled chair, shaking his head, mouthing the word.

Broken.

The orders and begging were flying thick and fast. Task closed his eyes to them.

'Don't listen to her, Task!'

'Kill her and Lash, I say!'

'Put an end to this madness!'

Voices squawking. Armour clanking. Hearts drumming.

He felt the shaking rise from ankle to knee, hip to chest. He railed against it. Lesky had been right. *He was no mindless machine!*

Something within him shattered like a pane of glass, fleeting enough to reveal his choices laid out plainly before him. Each shined with possibility. He counted, and found one more than he had assumed.

All too abruptly, it came for him: that flash of a match in the doorway, the shadowy figure pouncing. The world was deafening, but he was cold in his silence, like the absence of forest-song in the presence of a predator.

This was his blemish. His imperfection. And it was glorious. If a being was a product of its choices, then Task had chosen truth his entire creation; not chaos. He was not broken because of his rage, he was broken because he could choose to deny his purpose. Time and telling had distorted his story, but he could still remember Belerod's contemptuous sneer the day the rain came. Only now did he recognise the disappointment in it. The fear. The Realm's finest Windtricker had failed; but at the same time, he had succeeded.

He had given a beating heart to stone.

And how that heart beat now, pumping ferociously as the darkness descended. For the first time since his building, he gave in freely to the precipice.

The Task who opened his eyes was a different golem. He was a creature of rage. Cold-eyed, purposeful, heaving with low growls.

The yelling was reaching fever-pitch, the parties almost touching noses, and still the magic pulled him to Ellia and Lash.

The golem went after the magic as though it were an enemy line. With a loud snarl he wrenched his hands to his chest, attempting to clasp them. The magic sat like a metal sphere between them. Immovable.

The stones bunched around his shoulders, sliding to add weight to his quivering muscles. The ground quaked as he fell to his knees. A roar built deep in the golem's throat as he summoned every scrap of his might. His swollen arms pushed and pushed, crushing the stubborn magic in on itself.

In tiny, jarring increments, it began to show its weakness. The roar ripped out of him, quelling the entire battlefield with its rawness. The golem curled over his hands, feeling his fingertips scraping against each other.

The pressure inside his skull was immense. He felt like a keg of firepowder, sitting alone in a burning room, waiting to explode. And still the monster in him drove on, murderous in its intent to break the magic.

The golem's palms crashed together and the air snapped like a whip-crack. The shockwave drove him backwards, half-burying him in the earth. Everybody within a hundred foot-lengths was sent tumbling.

A vacuum descended over the field. Time slowed, slipping from one moment to the next. In his half-conscious state, the golem watched the blurry shapes scrambling to their feet.

Lash being hauled away. Ellia standing alone with fists clenched white, stuck between running and standing firm. Huff, shouting, dragging the tarpaulin from the nearby wagon before he'd even got to standing.

'You take my golem! I take yours!'

No! Surely Huff had no skill to toy with old-magic.

Other voices filled his ears.

'Charge!'

'Back to the fortress!'

'Attack!'

White bones caught the early sun. Had the sky been black with night, Task might have thought himself back in the Truehard camp, lying on the ground between a bone golem's punches. *It had all been a dream.*

The scraping whine brought him to his senses; as did the horns blaring from the rooftops.

'Not again!'

'Arise!' Huff was barking at the wheels of the wagon. The tarpaulin was ripped away as the creature reared up.

It was the audacity of it that brought the rage streaming back to him. Huff had perverted old-magic for his own cause; a filthy trick. He had dabbled in things he knew nothing about, like an untrained surgeon delving into an open chest cavity.

Task pressed his fists against the ground, shaky and uncertain. Power flowed through him; less intense than usual. Stones slipped from his shoulders as he took a step, then two, staggering towards Huff and his wagon.

Bone legs clattered onto the dirt, as tremulous as Task's. The golem looked disjointed. Its spine was crooked and more squat than he remembered, but it was no less fearsome. It looked around the field with hollow eyes; it seemed madder, more desperate.

'Kill them all!'

Huff was crawling away on all fours, hiding behind the wagon. Manx and Glum had scarpered. Both the Fading and the Truehards had begun to charge. In mere minutes, they would all be swarmed by soldiers.

Task lunged forward and broke into a sprint. The musketballs and arrows began to rain. As he laid hands on the wagon's rough edge, the walls of Safferon began to thunder. Cannon after cannon boomed. Iron crashed around him, ripping gouges in the earth. One cannonball clipped his shoulders and tore through the wagon's right side, crippling it. Another shot took a hand from Huff's golem. The air exploded with splinters of wood, bone and stone.

Huff was screeching.

'CHARGE!'

Task grabbed the wagon and spun it in a circle, using it like a club against the bone golem. The thing staggered backwards, howling. Task saw recognition in its eyes, as it fixed its gaze on him. It barrelled into the Fading ranks, slashing at the soldiers with its long claws.

Huff broke from the wagon wreckage and ran for his lines.

'Dartridge!' Task gave chase.

Cowards tended to be fast on their feet, but vengeful golems were always faster. As the spears and lances split for their general, Task caught up and cuffed him across the back, sending him sprawling into his own soldiers.

The golem didn't give the man a chance to utter a word. There was no explanation, no justification, no pleading. Just the gasping terror of a man watching a stone fist hover above him.

Even as the lances and musket balls bounced off his stone, Task looked down at the man's pale face and pondered, for a fleeting moment. He saw every master who had ever bound him. From Belerod to Huff Dartridge, he recalled every shade of iniquity they had taught him. He saw every burning town, every dead hand reaching for the sky, every child with their brains dashed out on the cobbles.

Perhaps Huff was not to blame for their sins, but he had to answer for his own.

The golem let the rage do the work for him. His fist hammered down. Only four times, did he strike the man, but it was enough to leave nothing but pulp.

Behind him, he heard the bubbling wail of the bone golem as it was severed from its master. It was enough to slow it, and let the cannons go to work. The iron began to rip its bones to shreds.

Task felt the severing, too, as if the ropes binding him had snapped.

THE HEART OF STONE

He stood alone in a circle of those who had seen their general's death. There was a terrible silence. A few dropped their weapons, but they were soon swept along by the others; those that were still intent on war and death.

'Stop! Stop charging!' he roared.

Not a single soldier listened. The golem tried to grab at them, drag them back, but they scrabbled from his clutches.

He spied a shape moving sideways across the charging lines. Ellia, saving her traitorous skin. With a trembling, dirty hand, he pushed himself from the ground, but his fist crumbled beneath him. He held up his hand to find two fingers missing.

He pushed with his legs instead, and began to run. He reached out to the ground for his pieces, but found them faint and slippery. He couldn't move them.

A cold rush of fear passed through him, making his stones prickle. He tensed as he pushed himself through the ranks, bowing his head as the cannon and musketballs crashed around him. Blood spattered his stones. Blades glanced from his back. Shouts of hatred filled his ears.

Ellia was climbing now, scaling the mountain rock to get above the army. With a great leap, Task bounded free of the Truehards, sending soldiers flying. He almost grasped her ankle before his footing gave way, more literally than he would have liked. His left foot had disintegrated into pebbles.

Digging his stump and remaining fingers into the rockface, he climbed, reaching the ledge she was scurrying across, over the heads of the rushing spears. Task felt the dawn light bathe him, unnaturally warm. Or perhaps he was burning up as he fell apart. He could already feel the anger beginning to falter. A weakness grew from his stomach, sharp and ominous.

He left a trail of stones as he chased her. As she jumped a gap, he leapt early, grabbing her leg and bringing her crashing to the rock. But he had sacrificed himself to do so, and now he fought to stay on the ledge. His claws scored deep marks in the stone.

Ellia, now free and standing, smiled as she dusted off her hands.

'It's been a pleasure, toying with you. It really has. I must admit the highlight was seeing you finally break your chains. As soon as I read Ghoffi's letters, I knew you could do it. To think, all it took was kidnapping a girl. Not driving you against Huff, not showing you the Fading, not even a bone golem. Just a girl. Part of me had hoped to claim you for my own, but alas, you were a disappointment. Now, I would love to chat more but, sadly, I have other matters that need my attention. Bigger, more important matters than you and your...' She waved a hand in the fortress' direction. 'This pathetic excuse for a finale. What did you think would happen? That Huff would really come to his senses? Laughable. At least the girl will live, I suppose, so long as Lash can hold off the assault.'

'Why?' said Task.

'Why? What a boring question. Why not, Task? I saw an opportunity and I took it. What more to life is there than having more? Acquisition, my dear golem, is perfection. Not the Architect's Blessed Manual, not royalty, not even the Fading's capitalist ideals. Personal gain is my religion.'

Task slid back, holding on with his elbows. Ellia came forwards to push him with her foot. 'It looks like you needed that magic, Task. You're coming apart.'

Task snatched up as he fell, pinching at her ankle before sliding from the ledge. The crunch of bone was a small reward.

He hit the boulders, and felt his back break, splitting him almost in two. His arm fell apart, then a leg. He was more porcelain than stone.

Again and again, he tried to pull himself together, straining at the thin air for his scattered pieces. He managed to make a few rattle, but moving them was impossible. He thought of Lesky locked somewhere in that fortress, of the Dregs, and of all the other innocents hurling themselves onto spears or being pulverised by musketballs. But none of it could repair him. His rage had dissipated like the morning mist.

The golem sagged, and resigned himself to the sky and the clash of battle.

He let his eyes roll up, and was taken by a silent darkness.

28

'The enemy of my enemy is my friend, but the friend of my enemy is also my enemy.'

DESTRIX MAXIM

1st RISING, 3782 - SAFFERON FORTRESS

His dreams were nothing but water. No memories. Just the ceaseless and casual flow of dark waters: blue, green, grey. They roared somewhere in the distance, like a threatening storm. The wind buffeted him as if he were standing on the deck of a ship. It had no words for him. No insight. There was nothing but salt and spray.

And there was no fear now. No panic. No vengeance in this water. The flow barely touched him. He hovered above; only there to watch and witness. He felt nothing but awe for its power. It was not magic; not the power of men and arms. It was the inimitable and senseless force of a machine more complex than humans could imagine. The sheer will of the earth beneath him. Seasons. Winds. Tides. Even the Rent. Mankind was no more than a parasite on the back of a wark, prone to bucking; lucky to survive between the whims of nature. This was the true and everlasting god, if there was such a thing. Task worshipped it with his stare.

Blue, green, grey.

Piece by piece, he felt himself come together.

He heard the voices first, arguing over his shatter. This way and that, they refitted, until he had taken a rough shape. With each fragment in place, more of the world made sense.

And yet, he still didn't feel whole. Awake, yes, but missing something. It was as if a colour had been stolen from him, in his long sleep. Or a missing limb was itching somewhere distant.

343

Task tried his eyes, finding them frozen by the cold. Fingers pressed in to help, and soon enough he was staring at a puzzle-piece of sky, its notches formed by the handful of heads peering down at him.

It took some time to focus, and an age more for his tongue to remember words. Scraping it along his teeth brought sparks of life, but the effect was muted.

'Lesky.'

'You're deffin' right.'

'Language, child!' Another voice, gruff, somewhere nearby.

'Hmph.'

'Can you feel your limbs, Task?' Another voice.

He could, and wriggled each to test whether they were movable. It was difficult, but he was rewarded with a scraping of stone. He didn't know what remnant of magic was keeping him together, but he decided not to question it.

'Told you the tongue still had magic in it. You fit to sit up?'

Task didn't know about that. He didn't know about it for a good while. He occupied himself by shifting stones around in his back, untangling the mess caused by the fall and the improvised repair. Clammy hands pressed down on him, and Task relished the contact.

The world spun twice, then settled. Soldiers dotted the scene; some standing on top of boulders, others crouching in the stone dust. They all looked exhausted, and carried the stink of battle; that blend of sweat and old terror, of copper and steel.

'You won,' he whispered.

'We won,' said Alabast's voice. 'Though there isn't anything to show for it.'

Task jerked. Her name came crashing back to him. 'Ellia? I lamed her.'

'Gone.' The knight shook his head.

Lesky tapped him on the arm. She hovered by his side, looking weaker than ever. She was still wrapped in bandages.

'What's important is you. What in Rent's name did you do?'

Task rolled onto his knees, dreading their crumbling. 'I broke the magic. I broke Belerod's spell. I saw my choice, and I made it, just as you said.'

'How are you still alive if you broke it?'

'I have no idea.'

Alabast played at being helpful. 'Maybe the Architect took pity on you.'

'He took pity on all of us,' said Lash, beckoning them to follow. 'I don't care how you did it, Task, but you survived, and that gives me hope. A rare thing, after the last few hours.'

Task found his balance with difficulty, and for the first fifty foot-lengths he staggered like a newborn.

Lash briefed him on the battle as they walked. It had stretched for a day, far into the afternoon and long into the night. In the early hours, the Truehards' spirits had broken under incessant cannon-fire and the lack of command. Manx and Glum had been left where they had fallen, running for their lives, an arrow neatly buried in the back of each skull.

He had seen countless aftermaths of conflict, but this one felt different. Bodies stretched from mountain to mountain, like another ring for the fortress. Broken spears poked up like makeshift gravestones. Hardly a patch of earth had escaped the litter of war. Alongside the crooked corpses lay broken shields, cannonballs and random body parts. Not a patch was without a splash of blood or effluent. Fading soldiers, hooded and bowed, wandered through the dead, poking and pinching at bodies. Healers and priests, too, each offering their own brand of medicine.

The scene was grisly. It tugged at his insides. Now that Task had found his heart, he was realising how capable it was of pain.

Faces stared up at him as he picked his way through the corpses. Every one he vaguely recognised, whether Fading or Truehard. Even the ones who were missing vital portions of their features, he knew them.

It was easy to feel responsible for their dead stares. He was even starting to think it was a mistake to break his bonds.

Task's only solace was that these men and women had been driven to fight by lies and habit. There was no honour or duty here, just raw human downfall. It was easier to hate an enemy than to forgive or understand them.

Huff had known that. He had put these corpses here, not through his stubbornness the morning of battle, but through weeks and months and years of lies. He had sold them the king and Council's story; fantasies of a glorious victory against the capitalist traitors. And these soldiers had believed it so much that even after staring into the cannon-mouths, after watching their general die at the hands of his own golem, they still charged. The Fading had been left no choice. *Survive or die.*

And behind it all, driving them together, had been Ellia. She had taken their valour and twisted it into something that served her alone. She had made their hope a hollow thing, bloated and ugly, like a poisoned corpse.

The secret to power was the ability of humans to convince themselves, and eventually others, of their own lies. In that respect, Ellia was a powerful woman indeed; perhaps more powerful than Task.

Without leadership nor patience, the Truehards had thrown themselves against the walls in a mad dash. Task could see it in the way the corpse-piles accumulated around the gates. They had been foolish. Safferon would have taken more than a day to crack without siege-engines. Or a golem.

Task looked to the creature slumped against the stone. Great claw-marks scarred the walls, above stumps of bone. The cannons and grenades had forced it back into oblivion. There was no chance of reassembling it now, yet he could still feel the residual hum of magic in the earth, old and strong. No wonder Huff had been seduced by it.

Prisoners tackled the bodies at the gates, clearing up their comrades into neat, grotesque piles. He just about recognised Lancemaster Taspin, drenched in blood and shite, trembling as he handled the bodies. Only once did his eyes rise to the golem's. They quickly fell down again, back to the Truehard dead. Task took no pleasure in his suffering.

Further along, Task spied Nerenna, missing a hand, and Cater, looking cannon-shocked and vacant. He paused to kneel beside them, and promised to see what Lash would do about a healer. Nerenna glared at him, but nodded all the same.

Safferon was devastated by the damage. Half of the keep was aflame. Soot-faced workers scurried around its parapets with buckets of meltwater. Cannonballs perforated the wall-tops. Entire sections had been blown clear by the Truehard cannons. Rubble-dust hung like mist in the morning air. The gatehouse was a shell, with bodies draped over its broken edges.

When they had reached the inner courtyard, Lash spoke up.

'Seeing as there's nowhere else to hold court, we shall do it here.' It was no more pleasant inside the fortress than out.

Shambling, they fashioned boulders and stone blocks into seats.

A knight. A girl. A lord. A golem.

A strange council, indeed.

Task realised who was missing. 'Westin?'

Lash shook his head. 'Cannon took his head clean from his shoulders. He was standing right next to me.'

Task noted the blood flecks on the lord's cheek. He had assumed it was his own.

'What is there to discuss now?' he asked.

'The final battle was won,' said Lash. 'But the war won't be truly over until the king surrenders.'

Task shook his head. 'From what I can see, you have no army.'

Lash countered. '*We* don't need one! We have you now. Free and unchained.'

'And me,' said Alabast, puffing his chest. 'Don't be forgetting me.'

'Who could?' muttered Lesky.

'There is the matter of Ellia,' said the golem. 'She has unfinished business. Important business, she told me. I'm starting to understand the web she snared me in, from the moment I set foot on the black sand of those slanted cliffs. Something tells me this was only the start.'

Lesky snorted. 'You got no idea.'

Alabast wasn't convinced. 'You really think so? If I was her, I'd be halfway across the Yawn by now. She's burnt all her bridges.'

The lord held up his hands. 'We all have reasons to hate her, but Lady Auger, or Zealot Frayne, from what the young girl has told me, is not lost in the wind. I understand she is riding to Caverill. For the Mission, or for the Boy King, we don't know. Her deceptions are long and tangled. A web, as you say, golem.'

'Trust me, she ain't done yet,' said Lesky. 'I saw her thoughts about the ambassador. The Khandri one comin' to inspect us. I think she might want to kill her. And there's that king still to deal with. She hates 'im, too.'

'In any case, the game has not changed,' said Lash. 'We must still fight to claim Hartlund before the Khandri arrive. Ellia has simply changed the enemy. The Fading will march on Caverill.'

Task had to agree. Time was a precious thing to him now, rather than something to endure. Mortality had knocked, and for once, he did not welcome it. It felt as if his stones could give up at any moment, before his work was done.

'That's the other side of the country, Lash,' said Alabast.

The lord ignored the knight's whingeing. 'Though it pains me, I've already appointed a new executor and captains to gather up the remaining soldiers. They will be ready to set out in three days.'

'Three days?' said Task.

'Fear not. We are riding out ahead of them, to stake our claim. We will be a day behind Ellia. If we travel fast, we can make it in under a week, in time for the ambassador's arrival. I will not allow the Boy King, or Ellia, to represent my country without my consent. Another war is not an option.'

Alabast held up his hands for sense. 'Did you take a knock to the head during the battle?'

Lash's face was cold. 'You are not expected to join us, Alabast. Your employment with the Fading ended when the last musket fired. You are released, Knight of Dawn. Free to go!'

Alabast looked uncomfortable, half-turning away.

'And you, golem. I hold no claim over you. You killed your own master. I imagine that frees you.'

'I imagine you're right,' said Task, though somehow he felt shackled to the job at hand. 'When do we leave?'

The lord couldn't help but look a little relieved. 'Within the hour. The firns are already being saddled. I've sent a rider to the Last Table. *The Bastion* will meet us in Caverill. Until then.' Lash pushed himself away toward the second wall. A gaggle of soldiers walked with him.

Task stood, not knowing what to do with himself.

'You're eager,' said Alabast.

'Did Ellia not wrong you, too?'

'Yes, but—'

'You're worried that you care, Knight,' said Lesky, propping her chin on a fist.

'I told you not to do that! And it's not that I *care*. It's because I'm no longer getting food and board. What am I supposed to do now?'

'You'll figure it out,' said Task, 'Right, Lesky?' The girl just rolled her eyes.

Alabast hunkered down, resting on his knees.

'What did she do to you, anyway? Lash hasn't said a word,' he said to Lesky. The bags under her eyes were a dark grey. She looked as if she hadn't eaten in a week.

Lesky scratched at something in her mess of hair. 'Made me fight a Mission glimpse, is what she did. And I did it, and more.'

Task tensed, feeling that tug at his insides again. 'Why?'

'So she could bridge with the Mission, and take over one of their people. She gathered these old men up, lit a fuse, and watched the whole place blow up, without even leaving the fortress. I ain't told Lash that part yet. Jus' what he needed to know.' She spoke with wide and distant eyes, still processing the memories.

'I saw it all, Task. Her entire mind, all naked and raw. I felt her hatred, and how it gave her these ideas that we've been playin' out like puppets. She's got plans, Task, big plans. For Caverill, the Council, the Accord... They were fuzzy, not as solid as memory, but I know they ain't good. She's been plannin' this since my da died. This has all been for him. Vengeance. I heard that word in her head, over and over.'

Alabast looked confused. 'What's your da—'

'It doesn't matter now. What matters is she's never going to stop. She's got a thirst for this now. First, revenge, then murder, now mego...' She frowned. 'Malago...'

'Megalomania.'

'Lash taught me that.'

Task would have laughed had he not been so afraid of coming apart. 'Any other skinbag like you would be cowering in a corner, shaking, over what's happened to you in the last week.'

Lesky shrugged. 'Mam says that fighters fight and survivors survive, but cowards cower. "You got to do what you are to be what you are", and I ain't no coward.'

'I've always said she's a wise woman.'

'And like I said, she's more than wise. You'll get to meet her soon, now the war's over.'

The tramping of feet summoned their gaze. Lash had returned with a score of soldiers and a familiar character shuffling in chains. Even smeared with dirt and wearing tatters, that circle of glass still clung doggedly to his eye.

'Task, I believe you know Councillor Dast?'

The golem caught the whiff of spirits as Lash pushed Dast into their circle. 'I do.'

'He was the one who surrendered the army to us.'

The old man looked sullen. 'Finally came to my senses, I suppose.'

'Dast and I go way back, don't we, Councillor? We both served Raspier in the golden years, when men had morals and their word was the truth. Baragad got to him, though. Hooked him with the unfortunate vice for wine.'

The councillor grumbled to himself.

'He'll be accompanying us to Caverill. He's going to inform the Council of its defeat.'

Dast looked up at that. 'I won't go.'

Lash prodded him. 'You will. Somebody has to account for Huff's actions, and as his minder, a trusted servant of the king, who better than you?'

Task towered over Dast, testing Lesky's theories of cowards and cowering. She was right.

'He'll go,' said Task. 'If I have to carry him myself, he'll go.'

Alabast must have assumed they were speaking of him. He snapped from his daze and surged to his feet.

'Fine! I'll help. You'll need a swordsman of my calibre on the road, not to mention the capital. Who knows what the bitch has planned for us.'

Task sighed with the others.

'What?' Alabast shrugged. He held out a finger to jab the prisoner.

'Who's the wrinkle?'

♛

She coughed again, spitting ash. The trees still smouldered in places. Lazy flakes of grey filled the air, dusting her hands and shoulders, coating her mouth as she panted.

The pain overcame her exercises. Her ankle was not so much broken as pulverised. It throbbed in a way that made her want to vomit. She could do nothing but slump over in the saddle, and let the jolting strides of the firn keep her conscious.

The beast needed no encouragement to run. The thunder of battle had chased them for leagues. Now, as they reached the edge of the roamwillow plains, the sounds had finally died. Only the crackle of old fires kept them company.

Ellia retched over the firn's shoulder, spewing all that she'd crammed down in the night. Precious fare for a journey so long.

She lolled back in her saddle, head back to keep from retching. She watched the ash-flakes drift like lost snow.

When the sickness had passed, she rummaged in her pack for some more droprose seeds, stolen from the Truehard healer. She chewed their bitter husks. They would numb her for a time.

If only she hadn't lost the girl. Lesky could have taken the edge off the pain, made her forget for a while.

Caverill filled her mind. The city was like a glorious buffet going untended; wilting and souring in her absence. She wondered if Gorder was handling it adequately, fending off the hungry.

With a cry, she shook the reins, spurring the beast into a gallop. She could see the spires of Gillish ahead, still smoking.

Ellia entwined her wrists in the leather straps and fastened herself to the firn's back. She did the same with her unbroken leg, closed her eyes, and let the droprose seeds lull her into a daze.

29

'Hartlund grew from the humble rebellion of sea folk against Destrix coastal raids. Riches stolen in the Diamond Wars built it into a power to be reckoned with. Ineptitude of its rulers seem to be its weakness. They are a feral people, and prone to war.'

GRADEN WRITINGS ON THE REALM

3RD RISING, 3782 - THE NALDISH LUMPS

As they journeyed south, silence reigned. For leagues after the crackle of the dead roamwillows, not a creature rustled nor squawked. Not a single traveller plodded along the road. Not a rattle came from a cartwheel or farm contraption. To Task, the countryside seemed dead.

It stayed that way until they heard the echo of hammers within Gillish, but they didn't stop to check who was hammering or why. Rain was approaching from the south, almost like it knew the north needed cleaning. They hoisted their hoods and cloaks and forged onwards through the deluge.

The rain chased them to the fringes of the Naldish Lumps. There it became hail; one last rebellion before Fading gave in to its passing.

To Task, hail felt bitter and angry, compared to rain; like a child throwing its spit-covered toys from its cot. He hated the way it attacked his stones.

Another night of restless travel saw the Lumps halfway-conquered, and by midday, they stood overlooking the Greenhammer, looking more like a Greyhammer under the monochrome sky.

One of the soldiers spotted a scouting party at the water's edge. Four lean looking firns and riders in Truehard colours.

While they waited for them to move west, they broke their fast hiding on a rocky tor of pale granite. Sparing no time for flame and pans, they ate something resembling biscuits from their packs, and meltwater from the hail. Councillor Dast was allowed a drink but no food. He constantly sweated, the booze seeping out of him. It was only fair to keep him watered, else he might have shrivelled up even more.

The golem sat apart from the group, hunched over, just another part of the scenery. His hands grasped the lichen-dressed granite, but he felt nothing but its cold texture. It was wind-cut, like him, but it did not speak to him.

The sun began to sink as they broke down into the valley and along the shore of the lake. Lash called for a camp among some old trees, and for the first time in three days, they stopped.

It was a good decision. The mist fell with the sun. The Rent must have been blowing hard in the Blue Mountain Sea, or so the soldiers said.

A bank of moisture came rolling over the lake. Just as the final tent was being propped, it hit like a chill; a wall of cold wet air that was so thick it could be carved into swirls. The soldiers called out as they pawed for each other. Someone lit a lantern and gave them something to huddle around. They flinched as Task reared out of the haze to join them.

'The morgs,' said Lesky, looking ghostly in the faint sulphur light. 'Thick fogs that come through the Darens every year. They're early, though.'

'They're inconvenient,' said Lash. 'Secure the councillor before he sneaks off.'

Dast had been edging away, even though he was firn-less, tied by the wrists and gagged. Two soldiers seized him.

Lesky was tired and aching from the ride, but she didn't look worried. 'They come quickly and they leave quickly.'

Alabast snorted.

'Quiet, Alabast,' said Lash. 'Light your lanterns if you have to, but keep them covered. This morg will keep us hidden for tonight. Rest. Alabast, you have first watch.'

As the soldiers dispersed, the knight took the lantern, grumbled something obnoxious, and walked into the mist. The lantern bobbed up and down as the knight's form faded.

'I'll watch him,' said Task.

'At this point,' said Lash, 'he can run whenever and wherever he likes. I don't care.'

'He's stuck around for some reason.'

Lash scratched at his moustache. 'Maybe you should find out why. If it's for more coin, tell him he can go hang.'

Lesky hopped up with a smile. 'I'll pick his brains for you.'

'Take the girl, Task.'

The golem had no objections. He may not have shared Lash's suspicion, but he was curious. He and Alabast did have something in common. *Redemption*, Ellia had called it. If Alabast was hunting for that, Task wanted to know more. It felt better than the hunger for vengeance.

They found Alabast hunched over the lantern, picking at a pipe-bowl with his fingernail.

'Spit on it. Back to harass me some more?'

'Nope,' said Lesky, plonking herself down next to the knight. She tapped her head. 'Don't need to now.'

'No, no, no! I'll have no more of that!' Alabast made to get up, but the golem rested a finger on his shoulder.

'Relax, Knight. She won't. On one condition, that is.'

'I'm getting bored of conditions. What is it?'

'Don't give her a reason to. You know you can trust us, Alabast.'

'Besides, we already know how much of a shitebag you really are, so you don't need to pretend.'

Shitebag. Task wondered why he had never thought of that. He liked it better than skinbag.

'What a charming mouth your pet has, golem.'

Task settled down at Alabast's side, poking the lantern shutters a little wider. 'Why are you still riding with us? You could have run at any time.'

Alabast nudged him with his elbow. 'I told you. You need me.'

Task sighed. 'Lesky?'

'Fine! If it'll help you sleep better,' cried Alabast, as he held up his hands. 'This mind is for adults only, not grubby, thinkpicking girls. You want to know, I'll tell you.'

'Well, you clearly know the gist of it already. I first want to say that it was not my fault the old beast was dying. If I'm to be honest, it was the kind thing to do.' He winced, remembering the amount of hacking it had taken. 'He even told me to take it, to make a name from his death. It was fate, and who am I to deny fate?'

Alabast looked at their blank expressions. 'You have no idea what I'm talking about, do you?'

Lesky stuck out a tongue. 'I only knew you were lyin' about somethin' dragon-shaped. I didn't know what. It was buried too deep. I was just windin' you up, Alabast.'

'You, Task?'

'I thought you were just exaggerating your feat. I thought maybe you'd poisoned the creature, or set up a cowardly trap.'

'How nice of you. Thank you.' Alabast sighed. 'And I thought I would be welcomed along on this journey, not pestered at every stop.'

'We're worried.'

'Lash is worried. Thinks I'm in league with Ellia. You two are just nosy.'

'We won't tell a soul,' said Lesky.

Alabast eyed the girl, and her look of practised integrity. The golem just waited patiently, like the lump he was. He seemed stiller, more ponderous than before the battle. Quieter, if that were possible.

The knight sighed. He had only told this story to one other; and the man had not lived long enough to pass it on. That in itself was a long story, but this was his deepest and darkest, and he hadn't had much practice at telling it. He'd buried it, piling on lie after lie until it was more of a dream than a memory. The details had changed over time, but sadly, the truth of the matter remained the same.

'A hunting party came back in one day. They said they'd seen a dragon in the forest, and that it had eaten half of their men. They were laughed straight into the Kopen madhouses. Nobody had seen a dragon in sixty years. A week later, the same thing happened, and again, until the city realised there was *something* in the woods. Soldiers were sent out to see, but two days later they came back running and bleeding. The challenge was sent out around the province. Slayers came from far and wide to test the dragon, but in a year nobody managed it. It couldn't be bested, they said. This old, angry drake. This Destrix Sheen. The last one of its kind.

'At the Bladehall, they teach you beast-fighting, and that's when the idea came to me. I could take the dragon! This was two years later, a day after a Khandri hunting band had come to try their luck, and brought the dragon out of hiding. It turned a village to splinters after it had dealt with the hunters. I decided it was my turn.

'The masters made a big noise when I marched out to fight it. Two days it took to reach the forest. All I had was this sword and a borrowed armour that chafed in places you wouldn't believe. I was exhausted by the time I reached its mountain. I set a fire in front of its cave and waited. I fell asleep, and when I awoke the fire was dying, and the dragon had not come.

'Took me about an hour to get in there, and when I did, he was all stretched out and limp, lying along the dirt and rocks. He had his eyes shut, and he stank. A mouldy smell. Old blood was on the stones here and there. I was looking around when he spoke.

'Now I never knew dragons could speak, so it came as a bit of a surprise. Even more surprising, he asked me to kill him. Right there and then, like a gift on a platter. He said he was dying, and tired of fighting off the hunters and heroes. He claimed he had never attacked without provocation. The hunters had unearthed him from hibernation, and when they couldn't kill or trap him the first time, they kept coming back, again and again. They made it look like the dragon was wild and hungry, when all he wanted was to sleep.'

The golem shuffled around, looking uncomfortable. Alabast imagined something was familiar about the story.

'We talked for about an hour about his life, how humans had once worshipped the dragons, then hunted them through centuries. He was older than you, Task, by about five hundred years. He had slept, cocooned, since before Kopen was a hovel on the riverbank. He told me the reason we humans struggle and fight is because we know the only immortal part of our mortal selves is our names. When it came to it…' Alabast paused, throat tightening as he remembered those silver eyes closing. 'He wished me well, and bade me to do something important. He was silent through the whole thing. Every strike.

'So, I'm a fake, but that doesn't mean I can't have another shot at honouring that old bastard's request. And I can do myself a favour too. Ellia said that it was time to add some "substance" to my life. I guess the best way to do that would be to follow you around, golem. Who knows, maybe Ellia's the monster who needs slaying now.'

His tone was lightening now; he had grown tired of storytelling, of being open. He clapped his hands and looked around at the mist. 'There you have it! The truth. And if you tell anyone, I'll—'

'Not looking for substance,' said Task. 'You're saving your backside again.'

'That's not true!' he snapped, locking eyes with the golem. Something in those glowing orbs seemed to understand how earnest the knight was. 'I know, I'm as surprised as you, golem. And as confused. Like you, I appear to care what happens next to this bastard island, and I'm buggered if I know why. I could have easily run for a ship, but somehow I didn't.'

The seriousness evaporated all too suddenly. 'And like I said, you need me. What if it turns out I'm the only who can save the day?'

The golem shook his head, but still the smile came. 'I'd be shocked, first of all.'

'Besides, if there's another war coming, I'd rather be rich enough to barter my way out of it. I think I've had enough of fighting.'

'I agree.'

The girl had been quiet, but now she got to her feet. 'Task, come with me.'

'Come with you where?' he asked. Alabast was clueless.

'I'll explain on the way. I just remembered somethin'. Thank you for tellin' the story, Alabast. You make a lot more sense now.'

The girl poked the golem into action, forcing him up and leading him into the fog. They vanished in three paces.

'Bye,' said Alabast with a wave.

He had poured his truth out, and they had fled. That's what he got for confiding in people.

'Where are we going?'

She guided him in the opposite direction of the lake. 'To meet my mam, like I said.'

The golem looked around as if she were hiding in the mist. 'Now? What about—'

'Lash won't know. We're just an hour's walk away. Maybe two. She'll really want to meet you.'

Task stopped, standing like a monolith in the darkness. 'No. We'll get lost. And there may be other Truehard scouting parties out there.'

Lesky gave him a tight smile. 'Don't ever doubt a Daren's girl on her own soil. Besides, you're a bloody golem and I'm a glimpse. Come on! For me.'

Task grumbled, but let himself be led.

The girl got a hundred foot-lengths before she started panting. Her injuries were persistent, stealing her breath. She took a moment by a boulder, shaking her head. 'I'll be fine. Just hang on.'

It was then that Task did something unexpected.

'Climb,' he said, sinking to a knee and stretching his arm out. Without pause, Lesky clambered onto his wide neck and sat with her legs either side of his head. He rose without effort, but as he did so, a few stones tumbled from his shoulders, thumping into the wet grass.

Lesky kept her mouth shut, hoping he had not noticed. She imagined he was too preoccupied with a girl on his back. She wondered whether she was the first girl to ride a golem.

They walked in silence for the most part, with Lesky giving him a few nudges left or right when he wandered off course. Even in the thick morg, she recognised the country. She had spent long days chasing snike through the shallows, making them jump onto the grass in fear and then gasp for air. She had always put them back.

She saw the crooked angles of Joker Oak, the enormous tree carved by lightning, broken in two halves like the cheeks and teeth of a crooked grin. It still sat proudly on a hillock, overseeing a realm of fields.

In less than an hour, thanks to Task's long strides, they came to the edge of Wittshire, where the flat earth turned hilly again, forming the northern border of the Darens. It was one of the smallest shires, but it was hers, and that's what mattered. The morg was weaker here, and the night revealed more of its secrets. She knew them all.

Nothing had changed since she had seen it last. Almost three years had passed and still the wagons lay upturned in the fields. Bunting still rotted on old pathways. Collapsed walls and burnt farmhouses lay scattered around the fields.

'What happened here?' said Task, booming through the night's silence and making her flinch. She shushed him.

'Same thing that happened to the rest of the country. A war broke out.' She eyed a rusted gibbet by the roadside; a skeleton still clinging to its bars even in death. That, she did not remember.

Sandwiched between the Six Sisters and the road to Safferon, the Darens had been hit hard by the first strikes of war. Since then, it had lain empty; a forgotten wasteland of unplowed fields and abandoned cottages, poking out of hills.

'When was the last time you were here?'

'I snuck back here three years ago, when the army pushed north again. Before that? The night I left it, two weeks after the Fading, or who we thought were the Fading, started burnin' towns n'such.'

'And your mam stayed?'

'Course she did. Her knees were all sore, and she didn't do much walkin',' Lesky felt a knot grow in her throat. 'Didn't like to travel.'

'But you went south?'

'Got on a wagon and went to see my cousin. Ganner's his friend, you see, that's how I fell in with the Truehards. Got stuck with that horrible slaver, when my cousin coughed 'is last with plague a few months later.'

Once again they fell into the rhythm of his monotonous steps, pounding on the cold earth. As they rounded a hill, they reached Witt. Even with the mist, Lesky could see her old village around her, plain as day. Her imagination filled the gaps.

Ole Coggins' house, with its thatch. The Reaping Pool, where she used to steal pinkies on Sunsoar's Eve. And *The King and Country*, the lean-to tavern that was never supposed to be permanent but had stayed that way anyhow.

'Where are we going?' said Task, as they came to a small sapling, broken halfway up its trunk. The rest of it lay on the ground, long-dead. 'I don't see any lights.'

'Just over there, forwards'n to the left. Just a little.'

Lesky guided the great golem to a tumbledown cottage, set back from the circle of the others. As it loomed, she saw its board roof had fallen in. The windows had been smashed so long ago their shards had gathered a film of dirt and mould. They looked like broken eyes, staring blindly into the night. The mist curled around its old stones.

'Lesky?'

'Keep goin'. Behind the cottage.'

Task plodded forwards, past the splintered fence and around to a tiny garden where the weeds had claimed the earth. He waded through them, snapping their stubborn stalks. Lesky found herself enjoying the noise.

'Just a little further.'

If Task had realised, he said nothing. He followed her instructions, slowing to a shuffle as he reached the centre of the garden. He looked around at the darkness, and for a moment, they both listened to the buzzing and slithering of the night creatures.

He knelt, holding out a hand to help her down. She stood in front of him, feeling the air move across her skin as he stood tall again. She took a few careful steps across the hallowed ground, and found the lump where weeds had strangled something small and solid. Lesky bent to it, tearing away the stems until she could spread her hands across the chiselled stone, fingers following the letters. She spoke in a half-whisper.

'I've brought you somebody to meet, Mam.' She turned to Task, finding his glinting eyes weaker than usual. His face had fallen. 'Task, meet my mother, Milla. Mam, this is Task.'

Lesky stepped away to let the golem shuffle forward. He was awkward, she could feel it, but he nodded to the gravestone all the same.

'A pleasure.'

'She died of a cancer in her lungs a week after the war started. Left me in the cottage on my own. But she had set me right, made sure I could look after myself. She was always teachin' me things. How to make a fire, or how to ride a firn. I can even skin a wark. But don't tell Shiver, wherever that little hound is. She always said I'd need those things one day, and she's been right so far.' Lesky smiled. 'She didn't suffer, and for that I'm glad. One day she was telling me about my da, and then...' Lesky snapped her fingers. 'Destroyer took her away.'

The golem nodded, and stretched out a hand to touch the gravestone. He twisted his head, eyes closed, as if he were listening to some distant song that was beyond her ears. He scrunched up his face, straining hard. He said nothing, and withdrew his hand.

'We buried her in the rain. No place wetter than the Darens. Figured she would like it. She always sang when it rained, so I sang instead. Yarger said a few words before we placed the dirt.'

Task turned to her. 'Why didn't you tell me?'

'Because I wanted you to meet her.'

The golem seemed to understand that. 'I imagine she would be proud of you.'

Lesky smirked. 'She'd tell me to comb my hair and wash the dirt out o' my ears.'

'And your father?'

Lesky bowed her head. 'Also dead, thanks to Ellia.'

'You're a brave girl, Lesky. Braver than most soldiers I've ever met. And that's a fair few.'

Lesky didn't feel brave. She just felt like Lesky, the same girl with the same mind she had always had. If bravery was what it was, then that was fine. She was just the product of her mother's words, and that was a better reason to be proud.

'She told me once I could change the world. I had no idea she meant with magic. She was magic, too. I realise that now. Not just in the way all mams are, but she 'ad something old in her blood. Maybe she was a gazer. She'd always guess things or see them comin' a league away. Her power was always bein' right. Da blamed it for all kinds of trouble. Made me think maybe she was right about changin' the world too. Made me think I might be different enough to do it myself. From what Ellia said, I might be a grim, so maybe I'm strong enough too.'

'The world doesn't want to change.'

'Don't you believe in people any more?'

'Look at Huff, and the Truehards. Charging when there was nothing to gain.'

'And look at Lash. Me. Even Alabast. The world will change if it has a choice. Right now it don't have one. It hasn't for the last nine years. Find it one, and we can stop the war.'

She bent down once more time to let her fingers linger on the grave, and then pointed herself back to the village. 'We should leave. Get back before they start to wonder.'

Task was silent and still for quite some time. His whisper, when it came, was barely more than the grinding of stone, but she heard it all the same.

'What kind of choice?'

'Guess we got until Caverill to figure that out.'

30

'Until now, Zealot Frayne has been an example of dedication.
Efficient in her guise as the baroness. Ruthless in executing her
orders. Eleven years, she has been with us now. She would have
topped Cane had she not fallen in with the likes of Techan of Witt.
The man is a rogue on more than one account, and prone to
disobedience. Make an example of him. It may teach our brightest
zealot the lesson she so desperately needs.'

A LETTER FROM CONSECRATOR LOCKYEN TO TREYARCH DASPAR

6TH RISING, 3782 - CAVERILL

Gorder winced as he stepped from his carriage. His gout was playing up in his knee, and he paused to massage it, wrinkling his lip at the way the half-road had already soiled his black shoes.

For the third time that morning, he wondered at Ellia's choice of rendezvous.

'That's it, Cap,' said Flummish, his driver, an old soldier he had once fought alongside. *'The Fat Fawl.* Just as you asked. Not a fancy establishment, is it?'

Gorder followed the man's gaze to the higgledy building wedged between two warehouses. It had thatch on its roof and soot on its windows. Black beams of wood poked from cracked grey plaster, and the ironwork had been eaten orange by the salt spray from the nearby cliffs. Though the paint on its sign had flaked away, Gorder recognised the arse-cheeks of a fawl when he saw them.

'Delightful, Ellia,' he said to himself. 'Door, Flummish!'

'Aye, Cap.' He pushed his way in with gloved hands, letting some of the stink out; mostly ash and old glugg. Gorder recalled his days in officers' messes, and breathed through his mouth.

He stepped under the low lintel and wound his way through the tables to the bar. Two bored-looking young gentlemen stood behind it. One picked bits from his teeth. The other was admiring some stick-legged thing he'd caught under a glass.

'I'm here for a Miss Frayne.'

'Room nine. Top of the stairs.'

'Wonderful,' said the Grand-Captain, heading for the worn steps that coiled into the ceiling.

'Shall I accompany you, Cap?'

One stair told him all he needed to know. 'Until the top, I think. The knee.'

Flummish obliged. With a good manner of grunting and puffing, they made it to the third floor, where the numbers reached ten.

Gorder patted Flummish on the shoulder and rapped on the door. His gout flared. *Architect, was he getting old.* He had heard old age referred to as graceful and dignified. He felt about as graceful and dignified as a soldier losing his bowels on parade.

'Enter!' She sounded tired.

Gorder ducked into the room. It was a modest affair with a sloping thatched roof kept at bay by a trellis of beams. In the corner, a fire smoked beneath a blocked chimney. Two chairs faced each other in its light. Ellia sat in one; her bandaged, splinted foot rested on the other. Her hair lay tangled about her forehead and neck. She wore a long robe, but he could still smell the road-stink on her. Her eyes looked smeared with boot-black.

'By the Rent, what happened to you?'

Ellia motioned with her pewter cup. 'A parting gift from our friend.'

'Which one?'

She slurped. 'Lash. A deffing cannonball. Surgeons say most of the bones are hopeless, but the meat can be saved. If I keep it still, it won't turn to rot, and I'll be able to walk by Sowing.'

'So it is done, then? We have managed it?'

Ellia nodded slowly. 'It is. Our new Hartlund will be born on the morrow, with us as its rulers. No Mission. No Boy King. No Baragad.'

'So my son was victorious?'

'Sit, Gorder, my friend.' She pointed to another chair and he claimed it.

'I'm afraid... that Huff could not be saved. Lash had him shot during the parley.'

He felt a musketball meet his stomach, stealing his breath. He could only summon one word.

'Parley?'

'The Fading's idea. They said they wanted to talk. It turned out to be a filthy ruse.'

'Filthy ruse,' Gorder echoed. It was as though the world had been turned around, made a little uglier. All the jokes and jibes at his foolish son turned bitter in his memory. All the missing mentions of "Father" in his letters. A helplessness set in.

'But he... we won the battle, at least?' It was a grasp for compensation.

'I could not stay to watch. Things turned quickly. All that planning was dashed in the mud. The golem cracked alright, as I'd hoped. But in doing so he went wild, refusing to crush Lash or his men. He crumbled instead. It was down to the army to finish the job. I am sure they prevailed over the capitalists.'

'Good news,' said Gorder, through a tight throat.

Ellia changed the subject. 'Can the same be said here?'

'Since you leapt ahead of schedule with the Blade, I had to improvise. It's fortunate I know the man in charge of the Council guard. Me.'

'Fortunate, indeed.'

'The powder is in place.'

'And the ambassador?'

'Due to arrive this evening. My personal guard will be at the docks, waiting to divert her to the west of the city. I have convinced our good Baragad to let me have that honour, what with the attack. The Council has no clue. They will be gathered and patiently waiting. It took some conniving.'

'I'm sure you were up to the task.'

Gorder nodded, his thoughts straying back to his son. 'He sent me a letter not too long ago. Full of defiance. Did he die quickly? Proudly?'

'The new meeting place? Where have you chosen?'

'A Mission church would have offended, so I organised the Museum of Antiquity, to let her see our pride in our Lundish culture.'

'A fine idea. Empty?'

'As a beggar's pockets.' This felt more like a report than a conversation. He reported to nobody. 'You evade my question, Ellia.'

She sighed into her cup, then tipped it out to let a single drip fall. 'Let us toast to your son's passing, and I will tell you. Would you be a kind soul?' She pointed to a pewter decanter on a stand near the fire.

'It's barely eleven in the morning, Ellia.'

'Then let's toast the day of our success, if that's more meaningful to you, Grand-Captain.' There was a sour edge on her voice.

Gorder rose with a harrumph and limped to fetch it. He found himself another cup, and rejoined her, pouring himself a liberal slog, and the same for her. It smelled like torig, and a cheap brew at that.

'That's more like it,' she said, sitting tall. 'To a day of changes, and to a future of our own design.'

She raised her cup, but Gorder stayed still. 'We'll hold a ceremony.'

Ellia coughed. 'And to General Huff Dartridge the Third! The man who won the war for crown and country.'

Gorder drank to that. He drank it all, swigging the fire down into his belly, eyes clamped shut. The gout would make him pay for that later, but it was for his son. *Huff.*

'Tell me. Did he die peacefully?'

Ellia thought about this, in a staring match with the fire. Perhaps she struggled to find the words. Her cup still lingered in her hand.

'No, actually.'

There came another musketball, this time lower down. 'Ellia?'

She shrugged. 'I lied. Lash didn't shoot him. In fact, the golem turned against him, battering him to death with his fists, right in front of his soldiers. Task turned his face and skull into a bloody paste, and they just kept charging. Not for Huff, but for their own reasons. They trampled his body into the dirt.'

Gorder felt a sickness. The kind that makes the hand shake, the vision swim. 'Why would you—'

'Because you should know the truth. How proud and spiteful you raised that little man to be. So cruel was he, that he broke a heart of stone. The golem hated him so much, he snapped free of his magic. Saved me a job really.'

'I did no so such thing…' Her words made no sense.

Ellia put down her pewter mug. It was still full. She reached for another one beneath her chair. She took a slurp. 'It doesn't matter, Gorder. You'll soon be too dead to worry about it.'

Now, he realised. It was not emotion that strangled and sickened him, but poison. *The torig.* Gorder began to spit and retch, trying to force himself to vomit.

'It's a shame it came to this. I'd hoped that we could go on, and share the new Hartlund as we'd always planned. But I'm afraid that after dealing with your son, well… The Dartridge name has taken on a sour taste. At least your garden will die with you, and won't go untended.'

He threw himself repeatedly against the arm of the chair, but to no avail. His stomach was a burning knot, his head fit to burst. With a gurgle, he sank to the floorboards. Spots of blood fell from his nose, crawling a path to Ellia. The Grand-Captain had never felt less grand in all his life.

He reached for Ellia with crooked hands, his joints frozen. She looked down and waited for him to die.

'I curse...' said Gorder, before his mouth closed up for good. The pain escorted him to a dark silence.

♛

In the sunset, Caverill looked like a living creature; something that had crawled to the edge of the cliffs but had lacked the guts to dip into the great crater of water that formed the harbour. The soldiers called it The Grave.

The city centre bore two tall horns. One was grey and proud, already sparkling with a hundred lanterns. The other was half-built, or broken in half, Task could not tell.

At their bases, the buildings spread out like three limbs studded with glowing eyes: two reaching arms and a fat tail, wrapped in a thick wall. The body of the city spread to the cliff's edge, where the ground rose upwards before dropping away.

In the light of the sun, the chalk of the cliffs glowed, making the city seem even darker against the landscape. Beyond them, the south coast of Hartlund peeled away, standing guard against the Blue Mountain Sea.

Once again, Task had to disagree; he would have called them the Grey Mountains. These Lundish seemed to have a poor understanding of colour.

The world was water from then on, and Task found himself peering to its very edge, where the ocean sloped away. All he could see of the God's Rent were the usual dark clouds gathering like worshippers.

'In another place, golem?' said Alabast. Task shook himself back to life.

'No. Just thinking.'

'I find that's a dangerous pastime. You always come back to the bad stuff.'

There was a time when Task would have agreed. But since being pieced back together, he didn't linger in the past. Even his dreams had turned calm and singular. He nodded all the same, and turned to see how Lash was getting on.

They had procured a wagon from a farm in the last league. It had been rickety, but with a clever bit of ropework, they had made it sturdy.

Lesky patted the wagon's side. 'That's what you get with island people. Good knots.'

The golem wasn't so sure, but the thing was holding firm for now.

The tarpaulin was made of soldiers' cloaks sewn together. It did a fine job of covering him. The firns, bar five, were released. They knew what was good for them, and galloped north.

The front soldiers had covered their armour with dirt or charcoal, swapping certain pieces to disguise them as mercenaries or soldiers of the shield line. The rest were covered with Truehard cloaks taken from the battlefield. A bit of mud and blood always helped. Pity would be their proof. As Alabast had pointed out several times already, it was a poor plan. But it was their only option.

'The gates will be shutting at sunset,' said Lash. 'We should get moving!'

So they did, setting out with four firns in the wagon's traces, and Lash leading them on a separate beast, looking like the sergeant of this motley crew. Beside him rode the councillor, now free of gag and rope. A soldier had a pistol primed and ready at his back. He knew the risks of spilling the ruse.

They walked quickly, eager to catch the light. The hill was tough for both firns and human legs. Task could hear their grunting and snorting under his tarpaulin. He tried to relax his stones, but stayed ready. He didn't like the prospect of having to use them, but then he never had. Death was still ugly, as it always would be.

They came to the gates just as the sun had dimmed to a sliver over the western land.

'You're cuttin' it close, squire!' came a shout. Task heard the chinking thump of boots and heavy mail. The wagon shuddered to a halt.

'You look rough, old fighter. What regiment?'

'The Iron Eyes, on dispatch to accompany Councillor Dast here,' said Lash, dropping his lord's accent for something grittier.

'No royal guards for the councillor?'

'All dead, sir,' said Lash. 'It's shaken the good man up.'

'Damn shame. How goes the war?'

'Tough. But we're winning. Thanks to the golem.'

'We 'eard about him!' came a yell further on. ''Eard 'e can kill a man with one look.'

If only.

'Pipe down, Babbit. That's rubbish.'

'He's mighty strong, that's for sure.'

The footsteps came closer, walking along the wagon's length. 'What you haulin', old fighter?'

'Bodies for burying. Truehard heroes fallen in battle. Noble-born fathers and mothers want them buried.'

'How nice for them,' said the guard.

'I wouldn't touch them,' said Lash. 'Not that the nobles would care. Begging your pardon, Councillor, but they rot just the same as us common folk. It's taken an age to tuck that cloth around it so it won't stink. They've been on that cart a long time.'

The guard resorted to patting the load instead, laying a hand on Task's knee.

The hand lingered, knocking twice.

'Still in their armour.'

'Feels more like stone t' me.'

Lash sucked his lip. 'Well, you know the sorts of suits noble-born coin can buy, That's why they want 'em back. And to tell the truth, a few are missing some skin around their faces. Could be bone you're feeling.'

The hand flew away.

'Well, don't let them stink up the city, mind. That Khandri Ambassador's ship was sighted in the harbour less than an hour ago. I'm sure you'll be needed, Councillor. Talk of Fading ships sniffing around, too. All the best, now!'

With a click of the guard's teeth, the firns were moving again. Task pressed himself to the wood as he felt the darkness of the gatehouse pass overhead. The firns' feet began to pad on something like stone or stamped dust.

'That was easy,' said Alabast.

'Never underestimate the effect of a uniform and a dignitary, Knight.'

'Why didn't you ever try this before? Sneak in, I mean. Do the dirty and end the war.'

'We did, against my judgement. Our mistake was that we never had a golem. Come on. It's this way. We don't have the time to waste.'

Task poked a hole in part of the stitching and watched the houses pass by. They grew taller the closer they came to the centre. Everything looked squashed, as if space was in short supply. One roof barely finished before meeting its neighbour. There seemed to be no symmetry or forethought. Lanterns hung from every available hook and pole, as if the dark was feared here.

The deeper they travelled, the more they had to meander into the knotted side-streets. Some sort of accident had happened recently, and Task glimpsed blocks of broken stone gathered in piles. Crushed glass sparkled in the gutters. There were suspicious gaps in the architecture where buildings had been flattened.

The tower. *Broken in half, then*, Task surmised. He heard the soldiers whispering its name. The Blade of something or other.

'What happened here?' asked Alabast of somebody passing by.

A woman's voice, squawking more than speaking. 'Blew up, it did! Barely a week ago. One night, we was all sleeping peacefully, then, *choooom!* There was an enormous blast and it all came fallin' down.'

'Thank you for your colourful description, madam.'

Lesky walked close to the tarpaulin. In the lengthening dark, he could see the concern on her little face.

'Ellia?' asked the golem.

The girl nodded, looking around as if she had lit the fuse.

The King's Council was at the top of a hill, overlooking the bay. It was a thick block of a building, hexagonal and plain but for the pennants and flags that streamed from its roof. It looked more like a keep than a council. Sometimes, there was little difference. Task eyed it from the gap.

Lash led them past it, not wishing to alert the soldiers that swarmed its steps. He guided the men around the side to a quieter spot. They let the golem loose, dragging away the tarpaulin and pointing him back down the street.

'Four years of complaining, and still they have these damn steps,' said Lash, as he was helped from the firn to his chair, which had been dismantled for the journey.

Task saw a nervousness in him. With no army at his back—no pounding of war-drums nor stink of firepowder—he felt the same. This was not like any battle he had ever fought before. The way Alabast and Lesky looked at him, they were feeling it, too. There was more at stake than personal survival, or the claim of a country. This was for everything.

'After you, Task, sir,' said Lash. 'As we discussed.'

Task nodded and spared a moment to flex his arms and roll his neck. He bit his tongue and felt the dance of magic. His stones drew in, tightening where they were loose, moving where they had wandered. For the first time since the battle, he felt whole. *Almost whole.* There were still gaps he could not point to.

Task strode down the street, feet crunching on the cobblestones. The soldiers filed in a single rank behind him. He could feel their heartbeats.

Without a word or wave, he emerged into the yellow lanternlight that bathed the steps. For a moment the guards just blinked at him, more confused than fearful. His approach galvanised them. Some began to back away, shaking their heads in disbelief as if the Destroyer himself had just ambled out of the shadows. Others lifted their halberds with as much relish as a condemned man inspects his noose. A few began to shout at the sight of the soldiers slipping out from behind.

Task charged.

With the steps cracking underfoot, his fists collided with the first two soldiers. One had his breastplate inverted. The other somersaulted over the heads of his friends with a wail.

That put the fight in them. Not for crown or country, but for their own skin; a pure cause to fight if there ever was one. But Task was inclined to let them live. He hadn't come here for carnage.

A halberd dug into his shoulder, dislodging a cluster of stones. He snarled, breaking it in half and pushing its owner to the ground. He turned to the next, and a flash of smoke and powder enveloped him as an iron musketball bounced off his forehead. The golem shook off the impact, and as the guard tried to reload, he dealt him a backhand that bent him at an awkward angle. He screeched, clutching his spine.

Bells were beginning to ring across the city. At the top of the steps, Task was about to lay hands on the wrought-iron doors when they swung inwards for him. Light spilled out like a wave, cutting silhouettes of the soldiers and short-cannons that lay in wait.

'Down!' said Lash, seeing all from the bottom of the steps. A Fading soldier beside Task heard the order too late. One of the cannons thundered, and the iron shrapnel reduced the woman to bloody ribbons.

'Grapeshot!'

The other cannon spoke, directing all its anger at Task. The golem slammed his forearms together to form a shield. Although the grapeshot was made for flesh, it still carved chunks out of him, adding his rock to the blast as it continued past him, to the sound of clangs and wet thuds.

He threw himself into the doorway before the muskets could fire again. He flew spreadeagled, crashing into the ranks of Truehards as they pulled their triggers. The hallway was swallowed by smoke. One of the cannons split under the golem's weight, igniting its powder, and half the doorway was blown apart in a burst of orange flame. Bricks flew into the night.

Task pushed himself from the marble floor, half-concussed by the explosion.

'Golem!'

Lash was yelling from outside. Task could hardly hear him over the ringing in his ears. He staggered through the haze, unsteady. The explosion had ripped away half of his thigh.

Lash was waving both arms, gesturing at the shapes massing in the street behind. Dast lay sprawled beside him, grapeshot embedded in his cheek. *That was the end of that.* Lesky looked unharmed, half-hidden behind a soldier.

Without a word or grunt, Task ran down the steps, lifted the chair and the girl and ran them both into the building. Only a dozen or so of Lash's soldiers remained, and they all sprinted into the smoke with them.

Coughing and spluttering, they rushed headlong down the marble corridor. With a spare hand, Task swatted at every figure who dared to step in their way. Every musket was snapped, every halberd splintered. Broken and gasping bodies writhed in a trail behind. Task left the killing to the Fading, and they took to the task with gusto, as if every guard was the Boy King himself. Alabast ran beside him, putting his starsteel to work with vicious efficiency. Battle-rage had gripped him tight; cold where Task's was hot, but brutal all the same.

'Forwards! Left! Down there!' Lash yelled in the golem's ear.

The lord brought them to another grand door, where ten guards had lined up against the wood, halberds propped against the marble, blades straight and confident.

Task had to admire their bravery. He turned his back on them, mid-stride, and used his weight to crush them against the door. The wood split under the force of the blow, and as the golem stumbled on something slippery, he brought Lash and the girl down onto the marble, safe and sound. His soldiers swarmed around him while Task saw to getting upright. A halberd blade had been driven deep into his shoulder. He snapped it free with a crunch as he looked around .

They were in a voluminous hall. Above, dark wood climbed the walls to form a vaulted dome. Gargoyles stared back at Task like distant cousins. At its far end, a balcony with mahogany seats had been built high above the marble below. At least thirty men and women sat on the balcony, all wearing looks of confusion.

Above them, bronze curtains fell around a tall-backed throne, also carved from dark wood, with silfrin patterns.

On the throne sat a chubby boy, no older than fifteen, toying with an ornate dagger. His crown was tilted to one side, too big for his head. He was practically draped in silk, staring wide-eyed at the golem and knight.

So this was Barrein.

A pole-like man stood near the boy, several steps below. He spoke to the Boy King behind a manicured hand.

Task looked around the Council, searching for Khandri cloths and colours. There was no sign of either. Lash had already realised this.

'Where is the ambassador?'

'Guards!' cried the skinny man. 'Seize the traitors.'

This was Task's cue. He strode forward, feet like cannon-shot on the marble. The guards who had been edging forwards soon changed direction.

'There'll be no throwing me out of the Council today, Baragad,' said Lash.

Baragad held his hands wide. 'Lord Lash. It has been many years. And is this the golem? How fascinating. You have turned traitor also, golem?'

Task didn't answer.

'Ten years, in fact. Where is the ambassador, Boy King?'

Barrein spoke up for the first time. His voice had yet to crack. 'You do not make demands of me!'

Baragad quietly congratulated him.

Lash turned to the golem. Task strolled forwards, making the councillors peer over the edge of their balcony. He crushed one of the supports with his fingers. The noise was loud enough for them all to understand.

'Delayed!' said a councillor.

'Delayed by whom?'

'You! We had assumed.' A shrill voice from the end of the balcony.

'Silence!' said Baragad.

'He's telling the truth, Lord,' said Lesky, sounding tiny in the hall.

Lash spoke to the Boy King. 'Your armies have failed. Your General Huff lies dead. Your golem has come to his senses. Even Councillor Dast lies dead on the steps outside. You have lost, Barrein. There is no hope in silence, as Lord Baragad would have you believe.'

Barrein was too busy pouting to answer. Task considered snapping all the supports and bringing the whole pompous lot down on their backsides.

Baragad was chuckling. 'You lie. Baroness Frayne mentioned no such defeat.'

'She's been lying to you!' said Alabast. 'Where is she?'

The councillor looked down his nose at the knight. 'And you are?'

'The man who will murder you if you don't start talking!'

Task broke another support for good measure. A worrying creak came from the construction.

'Tell us where she is,' said the golem, shocking them with the depth of his voice.

'She left not long since, looking into delays on the docks.'

'In which direction.'

'Who can know?'

Lesky scrunched her face into a deep wrinkle. 'West.'

The council tensed as they realised a glimpse was present. They were rich and deplorable, but they were not stupid.

Baragad came to the edge. 'Lash, what can you possibly hope to achieve here? Let us say that you have indeed defeated General Huff, and not snuck here as a last resort. This Council will have been surrounded by the entire city guard. You will not be able to escape, even with the stone monster and your shining knight. The word "futile" comes to mind, Lord Lash. It describes your struggle, now and always. I suppose we can watch as you finally get the final blaze of glory you always wanted.'

'The stone monster has a name,' said Lesky.

The golem stood so they could all see him. The precipice was there again, waiting, grinning with the promise of blood. He shook his head. *Not tonight.* He bit hard on his tongue to keep him steady. Words would do.

Task let his grinding words run free, spilling out from places long silent.

'The name is Task, a Blue Golem of Wind-Cut, built by Belerod of the Windtrickers. I assure you, if this is to be the end of me tonight, then it will be the end of all of you. I have grown tired of killing, but I am willing to make an exception for this group of parasites you call a council.

'Your kind does not deserve anything you possess. You deserve only the same as you offer those who depend on you, and that is plague, famine, struggle. It is death. These people behind me have helped me realise what needs to be done.

'If I had spit, I would use it on you. If I had the arms, I would strangle you all right now, and save this island, this Realm, the pain of your existence. Only your lofty location saves you, but not for long. You've climbed too high, and now it's time to come back down. Even you, Boy King. I have seen a hundred kings in my time. Like every one of them, you have no right to rule.'

Baragad leant back from the balcony, his face blotchy, torn between red and pale. 'You assume much, beast, I—'

'I said *assure*, not assume.'

'That may be so...' Baragad's mouth clamped shut, and he fiddled with the buttons of his fine coat. Lash made a gesture, and the other councillors began to file down the steps, joining the guards who were putting down their weapons.

'Task!' called Lash. 'Find the ambassador! My soldiers will hold the Council. Besides, I have some words of my own I would like to say.' He nodded solemnly. It was a gesture of gratitude, respect, appreciation. It was everything he had never received from a master.

Lesky and Alabast were already halfway to the door.

Task covered his eyes with a palm before joining them. Lash sent him off with a grin. It was his turn.

31

'Firepowder. The Graden say they made it first. The Borians say the same. The Hasp can make the only true claim. Dust that brings fire and thunder from nothing but a spark. Who else is devious enough for such invention? The Hasp barbarians have always excelled in the business of killing. Firepowder will change the face of this war. It makes quite the mess of everything.'

FROM WARTORN, BY GRAND-CAPTAIN TEMPLE, WRITING IN 3631

6TH RISING, 3782 - CAVERILL

Task mowed through the guards like a battering ram; head down, elbows tucked. Musketballs bit him all over, sending stone scattering.

Lesky ran close behind, hands up to fend off the smoke and chips with her hands. Alabast brought up the rear. He seemed to be in his element, a blur of starsteel carving out crimson arcs.

With a roar, Task burst through the ranks and out into the open street. The last glow of the sun guided them west. He began to outpace them, and Lesky cried out.

'Task!'

That's when it happened. The night turned to a fierce, white daylight. Then, a wave of thunder so loud she thought the air itself was ripping. It struck her in the back like an anvil, and threw her to the cobbles. She cried out, but her voice was stolen by the cacophony. Her lungs strained to burst. Blood streamed from a cut on her eye.

Debris came crashing down around her. Flaming wood, charred stone. A severed hand, complete with signet ring, flopped onto the cobbles near her face.

'Lash!' Task's roar was a distant echo to her whistling ears.

Before Lesky could crawl or try to stand, the ground trembled again. She looked up to see the golem, aghast at the flaming shell that had engulfed the Council. Lord Lash, the soldiers, the king and his councillors: they were gone. All that survived the blast was a roofless, broken ring of walls, gutted to the core and flaming. The anvil struck again; this time in her stomach.

The firepower didn't stink of sulphur or charred wood. It reeked of Ellia. *How had she not seen this?*

She had no time for gawping, nor wallowing in guilt. Huge hands scooped her up and flung her over a stone shoulder. She looked down to find Alabast limping alongside, with part of his hair burned away, leaving a raw scalp. He half-winked, half-grimaced. Lesky closed her eyes, feeling dizzy.

'Where is she, Lesky?' cried Task.

The girl calmed her thumping heart and reached for the void. It took some effort to quell her mind with the constant bustle of Task's sprint. She fumbled at first, slipping in and out until she managed to grab on tight. She began to tour the darkness, touching minds.

Most of them screamed at her, burning and dying. She flung herself out from the Council and into the city, skimming dreams and idle thoughts.

She quested for something familiar. All these minds glowed in different ways. Ellia's had always been bright and wavering. She hunted for it now.

'Lesky!'

'In a minute, Task!' She had almost grasped her. A mind glimmered for a moment before sputtering out, as if it had been abruptly shuttered. Lesky surged towards it, feeling the void obey her now.

She spoke.

Ellia.

There was nothing, and entirely too much of it. She was here somewhere; just hiding. Lesky threw herself at Ellia, but she was slippery. She scratched, and clawed, but there was nothing to purchase.

There was nothing, and entirely too much of it. She cast around, touching the minds of those nearby, seeing the smoky edges of buildings and streets.

'West! An old building, full of old stuff. I'll tell you.' Words were difficult, but she ground them out anyway.

Guiding the golem with taps on the back, she led a merry path through the streets of Caverill. The place was in torment: bells ringing, firns and fawls screeching, city-folk fleeing.

They sprinted on, Alabast looking more tired with every pace. He was limping badly now, almost skipping down the road, which had turned to stamped chalk.

Task ran without a sound. No grunts, no heavy breaths. Just cold silence. Lesky wondered what he was feeling. Anger? Or just an urge to finish this mess. She could understand. She could sense something dark and vengeful at the edge of the void.

Hatred! It was the first time she had ever experienced it: and all-consuming burn of desire to see harm visited upon Ellia. Even Ganner and his fists paled in comparison.

'Up ahead, Task!' she growled.

They came to a museum of sorts; another proud building with curled spires on every corner and vast signs proclaiming various wonders. They strode through its gates and into the grand atrium. A patchwork glass roof showed a little starlight, but there were lanterns to light the way.

Lesky slipped from the golem's shoulder, and marched for the nearest doorway, knuckles bloodless.

'She's here, Task. She's here, alright.'

Ambassador Fala was becoming irritated. Ellia could sense it in the angle of her chin, the stiffness of her gait.

She was a lithe woman, with sharp cheekbones and soft brown skin. Her eyes were the deepest a brown could be without straying into black, and how they stared. Ellia had thought her own gaze to be chilling, but this Khandri woman of the desert knew more about cold then she did.

Her robes were orange and white, woven from a complex lattice of strands that wrapped about her and trailed along the floor. Her black hair hung straight and seamless, like a stripe of paint from her head to her breast.

She wrinkled at her nose at something in a display case; an old wineskin, shrivelled with age. 'I maintain that was gunfire, Baroness Frayne. And not thunder as you think.' Her accent was clipped and polite, barely Khandri at all. It was more a mix of the entire Realm.

'Perhaps you are correct. Our victory is fresh, Ambassador, as I explained about the change in venue. But it could simply be the execution of a prisoner.'

'Is that how you deal with your delinquents?' she asked, almost purring. 'I find how a society handles punishment somewhat telling of its opinions on other policies.'

Ellia smiled. 'That is how we deal with our *traitors*, Ambassador Fala. We hang the rest.'

'I see.'

As she hobbled, Ellia looked back at the woman's guards, mingling with her own. Almost two-score men either followed them or stood spread around the museum hall. They were brutish types, clad in the same colours and wearing gold sabres at the belts. They seemed to look at nothing and everything all at once, and it filled her with suspicion. Magic was not reserved solely for the Mission. The Narwe Harmony worshipped the goddess of magic instead of the Architect. It was foolish to assume they did not still dabble in the old arts.

Ellia gestured to a door leading to another hall. 'Allow me to show you to a place where we can sit and talk.'

Fala was shown inside, but she did not sit. She stood like a pillar, hands folded in her sleeves, brown eyes surveying. There was not a scrap of the grand room her gaze did not cover; the fireplace, the expanse of marble floor, even the filigree on the pillars.

'When will the King be arriving?' she asked, once she was done.

'Forgive me, Ambassador. It seems I've confused you. His Highness won't be joining us this evening. He's given me total authority to speak with you.'

A deep boom rumbled through the city. Fala raised one eyebrow. 'More thunder? It seems your victory is too fresh, Baroness. Please explain.'

Ellia clicked her fingers, and a soldier bent over her shoulder. With a few words, he was jogging for the door.

'We will soon find out, Ambassador. Let's talk in the meantime. We are safe here.'

'I should hope so.' Her guards stepped closer to her.

Ellia held up her hands, inviting her to sit at the varnished table. A silfrin decanter sat at the centre, with two matching cups. She caught the look of one of Fala's guards, and felt somebody questing for her mind. She shut herself up tight, and feigned a smile.

'Come, Fala. Sit. Tell me what you have journeyed all this way to say.'

'Very well,' she consented, although the expression of displeasure remained. 'As you and your Highness should be aware, I represent the Narwe Harmony in its entirety. Like you, I have total authority.'

'Understood.'

'We of the Khandri come to you in hope of peaceful negotiation.' The Ambassador pulled a fist from her sleeve, and let sand dribble from her fingers. 'Dust from Haspia, Narwe, Ifl, Affela, and Khandri. In ten years, we have all seen our fields turn to this. The God's Rent sucks the moisture from our earth, giving it to you, the Accord, instead. Hartlund, I hear, is by far the wettest in the Realm. You and your allies have abundant fields, flowing rivers, fat animals. I have seen it from the Duelling Dozen to Braad, and I expect to see it here, despite your current... feud.

'We of the Khandri come with a proposition of trade and free passage. Long have you dominated the waters of what you call the Blue Mountain Sea. We call it *Yahlin*, the wet desert. We ask to be allowed to trade freely. We ask to be allowed passage to wetter lands in the name of peace, something our points of the compass have not known well. Should that not entice you, then perhaps profit might. You lusted for our diamonds, once, and we are willing to trade them for such an agreement.'

Ellia played at thinking, half-curious. 'How many others have taken the offer?'

Fala raised her chin once more. 'Begrad has offered passage to certain ports. Normont is undecided. Braad is not. The Destrix...' Here, she paused. 'The Destrix were very clear.'

Ellia winced. 'Not very prosperous, then. And Hartlund is the last on your list of places to come begging.'

The woman had control, that was for sure. Her face was set in stone. 'We do not come to beg, Baroness, I would remind you of that. We come to offer peace and profit. Do you normally look at such opportunities with bitter eyes?'

'I have never been in the business of peace,' Ellia replied. It felt like a confession.

'I see.' Fala cleared her throat. 'You are certainly correct. The Accord and the Harmony have never known such a thing. But perhaps they could.'

Ellia was enjoying herself, leading this stoic woman in circles. 'What are you prepared to offer?'

'For access to your ports and produce, we would offer one box per year. Three hundred stones.'

'One hundred boxes.'

That broke her. She narrowed those dark eyes. 'Outrageous.'

Ellia scoffed. 'You speak of profit, and yet you're unwilling to provide any. Think of the costs of expanding our ports, patrolling our waters.' She levelled a finger. 'You have been mining those mountains for hundreds of years. In Haspia I have seen children playing with diamonds bigger than their fists. One box is nothing to the Harmony.'

'Ten boxes.'

'One hundred.'

'You insult me.'

'I do.' Ellia leaned forwards. 'But that is my price for peace.' She had begun to hate the sound of the word.

'Did your great grandfather die by a Khandri sword, perhaps? Did your father tell you the story until a hatred of us settled deep in your heart? Is that what I see before me?'

'Not in the slightest,' said Ellia. 'I hate everybody equally.'

It was Fala's turn to lean across the table. 'We of the Khandri also have a price. One that will be paid by those who don't heed our offer.'

'And that is?'

'As I said, we are no strangers to war. We are prepared to wage another to save our lands.'

'The Harmony against the Accord once more.'

Fala didn't seem excited at the prospect, but she stood firm. 'If it should come to such a thing. Our ships are ready. Our soldiers trained. Our goddess is behind us.'

Ellia tapped her teeth in thought, wasting the ambassador's time, making her wonder.

At last she threw up her hands. 'I wouldn't want to test the goddess of magic. We have an agreement.'

'Ten boxes?'

'Why not.'

Fala extended a hand, and Ellia shook it too tightly, until the ambassador began to squeeze back. She was strong. Behind her, Ellia heard the sounds of sabres being drawn.

The soldiers remembered their orders. Pistols where whipped from belts. Musketballs found ribcages and skulls to bounce around. It was simple. A few put up a fight, but they were hacked down quick enough.

Ellia released Fala, and let her recoil. With a smile, she reached for a silfrin cup and the decanter.

'Would you care for some torig?'

Before she could pour a drop, more gunshots rang out. Though this time, they sounded far too close. She heard a dire wail, and was horrified to find it familiar.

'No... Seize her!'

Fala fought like a devil, lashing out with her nails and spitting at anyone who came close. A club finally made it through, catching her on the back of the neck. She collapsed onto her knees. The guards seized her by her obsidian hair.

As soon as the floor began to tremble, Ellia grabbed a knife from a nearby guard and held it hidden against her wrist. When the golem burst through the door, flattening two guards, she was standing beside the dazed ambassador.

'Task!' She called, as he shook off the splinters. A few guards tried their luck, but were batted aside like insects. 'What a pleasure to see you survived your fall. Even though you proved me wrong. I really hadn't expected you to survive, as well as break your magic. As soon as I read Ghoffi's letters about you, I knew you were special.'

'No talking, Ellia. Nothing but lies come from your mouth.'

She chuckled. 'It's taken you a while to realise. Ah! Alabast and the stable girl, too. How quaint. It's like the end of a fairytale, and I'm the evil witch. Did your da ever tell you such stories, Lesky?'

Task stepped forwards, and Ellia brandished the knife, holding it against Fala's throat.

'Might I introduce the Khandri ambassador. Dhoran Fala of Velons. Am I pronouncing that correctly?'

Fala spat on her, square on the cheek. Ellia had half a mind to spill her blood right there and then, but instead she wiped her face and smiled. 'Charming woman!'

Alabast took his turn to approach, but again she waggled the knife. A droplet of blood gathered on the blade.

Ellia felt Lesky rail against her mind. She set her jaw, matching the assaults. The girl was fierce. She had taught her well.

The pain shot through her skull, as Lesky flung the full force of her mind against her. For a moment, Ellia faltered. Her head felt heavy, but she rallied. Once again, she was steel. *Impenetrable.*

It must have seemed such an odd battle, the two of them staring at each other, lips working but wordless, eyes mad with concentration.

The girl came again, even stronger this time. Ellia winced. Her legs shook. Lesky had found a way in, and was prising her open like a purse. Ellia harried her, thinking nonsense, throwing up wall after wall. Like the golem, Lesky crashed through every barrier.

With a gasp, she was shaken to her knee, falling away from Fala. The guards pawed at her, but she swatted at them with the knife.

She strained, forcing the girl from her head. But she came back twice as strong, barrelling through her mind, shaking the walls. It was like she was trampling her brain with her feet, not her thoughts.

Ellia watched the blood drip from Lesky's nose through tear-blurred eyes.

Architect, she cursed. She was thirsty. Her throat felt like ash. She pawed at the air, gasping.

She barely heard the golem's growl over the pounding in her head.

'Lesky, what are you doing?'

Just a croak from the girl, deep in the void. She was barely in her own skull any more. She was in Ellia's, occupying every thought, overwhelming her.

'Water,' Ellia hissed. 'Flasks!'

None of the soldiers moved. None of them had a drop.

'Lesky?'

Task. Louder this time.

Ellia ached to crawl towards the decanter on the table. The thirst made her hands move, then her legs, until she was reaching for the torig.

Every fibre of her screamed no, but she could only hear Lesky's voice, repeating the same word over and over. The echoes built until they deafened her.

Drink.

Her tongue felt shrivelled. Her teeth were like desert tombstones. The silfrin was cold under her trembling fingers.

No! Again and again she yelled it in her mind. But she was now a slave to Lesky's whims.

'Lesky! What's going on?'

The girl managed one word through the strain.

'Poison. Foebane.'

The decanter wobbled over her open mouth, threatening to spill at any moment.

'Stop her, Task!' said Alabast. 'We want her alive!'

'I can't!'

Ellia felt the hold weaken, but not for long enough. The orange liquid dribbled down her fingers. *That was it*. All it took was a touch. Foebane starts working at the skin.

She saw Alabast out of the corner of her eye, moving fast. The sword sliced through her wrist so quickly, at first she did not feel the pain. Then it began to swell, alongside the realisation. The permanence of it was more painful than the injury.

Blood came fast, drenching her as she fell to the stone. She dragged her furs around her stump in an effort to quench the flow. Nausea overcame her as Lesky released her mind. Shadows clamoured at the edge of her vision. She had no words for them; just strangled cries of pain and frustration as Alabast wrapped a belt around her arm and pulled it tight.

'You're a... a grim, girl,' breathed Ellia, when the pain had started to dull. 'Always suspected your mother was... a gazer. Techan always hinted she had a knack...'

Lesky stared at her with eyes made of brimstone. There was no shock there. No wonder. Somehow, she already knew.

Ellia looked up at Task with dizzy eyes. 'You finally let loose, like I told you. Perhaps too much.' She pinched the air with her remaining hand. 'It would have been glorious.'

She thanked the shadows, when they came to take her. She did not want to live with failure.

'She'll live,' said Alabast, holding the back of his hand to her breast. 'Now the blood's stopped flowing.'

'I don't know why you would want her to,' gasped Lesky, half-collapsed on the floor, teetering on the cusp of spewing.

Task looked into her hard, narrow eyes, wracked with pain and anger. They were still affixed on the unconscious Ellia.

'And I don't know why you'd kill her. She should pay for what she has done.'

'She was about to. She needed slayin', like Alabast said!'

'Tried. Publicly. By the people. She will confess all. Lash wanted it that way.'

Alabast was wiping his blade. 'I know a monster when I see one, but I agree. I want words with her. I want explanations. Reasons.'

Lesky was adamant. 'She'll lie through her teeth.'

The brightly coloured woman coughed. She had a hand clasped to her neck, now that the soldiers had released her. They hung around, unsure of what do to.

'Will somebody explain what in Haspha is going on? You, Wind-Cut, who is your master?'

Task stepped forwards.

'Leave, or suffer me.'

The soldiers scattered.

Alabast knelt by the ambassador's side. 'Madam, it would take too long to explain to you, but believe me when I say that you should forget everything that has happened since you left your ship. This woman just murdered the entire council, and the king. She also sought to murder you tonight it seemed.'

'And set the Accord at war with the Harmony,' said Lesky. She tapped her head, looking woozy. 'I saw it before she got thirsty for poison.'

Task joined in. 'In short, don't believe a word of what she has said.'

The ambassador's expression was either one of shock or outrage. Task couldn't tell.

'You are no kingdom. You are rabble. Children and mercenaries. And creatures far too long-lived for their own good.'

Alabast spoke again, using his charms. 'Madam Ambassador, the Lundish, the true Lundish who have just won this war, wish for a peaceful solution. If you'll give us a day more of your time, you can talk to the Last Fading, the true successors to the king. Their council waits in the bay. Sail out there and speak with them. I'm sure they will convince you we are against further war.'

The ambassador thrust out her chin. Her dark eyes roamed over the three of them. 'You cannot offer what we need in your state. You are weak.'

'Then what an opportunity it will be to help us rebuild. Your name again, Madam?'

'Fala.'

'Ambassador Fala, you underestimate these people. They are stubborn. Their civil war has lasted nine years. Believe me, they will thrive with your help, and in return, you'll be able to feed your people.'

Fala thought some more, then shook her head. 'It would not matter. The rest of the Accord does not agree. Hartlund alone cannot feed the Khandri, nor the Affela, nor the Chanark, who cannot even kill their animals. We will be forced to take what we need from Graden, from Normont, instead of asking for it.'

Task rumbled. 'What would it take to stop the war from happening?'

'Can you reverse time, golem?'

'No, Madam.'

'Then you cannot go back to stop the old gods from breaking the *yahlin*, stop the Rent from taking the life from our lands. *Your* lands, golem.' Fala pointed a sharp fingernail. 'You are hardly in a shape to be stopping anything. Who made you?'

'Belerod.'

'The Hasp warlord.'

'The very same.'

'And how did you come to this land? Who is your master?'

'I was bought by the crown, sent to fight the Fading. My master was Huff Dartridge, but now I have none. I chose to break my chains and put an end to the fighting.'

'Why?'

'Cruelty. Injustice. Dishonour. Murder. Genocide. You may pick, Ambassador. I've seen them all, not just here. I'm not standing for it any longer.'

Fala looked him up and down, as if he wore an explanation. 'You're peculiar for a *makhina*.'

'You can blame my builder for that.'

The ambassador rose to her feet. She was taller than Alabast. 'You have a day.'

Task bowed deeply with a flourish of his hand, remembering his Khandri manners. Fala followed suit.

'That will be enough,' he said, catching Lesky's eye before turning to the door. She was kneeling now, slowly recovering. Her eyes were still as hard as his stones.

It would have to be.

32

'Freedom has a price, and a high one at that. Paying for it is the struggle of mankind.'

KING RASPIER, ADDRESSING THE ACCORD ASSEMBLY IN 3773

7TH RISING, 3782 - THE BLUE MOUNTAIN SEA

Golems and ships do not normally mix, as Task had said many times. But this stout mountain of a craft seemed to handle his bulk just fine. Even some of the doors were large enough for him.

He stood on the prow, watching Caverill flash in the distance. The Last Table had sent soldiers into the docks by boat and taken the city from the remaining guards. Like a fire that refused to go out, the fighting still raged. It looked so small from the mouth of the bay, so inconsequential.

The ocean waves were calm. They idly lapped at the thick hull of *The Bastion*, making music to pass the time. Task was enjoying it; losing himself in the sounds and textures as they folded into the rhythm of the sea.

Another ship was floating nearby; less mighty, more graceful, slimmer. Its triangular sails were slack in the still air. Every scrap of wood above the waterline was carved with faces and swirls; war-patterns, for luck and for keeping bad spirits away. Long cannons with mouths carved with teeth and lips poked from oval slits in the hull. They were for keeping people away.

Task had seen a hundred ships like it. The only difference was the Khandri flags, instead of the Hasp pennants.

'Botherin' you?' said Lesky, behind him. Her bandages had been changed, and even some of her colour had returned.

'Not at all.' Task patted a space on the railing. She hung over it to watch the oily waters.

'How far down do you think it is?'

'Can't be more than a few hundred fathoms.'

383

'What's a favom?'

'Fathom. Three thousand in a league.'

'That's a lot.'

Task murmured in agreement.

Lesky bobbed her head sternward. 'They're still at it. Talkin' for hours now. Probably gettin' nowhere fast.'

'What's got you so ruffled?'

'That ambassador's mind is set, I can feel it. There's this desperate part of her I can see.'

'I can still tell when you're lying. It's Ellia.'

Lesky glowered. 'Should have let me kill her.'

'I thought you wanted to be a stable girl, not an executioner.'

'I hate her. She deserved it.'

Alabast had been lurking nearby for a minute now.

'Maybe she did, but take it from somebody who's actually killed. Taking a life sticks to you like shite, Lesky. No matter how many times you wash it away, the stain is still there, and it still stinks.'

'Though I completely understand the urge...' Task reached out a hand and made a crushing motion. 'We would be no better than her.'

Lesky rested her chin on the rail, confused. 'I wanted it so much. It was like another me, pushing further and further. She called me a grim. Maybe that's what I am. My special gift, as mum called it.'

'I've got one of those,' Task grunted.

Lesky chuckled to herself. Moods of the young never stay put for too long. 'That's it. That's our fifth thing in common. We've both got something grim in us. Best friends at last. Mam would be happy.'

'I've got one too,' Alabast piped up. Seeing their disapproving faces, he quickly changed the subject. 'What do you think will happen here?'

'It doesn't matter,' said Task, once again drawing Lesky's attention.

'Why do you say that?'

Before Task could answer, the door under the ship's bridge flew open and a string of men and women came forth, shaking their heads. They went their separate ways, wandering off to different parts of the ship.

One man wore a bushy beard of grey. A thin pair of spectacles balanced on his red nose, and his eyes were quick and a bright leaf-green, despite his obvious years. He wore a long suit of dusky red, and a cloak for the cold.

He bowed. 'Task of Wind-Cut, I'm told.'

'You're correct.'

'My apologies for not introducing myself before. I am Master Corin Ebenez, Head of the Last Table. Lord Lash was a very dear friend of mine. I am sorry to hear of his death.'

Task thanked him with a short bow.

'What news?'

'Straight to the point, like Lash would have said. I'm afraid the news is not good. Ambassador Fala is convinced Hartlund cannot help. She has made one thing clear, however. She is keen to buy you.'

Task bristled. 'I'm not for sale.'

'That's what I told her. You aside, she is adamant on the whole Accord agreeing.'

'Told you,' said Lesky.

Ebenez looked around at the golem's companions. 'And you are?'

'Lesky of Witt.'

'I'm the Knight of Dawn.'

The master did not look impressed. 'Ah yes.'

Alabast crossed his arms. 'The one who brokered this negotiation, yes. We also caught Ellia.'

'The Lady Auger, yes I know. You did a fine job of it. You have our gratitude.'

'What'll happen to her?' said Lesky.

'Shot, most likely, for barbarous crimes against Hartlund. Although we do have her to thank for eliminating the Mission and the Council. Not to mention Huff.'

Lesky looked rather pleased with herself. Task could not share her elation.

'To *thank?* She killed Lord Lash, Master Ebenez.'

The man rummaged in his beard as if he were finding an excuse. 'Yes, well. Of course. I was merely pointing out the benefits of the situation.'

Task turned away from Ebenez, and leaned back on the rail.

Alabast guided the master away. 'He needs his sleep, sir. Yes... It sleeps. Now, as you know I'm a renowned monster-catcher, but recently I've been thinking of a career in politics. Seeing as I felled the mastermind behind this whole debacle, I was wondering...'

His propositions were lost to the slapping of the waves. Task shook his head.

Lesky hovered nearby, unsure of herself. Behind the weariness and injuries, she was the same as the first night they had met: a skinny waif, hair all wild, curious and fearless. Only this time, a fear was showing.

'What's in your mind, you big lump? You know I can't read you.'

The golem's voice was a low rumble; his version of a whisper. 'No, you don't.'

She nodded without understanding, and slowly backed away. 'Be sunrise soon.'

Task had spent the night in the prow, dozing, alone and unbothered.

His decision had kept him awake. He checked and re-checked, crawling through every part of himself until more and more meat began to grow around the bones of his inkling. He had nurtured it for days. Ideas were living things. They exploded into being, having evolved with time. They could blaze brightly or sour and wither away, like life. Because, like all life, ideas need to be fed to survive.

Task prised open his eyes to find the ship had drifted closer to land, bobbing around between the fishing boats and abandoned Truehard carracks. The Khandri ambassador's ship had gone at some point in the night. It must have slipped away in a moment of dreaming.

Dreaming. How his dreams had changed since Safferon. He only saw water now, pure and simple. Ever-flowing, always changing. There were no old memories dredged up to disturb him. It had taken a while, but he could finally see what they meant.

Lesky came to pester him not long after he woke. There was nothing sheepish about her this morning. She strutted up and sat down right beside him.

'Best friends tell each other everything.'

'And I will, I promise. Not yet, though. I need to talk to Ebenez.'

'The beard? Why?'

'I said I'll tell you.'

Lesky followed him all the way to the master's office. Only then did she leave him alone, citing they hadn't put him back together right.

Lightly, he knocked, and was urged to enter. He ducked under the door-frame and stood in the centre of the office, just to the left of a swinging lantern.

Ebenez came round to the front of his desk, hands clasped. His bald brow was sweaty. 'Mr G... Mr Task. Task? What do you prefer?'

'Task will do fine.'

'Task, what can I help you with? As I told the girl, there is nothing I can do to bring them back.'

'Lesky was in here?'

The master nodded. 'Half the morning. When I convinced her of the hopelessness of the situation, she moved on to telling me her plans to sort the army out and get it ready for another war. That girl has a sharp mind in her. She has big dreams. And oddly intuitive. I could use a girl like her in the coming years.'

Task found himself smiling. 'I came to speak to you about another matter.'

'And that is?'

'I'd like you to sail me south, until the God's Rent.'

'Why in the Realm would you ask that?'

'Because I have a way of stopping the war with the Harmony. For good.'

'Explain.'

'You merely have to trust me.'

'If I'm to sail *The Bastion* anywhere near the Rent, Task, I need to have a good reason.'

'Is the end of war not good enough?'

Ebenez started to reply, but found he had no words. He rummaged in his beard.

'Fine. I'll trust you, like the others have. It'll take three days.'

'Good enough. When do we set sail?'

Ebenez shrugged. 'Now?'

'Even better. Thank you... Master Ebenez.' The word was difficult, even out of context.

She was waiting for him when he ducked back onto deck. Arms crossed, face serious.

'Lesky—'

She cut him off. 'Afore you start, I know what's in your head. I can't read stone, but I can read a friend. You've decided on somethin' stupid.'

Task stared at her. 'I once told you what I wanted in life. I'm free, but I am still not finished. Fala was right. I'm too long-lived for my own good.' He gestured at his missing chunks; at the places where they couldn't find the stones to reattach.

'I broke the magic for *you*, Lesky. Not Huff. Not Ellia. It was only when she threatened you that I snapped. Although I'm not the golem I was, it has changed me, for the better. You said the Realm needed a reason. Find it one, and we can stop the war, you said. I've found one. In my dreams, Lesky. I was built to win wars. Well, what if I could win them before they started? Stop them altogether. Or at least until you grow and pass on to the next life. That would be enough. I couldn't save Orina, but I can save you. You could live to carry out what your mother told you, and change the world.'

'You're talking in riddles, Task.'

'I intend to destroy the Rent. Reset the world. Save it, Lesky. Peace, however brief, is still peace, and a beautiful thing I have never really known. Just like I never saved anything before you. You taught me the value of what it means to be, and that is to have choice. I've chosen my path, Lesky.'

They held each other's gaze. Lesky's eyes began to well up with tears.

'No! You made a promise, that night in the camp. You promised freedom, not death!'

'I know I did.' Task bowed his head. 'And as a friend, I'm asking you to let me break that promise.'

'How could you?'

'Because I can make a choice to do the right thing, like you taught me.' He offered a half-smile. 'And I get my wish.'

Lesky ran. No words, no insults, just the clatter of feet down the nearest hatch.

Three days passed, full of salt and spray. The Rent seem to know he was coming, and threw up every storm it could. *The Bastion* rode the swells like a boulder sliding down a mountain path, bullying its way through the worst of the waves.

Task spent the days on the prow, claiming it as his own. He let the sea and the rain and the wind wash over him. He had not known weather like this in decades, and he was intent on soaking up every drop.

Lesky had not spoken a word to him. She had not reared her head above deck since fleeing. He had tried to search for her, to no avail.

Alabast had come to join him once or twice, spending most of his time spitting sea-water. That was what he got for opening his mouth so much. He talked constantly, but never got to the point. The whole ship had learnt what the golem was intending to do. Alabast was just too afraid to say it.

Goodbye.

All he did was a raise a hand, and press it against the golem's arm.

On the morning of the fourth day, the nest spotted the Rent on the horizon. It sat flat on the ocean's surface, darker than all the clouds that gathered around it. The golem watched it creep closer with every gust of wind. The ship's captain kept the Rent on the starboard side, matching its swirl. Every good sailor knew that going against the current of the God's Rent was foolhardy.

One by one, they came to join him at the railing: sailors, soldiers, even the cook.

All except Lesky.

Alabast stood by the ship's wheel, gazing down the barrel of a spyglass.

Ships rarely dared to chance being snagged by the Rent. A ship would slip into an eddy, and all too quickly find itself in faster, uglier waters. As a Hasp captain had once told Task, there's only really one choice at that point: pray.

By the time the captain called for the sails to be changed, the rent had filled the air with its deep and eternal rumble. Task felt his stones resonating with it. The power thrummed through him.

At least twenty ships long and wide, the maelstrom churned in a constant corkscrew of grey-green water. When it had first appeared in the ocean, sailors thought it would drink the seas dry. Hundreds of years later, and its thirst was still as insatiable, but the waters remained. *Magic.*

The foam drew the curve of the dark mouth, and nothing ever tumbled until the last second. None had ever gazed directly on the abyss without dying shortly after. Through the waters, the shadow of a funnel could be seen burrowing to the ocean floor.

All eyes had turned on Task. Ebenez stood nearby with Alabast, hands clasped tightly and earnestly. 'You can change your mind, golem.'

But Task shook his head sternly. 'I choose this.'

The master nodded. 'Then if you are successful, we are forever in your debt. You will not be forgotten in Hartlund, nor likely the Realm.'

To a body, the entire deck covered eyes, saluting their most unlikely saviour. Task looked among them, thanking each with a nod, until he met a dark pair of eyes, misted with tears.

Lesky came forwards.

'You won't change your mind.' It was a statement, not a question. 'You won't change your mind even for me.'

'It's for you that I don't change it.' Task used a finger to gently raise her chin. Then, with a grunt, he plucked a sliver of stone from his chest, and placed it in her palm.

'To the little girl with big dreams.'

She smiled through her tears. Alabast laid an awkward hand on her shoulder. His armour had gone now, replaced by Fading garb. He bowed his head, and touched a hand above his eyes.

'And to the golem who just wanted to be free,' said Lesky. 'Now you can be.'

Task bowed deeply, and stepped into the reinforced dinghy, dangling by the bulwark. The cables creaked above him.

'We can all be,' he said.

'Lower the boat!' came the cry, and with a judder, it descended to the waters. Task glanced over to the whirlpool. *Not long now.*

He settled down, a hand balancing each side of his vessel. Like him, it had seen better days. White paint flaked where his cracked hands gripped the wood.

Faces crowded at the railing to watch him drift into the stronger currents. He didn't meet their gazes. He was fixated on the hole in the world, and how to mend it.

Half an hour was all it took to reach the edge of the Rent. Every foot-length he drifted towards it, the mightier the roar became; the more the sea kicked to spray, the more he could see of what awaited him.

With a slosh, the dinghy nosed into the vortex. It sounded as if a mountain were being twisted from its roots. The Rent's toothless mouth yawned wide, ravenous as the grave. Task stared down into the funnel, where the water spun at a blurring speed, bluer and greener.

The golem was mesmerised. It was everything he had seen from his dreams. Ever since Collaver had first mentioned the Rent, he had dreamt of this place, this latecomer to the creation of the world.

This lonely giant, like himself.

He stared into its great waters, and it stared back. It had waited an age for him.

As the waters quickened, faster and faster, and as the circles grew tighter and tighter, Task released his grip on the flaking wood and raised his arms to the spray of the maelstrom. He let its roar fill his mind, blotting out every soiled memory, washing away every spatter of blood.

At the last moment, before his dinghy tumbled down the churning wall, Task squatted, then jumped over the side.

For a moment he hung there in the mouth of the God's Rent, staring down at the blackness below.

The golem roared as he plummeted, and just for a moment, those upon *The Bastion* heard his voice, and shed tears of hope and sorrow.

EPILOGUE

The eyepiece of the spyglass was cold against her forehead, numbing her skin. She waited, biting her lip, but it was useless; Lesky couldn't help but take another peek. Another twist of the knife.

Every day she had taunted herself by staring through it, looking south. Every day it had been the same. The view was blurry, but the blotch on the far horizon remained. The clouds still lingered, more ominous than they had ever been.

She felt like dashing the instrument on the flagstones and stamping on its shards.

Of all the senseless deaths this war had caused, his was the most senseless of them all. The most painful.

She felt it more keenly than the rest of them. Perhaps it was because she soaked up their sorrow, and piled it atop her own. Try as she might, Lesky could not keep their voices out. Only when she slept, or worked, she could ignore them.

The curse of being a grim, she told herself, as she stalked indoors and slammed her door.

Lesky circled the sparse furniture, see-sawing between the bed and a table, strewn with parchment. She eyed the scrawl of numbers and names, amounts and supplies, and cursed.

Ebenez knew how to keep her busy. Barely two weeks, she had known him, and somehow he felt like the grim, not her. He knew exactly what kind of distraction she needed, and that was responsibility.

It was all she had ever craved, and yet even now, with a voice that the Last Table listened to, she felt empty. Her heart had been ripped clean from her chest, and the vacuous space that remained refused to be filled.

Lesky scattered the papers with her hand, filling the air with them as she vented a yell.

A thump came from the next room, and after a moment, a rapping at her door.

With a snarl, she wrenched it open. Behind it stood Alabast, arms crossed and face twisted with curiosity.

'What?'

'Heard you yelling.'

'I'm fine.'

'You haven't been fine for weeks. None of us have.'

Alabast pushed his way past her before Lesky could shut him out.

'Don't make me dig up summin dark and ugly out of your memo—'

The knight cut her off. 'I've decided to stay. Help Ebenez get this country back on two feet. Haven't got anywhere else to go. Besides, once the Khandri make up their minds, the Lundish'll need every sword they can get.'

'How long for?'

'Few months at least, maybe a year.'

'Finally negotiated a price, have you?'

He held up thumb and finger, touching them to form a circle.

Lesky snorted. Part of her wanted to pick his mind, but she knew how much he squirmed and complained.

'You must have asked for something. Heroes like you don't work for free.'

Alabast laughed. He stuck his hands in his jerkin pockets and moved to look out the window.

'Just the chance to take her head. No airs and graces, no playing the crowd, just the duty of ending her.'

Lesky narrowed her eyes. 'So they're finally doin' it.'

'Three days from now.'

'Should have killed her sooner. She doesn't deserve another day.'

'Ellia Auger lived three separate lives, Lesky. She was woven deep into the Mission and the Council. She pulled strings nobody knew existed. The Last Table wanted to know what else she could give them besides what you glimpsed. That took time. And some coercing, so I hear.'

'I would've done it. Would've searched her evil mind again.'

Alabast threw her a sly glance. 'No, you would have made her scratch her eyes out, or melted her insides or something. Ebenez is right; stick to helping with the rebuild. You're too young for murder.'

Lesky folded her arms. 'She killed him. Not personally, but with every lie and cheat, she killed Task. Just like she killed my father.'

The knight cocked his head.

'The Mission had him killed because he was... *involved* with her. Was 'gainst their rules, and they cut his throat for it. I saw it 'appen.' She tapped her head.

'Well,' Alabast sighed, looking out across the bay, dark and deep. 'Us parentless types got to stick together, I suppose. Especially now he's gone.'

There was an interminable pause. Lesky tapped her teeth as she waited for him to speak. She didn't trust herself to, not with her throat so tight. She held a hand to her chest, feeling the lump sitting against her skin.

The knight spoke without turning. 'I don't have to be a glimpse to see you're still hurting, Lesky. You've haven't changed your clothes in days. Barely eaten. I understand how you feel. He was a force of nature. A storm trapped in a body. He was, without a doubt, the most incredible creature I've ever met, but I guess he just wasn't a match for—'

'Don't.' Lesky ground out the word. 'You couldn't possibly understand. I know.' She jabbed at her temple again.

Alabast looked awkward, eyes sliding to the open door. She knew he contemplated escape. Consolation was not one of his skills.

It was at that moment they heard the clattering of feet in the hallway; half-sprinting, half-stumbling up the stairs. Alabast was at her side in an instant, hand on his sword-hilt.

A breathless, pudgy lad with red cheeks skidded to a halt in her doorway. He was wheezing so much a full sentence was beyond him.

'They're... the Table... docks...the captain said... aaahh....'

The man was useless.

'Spit it out!' the knight snapped.

Lesky was already moving, slow at first but accelerating quickly. She didn't have to wait for the message. The messenger's frantic mind had told her everything.

She barged past him, Alabast in tow, shouting her name. She didn't care. She sprinted down the staircase, then the next, and the next, until her feet squeaked on the marble of the atrium.

The street-noise struck her like a wall when she burst into the patchy sunlight. The streets are afire with the noise of hammering and bashing, sawing and yelling.

'Lesky!' Alabast yelled again, but it only spurred her on.

She raced down the walkways to the docks, zig-zagging across the chalk cliffs like an insect torn between two lanterns.

As soon as her feet touched the wooden planks, she looked for the ship. One with sails still raised, three masts, and a lightning bolt for a figurehead. She had seen it in the messenger's mind.

She spotted it instantly, and sprinted in its direction. Alabast had managed to keep up, but now she left him in her dust. She spotted a crowd gathered on the quay.

The entire Last Table were there, all twenty-seven of them, burbling excitedly and waving their arms. There was a heated discussion going on between Ebenez, standing tall on the deck with spectacles perched on his nose. He was arguing over a map with the captain of the ship. The feather in the man's cap wiggled as he nodded profusely, prodding again and again at the yellow parchment.

'Master Ebenez!' Lesky bellowed, making the crowd fall silent. 'Is it true?'

The master let go of the map, and took a moment to remove his spectacles from behind his ears.

'Lesky, this is Captain Jessob. I'll let him tell you.' Ebenez motioned for the captain to speak, which he did after much throat-clearing.

'Little lady, the Rent is dying!'

Lesky's heart tried its best to burst from her mouth.

'We saw it with our own eyes. Watched it for four days, we did. Though the ocean still turns, the mouth is shrinkin', gettin' weaker by the hour. *The Bolt* managed to get closer than any ship 'as in decades!'

Lesky's gaze switched to Ebenez, and she found him nodding, a smile tempting his lips and his eyes a-sparkle.

She began to laugh then, loudly and joyfully. She didn't feel the hands clapping her on the back and shoulders, nor did she hear the rest of the report. Even when Alabast came running up, a bemused look across his face, she simply grinned at him, and left him standing there.

As she walked back along the boards, she dug inside her shirt and pulled out the stone that sat against her chest. She watched it twirl on its string for a moment before she clutched it tightly, and pressed it to her lips.

The big lump had done it.

THE END

When I first put fingers to keys, I swore *The Heart of Stone* would be a standalone story. Writing this now, I know Task's last tale has been told, and that by choosing to end it how I did, I won't dilute his character, nor his struggle. However, a 400 year-old golem collects quite a lot of tales in his time, and they're currently tugging persistently at my sleeve. While I've no solid plans yet, I think we'll be glimpsing a younger Task in future publications, or perhaps an older Lesky...

In any case, I hope you enjoyed his tale, and thank you for reading. Feel free to share what you thought of the book in the usual places, or get in touch with me directly. I always enjoy hearing from people – it lets me know the apocalypse hasn't come yet.

I would also like to say a special thank you to the people who helped me polish and produce *The Heart of Stone*:

Andrew Lowe – **EDITOR**
Shawn T. King – **COVER DESIGNER**
Lawrence Gates – **PROOFREADER**

And to my great beta readers:

Meg Cowley Jolly
Josh Beysselance
Jordan Turner
Connor Eddies
Damien Duncan
James McStravick
Peter Hutchinson
Shane Shumaker

Thank you,

Ben Galley
FEBRUARY 2017

The HEART of STONE